PENGUIN BOOKS
THE FABULIST

Uthis Haemamool was born in 1975 in Kaeng Khoi district, Saraburi province in central Thailand. Among his seven published novels and four short stories collection, he became widely known for the *Kaeng Khoi Trilogy* containing the novels *The Brotherhood of Kaeng Khoi* [ลับแล, แก่งคอย], which won him the Seven Book Awards and the S.E.A. Write Award in 2009; *The Elegy* [ลักษณ์อาลัย], and *The Fabulist* [จุติ]. In 2017, his novel *Silhouette of Desire* was translated and published in Japanese, followed by an art exhibition of the same name that showcases his drawings and paintings. The novel was then adapted for the stage under the direction of Toshiki Okada, which premiered in Bangkok and staged at Centre Pompidou Paris in 2018 and Tokyo in 2019.

Palin Ansusinha graduated with a BA in English Language and Literature from King's College London in 2017. She translated several Thai short stories into English, including 'The World Shattered Yesterday', 'Tender Mercies', and 'The Weretiger Tale' by Phu Kradat. In 2020, she co-founded Soi Literary, a literary agency to promote contemporary Thai literature to an international audience. She currently lives in Bangkok, Thailand with her cat Jamu.

Ploy Kingchatchaval graduated with a BA in English Literature from the University of Cambridge in 2016 and an MA in Issues in Modern Culture from University College London in 2017. She translated the English screenplay for Puangsoi Aksornsawang's second feature film *I open a curtain to see a dead bird.* and Jirassaya Wongsutin's debut feature film *Flat Girls*, both in development. She currently lives in Bangkok, Thailand with her dog Tofu.

The Fabulist

จุติ

Uthis Haemamool

อุทิศ เหมะมูล

Translated by Palin Ansusinha and
Ploy Kingchatchaval

PENGUIN BOOKS
An imprint of Penguin Random House

PENGUIN BOOKS

USA | Canada | UK | Ireland | Australia
New Zealand | India | South Africa | China | Southeast Asia

Penguin Books is part of the Penguin Random House group of companies
whose addresses can be found at global.penguinrandomhouse.com

Published by Penguin Random House SEA Pte Ltd
9, Changi South Street 3, Level 08-01,
Singapore 486361

Penguin
Random House
SEA

First published in Penguin Books by Penguin Random House SEA 2023

Copyright © Uthis Haemamool 2023
English Translation Copyright © Palin Ansusinha and Ploy Kingchatchaval 2023

ISBN 9789815017052

Typeset in Garamond by MAP Systems, Bangalore, India

www.penguin.sg

And, of course,
For Al

Contents

Act 1: The Miraculous Old Woman

The high descends, the low rises with time

Look at you all, sitting here all innocent and wide-eyed. Your parents haven't got time to scold you: they're working their lives away like dogs, and that's why they ditch you mongrels with me when it suits them. Make yourselves at home, boys and girls. Piss around and tumble over wherever you like; I have plenty of space, just for you. And when you're done playing, I'll get a thermos full of iced water, cook you a full meal if you're hungry—fetch you some snacks too, shall I? There's plenty of room to sleep, so no need to bite each other's heads off over it. When you're with me, you help yourselves. I'm not wiping your arses for you *der*. You do everything yourselves. You fend for yourselves here. Entertain yourselves! Invent some mindless drama; make yourselves laugh, make yourselves cry. It's not my problem *ner*. I'm not promising I'll do anything for you. I'll do it if I feel like it, so don't you pester me. Remember that ner!

I don't care if your parents come back huffing and puffing when they see you catching on to my crude way of talking. They've coddled you enough already: don't do this, don't eat that, don't say this, don't touch that. They've wrapped you in cotton wool and monitored every single thing you do: what you eat, what you say, what you think. You're like raw eggs encased in stone. Can you even think for yourselves? I bet you can't. Tall enough for a dog to lick your arsehole, but you can't think for yourselves. You'll get yourselves a husband or a wife,

1

you'll have kids and you'll grow old, and you still won't be thinking for yourself. Parents these days are too overprotective. The next thing you know, some of them have coddled their kids till they physically can't coddle them anymore. Lucky brats. Blessed with 'good' parents: parents who end up raising good-for-nothing types, eh? Ha ha ha!

Where are you all from, anyway? How many of you are there? Five? Whose sons and daughters are you? There, this one's my great-grandchild, and that one lives next door. What about the rest of you? Are you all friends? Do you know why your parents have left you here? I bet you don't. They think you're too young to understand adults, so they're not telling you anything. But I know what your parents are getting up to. You want to know?

What? Look at you, all wide-eyed. Do you even understand what I'm saying? Oh, well. I don't blame you. I blame your parents for raising such incurious and unquestioning children; children who can't think for themselves, because all they ever did was mollycoddle you and figure everything out for you. Well, that's not happening with me. Do whatever you please, your majesties. And if your parents want to tell me off for encouraging indecency, then they can say it to my face. I'll be waiting on my pedestal, ready to deliver a whole sermon. Maybe I'll summon the guardian spirits while I'm at it, possess the hell out of them! Isn't that good? I see you nodding, eh?

Yeah, I think so, too.

Oh, well. Forgive my language ner: it's a habit of mine and it's not going to change. The only thing that needs changing are your ears. Replace them with a new pair, and maybe my words will ring more pleasantly. Sound good? Pluck the old pair right off and quickly stitch on some new ones. It won't hurt one bit. Come, *ee-la*. Let me do it for you. No? Ha ha ha! Then bear with me ner.

When I was around your age, I could do everything myself. Learn by myself, think for myself . . . Can you believe it? Well, believe it or not, you don't have much of a choice when you're in my house. If you don't believe it, you can leave. Sounds like I'm banishing you, doesn't it? Well, I am. And if you don't believe me, you can wander around until you find whatever it is that you believe in. I'm not banishing you because I own the place; I'm just encouraging you to do what I did. I've never owned anything in my entire life, not even now. This house I'm lying in, bedridden? It's my son's.

See the wrinkles on my arm? Come, take a closer look. Touch them if you want. I touch them every day to remind me of primordial times; a time before I was born, when I was merely a spirit, a spirit with a consciousness and memory. In its primitive age, Earth was one mass of land, its surface riddled with dents, pits, and ridges, both near and far. My spirit slumbered underground, inside the world's womb, for billions of years. Then one day, an explosion roared above, so deafening that its distance from me was indiscernible. It was followed by screaming. The screaming went on for a while. I trembled in fear, oblivious to what was happening above ground. After a while, all went silent, and I slept for another million years.

Meanwhile, movement stirred all around me; a passionate grinding, sliding in and out, up and down. The air shivered with pleasure, billowing with fiery heat. Magma oozed from volcanic craters, as it flooded across, froze over and filled up craters so they became plains. Lands became oceans, and oceans became land. Through extreme heat and cold, natural movements rocked Earth into conception, until the angels descended from the heavens, carrying diaphanous magic blankets. Once every century, the angels unfurled their blankets and swept them over mountains up to 8,000 *wa* high. Each time they arrived, they brought peace and harmony with them: a complete contrast to the chaos of nature. The angels performed this ritual every century, until eventually the towering hills were flattened, and the hollows in the ground rose to form new mountains. My once subterranean spirit migrated to the surface, where for the first time, I was able to perceive light and the land. The first thing I was able to see were hundreds and thousands of angels taking flight, swaddling the mountains with their magic blankets in ecstasy.

Can I claim to have lived here for a long time? Not really. I don't know for sure where I was before I began my existence underground. Upon surfacing, I noticed that the ground bore traces of fusulinid fossils. Do you know what they are? Of course not. It's not my job to teach you; you'll learn it in school someday. What about coral? Seaweed? Shells? Yes? Well, I was surrounded by those. I suspect that before I began, I had been in the ocean, carried ashore like those fossilized marine beings.

Once on Earth, my spirit resided in the core of a thlok tree. Each year, the tree grew, and my vision of the world grew with it. Don't even get me started on just how fantastic this world was! I could hear thunder and feel heat, feel the cold and the rain on my skin. I could see fruit-bearing trees, wheat, and lush plants growing in abundance. I could hear the rush of rising floodwaters, the echoes of the jungle, the sound of rocks splitting in two. I could hear wildlife searching for food, monkeys swinging from tree to tree, young deer skipping here and there . . . Bears, boars, rats, crabs, turtles, fish, nagas, flocks of birds soaring in the sky. I could see them all.

At night, the sky glimmered with starlight, and in the morning, the sun shone over the dew-bathed jungle, slicing through the trails of mist hanging over the leafy canopies. The jungle had a complex scent; delicate and pungent fragrances swirled together, with a whiff of damp earth. The fields, hills, and plains flickered, as if carpeted with diamonds; as the days went by, it was revealed that this glitter was in fact layers of the finest salt, accumulating over mounds of earth. The mountains and cliffs were no different. Rich in metal ores and all sorts of minerals, they clashed and flashed and reflected one another in the sunlight . . . Oh, never before had I seen such abundance!

Eventually, the first few humans wandered into the land where my tree stood. Some of them simply passed me by, while others saw an opportunity to settle under the hanging cliffs, inside the caves, and along the banks of the river and stream. Unlike other animals, humans get rowdy when they are in close proximity. From inside my thlok tree, I could hear them speaking to one another in their languages, which I eventually came to understand with time. I remember their voices and how they irritated me: not only were these humans boisterous, they were also possessive of the land they occupied. This land belongs to me! That land belongs to you! This is mine! That is yours! These were not merely empty words either; theirs was a language driven by an idea so terrible and violent. How do I know this? Well, because it happened to me.

These humans hollowed out cliffs and mountains, extracting stones and rocks to chisel into knives and axes, into murderous weapons. One day, they gathered around my thlok tree and watched as one of them struck my lower trunk with a bronze axe. There was nothing I could do but to helplessly watch too, as they mutilated my host. Despite all the times before when they had failed to fell my tree, breaking their axes in their attempt to hollow out more cliffs to make new ones, they were determined to do it. Eventually, they succeeded. The ear-splitting cry of my collapsing tree echoed for several days and nights. Not long after, I was spending sleepless nights listening to the sound of trees falling, one after another.

Utterly devastated, I became nothing but conscious spirit, unable to physically move on my own, forced to inhabit the body of one being after another. Out of desperation and deep sorrow, I prayed to the divine beings to grant me a body of my own so that I might seek the most enlightened being on Earth, the Lord Buddha. As soon I finished praying, a miracle happened. An injured naga, fleeing from the group of humans that had hurt it, suddenly collapsed from a spear wound by the large log where my spirit dwelled. I witnessed the naga's spirit depart from its body and extinguish; my own spirit migrated into the naga's lifeless body, bringing with it new life and energy. The body of the naga now belonged to me. I gathered all my strength and willpower and began to slither through the thick jungle with my new serpentine body. Suddenly, in the midst of the unfamiliar thrill of exercising my newfound ability to move, I felt a sharp pain in my left side. I found a safe place to rest, where I discovered that my body was drenched in blood. I licked my bleeding wound, which tasted strangely sweet, and felt a muscle throbbing violently in the hollows of my chest At that point, I realized that although I had a new life, that life also came with a wound . . .

Such is life, children. Birth and existence are imperfect.

What now, ee-la? You seem curious. You want to see my wound? You won't be seeing it now; it faded a long time ago. It was my body that was wounded, not my spirit. I'm not showing you my arm just to brag about my wound, you understand? I want you to contemplate these wrinkles; the deep channels, mounds, and folds. Look at them! Can you see them?

Every day, I look at the wrinkles on my arm as a reminder of the earth I once dwelled under and the very first time I surfaced upon it. The wrinkles on my arm today resemble the skin of the earth all those lives ago.

The arrival of the Lord Buddha

When I lived inside the giant thlok tree, I overheard a group of humans talking about the miracles of the Lord Buddha. Deep in meditation, he had travelled through the air from Jambudvipa to Kaattaka, which was also known as Mount Pattawee. Those huntsmen prowled around my tree, shouting over one another, each with their own elaborate version of the same story. I didn't know which one to believe. Still, I was able to piece together a few complete versions. Although they differ in motives, all of them share exactly the same beginning and end. Let me tell them to you.

The first version is set in the city of Parantapa, a region not far from here. There lived two brothers, Mahaboon and Julaboon. They were both merchants, who made a living trading with foreigners. Mahaboon, the older of the two, preferred to trade on land, so Julaboon, his younger brother, traded at sea, to ensure that their routes did not overlap. One day, Mahaboon travelled with a caravan of 500 carts to the city of Sawatee, where the streets were bustling with people carrying flowers, candles, incense, and other various offerings. They were all heading towards the Chetawan Temple, gushing about how much they wished to hear the Lord Buddha's sermon. Out of curiosity, Mahaboon followed them.

Inside the temple, he saw the Lord Buddha seated between Moggallāna and Sāriputta, his principal disciples. After listening to the sermon, a miracle occurred. Pintola, a Brahmin's son, felt his faith ignite upon hearing the sermon and, in that moment, expressed the wish to be ordained by the Buddha himself. Deeply moved, Mahaboon then invited the Lord Buddha to receive alms at his cavalcade of caravans.

The next morning, the Buddha and his disciples visited Mahaboon's caravan to receive their alms. Afterwards, they blessed Mahaboon. Overwhelmed with joy and ceaseless devotion, Mahaboon, like Pintola, was moved to express the wish to be ordained and to become one of Lord Buddha's disciples right there and then.

Once ordained, Mahaboon returned to reside in a temple in his hometown of Parantapa. *Uwa!* What a difficult name to pronounce. Let's just call it by its other name, Khitkhin. Not long afterwards, Mahaboon attained the spiritual status of an arhat. One day, during the rainy season, his brother Julaboon invited him for a meal at his home. Even during the rainy season, Julaboon was forced to trade at sea, despite the likelihood of a tempestuous journey. Concerned about his safety, Julaboon made his brother promise to rescue him and his crew if an unfortunate accident were to occur during their journey. Mahaboon gave his word.

A week into the journey, Julaboon and his crew had used up all the firewood and food on board. Forced to dock the ship to replenish their supplies, they approached a mysterious island. To their amazement, the island was abundant with red sandalwood, which was more valuable than all of their goods on board combined. It was then that Julaboon ordered his crew to replace all of their goods with red sandalwood from the island. However, Julaboon's ransacking of the red sandalwood had infuriated the island demons, whose wrath manifested as a violent storm that capsized Julaboon's ship. On the brink of death, Julaboon prayed to his brother. Mahaboon miraculously appeared out of thin air and rescued the entire ship from falling prey to the demon's lethal claws. Safely back in Khitkhin, Julaboon offered his brother his entire supply of red sandalwood as a sign of his gratitude. Mahaboon refused, for the red sandalwood had been stolen from the island due to greed; instead, he expressed his wish to invite the Lord Buddha to impart his teachings to Julaboon, his crew, and the rest of the people of Khitkhin, which included a hermit named Sajjapan.

From the supply of red sandalwood, Julaboon built 500 pavilions to celebrate the Lord Buddha's arrival. The people of Khitkhin listened to the Buddha's teachings with great delight. Afterwards they watched him perform a miracle, impressing the shape of his shadow and right footprint onto the rock face of Mount Pattawee for the people to worship and commemorate him by.

In another version of the huntsmen's story, it was rumoured that the Buddha had put Pintola, the newly ordained son of the Brahmin, under the tutelage of Moggallāna, so his principal disciple might support the new monk's spiritual journey towards becoming an arhat. As days went by, Moggallāna saw that his student needed to practice basic meditation, so he took Pintola across the forests and mountains of Jambudvipa so he could meditate in solitude. However, Pintola was not able to reach a new level of enlightenment, and Moggallāna wondered if he would benefit from somewhere even more isolated, like the borders of some faraway land. After telling Pintola his plan, Moggallāna cast a spell, shrinking Pintola to the size of an Indian gooseberry before tucking him inside the hem of his robe and taking flight towards the land of Suvarnabhumi.

They arrived, and Moggallāna saw that the lush and sequestered surroundings of Mount Kaattaka were indeed suitable for Pintola's meditation practice. There was also a community of people there, led by a huntsman named Kaattaka, who Moggallāna felt would benefit from the teachings of the Buddha. As they descended onto the mountain, Moggallāna transformed Pintola back to his original size, and the two of them made their way to pay a visit to the huntsman.

It was dark by the time the two monks arrived at Kaattaka's house. After a full day of hunting, the huntsman was relaxing in his home, his bow and arrow leaning against the wall.

'Good host,' Moggallāna said, greeting the huntsman. 'We have lost our way, and fear that it may be dangerous to continue our journey in the dark. If you don't mind, may we rest here for the night?'

Upon seeing the two monks, Kaattaka was startled, for he had never seen a religious being in the flesh before. Both of them emanated a mysterious aura, and Kaattaka wondered whether they were even humans at all. How had these two strangers even managed to pass through the village gates? He suspected that they were evil spirits, full of ill intent.

'You villains! How did you trespass in here without being stopped by my servants? Wandering in here and asking for my hospitality at your leisure. The audacity! What monstrous and evil beings you are. If you continue to insist on resting here for the night, you shall find yourself asking for permission from my bow.'

'Look, nobleman. We are monks; our actions are nothing but peaceful. We did not mean to offend you by trespassing onto your land. Our intentions are sincere and kind: to enlighten others about the nature and causes of happiness and suffering. You too have displayed the kindness within you by allowing us to ask your bow for permission to rest here for the night.' Moggallāna turned towards the bow.

'Loyal bow, I ask you to perform your duty to your true master as you always have. May I ask you to transform yourself into a bed and a roof to shelter us both for the night?'

Suddenly, the bow transformed into a bed.

Moggallāna led Pintola towards the bed, and two of them began to meditate through the night.

The miracle performed by the two monks alarmed Kaattaka, affirming his suspicion that they were evil spirits in disguise. The incident left him tossing and turning all night. In the meantime, his wife, children, and servants had begun to spread rumours of the monks' arrival, and the villagers were curious to see the pair for themselves. When dawn broke, Pintola fell from the bed, exhausted from meditating all night. Moggallāna reprimanded his student for his lack of concentration, telling him to stay focused at all times.

Kaattaka saw his chance and strode towards them. 'Evil spirits! You are bringing ill fate upon my land. Leave now, so I may use my bow as I please!'

The two monks transformed the bed back into a bow, expressing their gratitude to the huntsman before heading back to the tranquil peak of Mount Kaattaka. A few days and nights passed; finally, Pintola successfully attained the spiritual status of an arhat, and both monks travelled back to Jambudvipa together through the air.

Once they arrived at the Buddha's abode, Moggallāna recounted their entire journey, telling him about the recalcitrant huntsmen they had encountered. Moggallāna thought that Kaattaka would greatly benefit from the Buddha's guidance, and saw this as an opportunity for the Buddha to personally impart his teachings to the people of that region, so that they might find peace and happiness in the years to come. After listening to Moggallāna, the Buddha decided that he would travel alone to visit the huntsman and the people in Mount Kaattaka the very next day.

When morning arrived, the Lord Buddha traversed through the air and alighted gracefully onto Mount Kaattaka. The entire area was suddenly bathed in his serene light, and the lush forest blossomed with freshly ripened fruit, satiating the hunger of countless animals who no longer needed to encroach on the lives of others for survival. The Buddha dimmed his aura and disguised himself as an ordinary monk before heading to visit the huntsman.

Kaattaka was relaxing in his front yard once more when he saw the Buddha approaching him. *There were two of them yesterday, and here comes another one*, he thought to himself, agitated. *These scoundrels are definitely trying to ruin my life.*

'Good man,' the Buddha said, greeting Kaattaka. 'Would you be so kind as to offer me refuge for the night?'

'Stop it, you villain!' Kaattaka snapped. 'I won't be disturbed again by the mayhem the other two of you brought upon me last night.'

'If you do not permit me to rest here, will you allow me to rest by the cliff's edge?' asked the Buddha.

'As you please,' Kaattaka said, shrugging.

The Buddha then made his way to the cliff. He was determined to quell the huntsman's stubbornness, and to liberate his servants from their master's savagery and wickedness. With all his might, the Lord Buddha conjured dark clouds to cloak the entire sky. For three days and three nights, torrents of heavy rain poured down from the heavens. To shelter himself, the Lord Buddha bent the cliff's edge into the shape of a cobra's hood, where he remained completely dry throughout the storm. The storm was catastrophic for the huntsman and his servants. A flash flood flowed out from the nearby jungle, sweeping away their homes and prized possessions. Frantic, the villagers tried their best to salvage what was left of their belongings and supplies.

Once the villagers caught sight of the Buddha, the cliff arching over him like a cobra's hood, their imaginations ran wild. Some were convinced that the monk was responsible for this miraculous metamorphosis, but others feared that he would bring about disaster. Frustrated, Kaattaka yelled at the Buddha.

'You deceitful fiend! You have brought this downpour upon us, and look how you have deformed my cliff. You did not keep your word about staying for only one night; instead, you have stayed for three. Now get out of here! Leave, as you promised you would!'

'Good huntsman,' the Buddha replied. 'It is true that I only asked to stay for one night. However, the rain did not permit to leave, and although it has now stopped, everywhere else has flooded. May I please stay here another night?'

Kaattaka was too agitated to continue arguing with the Buddha. He decided to return to his house with his servants.

That night, the Lord Buddha performed another miracle. He summoned the angels and the Brahmins, who flew to assemble around him, illuminating Mount Kaattaka with their sun-bright auras. Their brilliance woke the huntsman and his servants. At first, they were alarmed, mistaking the light for a forest fire but, after taking a closer look, they realized that the canopies and hills before them were beaming with celestial light. This extraordinary sight finally convinced the huntsman of the Buddha's miraculous powers.

The next morning, the huntsman and his servants went to pay their respects to the Buddha by the cliff. Upon hearing the Buddha's story and his teachings, they and their families turned to a devoted life of goodness, swearing never to harm other beings for as long as they lived.

Profoundly overwhelmed with reverence, Kaattaka expressed his wish to be personally ordained by the Buddha himself. Not only did the Buddha immediately grant Kaattaka his wish, he also advised Kaattaka to practice meditation, which would help him expel his greed and start him on the path towards enlightenment. With the swiftness of a banana tree felled with a single swing of a sword, Kaattaka became an arhat. He exclaimed with joy:

'I used to live a sinful life of ignorance, killing many animals, but now that I have come to understand and appreciate dharma, I vow to abandon my old ways and free myself from all suffering. I am truly at peace.'

Not long afterwards, the Buddha told Kaattaka that his mission here was complete, and that it was time for him to return to India. Kaattaka asked to follow him but the Buddha refused, instead advising him to remain on Mount Kaattaka to bestow Buddhist teachings upon others in the region, so that they too might abandon their sinful and corrupted ways. Entrusted with this duty, the huntsman agreed to remain on Mount Kaattaka, but asked if he could have something to remember the Buddha by. And so, the Buddha imprinted his image upon the cliff face before gliding back to Jambudvipa through the air.

Unlike the first two, the final version of this story has no complicated plotlines. The Buddha simply knew, through his meditation, which region would most benefit from his teachings and pass them down for years to come. As he meditated, a vision of the small hills of Pattawee came to him, and so it was there that he made his journey.

He arrived in Pattawee in the middle of a raging rainstorm, so sought refuge under a cliff's edge. His holiness shielded him from every single drop of rain, and his radiant aura left his image permanently seared onto the cliff face.

When the rain subsided, the Buddha travelled to Mount Suwan, where he stood on a flat piece of stone at the top of the mountain. A huntsman named Sajjapan was hunting in the area where he came across the Buddha, bathed in brilliant light. Never had he seen such a miraculous being before. The huntsman approached him with a gesture of reverence, asking the Buddha to leave his footprint on the stone as a token for the angels and human beings to worship forever.

Before consenting, the Buddha asked him to abstain from the sin of killing, and the huntsman willingly agreed to do so. The Buddha then placed his right footprint at the top of Mount Suwan, where it would be worshipped by his devotees.

He later travelled to a town nearby, where he stopped at a large tree. There, he performed another miracle, where he appeared to be walking, sitting, and sleeping on the treetop. Awestruck by his powers, the people and the angels in the area gathered together to pay their respects, offer alms, and listen to the Buddha's teachings.

As the angels and townspeople congregated beneath the large tree, the Buddha smiled at the sight of a goat grazing nearby. Anon, his disciple, saw him smile; curious, he asked the Buddha what he had seen. The Buddha replied that he had seen a vision of this goat reincarnated as a great king, a ruler of the region who would preserve his image and his footprint for generations to come.

These are the stories I gathered from the huntsmen about the miraculous powers of the Lord Buddha. To this day, some people are reluctant to approach the Buddha's image and footprint, since those who had done so in the stories had had their lives completely turned upside-down by the Buddha's powers.

As I dwelled in the thlok tree, I contemplated the three versions of the story recounted by the huntsmen over and over again, until a question occurred to me. How could three different encounters with the Buddha all happen at the same time? The hermit named Sajjapan, the huntsman named Kaattaka, and the other huntsman called Sajjapan: all three of them had asked the Buddha to perform the same miracle, to leave his image and footprint. For a single piece of evidence to be introduced by three different people who all happened to meet the Buddha in near identical situations, I realized that these three different people had to be the same person!

So, Mount Suwan is Mount Pattawee, and Kaattaka refers to the huntsman of Mount Pattawee, whose name was actually Sajjapan.

As to whether he was a hermit or a huntsman, I know only what I heard from those men. It could be that Sajjapan was a huntsman before he became a hermit. But if you really want to know, light some incense and summon his spirit, and you can ask him yourself. His spirit rests in his abode at the Temple of the Buddha's Footprint. You can ask your parents to take you there.

Upon hearing these stories from the men, I too came to regard the Lord Buddha with reverence. I had wished desperately to follow his path; once I had been blessed with the body of a naga, I was determined to seek out his footprint on Mount Pattawee.

I knew I had arrived on Mount Pattawee when I felt an extraordinary calm settle over me. As I slithered past the foot of the mountain, my heart brimmed with an inexplicable sense of serenity and contentment. *This is the mountain*, I told myself. Meandering up the steep ascent, I finally arrived at the top of the mountain. There, I saw his footprint on a piece of stone. It was not too deep, and was about three *soks* long and half a sok wide. I slithered closer, and as I looked at the crystal-clear water trapped inside the footprint, an image of the Wheel of Dharma appeared at the centre. I bent down for a sip, catching sight of my own serpentine reflection, and began to lap at the water with my tongue, quenching the immense thirst I had carried with me throughout my long journey.

As I lifted my head, the delightfully pure taste of the water spread through the entire length of my body. Then and there, a miracle happened. The pain from the wound on the side of my body completely disappeared, and the ruptured skin instantly began to heal. I was suddenly reinvigorated, every muscle in my body pulsing with energy. This blissful state remained with me for centuries.

Wandering

The sacred water from the footprint kept me alive for hundreds of years; in other words, I became immortal. You may think of immortality, of not knowing pain or death, as a blessing: death, perhaps, but that pain had burdened my heart for centuries.

It happened right after I discovered the Buddha's footprint. I had decided to remain in the area, hoping that the footprint's miraculous power would protect me from harm. However, the footprint had already been claimed by humans. The few times I tried to drink from the footprint, a group of them—huntsmen and villagers alike—would chase me away, throwing rocks and all sorts of other things at me. Since it was too risky to venture near the footprint during the day, I would hide until it was safe to return at night, slipping past the watchful human eyes that guarded it.

One night, without warning, the angels appeared together on Mount Pattawee without prior arrangement, illuminating the entire mountain with their glowing light. They had come to mourn the passing of the Lord Buddha. Oh, how my heart broke!

I, who had patiently waited by his footprint in the hope that one day I would be blessed enough to welcome his return . . . I, who had prayed for a chance to follow his path with the body that I now possessed . . . My utmost desires were completely shattered. I mourned for many days and nights in total despair until one morning, when I decided to shake myself out of my own misery. I scaled down Mount Pattawee with a newfound purpose: to journey to every corner of the region, following in the footsteps of the late Lord Buddha.

I first headed towards the district where the Buddha had once performed his miracles on the topmost boughs of a large tree. Just as I was about to arrive, I saw that the village had become a kind of bustling meeting-place; a market, almost. In my current form, close proximity to humans was simply asking for capture, so I turned instead towards Khitkhin. To my surprise, Khitkhin seemed more crowded than the previous place. Too exhausted to go any further, I retreated back into the jungle.

Dejected and alone, I slithered along the banks of the Pasak River until the guardian spirit of the mountains revealed himself to me.

'My dear child,' he asked, 'what caused your loneliness and misery?'

I told him my truth. Taking pity on me, the guardian spirit said, 'My child, head east towards a mountain and there you will find a cave. They call it Phra Ngam Cave, where all those who venture inside marvel at the beauty of the Buddha image within, carved out of stone. Go and see it for your own good, my child. And when you reach the foot of the mountain, you will pass a Mon village. You need not fear the Mons, for they are devout Buddhists who would never harm a soul. When you reach the mouth of the cave, take some time to compose yourself. Steady your mind, then kneel down to the ground to pay respect to the cave's caretaker, a hermit. Tell him of your good intentions and he will grant you the chance to be close to the Lord Buddha.'

I thanked the guardian spirit for his guidance before resolutely making my way to the Phra Ngam Cave.

Oh, dear child! I spent so much time lost in the mountains! It was not because of the unfamiliar terrain, but because the forest spirits sensed that I was lost and played tricks on me to lead me astray. Time was wasted, and it took so long that I could feel that my strength had subsided and my skin that was once plump had sagged. My immortality was waning.

I was wallowing in the swamp when the Mud Lord suddenly appeared. He dragged me under the surface, threatening to hold me captive as his wife in his underwater kingdom. I begged for mercy: 'Please, no. My life on land began not so long ago.'

I struggled for my life but to no avail: only when I stopped moving did the Mud Lord finally loosen his grip.

One day, I could hear noises coming from afar. It sounded as though thousands of people were marching through the jungle. Suddenly, a voice rang out over the cacophony of human cries and beating shields.

'Whose territory is this?'

The crowd responded to the call as one. 'The great Khmer people!'

They marched on, shouting and pounding their shields. 'The Mons have fallen! The Khmers have risen to greatness!'

Expanding their rule and claiming sovereignty over this region, the Khmers called for the villagers to pledge their loyalty to the new kingdom, to do their part in helping to restore the prosperity of Buddhism. The name of this new kingdom was Lawo.

The Mud Lord, listening to the throng of marching Khmers claiming the territory as their own, suddenly grew agitated.

'Uwa! I have lived here for years and have never laid claim to anything. And yet, I now belong to the Khmers!'

I seized this opportunity to free myself from his grip. Leaving the dismayed Mud Lord and his fury behind in the seething swamp, I managed to make it back on land.

I resumed my journey, praying desperately to the divine beings: 'Please, let nothing else hinder me from reaching my destination. Please, let any wicked spirits with harm in their hearts be defeated.'

As I meandered my way through the forest, I heard some strange huffing and puffing. The sound was coming from a nearby bush, which was shaking vigorously as though possessed. It sounded like someone furiously eating: huffing, puffing, and eating. Timidly, I asked that someone whether he had good or ill intentions. The eating sounds came to an abrupt stop. A voice rang out from behind the bush.

'Good.' The voice then told me to stay as far away as possible, as it could cause me harm. I did as I was told, taking several steps back.

'Where are you off to?' I asked.

'Lawo. My father banished me there.'

'That's strange. Why would a father banish his child?'

'None of your business. Stay away unless you wish to be harmed.'

'But you said you were of good intentions. How could you possibly harm me?'

'Who are you to ask so many questions?'

'I'm a naga,' I replied. 'I'm on my way to Phra Ngam Cave to admire the image of the Buddha.'

'Oh. We are heading in different directions but we share the same purpose.'

The voice behind the bush softened as we began to converse. He told me how his father—the god Shiva—had come to banish him to a palace in Lawo. His father, struck by a violent rage, had given birth to him from between his eyebrows. Once born, he fell to the ground. The moment he opened his eyes, he found himself furiously ravenous. He began to consume everything in his wake, day and night, but nothing could fill the void inside him.

His hunger grew so uncontrollable that one day, he began to devour his own limbs. His father soon realized that it was his own virulent fury that had given birth to his son: the kind of fury that eats itself alive.

'My son,' his father said. 'You must go and station yourself at the gates of Lawo. You must serve a reminder of the destructive power of rage and hatred.'

He'd obeyed his father's wish, making his journey to Lawo.

'What is your name?' I asked him.

'My father calls me Kala,' he replied. 'All right, inquisitive naga. It's time for you to leave. You've taken up enough of the time I should've spent eating.'

'Are you eating yourself right now?' I asked out of curiosity. Without thinking, I moved closer to Kala, craning my head and peering through the bush. Kala was indeed in the midst of eating himself. He sat devouring his own torso until he realized that he was being watched. He lifted his head and snapped at me.

'Get away from me, you nosy naga!'

Our eyes met.

Kala's face was grotesque. It was flat, studded with a pair of bulging eyes and a mouth that slashed across the skin from one ear to the other. Canine teeth protruded from his gash of a grimace. All that was left of his body was that face and two arms. Once he saw me, he let out a howling cry, full of pain and sadness.

'My dear naga, you've brought this upon yourself. There is nothing I can do to help you now. What will be, will be!'

'What are you going to do?' I asked, alarmed.

'You have seen my face. Now, I will have to devour your Time.'

Terrified, I fled as fast as I could, screaming at the top of my lungs. I could hear Kala screaming too, his gaping mouth gulping down my Time, one year after another, until suddenly he fled in another direction.

Finally, I emerged from the jungle. Never in my life have I felt as drained as I did in that moment. My once-vivid memories began to fade; my once-fading memories disappeared entirely. My surroundings slowly untwisted, reforming into unfamiliar terrain. It began to dawn on me: while I had been fleeing from Kala, 700 years of my Time had fled from me.

I am the goat in the Lord Buddha's prophecy

I staggered out of the jungle and onto a vast plain. Before me was a scene I had never encountered in any of my lives. Stretching as far as the eye could see were fields of grass, rice, vegetables and crops, separated by deep furrows in the earth. Starving, I slithered towards them to feed, but was swiftly chased away by villagers. When they realized that the creature grazing on their crops was in fact a naga, the villagers called for their spears and bow and arrows, intent on either killing me for food or keeping me as an exotic pet. Luckily, I managed to escape those wicked humans; before I knew it, I had reached the mountain that led to Phra Ngam Cave.

A forest blanketed the foot of the mountain, with villages scattered throughout it. I felt much more at ease, moving inconspicuously along the forest's many hidden pathways and trails. Not far up the mountain was the mouth of the cave. I discreetly crawled my way inside and was suddenly cocooned by damp cave air. Even inside, the cave was well-lit. It was full of stalagmites and stalactites. Oh child, what strange beauty that was! But what was even more exquisite was the Buddha's image carved on the cave wall. I believe that the carving is what gave the cave its name, because, child, I was truly mesmerized. It was as if the Lord Buddha himself sat before me, ready to give his sermon.

The carving depicted the Lord Buddha cross-legged on a lotus flower, with a halo around his head and his hands raised in the attitude of teaching. Around him were carvings of angels and human devotees, listening to his sermon with rapt attention. The scene was a recalling of the Lord Buddha's journey to Mount Pattawee, where he had brought Sajjapan the huntsman to Buddhism and the angels had gathered around the mountain, illuminating the night and the surrounding region with their radiant light. I admired the carving, overcome with peace. Slowly, I curled up underneath the carving and fell asleep.

A muffled chanting woke me. I lifted my head to see the hermit in the midst of meditation, murmuring incomprehensibly. Not wanting to disturb him, I continued to lay there, watching. A moment later, he spoke to me, eyes still closed.

'What was it that you fled from, my child?'

The Khmers, I thought silently. *I ran away to seek the Lord Buddha's protection.*

He nodded in understanding. 'Don't be afraid. The Lawo kingdom is long gone.'

But I just escaped from those Khmer troops marching through the jungle, I told him.

'That was 800 years ago, my child,' the hermit replied. 'My visions tell me that your Time was devoured by Kala. The Khmers have been all but wiped out; the few that survived sought refuge in the villages by the foot of this mountain.

But did the jungle and the mountains recover after the fall of the Lawo kingdom?

'My child, the jungle and the mountains belong to the Kingdom of Ayutthaya, who has ruled this land and its people for hundreds of years. It doesn't matter who you were before, because now, everything belongs to Siam: the mountains, the trees, the streams, the ancient places of worship, and the lives of all peoples.' The hermit went silent for a moment before adding, 'You, too, are a creature of Siam.'

So are you, I teased back.

'Uwa! A witty creature too!' He chuckled. 'Dear child, do you know how territories were claimed?'

I did not.

'By those who claimed they were the Buddha's goat,' he laughed.

The hermit was a generous storyteller. As night fell, he shared with me tale after tale.

He began with the Buddha's arrival in Mount Pattawee and the miracle he had performed for the world to see, on top of a large tree in the Nhong Sa-no district. Looking down from above, the Buddha caught sight of a goat grazing in the area and smiled to himself. Anon, his disciple, saw him smile; curious, he asked the Buddha what he had seen . . . 'This goat,' the Buddha replied, 'will be reborn in its next life as a mighty king, destined to ensure the prosperity of Buddhism in the distant future.'

During the Lawo kingdom's reign in this region, two other kingdoms had also risen to power: the Haripunchai and Tambalinga kingdoms. The Haripunchais were former Mons who had been driven from their territory by the Khmers. They had regained their strength and were fighting back to reclaim their land. During this battle, the Tambalingas marched their troops from the South. They waited until the other two armies had exhausted one another before seizing the opportunity to conquer them both. As the victor of the War of the Three Kingdoms, the Tambalingas made Prince Kampote, the son of their king, the new ruler of the Lawo kingdom. The Tambalingas continued to rule Lawo for many years, until an outbreak occurred in the capital during the reign of King Srithammasokkaraj. The entire kingdom was forced to migrate back to the South, re-establishing their capital in Nakhon Sri Thammarat.

The city of Lawo was abandoned, but new kingdoms continued to emerge across the Suvarnabhumi region: Sukhothai, Lanna, Nakhon Sri Thammarat, and Pipeli in the city of Phetchaburi.

The Srithammasokkaraj dynasty and the U-Thong dynasty shared a close relationship and strong trade agreements, as their two kings were both of Khmer descent, or so they say.

The new kingdom in the South, erected by the Srithammasokkarajs, grew prosperous. King Srithammasokkaraj's might was renowned throughout the region: this was a king who had conquered twelve cities, naming them after the animals of the Chinese zodiac, and had successfully strengthened the Buddhist faith by summoning Lord Buddha's remains to the city of Nakhon Sri Thammarat, where they were to be preserved.

One day, before an assembly of courtiers, Brahmins, and ministers, King Srithammasokkaraj announced that he was the reincarnation of the goat from the Lord Buddha's prophecy. Not long after this, King Srithammasokkaraj passed away, and his throne was passed down to his viceroy.

The city of Pipeli and the Nakhon Sri Thammarat kingdom agreed to an amicable division of their territories. The two allies agreed that, going forward, the Southern region would belong to Nakhon Sri

Thammarat and the Northern region to the city of Pipeli. The treaty was sealed with a marriage between the sons and daughters of the two royal families. When the king of Pipeli met his end, a new king named U-Thong ascended to the throne.

However, not so long after the succession, the city of Pipeli faced crippling waves of famine and plague. When people and animals began to collapse once more—a sure sign that another cataclysmic episode was on the horizon—those still left alive were desperate to leave. King U-Thong decided to relocate the capital. He convened with his wise advisors, who pointed to an area northeast of the city of Lawo: home to Mount Pattawee and Mount Suwanbanpot, where the Buddha's shadow and footprint had been impressed onto the rock. Nhong Sa-no District—where the Buddha had performed his miracle on the treetop and delivered the prophecy of the goat reincarnated as a powerful king—was also nearby. Upon hearing this, King U-Thong proclaimed that he himself was the goat from the Buddha's prophecy. He was determined to take his army and loyal subjects with him on a pilgrimage to worship the sacred traces of the Lord Buddha.

Well into his journey, after visiting the many sacred sites, the king had set up camp by a river in Nhong Sa-no when suddenly, an enormous catfish leapt out of the water, capturing everyone's attention. As if by the miraculous stroke of an invisible hand, a gong sounded at the exact same time that the fish uttered words that echoed throughout the entire region: 'This district is fit for a capital.' Struck by this auspicious sight, the king prayed and tried his luck: he threw his sword, vowing that its landing place would mark the new capital. It landed in Nhong Sa-no.

Suddenly, in perfect synchronicity, the king's men broke into a deafening clamour. 'Only one who is blessed with sufficient merit is worthy of building a capital in Nhong Sa-no! Such worth can only be proven by the ability to ingest iron and a talent for archery! The blessed one must shoot an arrow and watch it return to him without moving a muscle!'

Upon hearing his men begin this eerie and tumultuous refrain, the king knew that the guardian spirits of Nhong Sa-no were speaking to him. They had ventriloquized his men in order to demand proof of his worth; of his merit and might. 'I am the goat from the Lord Buddha's prophecy,' the king then declared. 'I am able to ingest iron and my loyal arrow, once released, returns to me with ease.'

The king then ordered his cooks to grind a piece of iron into dust and mix it into his food, which he ate for all to see. From then on, all of the king's meals were served dusted with iron. He even claimed that it improved the taste of his food and immunized him from all kinds of illnesses. After eating the iron-dusted food for the first time, the king made his way to the riverside, bow and arrow in hand. He shot the arrow against the current, and watched as the river returned the arrow to his waiting hands. His men cheered, delighted by the king's wit.

Thus, the new capital was built, along with many palaces and temples. It was named Krungthep Mahanakhon Bavorn Tavaravadee Sri Ayutthaya Mahadilok Bavorn Rattanaratchathani Burirom, or Ayutthaya for short, which meant 'invincible city' in Khmer.

The city enjoyed many prosperous and peaceful days, impervious to external threats and enemy attacks. However, the king had yet to be formally crowned by the pure-blooded Brahmins. He sent an ambassador to central India to ask the King of Varanasi for permission to bring the Brahmins to Ayutthaya to conduct the coronation ceremony.

And so, the inauguration of the Kingdom of Ayutthaya came to pass. Forming alliances with the nearby cities of Lawo and Supanburi, the kingdom went on to colonize sixteen cities. Word of King U-Thong's greatness travelled throughout the region, as he waged war after war and conquered land after land. The capital of Ayutthaya established itself as a formidable force in Siam and its neighbouring countries, and the king became widely referred to by the people as Phra Chao Paen Din, or 'divine ruler of the land'.

My child, do you see the injustice that appears time and time again throughout the ages? Kings fought other kings, all proclaiming to be the goat from the prophecy. They waged wars to conquer lands, costing many lives, and built kingdoms, their subjects powerless to resist strict laws and regulations. However, things were different in the early days, when the world was newly created: a complete reversal of the order of things. The word 'king', or *rajah*, was commonly used to describe someone respectable and just: put simply, it was a word used for one who brought happiness to others. It was a word created and constituted by the people, as was written in the Sutta Pitaka, one of the three divisions of the Pali canon known as the Tipitaka. The Tipitaka contains the Vinaya Pitaka, the Sutta Pitaka, and the Abhidhamma. The Sutta Pitaka is categorized into five collections, and one of those—the Digha Nikaya—recounts the creation myth of the world as follows:

The world as it once existed was pure, unmolested by classification. It was unbounded by time, devoid of day or night. Gods with luminous, translucent bodies—neither male nor female, neither good nor evil—dwelled in the heavens, drifting and gliding with great joy.

As time passed, the earth began to lactate; moss, lichen, and other vegetation began to grow. Curious, the gods eventually tasted the fertile land, relishing the sensuous flavours, aromas, and colours. They became addicted to eating the earth's greenery, searching high and low, in every crack and crevice, for more. Gradually, their luminous auras dimmed, as their celestial bodies grew swaddled in flesh. Their appetites grew insatiable; they were no longer sated by their own happiness. Their waning light was no longer bright enough to illuminate Earth, and they were replaced by the brilliant sun and moon; hence, day and night came to be. Time was divided into days, months, years; seasons came into existence. Divine beings became humans, separated by gender and bound by time, imbued with carnal desire and the ability to procreate.

Humans had to survive on whatever nature gave them. They gathered plants and rice and stored food for days in order to feed their children and other dependents. When human demand grew beyond what nature could provide them with, agriculture came to be, and land became a valuable commodity. There were those who could obtain land and those who couldn't, and thus evil arose. Cheating, stealing, and competition became common practice, as did punishment, perjury, revenge, and murder.

As things continued to escalate, some humans convened to find a respectable and just figure to preside over the growing conflicts. It was unanimously understood that this respectable and just figure—the king—would belong to the second caste and would be given the task of restoring justice to the community. Once justice prevailed, the community would reward the king with a share of their crops or land. This was the concept of kingship or monarchy at its most fundamental.

Nevertheless, like all those tethered to power, most kings were unwilling to cede their positions of privilege, seeking to expand and consolidate their power through the murder of other rulers and the colonization of other kingdoms. To prevent dissent, succession was a process formally passed down through bloodlines. However, evil persisted with power as children and grandchildren killed each other for the throne.

Ever since the Sukhothai Kingdom, the right to the Kingdom of Ayutthaya belonged solely to the king, or Khun Luang, as the people called him. (My child, your memory of this era was also devoured by Kala.) The system of governance between a king and his subjects was once similar to the relationship between a father and his children; then, the people had called their ruler Phor Khun, or 'Great Father'. It was different from the absolute monarchy devised by the Khmers: a system heavily influenced by the Brahmins, where the king was seen as the avatar of the gods. The Khmers ruled their subjects as masters ruled their slaves. Within the territories they colonized, people were forced to worship in the king's faith: buildings, temples, and Bodhisattva figures were erected to honour kings as reincarnations of the gods.

However, things were complicated. Although the Siamese considered the Sukhothai kingdom to be their own, Mon-Khmer influences were ever-present in Siamese customs and daily life. Monks continued to write and record the names of Sukhothai kings in an ancient Khmer dialect, and royal terms remained Khmer in origin. The use of royal language was common during the beginning of the Ayutthaya kingdom, but, my child, it was too complicated for commoners, who simply preferred to call the king Khun Luang. Despite coming into use during the Sukhothai era, the term Khun Luang became most established in the Ayutthaya kingdom. In the Ayutthaya era, the kingdom was able to expand its territories further than ever before. Khun Luang of Ayutthaya became a title that transcended other titles in any country or language.

The father of his subjects eventually became the father of the land. The king not only presided over his subjects, but also his territories. Land became clearly demarcated—'This land belonged to Siam,' they said, 'this here is Siamese land.'—and King U-Thong understood the significance of this, my child. Once he became King of Ayutthaya, a law was issued as follows:

'All land within the Kingdom of Ayutthaya belongs to the king; subjects do not possess the right to land ownership, despite occupancy.'

From that moment on, the king has possessed absolute power over capital, property, the lives of his subjects and all Siamese territories. The people gave their king the new name of Phra Chao Pan Din: divine ruler of the land.

Naming the city

The hermit stayed up, telling his stories until the break of dawn, as if conversation was the only thing he had hungered for all these years. Every episode he recounted left me awestruck. Kala had taken the span of an entire kingdom from me, but he hadn't stopped there: he had ingested the conquering of Ayutthaya too!

The land of Suvarnabhumi was in constant contact with other ruled territories, from neighbouring kingdoms like Hanthawaddy, Lanna, and Lan Xang to the Khmer Empire and the kingdoms of China. Sometimes, they reached out in peace; at other times, they waged war. Siam itself was not always a harmonious entity: internal politics were rife between several colonies—Phitsanulok, Nakhon Ratchasima, Myeik, and Nakhon Sri Thammarat—who fought for autonomy and personal benefits over the interest of the kingdom as a whole. These matters were handled either by force or by diplomacy, with rulers sending their children and other members of the royal family across colonies to tie artful knots of arbitration. Nevertheless, the latter often devolved into eventual bloodshed; fathers, mothers, children, siblings and relatives continued to fight one another to become Ayutthaya's Phra Chao Pan Din.

Chaos preceded the fall of Ayutthaya. The Hanthawaddy kingdom had already invaded the capital twice. The first invasion had been triggered in the city of Chiang Kran, where the Mons pledged their loyalty to Ayutthaya over Hanthawaddy. The second invasion had occurred when during Ayutthaya's weakest point; with aid and additional troops from the northern city of Phitsanulok, the capital had managed to resist the attack led by the King of Hanthawaddy. However, in the battle that ensued during the second invasion, Ayutthaya lost its queen. Following the great loss of Queen Suriyothai, King Maha Chakkraphat of Ayutthaya consulted with his advisers before building more cities around the capital, fortifying its defence against any future battles with Hanthawaddy.

This very land had been called many names, but none of them had truly stuck. Villagers continued to live off the land, but fled into the jungles and mountains whenever faced with epidemic or war. With its fertile earth and strategic location along the route from Nakhon Ratchasima to Cambodia, the land was more than suitable for growing rice and crops as food supplies during wartime. The king saw this and proceeded to carve out parts of the surrounding cities—Lopburi, Nakhon Ratchasima, and Nakhon Nayok—to form the new city of Saraburi. The city became the kingdom's repository and outpost, a place from which to monitor potential threats coming from the direction of Nakhon Ratchasima and Cambodia.

All right then! Now, you all know that this place is called Saraburi: a land twice severed and sutured simply to be named for your tongue's convenience.

I'm tired of telling you about Ayutthaya. If you're keen to know more, do yourself a favour and go read about it. Or you could ask your teachers, but be sure to tell them to teach you well. Tell them not to teach you to hate the Burmese, the Mons, the Lao people, or the Khmers. It's not as simple as that. Our histories are deeply entangled and their kingdoms were among the greatest of them all, even greater than ours. They are Buddhists like us—no—actually, we are Buddhists like them. The Khmers were the first to convert to Buddhism and

Brahminism, and we in turn inherited all that from them. You can see it in our language of hierarchies, especially in the royal language. The Lao people used to be our beloved kin: ask your parents to take you to Bangkok, to see for yourselves just how beautiful the Emerald Buddha is. As for Burma? They were once our close friends, but, as in all relationships, there were times of conflict that turned chivalrous men into ruthless patriots. It's not that they're evil. We're evil to them too. So, you tell your teachers to teach you these things, ner.

Now, you must be wondering how old the hermit was. That's something I don't know for certain, although I spent a long time with him indeed. From listening to the stories he recounted, as if he'd been there to witness them himself, I can only assume that he had spent at least 400 years alone in that cave, practising the skills he needed to reach enlightenment. He was a true master of his body, with a spirit full of determination and might. Each day began with yoga or walking meditation. Sometimes, he'd travel through the air for days, returning with a bunch of bananas, wood, or some herbs. He was always mumbling to himself; sometimes disappearing, turning himself to stone, or setting himself ablaze.

Sometimes, after disappearing for an entire day, he would return with news from the capital. He did this after Hanthawaddy enthroned Maha Thammaracha as Ayutthaya's new king—an unexpected event in the history of the kingdom—and after the Black Prince's coronation. Later, when he was succeeded by his brother, the White Prince, the hermit would do the same. He would say all of these things aloud, without really addressing anyone in particular. His voice would echo inside the cave and I, the only living creature present, would listen.

As I've said before, my spirit is immortal, but my physical body—where my spirit resides—deteriorates with time. After about thirty years of living with the hermit, my naga body eventually wore itself out. All I could do was curl up and rest inside the cave, waiting. The hermit saw the state that I was in and pitied me. One evening, he returned to the cave carrying the carcass of a tiger. He beckoned me closer and began to cast a spell that transferred my spirit out of the naga's body and into the tiger's. The abandoned body of the naga disintegrated into dust before vanishing into thin air.

'My dear, you are burdened with sin,' the hermit lamented. 'Fated to live an immortal life without any purpose.'

Upon hearing the hermit's words, I suddenly realized—after all this time—the kind of life I had been yearning to live: a life devoted to him. Now that I had the body of a tiger, I could carry him on my back during his meditation trips to the jungle. The hermit chuckled upon hearing my wish. Despite having the power to teleport himself, he allowed me to express my gratitude to him by performing the role of his carrier.

The tiger's body was already old and lifeless by the time the hermit had procured it: never would he commit the sin of murder, let alone for the mere purpose of bringing me a new body. I was living inside the walls of a corpse; the body was beginning to cannibalize itself, taking with it my ability to see and hear. Soon, the hermit had to search for a new body once again. This time, he returned with the carcass of a young, stillborn deer.

'Do you feel disheartened, having to live through the bodies of others, one after another?' the hermit asked.

I did not know how to respond.

'Have you ever wanted a life of your own?'

'Will it be one where I get to live with you forever?' I asked him.

'Live for your own sake. Why do you need to live for me?'

'To pay my thanks to you for looking after me all these years,' I replied.

'You don't owe me anything,' he said. 'Everything I've done for you was for my own happiness, and that's enough for me. Don't try to impose any unnecessary, complicated bond between us. If you feel the need to give back, I'd rather you give for the sake of giving without expecting anything in return.'

'Then I don't want a life of my own,' I protested.

'Your spirit binds itself to things beyond the body it dwells in,' he said in contemplation. 'Soon I'll be gone. What will you do then?'

'What are you saying? If you leave, then I want to leave with you too.'

'That is impossible because you are immortal. Your spirit is bound to dwell on this earth for eternity. Where I'm going, spirits are extinguished and released from all previous ties. You cannot come with me because your spirit is inextinguishable. Do you understand?'

'Will I ever be extinguished?'

'You will have to die and be reborn again,' he replied. 'To secure a successful rebirth, in the moments before you die, you must direct your consciousness, heart and mind towards the purpose of your next life.'

The hermit then confided that he had a bundle of herbs with him. These herbs had the power to release me from all the pain and suffering of immortality, to usher my spirit into the cycle of life and death. However, the hermit refused to give me the herbs until I was able to tell him why I wished to be reborn, and for what purpose.

I had laid this matter to rest decades ago. I was quite satisfied with my life then; living in my deer body, keeping the hermit company day by day in the Phra Ngam Cave. All the while, our bond grew stronger with each passing day. I watched his human form move with such grace and agility—the firm reach and grasp of his mercurial hands—and imagined how wonderful it would be if I, too, were able to operate the human physique. I would be able to tend to him better, and that was truly my only wish: to be reborn as a human so I could care for the hermit for the rest of my human days.

A strange feeling stirred within me. It happened the day I left the cave to hunt near the stream. I was happy until I felt my heart plummet to the ground. I stood there by the stream. What had I just lost? Nothing at all. Nothing had been lost; rather, it was the fear of loss—of losing someone—that had taken hold of me. From that seed of fear and trepidation stemmed my worry: a foreign and feverish sensation that had admittedly grown out of the love I had for the hermit. Distraught at the prospect of losing him, I stood there and wept.

I was seized by this feeling for a long time, letting it consume my appetite and keep me awake at night. I refused to step out of the cave, planting myself next to the hermit whenever he was there. From that moment on, I was aware of every movement he made, no matter how slight.

And suddenly, on a day just like any other, he disappeared. It didn't occur to me at first that he might not return but, as time passed,

I grew tormented. Days dragged into weeks into months into years, and still, there was no sign of him. Time flew past, and suddenly there came a day when a monk appeared in the cave, looking for a place to rest. I quickly fled into another nearby cave to hide, but kept careful watch. From that day on, more monks began to arrive. Eventually, they started to build a monastery, which later became known as the Temple of Bodhisattva Cave.

I remained there after the monastery was built, relying on the cave's many crevices for shelter while I waited patiently for the hermit. The monks noticed my presence but they were kind enough to let me be, lingering by the cave's mouth in anticipation for the hermit's return.

Not long after this, a group of villagers began to visit the monastery to pay their respects to the monks, giving alms and listening to sermons. They all found it strange to see a deer stationed at the mouth of the cave, lying still as a rock. Soon, through word of mouth, the story of the deer waiting at the cave spread to the villagers. Eventually, people started to call the district Thap Kwang,[1] which means 'village of the deer'. I was the deer that lingered.

One night, the hermit came to visit me in my dreams. He told me that my wait was in vain because his spirit had already departed from this world. He had watched me all these years and, moved by pity, felt the need to finally explain what had become of him. His spirit had been extinguished and he had reached enlightenment, never to return to this world. He had reached enlightenment while meditating at Mount Suwanbanpot; then, he had departed his physical body and this world. He told me to find my own path and reminded me of the bundle of herbs hidden in the base of the Buddha carving in the cave. 'Set your spirit toward the cycles of life and death,' he said, 'and take the herbs.

[1] The present belief is that this subdistrict was called Baan Lao due to the influx of Lao refugees who migrated there during the war in the city of Viang Chan (now Vientiane), after it was invaded by Prince Maha Kasatsuek and his army, under the King of Thonburi's order. It was also when the Emerald Buddha was summoned from the city to return with the prince's army. During the reign of Rama V, the subdistrict changed its name back to Thap Kwang, its name prior to the Thonburi era. The name change was ordered by Prince Damrong Rajanubhab, the defence minister at the time, to alleviate ethnic conflict between the Lao and Thai inhabitants.

Set your heart in the direction of what you desire to be and achieve in your next life. This is what I came to tell you, my child.'

The dream startled me awake. I burst into a painful howl that echoed through the mountains. His body, I thought, was the last physical thing I could cling to; I darted out of the cave, desperate to find the hermit's remains in Mount Suwanbanpot.

Obscured

I ran without stopping for two days and nights, tracing the scent of the hermit's remains, which finally led me to the foot of Mount Suwanbanpot. I stopped and looked around, to make sure that it was safe to lie down. An immense wave of exhaustion surged through my entire body and my limbs shuddered as if on the brink of paralysis. Before I knew it, I was asleep.

I woke, feeling a little more refreshed, and walked around a small enclosure surrounded by towering trees. I sniffed the earth, using my snout to desperately rummage and ransack through the piles of leaves, searching for the hermit's scent. I was certain that his remains were buried underneath a large stone where the gentle fragrance of lotus flower was strongest. This was where he had departed, I was sure of it. I started digging into the earth with my two hooves, hoping to see his body once again.

I was about half a metre deep when a sharp pang struck me on the side of my body: an arrow, lodged inside me, blood trickling down from the open wound. What cruel huntsman would do such a thing? I scurried into the forest, afraid for my life. I reached the edge of the mountain and discovered a small pond, as if guided by some miraculous force. *It must have been the hermit's spirit,* I thought. I crept nearer to the pond. As I lowered my head for a drink, I realized that the pond had formed from the Buddha's footprint, similar to the one I had first encountered in Mount Pattawee. I had known instantly that the water in that pond was sacred, since it healed my wounds and immortalized me for hundreds of years. Convinced that this pond was as sacred as the one on Mount Pattawee, I prayed for two things as I drank. First, I prayed that my wounds be remedied and, second, I prayed for a new body that would betray me less: a body that would be truly mine, so I would no longer have to live off the bodies of others. As I bent down to take a sip, I noticed the elaborate grooves and patterns impressed on the banks of the pond from the weight of the Buddha's footprint. They were even more striking than the ones on Mount Pattawee. After the first sip, I felt life and exuberance resurge through my entire body. Frolicking through the bushes, I ran straight into an ugly-looking huntsman who had followed me into the forest, a bow clutched in his hands. It was he who had tried to kill me.

The hideous huntsman was stunned at the sight of me bounding out of the bush. He stood there for a moment, dumbfounded as to how the deer he had shot was not only unscathed, but alive and leaping as if it had been given a new life. It might have been confusion that drew the huntsman's attention away from me, because he began to make his way into the bushes where the Buddha's footprint was. Never before had I felt so brave. I was no longer afraid of the huntsman, so I tiptoed after him and kept watch behind the bushes. Oh, children, he looked so bewildered, so lost in thought. He squatted next to the footprint and doused his arms, legs, face, and body with the sacred water. Miraculously, his skin—which had been plagued with some sort of disease—was transformed anew. I could see that the huntsman was pleased, but at the same time, another transformation was taking place inside me. I could feel waves from the sacred water surging inside me, one after another. The first wave restored my energy, but the second— more violent than the first—left me feverish and dizzy. Before I could take another step, I fell unconscious.

I lifted my eyes, still heavy with slumber, to find myself lying on the wooden floor inside a hut. My body was relaxed; I could move my head and lift up my hands—my hands! They were human hands, every inch of them! Oh, my child, through the power of the sacred water from the Buddha's footprint, I had received the beautiful body of a human woman.

Another human figure appeared. He seemed to be preoccupied with cooking something. When he noticed that I had begun to stir, he told me not to be afraid, and introduced himself as a well-intended local huntsman called Boon. He had seen me lying unconscious in the jungle while out hunting. He hadn't recognized me and assumed that I wasn't from here, but noticed that I was still breathing, so had decided to take me to his hut in the middle of the forest to look after me. As he explained, he handed me some herbal medicine.

I looked at Boon. He was quite handsome, and he was also kind. I drank the medicine, choking a little at how bitter and hot it was. Afterwards, a warm sensation filled my insides: a sensation that I had never felt before. *This must be how humans feel*, I thought to myself. Once I finished the medicine, I remembered the Buddha's footprint. I recounted to Boon all the miraculous stories I knew about it. He must have found me odd, having heard the stories, which—as I told him—were all true. I even told him about the other footprint I thought I had seen on Mount Pattawee. Boon looked confused and quickly changed the subject, telling me to rest in the hut and avoid being seen by anyone. I listened to him, believing that he meant well.

Boon came and went as he pleased. He would sometimes disappear for a while before returning with food and clothes for me. I lived with him and slept with him. He was my first.

He was sly, too. He already had another family living somewhere else. Our hut was his little hunting hideout. Eventually, he found more honourable work and gave up hunting. He became a somebody in the area, and I was his mistress, a part of his secret life. I eventually came to suspect this after gathering bits and pieces of stories here and there.

One day, I returned to the Buddha's footprint on Mount Suwanbanpot, only to discover that things had changed drastically. The foot of the mountain looked bizarre, crawling with officials. A wooden pavilion had been erected over the Buddha's footprint, signifying it as an important royal site. Visitors paying respect to the footprint turned to tell me that a huntsman called Boon had discovered it while out hunting a deer. The huntsman had reported this discovery to the Saraburi authorities, and the news had spread to the capital of

Ayutthaya to the ears of King Songtham, who had then travelled to Saraburi with his troops. Boon had volunteered to take the king up the mountain to see the footprint himself, and he had been amply rewarded for his service. The king had ordered a royal pavilion to be built over the footprint to commemorate the discovery. He'd appointed guards, invited foreigners from Holland with their binoculars to survey the area and construct roadworks, and even ordered a royal residence to be built in anticipation of his future visits. All this grandiosity!

As I listened to the story, I thought about the two footprints: the left on Mount Suwanbanpot and the right on Mount Pattawee. But when I asked the visitors about the right footprint on Mount Pattawee, they all looked confused. They'd never heard about a footprint on Mount Pattawee, they said. They only knew of the Buddha's shadow that had been imprinted there.

Keeping the rest of my questions to myself, I decided to head to Mount Pattawee to see the footprint with my own eyes. So much development had taken place that the area was almost unrecognizable. I approached a monk who seemed to be a powerful and reclusive arhat, who was silently meditating in an abandoned cell at the back of the temple grounds. After paying my respects, I asked him about the Buddha's footprint that I had once found so long ago. The arhat assured me that it still existed, but was hidden. A mandapa had been built over the footprint to obscure it, making the people believe that there was only one footprint in Mount Suwanbanpot. Since Mount Pattawee was already home to the imprint of the Buddha's shadow, they had decided to cover the footprint on Mount Suwanbanpot with sand, poured cement over it and fabricated a more unassuming footprint in its place. Out of respect for the king, the villagers agreed to it and, instead, built the mandapa as a courtesy to the Buddha. The villagers had agreed to keep everything a secret, making the job of archivists and historians much easier. So that was what had happened, my dears. Perhaps the footprint on Mount Suwanbanpot is considered to be more auspicious today because it was discovered by the king, or perhaps it is because the king's courtiers and Boon the huntsman had conspired to conceal the right footprint from the king. No matter. Artificiality obscures but eventually deteriorates. Authenticity is what remains. The truth often reveals itself, sooner or later. That is what the arhat told me.

If my memory serves me right, my dears, the footprint on Mount Pattawee was rediscovered 400 years later in 1994, by the state's fine arts department in the Rattanakosin era. They had initially come to the area to carry out some minor maintenance work on the pavilion's exterior, and hadn't anticipated the important relic obscured underneath it.

I had been naive about these things back then. I didn't care to understand why people would manipulate and distort things, and for whom they would contort and conceal reality: all for the purpose of flattery. I hadn't been human for long; all I knew was how difficult it was to understand humans, how complicated their affairs were. But living with Boon made me realize how manipulative and cunning they can really be.

I slowly collected my thoughts, summoning the conviction to tell others that it was I who had seen the right footprint all those years ago. But no one believed me. They thought I was mad. 'If what you're saying is true,' they said, 'you would have been alive thousands of years ago.'

'Of course,' I nodded. 'Before I was human, I was a spirit inside a thlok tree, a naga, a tiger, and a deer.' People laughed at me, calling me delusional, a madwoman, a Khmer who had lost her mind from too much black magic. They regarded me with derision and fear, and my stories—my own experiences—were nothing but lies and fables to them.

They accused me of taking age-old myths passed down by their elders and turning them into brand-new lies, of tainting written accounts recorded by previous generations in order to take all the credit for myself. Things were twice inverted: the more stories fell from my dampened lips, the further truth slipped away from them. Later came the historical annals and books; the written texts that your generation have so much faith in, all while dismissing the stories told to you by your elders. Things become visible only when those with authority—those esteemed with such-and-such position—write them down, like the story of how the Buddha's footprint was discovered by King Songtham of Ayutthaya. You only see what the Phra Chao Pan

Din sees: whatever eludes his sight eludes yours too. They wrote that the Buddha's footprint was found on Mount Suwanbanpot and that the imprint of the Buddha's shadow was discovered on Mount Pattawee. When they omitted the footprint on Mount Pattawee in their records, the actual footprint ceased to exist too. Perhaps they had written it down somewhere, but it was erased or edited through the ages. I have seen history purging itself with each new monarch, and you may well still be circling in its cesspool.

Just look at that footprint on Mount Pattawee! They rediscovered it in 1994 and proceeded to record it as such. But when you take the time to actually look through the annals of history, you'll find that the footprint existed long before it was recorded. There's nothing wrong with not knowing the genealogy of things: that's what research is for. But when you start reappropriating this story and that story into a new myth, all out of ignorance? Well, that just hurts my head. If you want to know how it feels, go and ask your parents to tell you about the two legends behind these two footprints. Did you know both of them are based on the same legend? Legend has it that the Buddha travelled to the mountains and left his footprint there—a single footprint, mind you—and then what? Then there's a mysterious gap in the story, followed by the discovery made by Boon the huntsman and King Songtham, and then another gap before the conclusion, which is that the pavilion was built to preserve the footprint, which has been safeguarded by every monarch that has come to power since.

I'm telling you all this but the question is, which foot was put in writing? Which one was it that was written up in the legend?

Out of convenience, these obscure gaps that punctuate the story of the Buddha's footprints are glossed over by a single legend, a single version of history. But do you see how the lines of history are dotted throughout? I like to imagine Kala sinking its ghastly teeth into the edges and folds of time, like a cockroach gnawing on a piece of fabric.

Your sense of history and time is muddled. Your memories are tied to time, and so are your lives, which—if you believe what I just told you—will be severed short; as humans, you are only able to live to about a hundred years. I can see that the human lifespan keeps on diminishing; it used to be two or three times as long only two or three thousand years ago.

My life is as much a life as yours are, children. In the most fundamental sense, the lives of humans, animals, the earth, and the plants exist on different scales and cycles, with the earth being the oldest among us. Born out of the earth and later transformed into a human, my life is longer than any of yours. Now you understand why I am still alive today.

Now, let me return to Boon the huntsman. I revisited different places in Saraburi, observing the transformation and development of its communities, listening to numerous stories told by people like the arhat. After much consideration on my part, I came to wonder why *this* Boon, the huntsman in the stories people had been telling me, shared exactly the same name as the man I was living with. (Dare I consider the possibility that the man I was living with had a family and people of his own? That he looked down on me, saw me as a serf?) I thought about what Boon had told me after I woke up in human form. It occurred to me that my Boon must be the same Boon from the legend. Then I remembered being shot by the huntsman, and the arrow that had pierced my deer body while I drank the sacred water from the Buddha's footprint, the sacred water that had granted me my human form. The same water that had also cured the ugly huntsman's skin ailments. Was I right in thinking that the sacred water, which possessed the power to transform me from a deer into a human, could also easily turn a hideous huntsman into a handsome one?

I was shocked by my realization. Boon had been that huntsman all along.

I began to look further into his identity, into his family and the land that he lived off. That was when I learned of what it meant to be enslaved, and the difference between a mistress and a wife. After a period of exhausting and painful rumination, I finally realized that, simply put, a life with Boon meant a life of shame and manipulation. And so, I mustered the courage to leave him for good. 'We don't owe each other anything now, Boon,' I lamented, as I fled from the hut.

Rebellion and time

It is not just our relationship to time that differs. As a human being in nothing but name, the ties that bind me are of a very different nature to yours. Nowadays, humans like you tether time to parents, relatives, homes, systems of governance, making a living, money, and so forth. These are the kinds of things that you humans have latched your lives onto.

As for me, I am not bound to any of these things. My time is much freer, longer. My life is bound to nature, to the mountains and the jungles, and this is the major difference between us. You left the jungle to build yourselves a community, establishing rules to follow and laws to abide by. Your construction engineered a different flow of time. You left the jungle long ago, and you frequently returned to invade and conquer it. In doing so, you altered the jungle's time—primordial Time—to keep pace with your own stipulated sense of time. Your ancestors relentlessly dismantled and distorted the world's sense of time. If I remember correctly, King Prasart Thong of the Ayutthaya Kingdom invented an entire chronology of his own, although he was not pleased that neighbouring kingdoms like the Mons and the Burmese refused to recognize it, let alone abide by it.

Perhaps you'll find it easier to understand when I say that my time oscillates between two different spaces—the city and the jungle—that move at two very different paces. Do you notice how time flies when you are in the city with your parents, how everything passes in an instant? But when you're here with me in the countryside, you think to yourself: why does it drag on? This is how it feels: this sense of drag, these barely palpable remnants of the past.

I'm telling you this because the days and nights I spent in the jungle were nothing like the days and nights I spent in the city. One night in the jungle might have felt like a year in the city, but there is no way of knowing the difference, especially when we're so immersed in it. It was not until many things happened that I was able to calculate that

150 years had gone by for humans living outside of the jungle. The Ayutthaya Kingdom had transitioned into Thonburi and eventually into the Rattanakosin era, where we are now.

What changes took place during those 150 years and how was I involved in them? Let me tell you now.

When I fled from Boon, I headed to Pasak River. As soon as I arrived there, there was a sudden and deafening earthquake: *A sign from the angels*, I thought, *telling me to stop and rest right where I was.* There, I built a small hut for myself by the river bank, surviving on the river's sustenance.

One day, the sounds of marching footsteps and banging shields, drums, and gongs echoed from the jungle. Curious about what was happening, I came out to see an army of men—thousands and thousands of them—marching towards me. Marching along with them was an elephant with a many-tiered throne on its back, an elaborate umbrella shading the dignified figure sitting beneath it. I had never seen such a spectacle before, and thought that the man sitting on the elephant must be some kind of saint: a king, perhaps. Yet, there was something unusual in the way they were rallying the villagers, who all stopped what they were doing to join the crowd, arming themselves with scythes, swords, and spears. Some even joined empty-handed.

As the crowd passed, a group of people beckoned me to join them. Confused, I asked them where they were going. 'To reclaim our land,' they replied.

'Who are you reclaiming it from?' I asked.

'From the current king,' they said, as if it were obvious. 'Join our rebellion, mother, and you'll be rewarded with a better life when it's over.'

I asked them about the figure sitting on the elephant, and they told me it was Prince Phra Kwan on his way to reclaim his rightful place on the throne. 'The prince has great merit,' one of them said as they beckoned towards me. 'Join us and we'll tell you the most extraordinary stories about Prince Phra Kwan.' And so, I joined them on their walk towards the capital.

They told me that Prince Phra Kwan was the son of the late king. His birth had been announced by a violent earthquake, which reverberated rumours throughout the palace that he would one day inherit the throne, making him a well-respected figure from the very start. After King Jian passed away, the king's viceroy had come up with a scheme to usurp the throne, which involved tricking the prince into being alone with him so he could strike him to death with a log of sandalwood. The viceroy then became king. However, thanks to his merit, Prince Phra Kwan miraculously survived the assassination, and was taken away by angels, who nurtured him and trained him with incredible spells. The prince quickly called upon the former king's governors, recruiting them as allies, and assembled villagers like us to march together into the capital to reclaim the throne.

And that was what happened. I lived with the people of the rebellion as we moved towards the palace. There were around 2,000 of us, from Nakhon Ratchasima, Nakhon Nayok, Lopburi, and Saraburi. We walked day and night, listening not only to tales of Prince Phra Kwan but also tales of the present king, who I was told was named King Suea. Vicious and ruthless like his name, which meant 'tiger', King Suea was known for his might and charisma. According to the stories, he was the late King Narai's bastard son and, like his father, was well-versed in magic, capable of flying through the air and taming all kinds of wild beasts. He was a philanderer who took pleasure from keeping sharks in captivity and feeding them with the still-kicking bodies of those who wronged him. It was also said that when he was young, he had dared to kick Chao Phraya Wichayen Pitchayen—a Western courtier and a favourite of King Narai's, also known as Constantine Phaulkon—directly in the head. Later, this foreigner was caught committing treason: King Suea's kick was then interpreted as a foreshadowing of the courtier's future misdeeds. Towards the end of King Narai's reign, an influx of Westerners caused widespread fear that the Buddhist kingdom of Siam would be converted to Christianity. In response to this, all Westerners were banished from the kingdom by King Petch Rajah, King Narai's successor. However, when King Petch Rajah fell ill, his viceroy, none other than King Suea, had seized the opportunity to oust Prince Phra Kwan from the throne.

We would huddle together and listen to these stories, enthralled from beginning to end. We all felt the passion and rage that was boiling under our skin and through the lengths of our bodies, roused by a cause that stirred our flesh and blood together as one. The next morning, we marched into the capital of Ayutthaya with fiery determination.

We reached the bridge that would take us to the palace gates. Things seemed serene, unperturbed; it was as if no one inside knew that a rebellion was coming. Prince Phra Kwan halted his elephant, talking briefly with his advisors before commanding the troops to invade. We charged across the bridge towards the palace. Suddenly, we heard the sound of cannon fire coming from a fort above the city wall, and Prince Phra Kwan fell from his elephant, dead in an instant. We were momentarily stunned. Then, panic ensued. Those who were charging towards the gate continued in their crusade, while those that hadn't yet crossed the bridge were stupefied. Some lost their minds along with Prince Phra Kwan's life. At that moment, soldiers from the palace charged forth, capturing our elephants and the remaining leaders of our troops. The villagers who raised their swords to fight were killed; the others dropped their weapons in defeat.

I was in the midst of the crowd and hadn't yet crossed the bridge when news of Prince Phra Kwan's death travelled down from the frontline.[2] As soon as they saw the soldiers rushing out of the palace, the people next to me fled in an instant. At first, I was confused, but I decided to run after them.

I returned to the jungle, where peace was restored in my heart. Our world had turned upside down. I caught a glimpse of the capital, mesmerized by the beauty of the temples and the palaces but horrified by the soldiers, the chaos, and the death that surrounded me. My hair turned completely white. Can you believe that? Afterwards, I returned to my riverside cottage, where I had lived before the attempted rebellion. A long time passed before the colour returned to my hair. I can still remember the day it turned back to black. It was the same day that the western sky had turned red as it shifted from day to night. An eerie and ominous blood red, as if the sun were setting the earth ablaze and shooting sparks into the sky. Not long after that, the jungle was

---

[2] In truth, it was Thamthien, Prince Phra Kwan's former governor, who disguised himself as the prince and incited rebellion, not Prince Phra Kwan himself.

swarming with people who had fled from other villages, carrying their children and belongings with them.

The villagers cried and cursed at the sky, lamenting that the land had turned against them. They cried over the damage that had been done to the Buddha's footprint on Mount Suwan, blaming the ethnic Chinese from Klong Suanplu Village. They claimed that 300 Chinese robbers had stripped the silver plating on the base of the Buddha's footprint and the gold plating from the pavilion before setting the entire thing on fire. Such a profane act will bring about the end of Buddhism, they protested.

'Where were the authorities when this happened?' I asked.

'They've all been called away to fight against the Burmese,' the villagers said. 'The king is dead, the capital is in ruins, and the kingdom has been burned to dust by the Burmese army. Can't you see it? The sky in the west is red. The Ayutthaya kingdom has been consumed by a sea of flames.'

I watched these villagers turn into war refugees, feeling a bitter heaviness in my heart. They had had a home to call their own once, and now they had nothing, their peaceful lives turned into predicament. Men—former patriarchs of their families—had all been conscripted into the king's army and killed in battle. It is the commoners who have to bear the consequences of a war declared in the name of the kingdom, since it is the commoners who are the backbone of any army. When there is victory, the people commend their king, with whom they must plead for his divine protection. But when the king dies, the people are left to drown in perpetual chaos.

Not long after, the villagers left the jungle and returned to the city. It was said that a new ruler had defeated the Burmese army, forcing them to withdraw their troops back to Burma. As Siam slowly recovered from its war wounds, the new king established a new capital, further south from the previous one. This new capital was named Thonburi.

A huge Siamese army eventually marched through Saraburi once again, during one of the most significant events in the city's history: one that changed the fate of Saraburi forever. Led by two brothers, Prince Kasatsuek and Prince Surasi, the army headed to wage war upon Viang Chan. They returned victorious, with Lao rulers and their subjects in tow as prisoners of war. They also brought back many precious items they had plundered, including the Emerald Buddha and Phra Bang. The Siamese king forced many of the Lao families from Viang Chan to settle in Saraburi. Eventually, the Lao community grew into one of the largest and most diverse collectives in the land. Communities such as the Lao Pung Dam, the Lao Viang, the Lao Puan, the Lao Ngaew, and the Lao Yaw made a life here. After each Siamese victory in the wars against the Laos and the Khmers, Lao refugees were sent to Saraburi. Later, some of these refugees would be appointed as governors, and promoted into various positions of authority in Saraburi.

People say that King Thaksin was a great admirer of the Emerald Buddha, for its arrival had brought great honour to his kingdom. Towards the end of his reign, news of the king's lavish celebration planned in honour of the Emerald Buddha spread to the people in Saraburi. They began to complain about King Thaksin's neglect of them. King Thaksin had never stepped foot in Saraburi to pay respect to the Buddha's footprint as his former predecessors had done. After the devastating pavilion fire, the king did nothing but order a replacement roof.

Upon hearing yet another story about the footprint, I couldn't help but wonder why the villagers hardly mentioned the other footprint: that one next to the imprint of the Buddha's shadow. Imagine how peaceful that place must be, safe from any threats of destruction, its whereabouts unknown to most people. I thought of the arhat that I had spoken to, wishing that I could return to pay my respects to him and Bodhisattva Cave. Since becoming human, it felt as though I had become distant from my fate, entangled in the struggle to merely subsist, with all sorts of desires and passions stirring deep within my heart. I realized that these things had become more important to me as a human, giving rise to peculiar feelings I never had as an animal.

Perhaps it was the present chaos around my cottage that caused my heart to stir at the thought of these holy places. People had begun to settle around my cottage. A few houses grew into a community, and I felt anxious and fearful at the prospect of meeting them, regardless of their ethnicity. My fear of humans remained; I still felt unable to decipher what they were thinking, so it was best for me to keep my distance. One day, I said to myself, *I'm not having it anymore. I'm not going to live here anymore.* I wanted somewhere with more peace and quiet. I thought of Mount Pattawee again, of fulfilling my desire to return and pay my respects to that holy place before finding a place where I could settle. I decided to begin my journey.

To get to Mount Pattawee, I headed south for two days and two nights. However, just before arriving at the mountain, something caught my attention while making my way through the jungle in Khao Noi. There were seven or eight men: not common villagers, powerful people, with elephants and horses in tow. Most of them looked like low-ranking soldiers, while two were clearly of higher ranking. One of them seemed like their leader: the rest of the men referred to him as Prince Chui,[3] and approached him with reverence. As I nervously observed them from afar, I began to wonder if they were conspiring to commit treason. My experience with Prince Phra Kwan was still etched into my memory, reminding me to stay as far as possible from such royal affairs. I decided to let these people be, and resumed my journey.

The arhat was no longer in Mount Pattawee, but I was still able to pay my respects to the Buddha's shadow and footprint, which filled my heart with joy once again. I made my way back down the mountain.

As I approached the area where I had seen Prince Chui and his men, I realized that the path had been cordoned off by thousands of soldiers, surrounding the forest with their elephants and horses. What an intimidating sight it was, with every soldier fully armed. One of them gestured at me and told me to leave, that the king's viceroy had ordered the capture of Prince Chui and his men. I immediately hurried away. This time, the king didn't have to wait for the conspirators to come to him; this time, it had happened the other way around. It occurred to

---

[3] Prince Chui, also known as Prince Indraphitthak, was the eldest son of King Thaksin of Thonburi. The fictional account above is based on the events that unfolded after the execution of the King of Thonburi and many of his male heirs, carried out by Somdet Chao Praya Maha Kasatsuek and Chao Praya Surasi. The two had returned to Thonburi after their victory to seize power from the king, the former crowning himself the first king of the Chakri dynasty. After Chao Praya Surasi found out that Prince Chui was hiding in Khao Noi, he commanded his army to capture the prince and his supporters in order to bring them back to the royal city for execution.

me that it seemed as though no one could escape the consequence of their karma.

Gilding the core

I rerouted north, intent on visiting the ancient city of Khitkhin: the city that I had not been able to explore as a naga. Now, in my human form, I was free to do just that.

My journey towards Khitkhin took one night and two days. I travelled across jungles, villages, orchards and farmland before arriving at the village of U-Tapao, which was swarming with centipedes. One of them bit me, and I let out a sudden cry. A villager must have heard me, for he quickly found a crab in a nearby river, cracked its shell open and rubbed its roe on the centipede's bite. The crab roe instantly soothed the pain, and the swelling on my leg quickly subsided. The villager asked where I was from and where I was heading, so I told him that I had come from the Buddha's shadow and was heading to Khitkhin. It seemed as if he had never heard of the city's name before, but he did not ask any further questions. Once my leg had healed enough for me to resume my journey, the villager handed me a crab and told me to keep one close at hand until I made it out of the village. He told me that the centipedes in this village were afraid of crabs, and so every house in the village was guarded by amulets of hanging crabs in order to scare them away.

The villager also told me that there was a river buried underneath the land where I was sitting. He pointed to a pole sticking out of the ground: a mast belonging to a sunken trading boat, he said. According to the story behind the shipwreck, this place had once been an ancient crab colony which was later invaded by an army of centipedes that forced the crabs to retreat into the river. As time passed, humans colonized the land, forcing the centipedes to scatter. The humans killed some of the centipedes during the conquest, suffering from severe bite wounds as a result. Later, they discovered the healing properties of crab roe and began to catch crabs, extracting their roe for medicine. The crabs grew so vengeful of the centipedes that they would fatally attack any centipede that came their way. One day, a trading boat was making its way across the river when the crabs, looking up at the surface of the water, mistook the rowing paddles for the legs of a centipede. The crabs attacked the ship until it sank: an event that has terrified the centipedes to this day. Knowing of this rivalry, the villagers continue to carry crabs with them wherever they go, to protect themselves from the centipedes.

His story made sense. I thanked him before resuming my journey towards Khitkhin. Once I made it out of U-Tapao, I released the crab back into the river where it belonged.

My journey had led me back to Pasak River once more. During the dry season, there was hardly any water, and it was easy to cross; now, however, it was overflowing. It was impossible to cross the river to Khitkhin by myself, so I decided to walk along the river bank to the old town centre of Saraburi, an area known as the Sao Hai district. Before it was named Sao Hai, this area was formerly known as Pai Lom Noi Village. How did the name Sao Hai come about? Well, you kids just listen to what I'm about to tell you.

I met a man who offered to row me to the other side of the river with his boat for free. At first, his manner seemed generous and friendly. He asked how a young woman like me knew about the city of Khitkhin, and whether I had a man and children of my own. Rowing the boat across the river, his eyes roamed over me. I began to doubt whether he was truly trustworthy. He kept asking questions. Did a 'young woman like me' feel lonely travelling by myself? A 'young woman like me' couldn't possibly make it back to Pai Lom Noi Village on my own, he said, and he offered to wait for me by the river bank when I returned from Khitkhin. By the time we reached the shore, I knew to quickly hop off the boat, thanking him before hurrying away.

The city of Khitkhin that I remembered as a naga no longer existed. It was once crowded with people, but now it was completely abandoned. Ancient buildings had toppled over one another, buried beneath mounds of earth that now enriched the villagers' fields and orchards. The past had seeped back into the earth, entombed by the livelihood of the present. The old city had been reduced to a small shrine in the midst of agricultural land.

Such is change . . . And change is incessant.

That moment where I stood was the beginning of King Rama I's reign in the Kingdom of Rattanakosin. Saraburi became a settlement populated by prisoners of war from every battle won by the Siamese king, driven from their homes in Lan Xang and Chiang San. It was home to many Lao and Vietnamese communities, not to mention the Mons and the Khmers who had come before them. Saraburi has held an ever-accumulating strata of histories and peoples; those who originated here married Laotians, Vietnamese, Mons, and Khmers, bringing about generations of mixed ethnicities who became Thai citizens as we know them today. People are not simply defined by their ethnicity: they are also defined by their nationality, that which is given to them by way of where they live. They are Thai because it is on Thai land that they live.

This land has witnessed the comings and goings of generation after generation of humans, the ebb and flow of different kingdoms, constructions and reassemblages, changes that occur and recur and will keep on recurring.

Here where I stood, by the banks of the Pasak River after my return from Khitkhin, during the reign of King Rama I of the Rattanakosin kingdom, was when the city was heavily populated with Lao people. Naturally, the names of temples, canals, swamps, hills, communities, villages, sub-districts, and towns often change to reflect the identity of those who live there. Names are ephemeral; they tend to change over time. What was Lao became Thai: Sanom Lao Temple became Thai Ngam Temple (and later it was mispronounced into the Sai-Ngam Temple), Sanom Lao Village became Nong Sanom Village, Sala Ree Lao Subdistrict became Sala Ree Thai Subdistrict, Muang Lao Subdistrict became Muang Ngam Subdistrict, and so on and so forth.

Names of places also change according to the contexts of different eras. Conflicts and disagreements often occur in diverse areas, and these trivial misunderstandings at times may escalate into full-fledged discrimination. In situations such as these, places are sometimes given new Thai names in an attempt to ease and prevent future conflicts. It all seems confusing to me, to be honest. They were all born from the womb of mixed ancestors, but they identify as Thai only because their official documents say so. They use this documentation to justify their hatred and their prejudice, not realizing that nationality came much later. You are all humans; your blood bleeds the same red, and you are equally fated to follow the same sequence of birth, old age, sickness and death.

Do you remember the Thap Kwang Village, where the cave with all the Bodhisattvas carvings is? I already told you that they named the district after me, back when I was a deer waiting at the cave's mouth for the hermit. Eventually, when the district came to house mostly Lao settlers, its name was changed to Lao Village. Unsurprisingly, however, the name sparked some conflict among the people who lived there, so they changed the name back to Thap Kwang once again.

Let me tell you, this is not the only district that has taken its name from parts of my personal history. But enough about that for now, and let us return to it later.

Now, let us go back to when I was standing by the banks of the Pasak River after returning from the city of Khitkhin. Avoiding the place where I had left the dubious man with his boat, I changed course, walking until I reached the end of Pai Lom Noi. As I meandered through the dense jungle, darkness veiled the evening sky, engulfing me in it. I decided to rest by the riverbank for the night, and start my journey again at dawn.

At dusk, the entire jungle pulsated with noise: the sounds of crickets and other insects, the moaning and roaring of animals, and the flapping of winged creatures. Dark shadows lurked behind bushes, flickering with the red glint of animal eyes out hunting. I wasn't afraid, as I had taken shelter beneath a huge teak tree. Under it, silence reigned, and all that could be heard was the gentle and continuous sound of the flowing river.

But suddenly, I heard someone crying in the distance. As the sound drew closer and closer, I could tell it was coming from a woman, and that it was coming from the middle of the Pasak River. I got up and looked across the water to see her on top of a floating log. What a strange sight it was; the log motionless against the current as her cries echoed, cutting across the heart of the jungle.

I walked to the riverbank and called out to her.

'My dear, what has caused you such grief that you find yourself weeping in the middle of the river?'

The woman paused to look at me for a moment, before letting out a cold sob.

'Please come up ashore, my dear, so that we can talk,' I told her. Something about the way she was sitting on the log was making me uneasy. It was a large log, but somehow, it was completely still and stable, floating effortlessly despite the current. *That woman,* I thought, *must be the guardian spirit of that log.*

She accepted my invitation, appearing suddenly beside me. Her face was hidden behind her long, flowing hair. She brushed it back behind her ears to reveal a stunning face that was clouded over with sadness.

She told me that she had been the guardian of the Golden Takhian tree, where she had lived for thousands of years in the distant jungle. One day, someone came to ask for permission to fell her tree. They admired its grace and beauty, and hoped to use its trunk for the pillar ceremony to construct the new capital of Rattanakosin. The woman had gladly granted them permission, knowing how auspicious this honour was. They felled the tree and stripped off the bark, revealing the luminous wood inside. They floated her down the Pasak River together, carried by the current towards the city of Rattanakosin. However, just before she reached the city, she was told that another log had already been procured as the main pillar of Rattanakosin. Stranded in the middle of the river without any help from anyone, she decided to paddle her naked log back upstream to their previous dwelling, but it was no use: by the time she reached Pai Lom Village, she was beside herself with grief. She was not able to accomplish what she had intended to do, but neither could she return to the jungle in her current state. She was forever marooned in the middle of the river.

'Oh, my dear,' I said. 'I have nothing but sympathy for you. Like you, I was once the owner of a tree before I was transformed into a human by the miraculous power of the Lord Buddha; like you, I am also without a home. Seeing as we have been dealt such similar circumstances, let me go upstream with you to where you used to dwell.'

She gave me a brief smile and praised me for my generosity before telling me that she was simply too weak to go any further. She returned my kindness by pointing me in the direction of an abandoned boat parked by the riverbank not far from where we were. I could use the boat to go upstream as I wished.

We ended our conversation and exchanged our heartfelt thanks. The woman returned to her log in the middle of the river. I stood and watched her for some time; she started sobbing once more, letting out a piercing howl that cut deep into the jungle and mountains, the villages and towns. Not long after, she sank into the depths of the Pasak River, taking her Golden Takhian log with her.

Those who lived in Pai Lom Noi Village started hearing the weeping woman's cries in the middle of the night. Days, months, and years passed; the village became known as Saow Hai Village, or 'the village of the weeping woman'. I was not the only one who encountered her there; the villagers came to know her too. Eventually, through word of mouth, the village's name morphed into Sao Hai, or 'the village of the weeping log'.

The villagers had agreed to summon the woman's spirit from the river and to enshrine her on land, so that everyone in the village could pay their respects. It seemed that the Golden Takhian woman would be freed from her suffering at last; finally, she would know peace. But 170 years passed before the ceremony took place. The Golden Takhian log had sunk to the bottom of the river during the reign of King Rama I, but it was not rediscovered until 1958, during the reign of King Rama IX.

When the villagers found her, she was in a most dilapidated state. She was scarred and wrinkled after 170 years of being submerged in the Pasak River. Her skin, once smooth and youthful, had now dulled. More noticeably, time had compressed and contorted her; she had shrunk substantially in size. She was so different from the first time I had seen her.

After bringing her up, they encased her in gold leaf as a token of their reverence; the pure gold coating made her even more sacred. They gilded and painted the entire length of the log, transforming her physical body just as they were rewriting her legend anew. Indeed, a myriad of stories and theories appeared in an attempt to explain why she had been turned away from the inauguration of Rattanakosin. Some said that the current had been too slow to carry her to the city (blaming her for taking too long to drift downstream), while others pointed out that her log was crooked at the end (blaming her for her own imperfections). While there was visible proof that her log was indeed crooked at the end, the historical records show that the capital required the most beautiful log as the city's main pillar. Saraburi had always been known for its unmatched trees. Doesn't it seem implausible to you that those people would have chosen a crooked log as a candidate instead of the most beautiful ones they could find? Do you see what I mean?

I will tell you this: that Golden Takhian log was perfect. I saw it with my own eyes the night I encountered the weeping woman. By the time they rescued her from the river, the log had become crooked from the strenuous conditions it had suffered. Withered from exposure, it had been eroded by water and devoured by time. It is natural for fresh wood to disfigure as it dries. They found her 170 years after she had first sunk. They went on to make up stories about her, writing in their records that this was how she had always looked. Does that seem fair to you?

That's my take on it. Let me tell you now that the legends they tell of Sao Hai are entirely fictional. You can choose what to believe, but you should know that the Golden Takhian woman and I suffered similar circumstances: I feel I can speak for her.

Birth

In the early hours, when light began to leak through the trees, I made my way down to the riverbank to find the abandoned boat. It had capsized long ago and was covered in thick vines, just as the Golden Takhian woman had said. I uncovered the vines and turned the boat over to inspect its condition. It looked old rather than dilapidated, and there was a sturdy paddle that looked as though it could take me quite far from here.

I dragged the boat into the Pasak River, saying a silent farewell to the Golden Takhian woman before climbing aboard. I prayed to the divine beings, asking them to protect me from harm and to guide me somewhere safe and peaceful. I also prayed to Ganga, the guardian spirit of the Pasak River, asking her to carry me to a place of abundance, somewhere I could live a life free from sickness. I climbed into the boat, pushing against the bank and making my way upstream.

After half a day on the river, the landscape around me slowly cast off its layer of villages and towns to reveal a marvellous, mysterious view of ancient forests. The river seemed to be in constant flux, changing from deep and stagnant to shallow and stormy as it bent and stretched with the shifting terrain. The sun was scorching hot but the jungles emanated cool air, reverberating with the roaring of tigers, the songs of pheasants, and the wails of monkeys and gibbons. My heart swelled as I listened to this cacophony of creatures. I ate a bunch of bananas and drank the most pure-tasting water from the river itself. Oh, you can't even imagine how fresh everything was!

How brief that blissful moment was! It was not long before I heard a painful cry from the riverbank. A figure emerged from the shadows of the forest. It appeared to be a young man, running as if he were being chased; he seemed badly injured. He cried out to me for help, telling me that he refused to die here and that he had to return to his homeland. He promised me that he was a good man, that he would be forever grateful for my assistance. Hearing his pleas for assistance, I couldn't help but steer my boat towards him. He rolled from the hills right down to the riverbank, crawling onto the boat so abruptly that it almost capsized. He urged me to paddle fast, as he was being pursued by people who were coming for his life. 'Quick, woman! We must leave now!' he cried. Once I had paddled to the middle of the river, he thanked me before falling unconscious.

He laid unconscious the entire night, as if he was already dead. Despite his presence, I felt as though I was alone. The stranger slept on his side; his body curled up in a way that occupied most of the boat, leaving only a tiny space for me to sit and paddle. I inspected the bruises on his face and the trail of dried blood from his ears to his neck. He clutched his belly with his hand; he seemed to be in pain. His hand kept some kind of grass or herb pressed tight against the wound. It looked serious: his torso was soaked in blood and his clothes and hands were dyed crimson. He moaned from time to time, which reassured me. At least he was still alive.

The next morning, we drifted past a remote part of the jungle. I was exhausted from lack of sleep and concerned about the uncertain fate of the comatose stranger lying next to me. I had begun to doze off when, suddenly, we were both startled awake as the boat crashed into an underwater boulder. The stranger let out an agonized cry; the impact had probably worsened the pain in his belly. I used the paddle to inspect the water's depth and found that we were now in the shallows. The current had become too strong, swerving the boat left, then right, knocking into rocks on one side, then the other. My heart pounded with anxiety. As the sky lightened, I could see the cluster of rocks in front of us, protruding from the water. It was impossible to paddle back, so we simply kept on crashing into the rocks, jolting us both each time with aggressive force. I had never encountered such difficult and rocky terrain before. The stranger pushed on each side of the boat, holding himself upright; this sudden movement shifted the weight of the boat, we veered straight into a huge rock. I thought the boat would split in two, but before I knew what was happening, I was thrown overboard, hitting my head on a rock. I was knocked unconscious.

I woke up on land, warm from the heat of a nearby fire that was keeping the mosquitoes at bay. I wasn't alone. The stranger was there, watching me with attentive tenderness, despite his own injuries. *He must have saved me from drowning in that wild current*, I thought. *He hadn't abandoned me in my moment of need, just as I hadn't abandoned him in his.* My appreciation for him grew stronger. I watched him feed the fire, grill some fish and gather some root vegetables as he waited for me to wake up. He was hurt too, and still, he took care of me. He must have carried me to this rocky beach, underneath the leafy forest canopy where we were shielded from the heat and rain. He looked at me, his big round eyes glinting in the firelight; for some reason, it roused a new sensation within me. Feeling hot and flustered, I shifted my body away from him, diverting his gaze.

He tended to me until both of us recovered. We stayed on that beach for many days and nights, without thinking about taking our journey elsewhere. We spoke very little to one other, but shared a quiet understanding that we needn't rush, that we ought to wait for his wounds to heal completely before continuing our journey. I foraged for food and tended to the fire, while he went into the forest, returning with timber and grass. He started building a hut by the shore, large enough to shelter both of us from the weather.

One day, he told me that he was a former Lao subject. After losing the war with Siam, he had been exiled from Viang Chan along with King Anuwong of Lan Xang. The Lao king was kept as a war prisoner in Bangkok, while his subjects were sent to settle elsewhere throughout the kingdom. Later, the right to rule over the capital city of Lan Xang was restored to King Anuwong. As one of the king's aides, the man had had the chance to return to his hometown. During the reign of King Rama III of Siam, King Anuwong and his men had travelled back to Siam to attend the funeral of the late King Rama II. King Anuwong took this as an opportunity to ask the Siamese king if he could bring some of the Lao people back to Viang Chan with him, as so many of them had been forced to settle in Siam after so many wars. The Siamese king refused King Anuwong's request. Frustrated, King Anuwong told his men during their journey home that he had had enough of Siam, that they had colonized Laos and turned them into Thai subjects in order to exploit them for labour, that they discriminated against Lao royalty and commoners alike. The king then commanded his best soldiers to spread out across the Siamese kingdom—from Saraburi to Nakhon Ratchasima, from Nong Bua Lampu to Kukhan—and keep watch in disguise. They would report back to the capital, Lan Xang.

The man, along with some of his fellow soldiers, were posted in Saraburi, where they were on friendly terms with Phraya Surarachawong, Saraburi's governor, who was also of Lao ethnicity. One day, news came from the soldiers keeping watch in the capital of Bangkok: Siam was unable to come to an agreement with the British on the trade treaty. Fearing potential war, they'd sent confidential messages to the Lao spies stationed in other provinces, so they could later deliver the news to King Anuwong. However, the news was intercepted by the Siamese officials in Saraburi. All of his fellow soldiers had been arrested and killed. The man was the only survivor; the only one who had escaped, the only one I had rescued from death by a hair's breadth.

His tone was vindictive, full of bitterness and defeat. Tears streamed down his eyes as he cursed the Siamese, the way they saw Lao people as lesser than and treated them as such. The passion and fury that had been bottled inside him now burst forth. He had barely spoken a word before this, but now every sentence cascaded out of him like the rolling of a relentless storm. I couldn't help but carry his pain as if it were my own. All I could do was console him. 'There, there.'

I told him how fortunate it was that he had survived, despite all that he had lost and all those who had died. Thai, Lao, Vietnamese, Burmese, Khmer: none of it meant anything to me. I asked if he wanted to stay here, to be with me in this place. 'Look at where we are: a rocky beach by the Pasak River, surrounded by verdant forest. We are probably the only humans here among the wild animals; we, too, could live like wild animals, with a habitat of our very own. We could subsist on only what we need. We could protect and live off this piece of land given to us by Mother Earth.'

He sobbed and nodded in agreement, and that was how we came to live together.

He left the hut every day; sometimes during the day, sometimes at night. His heart was not made for a peaceful life: it quickened at news from the outside world, it yearned for human contact. One day, after having rallied Lao people in Saraburi, he told me that he had almost managed to convince Thao Noree, the head of the district, to ally with him. He had been told that King Anuwong was finally leading his army from Lan Xang to fight for independence, and that it was his duty to assemble the troops in Saraburi.

The day before he left me, he told me that this plan was destined to succeed. He tried to make me understand that this land was not truly his; he was neither born nor raised here. He tried to convince me to go and live with him in Lan Xang where he truly belonged. There, he said, he was a respected figure, and he promised to give me the life I deserve as the wife of a wealthy and powerful man.

His words may have captivated those as passionate as he was for success, but not me. I didn't need to be anything other than what I already was. So, I asked him how he could abandon me after all this time we had spent together. He said he wasn't abandoning me, but that he had an important mission he needed to complete, and that he'd be back for me. He promised that he would return.

That morning, he left the hut. 'Wait for me here,' he said. 'It's safe here.' No one knew he had been living in this small cottage. He'd been vigilant about covering his tracks every time he'd left the hut, so he could make sure that no one could get to me.

'Wait for me here der,' he repeated. 'I'll be back,' he promised.

The war for independence that he told me about—you'll soon learn about it in your Thai history lessons—came to be known as the Anuwong Rebellion. King Anuwong marched his growing army into Siam, rallying Lao subjects along the way; indeed, the majority of those who joined him were Lao exiles. King Anuwong made a declaration to all of the provinces around the kingdom that the Lao army was marching to aid Siam in the war against the British. He continued gathering men, supplies and weapons until they reached Nakhon Ratchasima. There, it was announced that Siam had successfully come to an agreement with the British regarding the trade treaty: just as King Anuwong was about to dispatch soldiers to Saraburi, in order to rally more men. King Anuwong decided instead to retreat back to Viang Chan.

Not long afterwards, the Siamese king found out about the attempted rebellion and was vexed. He'd been on friendly terms with King Anuwong during his time in Bangkok, and he felt betrayed: he had been kind enough to reinstate the Lao king as the ruler of Lan Xang, but his generosity had been repaid with mutiny. The Siamese king commanded his army to attack every province with Lao military presence. They crushed King Anuwong's army before invading Lan Xang and destroying the capital. Raging with anger, the Siamese king had ordered his men to burn everything to the ground, to obliterate the kingdom from history; true to his word, the city's wall and its temples were incinerated to dust. And that was the end of Viang Chan. King Anuwong fled to Vietnam, but he was soon captured and executed along with his family in Bangkok.

The Lao king was dead, and it was likely that my lover had died with him. But I knew none of this at the time. I am telling you kids this story with the help of hindsight, so you can place into sequence what I couldn't. Now, let us return to that day: the day he left the hut.

I am not a stupid or naive person, but looking back, it seems that I truly acted like one. He had told me to wait for him there, and so I did. One night passed, then so did three more; many nights came and went with no sign of his return. I'd never known what it felt like to truly love someone, and how precious a promise could be. I'd slowly nurtured these feelings inside me until before I knew it, they had grown into something I had no choice but to harbour. Love and Promise had slowly taken shape and solidified in my womb, heavy as stone. Every night I sat outside the hut waiting for him, my eyes drifting with the current of the Pasak River, towards the rocks that protruded from the surface of the water. It felt as if one of those rocks was forming inside me as I waited.

I was not merely stupid or naive. I was tempestuous in a way I had never been before. I howled with the wild animals at night, violently swinging between frustration and rage, sorrow and despair. I had to let the emotions out somehow; otherwise, they would suffocate me to death. My cries cut through the rapid shifts and changes in my environment. Dead bodies were drifting down the Pasak River almost daily. There must have been some epidemic or war taking place beyond the seclusion of the jungle. Bodies were being thrown into the river to meet a gruesome fate: dozens of vultures, circling in the sky above, waiting for the opportunity to swoop down and tear through the sea of skin, to peck through the flesh and guts. It was a terrible sight to behold.

The place had begun to grow hostile, but my body was too much of a burden to go anywhere else. I wouldn't have left even if I could've, because he had promised me that he'd be back; he'd told me to wait here. That promise bound us together and bound me to this place, the love between us ripening until the night I gave birth to our baby.

A baby girl. She was so tiny that she could fit into my cupped palms. She came out of me as still as death; unmoving, silent. I didn't know what to do.

I held her close. I tried shaking her gently to wake her up. I wiped the mucus out of her eyes, nose and mouth. My entire body was sore; the experience of childbirth had wrung the life out of me. *She isn't awake now, but she might be by tomorrow,* I thought to myself. Exhausted, I fell asleep with the baby lying still in my arms.

Kaeng Khoi

I woke with a sharp pang, as if I was being yanked by something. It was already light, the sun hovering directly above my head. As I drowsily pulled myself up, I realized that my baby was no longer in my arms. Where had she gone? Another shooting pain tugged at me again before I realized that it was coming from the umbilical cord that still tethered her body to mine. The cord had stretched all the way down to the water's edge, where I saw a vulture trying to rip the cord apart.

There was a whole flock of them, pecking and feeding on something down there. I saw my baby at the end of the umbilical cord, and screamed at the top of my lungs. Those vultures had stolen my baby from me and were feeding on her as if she were a piece of flesh. Frantic, I rushed towards her, flailing my arms in a desperate attempt to drive the abominable creatures away. At first, they refused to move; I charged straight into the flock, wrestling with the birds until—finally—I reached my baby. I clasped her tightly to my chest and crawled back to the front of the hut.

My baby—my love, my promise, my devotion—my baby was dead. Those vultures had pecked at her soft flesh, tearing my love to shreds like it was a tattered rag. Grief devoured me whole. I spent every waking hour weeping, wringing what was left of my sanity dry. I wept until my heart disintegrated; until my head boiled over and exploded into pieces. I wanted my screams to slice through the skin of every creature in the jungle so they too could feel the wound gaping in my heart. I howled through the jungle like a deranged beast so any and all other humans would know that it was them, humans, who took my man away. I had been waiting for him: he who had yet to return. I wanted my cries to turn to ice, to keep every fucking one of them awake at night, shivering with cold and fear; I wanted every fucking day of the rest of their lives to be full of unease, of restlessness and despair. I wept like this for three days and three nights.

The next morning, I woke, soaked in my own tears. I had wept until my tears had turned into rivulets of blood. My body was parched, my skin and flesh withered like the marrow in my bones. The state of my baby I had kept clutched in my arms all this time had started to alter. Soon, those cursed vultures were flocking above us again, anticipating their next meal. Some were waiting by the beach, while others were perched on rocks. My gaze was fixed on them, my eyes burning with vengeance.

'You'll never fucking have her! Never!'

In that moment, I made a decision. This little baby was mine. She had been born from my own body and no one was going to take her away from me. I refused to let her be eaten by any depraved animal. And so, I returned her to me.

The villagers in the distant jungle had heard me howling for the past three days and nights. South, North, East, West: they'd come from all the different parts of the river, following the sound of my screams to find me. Although they had stopped at a distance and were watching from afar, I could see that they knew exactly what I was doing. I could see it in their horror-struck faces, full of pity and disgust.

As soon as I saw them, I asked if they had seen my man; my man, the one who had told me to wait by this rocky beach. 'Have you seen him?'

None of them responded to my question; instead, grimaced and retched at the sight before them. They stood there, utterly stupefied. Suddenly, one of them shouted.

'You ghoul!'

Another one followed.

'You hellish freak! How can you devour your own baby?'

They all cursed at me; they told me to burn in hell, to turn into stone. But their words didn't stop me from continuing what I had set out to do: to return my own flesh and blood to my body. Slowly, the villagers left me alone, unable to watch such a sickening sight.

Since then, word spread about the woman who waited for her husband to return, who had eaten her own baby so the vultures couldn't. The story travelled far and wide, etching itself into the memories and imaginations of those who lived there. Later, they came to call this place Kaeng Khoi, or 'awaiting islet', and my legend is still told today.

What used to be a remote and often overlooked area has since acquired names, the vast and verdant jungle included. From there, various subdistricts and villages followed suit. I will tell you how they got their names.

I had taken my baby's flesh, blood, and skin back into my body; all that remained were pieces of bone, which I could not ingest. And so, I detached what used to be an arm and threw it with all my might. It flew southward into what used to be called the Old District, or the Gao District. It hit a sugar palm tree with a loud thwack before landing in the fields below. The people eventually came to call it Khon Kwang Subdistrict—the Flying Limb District—and then, even later, Tan Diew Subdistrict, or 'lonely sugar palm tree'.

I detached another skeletal arm, throwing it southwards again. It landed in a brook that was often frequented by nearby villagers. As soon as the bone touched the water, the entire brook dried up, as if by magic. From then on, the villagers called their subdistrict Huay Hang, or 'the dry brook'.

Then, I snapped off the right leg bone and hurled it eastwards, over some small, interspersed hills. It landed in the middle of the forest, in an area dense with towering klor trees. The leg bone hit one of these trees, causing it to collapse; the tree landed directly over a stream, forming a bridge. It was then named Tha Klor Subdistrict, after the klor tree.

I threw the left leg in the same direction as the right. It flew over the same small hills, but the wind carried it further. It came to land along a narrow, meandering bend of the Pasak River. The leg bone hit one of the immense banks that towered over either side of the river like cliffs. There was a loud sound, and the bank crumbled down into the river, small rocky islets that scattered across the surface of the water. The people in the area named their subdistrict Hin Son after these newly formed hidden rocks.

I cast what was left of the torso—the spine and the rib cage—further away. They were struck by lightning in mid-air, splintering into three separate parts. The first landed in a grove of bael trees, which miraculously began to grow in lush abundance: the subdistrict was then named Tha Matoom after the bael trees. The second part landed in the middle of the jungle, on the edge of Dong Phaya Fai Forest, a remote area where very few dared to tread. The villagers grew even more fearful after the bones landed there, avoiding the area completely. It came to be known as Baan Pa, or 'wild village'. The third part—the torso bone—was planted in the ground. Perhaps it had been struck by lightning, but for some unknown reason, the bone brought fertility to the land it touched; an abundance of plants and crops sprung forth from the earth around it. It had fallen onto a mound of dirt which, over time, was layered over with years of dirt and soil. Eventually it formed the shape of a stupa. The villagers therefore called their subdistrict Baan That, a derivation of the Lao term for 'stupa'.

I threw the pelvic bone across the Pasak River. It landed on the roof of a house owned by a man named Song, before ricocheting into another house nearby, which belonged to a woman named Khon. The two of them were deeply in love, and the incident was seen as a sign of their auspicious partnership and a foreshadowing of their prosperous future. They went on to have many children and grandchildren, all of whom grew up and lived in the area. It was later named Song Khon, or 'two people', after the couple.

I threw my baby's neck bone westward, to the other side of the Pasak River. It flew into an area occupied by a community of blacksmiths, landing directly in one of the furnaces. Instead of turning to ash, the bone miraculously hardened, turning into a black disc similar to a metal amulet. The blacksmith who owned that furnace kept it and worshipped it; it was rumoured that he became invincible and skilled in powerful spells. That subdistrict was named Tao Poon, after the cement furnace.

I cast the tailbone southeast, where it skimmed across the surface of the river, refusing to sink. The bone tore clean through a leafy plant, which scattered in the wind, dispersing over rice fields, farmland, and the fences surrounding people's houses. Despite being ripped to shreds by the tailbone, those scraps of leaves sprouted wherever they landed, becoming a plentiful source of food for the villagers. The subdistrict came to be called Cham Pak Paew after the species of plant that had brought abundance to the area.

That left the last piece of bone: my baby's skull. I hurled with all the strength I could muster. It flew the furthest of them all, landing right in the middle of Dong Phaya Fai Forest. The army had once moved its troops from Nakhon Ratchasima to the capital through this forest, and many of them had died along the way from malaria. What remained of their weapons and uniforms were still scattered across the forest floor. My baby's skull landed on one of these abandoned helmets, triggering a howling scream that shot right through the forest, reaching villages at the foot of distant mountains. One day, a travelling huntsman found the skull and the helmet. He believed that he had encountered the spirit of a dead soldier pleading for his life. The subdistrict was later named Mhuak Lek, or 'steel helmet'. Later, when the area was divided to form another subdistrict, its name morphed slightly and was known from that point onwards as Muak Lek.

All of these names were derived from the consequences of my actions, tokens of my own karma. And so, the entire jungle came to be divided into distinct territories.

After tending to my baby's little life, I felt a brief moment of relief, but grief and despair continued to eat at me from within. I sat in front of my hut, staring blankly at the flock of vultures still circling the sky. They had been denied the child, so now they wanted the mother; they waited patiently for me to die. But they never got that satisfaction. I did not die as prey because I could not die. I still had hundreds of years left to live, so that I could one day recount my stories to you all.

Did you forget that my spirit is eternal, inextinguishable for as long as I remain on this earth? But immortality, like everything else, is also susceptible to change; subject to transformation, deterioration, and decay, just like the wrinkles I had gained and the wounds that others had left in me during this traumatic time.

At first, I had only myself to blame. The loss of my baby daughter had crushed my spirit to the ground. I had wept for days and nights, tears seeping from every pore on my body, until all that was left to run was blood, trickling down before rising into hot vapour around me. I had bled myself dry, my once-soft skin ossifying into insignificance. I had descended into a fragile and mutable state that anything could slip right through me. When that group of villagers had seen what I had done with my baby, they had projected their curses onto me. Just as the consequences of my own actions had led to the naming of new lands, the villagers' words turned to action, naming me, in my vulnerable state, into a new being.

Their curses had taken hold of my spirit, and I transformed into the very thing they had damned me to become: my entire body gradually hardened into stone. I became a statue, firmly bound to the beach they had come to call Kaeng Khoi.

Incantations

The moment I became a statue at Kaeng Khoi Beach, I felt immense relief. The curse of paralysis had actually liberated me from my struggle for survival. Everything else around me was continually moulded by the touch of time. A dock was built on the beach, allowing people to travel across the river, from north to south, upstream as well as downstream. The once dense jungle slowly began to recede, villages growing in its place; trade routes formed around the river's strong currents, bringing with them travelers in transit, who in turn brought goods to be sold and exchanged. I witnessed these changes unfolding along the river. Some of those who had once cursed me began to worship me. They prayed for me to grant their wishes, to bless their journeys; they offered me food and bathed me in the sweet scent of flowers, of candles and incense. They brought me dolls, tokens of the child I had lost, as well as blankets to kept me warm during the colder months. As you can see, I was spoiled rotten with offerings.

Not long afterwards, I overheard the villagers talking about King Pinklao, who was residing at Sri Tao Palace in the subdistrict of Song Khon. It was rumoured that he was surveying the area for Siam's second capital. The king feared that the Chao Phraya River might fall into the hands of Westerners, and that the riverside capital of Bangkok would then fall prey to their cannons. King Pinklao had been eyeing Saraburi as a potential new capital, building a palace in the Khao Kok area and using it as an army in preparation for the war against the West.

However, this war ultimately did not take place during King Pinklao's reign; instead, it happened under the rule of King Rama V, as did many of the events that followed.

King Rama V was known for travelling all over the kingdom, and although his trips seemed recreational, they enabled him to claim ownership over his territories, inscribing his name onto many important places throughout the kingdom. He also built Siam's first railway line, which cut through Kaeng Khoi, bringing with it development that spread into many of the surrounding regions. He also abolished slavery and reformed the country's systems of governance, centralizing all governing powers so that every region in the kingdom was run by a capital-appointed official. What were once known as colonies, as inner and outer provinces, were given new names: counties, towns, districts, villages, subdistricts. Borders and boundaries were strengthened, and uncivilized practices were outlawed to safeguard Siam's sovereignty and ensure lasting independence.

And so Kaeng Khoi became a district, while other villages became subdistricts. However, Siam had shrunk following the redrawing of our borders. There were no more Siamese colonies under the threat of France and Britain, who saw us as savages and saw themselves as duty-bound to civilize us. The king had to surrender all our former colonies to the Westerners. Siam underwent significant reforms, but lost substantial land in the process. But alas, it's hard to imagine not going through these changes.

These changes occur as Earth revolves, and we must find ways to change with it rather than resist it. Such is the nature of Earth and the transience of its eras. What was once high as the sky eventually descends, sinking low as the depth of the ocean; the land shifts as Earth's core twists from left to right. Buddhism takes the transient nature of Earth as its inherent truth. The Buddha says that nothing is permanent, that it is only those who idealize that suffer. The changes made on this land are constant; even the king, who used to be the avatar of God, became Phra Chao Pan Din. Since the possession of land determined a kingdom's prestige and prosperity, modes of governance became an indicator for each country's civilization. That, then, was how the regime of the monarchy was established in Siam, before we made our way to constitutional monarchy.

Alas, when someone is rendered silent, fixed in place, they can become enwrapped in the stories told of them by others. Travelers tell stories plucked from their own experience, while it is easier for settlers to take the words of another and weave them anew. The original stories are not theirs, but they can tell their own versions with the certainty of a tidal wave coming into shore. Being anchored in place has its disadvantages: the ramblings you hear tend to be the opposite of the truth. Those who are inside talk only of the outside; those who are below talk only of what is above. As for me, I blather about things that move and vary, all while standing immovably still. It wasn't all blather, though; I am made of change, after all. I had been cursed into stone but only for a period of time.

The curse had not compromised my beauty. I was renowned for my womanliness, my curvaceousness. I am not saying this to flatter myself. I am saying it because it's true. Things turned upside-down when I turned to stone. Young couples came for my blessing, and those suffering from infertility prayed to me, begging me to grant them a child. How could I possibly give them what they wanted: I, who had neither child nor husband? But alas, it is what they wanted to believe and it would have been sinful to refute their faith.

While most came for my blessing, some came to satisfy their own wants and needs. Perverts touched every part of me, feeling my arms and legs and molesting my breasts. My rough stone skin grew smooth from constant touch, slippery and shiny. I glowed more than ever before.

Beauty is dangerous. Stasis is dangerous. Being worshipped— being a vessel for other people's hopes and dreams—is dangerous too. You never know what kinds of desires and behaviours you may be subjected to. How can you tell who means well and who doesn't?

And then that day arrived: the day I transformed back into a human. I disappeared from the beach at Kaeng Khoi, leaving nothing of me behind except the stories told by others.

It was the night of the full moon. Its brilliance blinded the stars, which faded into the depthless night sky. The beach was as bright at night as it was during the day. The lead-coloured Pasak River oozed silently. I had a premonition. Something was about to happen to me. I sensed it: something bizarre, something mysterious yet full of purpose. Something was watching me with glistening eyes that were neither human nor animal, but something in between. The eyes radiated authority, power, and might. My entire body suddenly felt hot and feverish. Strange, very strange indeed. I was spellbound, captured by this pair of possessive eyes.

The sky above me was changing too. Dark shadows slowly engulfed the full moon, forming a lunar eclipse. Little by little, the entire orb was eventually swallowed whole, its brilliant light turning red as blood. At that moment, something stepped out of the bushes and began to walk towards me with intent. I could only see the whites of his eyes, the piercing gaze that emanated from this resinous black figure. He stared right at me, raising both of his hands into prayer position before beginning to mumble. His mumblings grew louder, turning into something almost akin to a howl. He would stop at intervals to blow at me. I felt the oddest sensation, shivering first with cold then burning hot with desire. I grew lustful as his words fondled me.

In the eerie darkness of the lunar eclipse, I yearned for him with a fervour that penetrated deep into every one of my previous lives. His black magic infiltrated my memory like a parasite. Leechlike, it replaced and rearranged my understanding of my own past. It didn't change everything: it took and transformed only what he needed from me. He instilled himself into the deepest part of my memories. *He was the promise of return*, the parasite told me. *It was he who made this promise, and now he has come back.* The shadows slowly released the moon from its grip, first illuminating the atmosphere, and then a familiar face: his face.

Water surged through my entire body. Tears streamed from my eyes and down my cheeks. He was standing right in front of me.

'My love,' I cried. 'You've been gone for so long.'

I rushed to tell him that our child was gone.

He said nothing. Instead, he walked towards me and picked me up. He wiped my tears away and looked closely at me. I put my arms around him, holding myself upright. His eyes were gleaming, wild and powerful.

'Beautiful. More beautiful than I could have ever imagined,' he said. His expression conveyed the full force of his animalistic desire. Suddenly, his lips began to move, forming whispers blowing directly into my face. I suddenly felt drowsy, and was soon unconscious.

He took me to his home, deep inside the jungle, somewhere in Dong Phaya Fai Forest. Inside, it was dark and overcrowded with a miscellany of eccentric objects: herbal baths, an altar dedicated to Kali, Shiva linga, talismanic cloths, and amulets. I could feel the presence of invisible servants roaming the house. A bilious stench—a mix of oils, pungent herbs, candles, incense, and nocturnal flowers—rendered the air inside viscous and nauseating.

I woke to find myself still in his arms that lowered me into the herbal bath. He started chanting a spell, washing away the top layer of my skin, which slowly flaked away to reveal the smooth, honey-toned complexion beneath. Once I was clean, he lifted me from the bath and carried me to bed. All this time, I had not said a word. His mumbling was a continuous hum; something about the sound compelled me to act in compliance. He mounted me before lustfully devouring every part of me. I was enraptured, caught entirely in the bizarre moment. Waves of pleasurable weakness surged beneath my skin, over and over. The waves didn't seem to cease for him either. He took what he wanted until dawn broke.

I slept for an entire day and woke again at night. As soon as I woke, he expelled his incantation over my body; I was overcome with desire once more. He took pleasure in me night after night until I fell pregnant. Fortunately, this seemed to relieve him of his thirst for me. He looked forward to having the baby, and waited patiently. He occupied himself with his incantations; with his attention no longer on me, I managed to regain some consciousness and realized that he was not my real husband. This man had submerged himself in menace and dark magic. When I compared him to my memory of the hermit from the cave, all those lives ago—the light and purity that emanated from his body—I knew it was true. This man was clouded with darkness and unscrupulous desires.

My suspicions were confirmed on the night when I woke in horror to find that my baby had been gouged from my womb. He had taken the premature baby to the altar to conduct his vile rituals. He was turning my baby into one of his servants. He saw the panic in my eyes; I tried to resist, but he began to chant his spell. I fell unconscious.

It became clear that one child was not enough for him: he wanted more. When my body had recovered enough for him, he raped me. I fell pregnant again. When I was not under his spell, I was able to piece together some of my scattered thoughts. I remembered the night of the lunar eclipse, when he had appeared before me in the guise of my man, seducing me with his incantations. Once I had pieced the entire story together, I conceived of a plan to destroy him, but it would only work if I could resist his spells.

The next day, I woke at noon to find him asleep in front of the altar. He did not sleep with me when I was pregnant. Despite the common use of the Yoni in black magic, those who practice it believed that elevating the female sex above the head yielded catastrophic consequences. I'd heard before that all powerful spells dwindle when tainted by women. I crept up to the altar and mounted his sleeping frame. I took the Yoni from the altar and crossed it above his head.

I prayed that it would work, that it would corrode the evil that had accumulated within him across his lifetimes and render them obsolete.

Anxious, I looked at him. *Could I really do it?* I took a knife from the altar, but my grip on it felt clumsy, uncertain. Suddenly, he opened his eyes. He seemed completely unsurprised to find me trespassing into his sacred space. He looked directly at me, his face full of contempt.

'You vile bitch,' he said. 'What are you doing in here?'

He was still lying down; he began to mumble his incantations at me, almost lazy in his confidence. It was then that I knew my plan had worked: his breath was nothing but bilious air. He swore several times as he tried desperately to lift himself from the ground, threatening me all the while. He was still distracted by his failed incantations when I took the knife in my hand and stabbed it into his chest. It passed through his ribs with ease before directly piercing his heart. He jerked still before collapsing onto the altar, his eyes wide open. He died instantly.

The spirits he'd held captive as his servants began to howl, resounding throughout the forest. Their howls turned into rapturous cries as they were finally freed from servitude. As the spirits began to drift away, I too started to make my way out of Dong Phaya Fai Forest.

Twins

As I stumbled out of Dong Phaya Fai Forest, I came across a man foraging. He asked where I had come from. Dong Phaya Fai Forest, I told him. He corrected me, saying that the forest was now known as Dong Phaya Yen. It didn't do much to bother me; the forest was still the same, no matter how many new names it was given.

Getting out of the forest had been my first priority: it was far too dangerous to remain there. I wasn't travelling alone any more: my womb was heavy with child again. I had already lost two babies: I could not let it happen again. I felt as though I already knew the living thing inside me, knew how to keep it safe, what to avoid and how best to nurture it. As my belly grew, so did these feelings within me. All I wanted was to take care of my child, despite the fact that it had been conceived with that monstrous shaman. Above all else, the child was still mine. Trees bear fruit fertilized by drifting spores, set adrift by the wind. You can't do nothing to force nature. It's not important where each of the spores came from: the fruit grows from the tree, bound to one another until the fruit falls, their seeds dispersed and grow into a new tree, bearing more fruits of their own.

I did not abandon the forest entirely; instead, I settled right along its seams, where its borders touched the community: an area near what is known today as Muak Lek Waterfall. I built myself a simple hut, with easy access to food and water, which was plentiful. This pregnancy felt completely different to my earlier ones: my belly grew so large that I felt it might be on the verge of exploding. Labour was excruciating. I felt the child violently kicking and pushing against my womb for weeks before I finally gave birth. To my surprise, I had twins: both male. The elder one looked thin compared to his plump little brother. Their arrival explained the pain I had endured while carrying them: they'd been fighting with one another from the very beginning, even before birth.

I wiped the mucus out of their eyes, their noses, their mouths. When I cut the umbilical cord, they began to cry, their wails piercing through the forest. Their little limbs shuddered. *There, there. I didn't cut you off from me. Look, here, suck on my breast.* I looked at the two babies, these two living creatures of mine: my children.

I raised them without proper names until they were around two or three years old. I called the eldest one Dang and the younger one Dam, according to the colour of their skin.

One day, a group of people arrived to survey the edge of the forest. They didn't look like the local residents who often foraged in the area. They seemed anxious, as though they were looking for something. They headed towards my hut. They were polite enough in their greeting, but their news was unpleasant. They told me I could no longer stay where I was. I asked them why, and they told me that this was a non-residential area, that I would have to relocate to a residential zone and become part of a community. I told them I had never been part of a community, that I had lived in the forest all my life. They refused to listen. They told me that this area bordered the national park, a lush forest with wild plants and animals that had to be protected from human activity. They said that there were plans to build a botanical garden right where I was living, that there would be no humans allowed. I argued, telling them that I'd lived amongst the spirits of the forest and the mountains all my life, but they were insistent. 'Who do you think you are, telling me what to do?' I asked. They told me they were state officers.

'What state?'

'The Thai state.'

'Which Thai state? This is Siam, is it not? This land belongs to the King of Siam, does it not?'

They laughed at me and said that the land might still belong to the king, but that the state now had authority over it. They told me that Siam had changed its name to Thailand and mocked me for my ignorance, saying that I had been in the forest too long.

Well, at first, it didn't interest me whether or not Siam had changed its name, since the land was still as it was, as it ever had been. However, the name was not the only thing that had changed: its governance had too. Forested land had swiftly been replaced with ever-expanding residential areas, to the point where what was left of the forest required protection and preservation. I was a part of the jungle, but I was in a human body, with two little human children, and so I had to leave, to assimilate into the human community. My body was bound to nothing except my two children.

Not only did they evict us, they branded us too, commanding us to register as citizens of the Thai state. I had to write my children's names on a registration form. It was then that I named the elder twin 'Siam' and the younger twin 'Thai'.

With my two sons in my arms, I travelled downhill, out of what was to be the Muak Lek botanical garden and towards the lower lands. There, I found a field shaded by various species of jungle plants and trees. The three of us began our lives there. There'd been no need to worry: Siam and Thai grew into strong and healthy kids, with natural survival skills and a restless sense of curiosity. As soon as they were able to walk and run, the two of them would disappear for hours before returning home covered in dirt and mud, carrying armloads of root vegetables and game. But for me, being away from the jungle and being forced to live amongst humans had led to strange and drastic changes. I felt weak. My skin, once plump and full of life, became dry and wrinkled. My youthful beauty waned; in the space of only ten years, I had grown old.

Every part of my body had aged, with the exception of my spirit. But even then, I could argue that my spirit has lived through thousands and thousands of years. My ancient spirit has outlived many things, but it has never weakened, nor withered away like any of my physical bodies.

Both of my sons turned out to possess a talent for fishing as well as a thirst for knowledge. They liked to play at a nearby temple, where they would spend all day helping the monks, listening to their sermons and memorizing them. The monks, having grown fond of them, taught them both to read and write. There was a small school run by the temple, and the abbot enrolled my sons there without charging a single baht. Every day, they would return home with a tiffin box full of food from the kindly abbot, and tell me the things they had learned at school that day. I was proud of their cleverness and curiosity, that they were helping me put food on our table.

After many years of living in that shaded field, a man approached our hut. *Not those damned officials again*, I thought to myself. He told us that we had to move. I replied that our hut had been built on independent land, that it was part of the jungle and therefore did not belong to anyone. He told me that he was the owner of the land, and that this place wasn't part of the jungle; rather, we were in his orchard, where he grew all kinds of fruits and vegetables. He had known about me for a while, he said, but hadn't thought that I would stay for this long. We had been living off his crops, leaving him with much less than he ought to have. He was not happy, and so, he wanted us to move. I asked him where we ought to go: everywhere we went was already owned by someone else. He said he didn't know, that all he knew was that he was the rightful owner of this land. 'I have evidence,' he said. 'It's written down on the deed.'

If we didn't move out, he said, he would call the police to arrest us and they would lock us up.

'Oh,' I cried, 'aren't you overreacting? The earth belongs to all living creatures; why do humans insist on claiming sole ownership of land that should be for everyone? I don't understand.' He told me that he didn't want to listen to any of my preaching, and that he, as the owner, had every right to live off this land, while I was an intruder. Leave, he repeated, telling us that he was asking nicely. And so, my sons and I were on the move again.

Sons grow up to be better versions of their parents: a golden boy-child. Once they learned that we had to find a new place to live, Siam and Thai were determined to help me

'Mummy,' Thai said to me one evening. 'The abbot said that we could build a small hut for ourselves on the temple grounds.'

'Mummy, the abbot told me first,' Siam said, chiming in competitively. 'I'm the one who told Thai. You were supposed to hear it from me first!'

'What are you talking about?' Thai countered. 'The abbot told us at the same time! We both have the right to tell Mummy. I just told her first. You lost! Don't be a sore loser!'

'There, there,' I soothed. 'I love you both equally.'

I put my arms out to both of them, but Thai reached me first, pushing Siam away. Siam, who had been the weaker one ever since they were babies, tried to snuggle up again, but Thai kicked him away. Secretly, I felt sorry for him. 'Mummy?' Thai said.

'Yes, baby?' I replied.

'One day, I'm going to find you a place to live where you won't get thrown out. Just you wait.'

I remember his words to this day, and the way he said them with a seriousness and commitment far beyond his years. I was so touched, eyes brimming with tears. 'One day, I'll buy all this land for myself,' he added.

I held my youngest in my arms, but my eyes watched my eldest, who was sitting with his back turned vexedly towards me, eyes turned towards the fields outside. He must have thought that I loved him less than I did his brother. Not at all, my dear son, I love you both equally; admittedly, I worry about you more than I do your brother. Siam's fate drives him away from his mother. I could sense him watching me, hoping for acknowledgement, for recognition of all the things he tried to do for me. He looked at me without looking at me, his gaze still fixed on the horizon beyond the jungle. His face was full of intent, as if he was trying to command the thunder to roar, the clouds to move, the sky to change colour; as if these signs would make me realize that he could do great things for me, miraculous things: all without having to look at me. All of this for his mother.

A decade later, Siam would say to me: 'A human's worth is determined not by how he talks about himself, but by how others talk about him.' My dear son, Siam.

The three of us moved onto the temple grounds. We built a small hut by the graveyard, near a forested area. Wearied by old age, I could no longer walk briskly or carry things like I used to do. Still—as someone who had always done everything by herself, for herself—idleness didn't sit right with me, and so I volunteered to help with the temple activities as much as I was able.

Siam was bright, and Thai was determined. Their respective qualities led them down different paths in life. The abbot saw a bright future ahead of Siam; when he had nothing left to teach the child, to satisfy his insatiable hunger for knowledge, the abbot sent Siam off to Bangkok to pursue higher education. The abbot had offered to send Thai to Bangkok too, but Thai wouldn't go. He was too attached to me. Thai was pleased for his twin brother, he said, but he'd rather stay and look after me, and make me happier than ever before: just wait and see! He took advanced vocational courses at a local college in town, coming home to me in the evenings. He did his best to look after me and the abbot. Thai has always been persistent: when he sets his heart on something, he makes sure that he gets it. When an opportunity arises, Thai is always ready to seize with his claws, his eyes as sharp and ready as an eagle's.

Thai found a job at a cement factory. He had worked there for less than two years before being promoted to division head. The job paid well, and later, at the start of that following year, had been able to buy a small piece of land near the river in the subdistrict of Baan Pa. True to his promise, he built me a small house, surrounded by orchards. The two of us, mother and son, gave our thanks to the abbot before moving into our house, built on land that was ours, thanks entirely to Thai's effort and hard work.

I was content enough, but I still had concerns. The older I got, the more anxious I became about not having anything to do. I tried to keep myself occupied around the house. 'You're a grown man now,' I said to Thai. 'You need to do things that will make you happy. No need to take care of me. I'm fine on my own. You've built me a house. Go on, live your own life.'

As for Siam, he rarely returned home after leaving to study in Bangkok. Every once in a while, he would come back to visit the abbot and to spend a few nights at home with me; before I knew it, he would be off again. It might be a year before he returned again. He wrote to me occasionally, telling me that he might study to become a teacher, before writing again to say that he was now thinking about studying politics. With a capricious mind like his, it seemed unlikely that he would complete his studies anytime soon. In his letters, Siam described to me all that he had encountered, the experiences he had gleaned, and the journeys he had taken in search of the meaning of life. Thai would read them out loud to me.

'Don't you see, Mummy?' Thai said mockingly, as he read one of the letters to me. 'I wasn't wrong when I said he'd end up a good-for-nothing type.'

After that, no news came from Siam for a long while. When his next letter finally arrived, he told us that he had joined his fellow students in their political demonstrations, but had had to flee into the jungle once the military crackdown had been announced. He would never going to complete his studies. Nevertheless, he wrote, the world was his oyster, and education was certainly not only confined to the walls of the university.

'What nonsense!' Thai said, laughing derisively at Siam's letter.

Siam had also written that he had spent two years abroad and returned to Thailand when the political climate was calmer. He was starting his life anew. It had been a wonderful experience that allowed him to truly understand the life and spirit of the working class. 'No need to worry about me, Mum,' Siam wrote. 'This son of yours has many lives, and when the time is right, I will return home to give thanks to you.'

Thai had nothing kind to say about his brother. He continually complained that Siam was unreliable and that he was wasting his life. I told Thai not to be so hard on his brother.

Deep down, I felt that Siam and I shared exactly the same spirit. He was spending his life traveling from one place to another, and I had done the same. He said he had many lives, and so do I. I had no objections to the way Siam had chosen to live his life, but I kept my approval a secret from Thai, so he would not accuse me of favouritism. Thai couldn't accept that someone else might love his mother as much as he did, and he couldn't stand sharing his mother's love with anyone. That, he got from his father.

My concern for Siam also stemmed partly from the inexplicable sense of foreboding I had always had about his future. Since we were so similar to one another, it was almost as if I could tell what was about to happen to him, as if my own life were a blueprint for his fate.

Thai later bought another piece of land near a main road in the subdistrict of Thap Kwang, where he started his own garage business. He found himself a wife, who I'd heard was a land broker. Thai built them a home on his new land. Since then, he stopped visiting me as often. I was happy for him, and no longer worried about him. I had told him to find happiness for himself and, sure enough, he had followed my advice. I was pleased that one of my sons had finally settled down.

Still, I had my elder son to worry about, and he was about to come home.

Homecoming

It was already late in the evening when Siam returned home. I heard him calling for me—'Mum! Mum!'—before he had even climbed up the stairs. I could hear the apprehension in his voice. By the time I'd responded to him, he was already sitting in front of me and asking me question after anxious question. 'How are you? Is everything okay? I'm glad you're all right. I was so worried about you.'

I was pleased to see him, and examined him from head to toe with what little eyesight I had left at my age. Look at him! He left home a scrawny teenager and has returned a middle-aged man. His freckled skin was well-worn and weathered with age, but he still referred to himself as my little boy, and I knew that my baby was still there, still just the same, living a body that had changed with the passage of time.

I asked him what the matter was. He told me that, on this journey home, he had been troubled by a feeling: a sudden fear of losing his loved ones. He didn't want to imagine such awful things, he said, but he couldn't help worrying about losing me. I laughed and tried to comfort him, saying that when my time came, it would be right, for I had lived for so long: long enough to see him grow old. In ten years, he would look as I did now, and it would be painful to see him grow older than me. It would be absolutely unbearable to see my children die before me. I wouldn't be able to accept something so unnatural.

Siam rested his head on my lap, looking up at me innocently like he really was still my little boy. 'I know you'll live forever, Mum,' he said. 'You're immortal. You told me so yourself.' I laughed at his attempt to flatter me. He knew just what to say to please me.

'Yes,' I said. 'I'm not dying soon.'

He then asked me: 'Thai doesn't have an immortal spirit, does he? You only gave it to me, right?'

I told him that Thai got the best of their father's qualities. 'Your father may have practiced black magic, but once he had his heart set on something, he wouldn't stop until he got it. Thai is strong-willed like his father was. He's done well for himself. He's got a wife and kids, did you know that? What about you? What have you got?'

He replied, slipping back into his native dialect, 'I've got my love for you, Mum.'

I chuckled, 'Don't you try to sweet talk me!' Then I told him to wash up and find something to eat.

The next morning, we learned that the abbot who once supported our family had passed away. Siam and I left my home in the subdistrict of Song Khon and headed to the temple in Muak Lek District to attend his funeral. Thai and his wife also travelled from their home in Thap Kwang Subdistrict to the temple. It was a grand funeral, with guests from all over. A huge statue of the abbot had been built, enshrined inside a pavilion where people could pay their respects. The late abbot's assistant, who had officially become the temple's new abbot following the funeral, turned out to be a previous classmate and good friend of Siam's.

When Siam and Thai saw each other at the temple, Thai asked his brother how he was earning his living and why he never told me anything about what he was up to. Thai worded his questions carefully, as if he knew something I didn't and was backing his brother into a corner, forcing him to explain himself to me. Siam said he did all sorts of things and all was well. He'd been busy taking care of several businesses, travelling all over the country and overseas to negotiate deals. He claimed to be a well-respected man who knew people from all walks of life from those on the lowest rung of the ladder to the highest. According to him, he knew a lot of people and was well-respected by them. He also suggested that when a person reached a certain stage in life, perhaps it wasn't enough to think about only himself and his family if he wanted to improve the lives of his fellow compatriots. He said he wanted to get involved in politics, which seemed to me to be the latest challenge had had set himself. Siam told his brother that he wanted to help others, but at this, Thai sniggered, not convinced in the slightest. It seemed that my two sons could not see eye to eye, even now.

When I was alone with my eldest, I asked him if he was really serious about wanting to help his compatriots. Wouldn't he be stealing the king's job? He laughed, saying that these days, the king was above politics. Instead he was a pillar of the nation, allowing his government to deal with the day-to-day administration of the country: a government that was now elected by the people. Siam tried to explain that Thailand was now a constitutional monarchy.

'What you're saying sounds so complicated and impractical,' I told him. 'Things used to be much simpler. When did it all get so messy?'

He replied, 'The world never stops changing. Nothing is permanent. Don't you believe that?'

While I agreed with him, I told him that I wasn't sure if this change would lead to something better. He responded by saying that doubt always leads to better things. 'All right, fine,' I said. 'You're so good with words.'

I paused before asking him another question. 'Why do you want to help humans and not other living beings? Humans are not easy to deal with; they bicker with one other like dogs. The word "khon", or "human", refers to a mongrel, a mixture of all sorts: we know nothing about where they all came from. But all they do is cause trouble on Earth because they think they're superior to all the other creatures. They take all that they can, they draw imaginary boundaries to claim dominion over kingdom and country. They created concepts like nations merely to justify their invasion of other lands. All I see is that things have gotten more and more complicated. I have seen how humans hunger for control: their passion, their love, their misguided pursuits for power. I've seen it all. As their lifespan grows shorter, their desire for immortality intensifies. They'll do whatever they can to make themselves feel as though they could live forever. What good is living forever? No one ever asked me what it feels like. It's not good. With an immortal spirit, one has no choice but to struggle to get by. The truth is, a long life isn't a happy life, but discovering happiness makes you want to live a longer one. Once you experience happiness, there is no such thing as getting enough of it: very few people learn to be content with what they already have. I think that contentment is what allowed the hermit and the Buddha to rise above ordinary people. So I just can't help but wonder why you want to help humans instead of other living beings.'

'Because we're all a mixture of all sorts, Mum. What's more, humans actually need to be mixed well. The word "khon" comes from a verb meaning "stir"; before we can become truly human, we must be stirred together. Humans have the capacity to learn, to understand, to correct past mistakes. Change isn't easy for humans. It's challenging but it's necessary too.' He paused a moment before adding: 'Won't you be proud if one day, in the future, people remember me? Talk about me? A human's worth is determined not by how he talks about himself, but by how others talk about him.'

'You always come up with all sorts of explanations.' I said. 'Still, I love you no matter what. You know that, don't you? I was born from the earth, and a mother is worth as much as the land from which you were born. I hope you realize that you don't have to do anything to earn my love, because I have always loved you.' I continued: 'But please, don't use my love to justify your actions. Don't claim that you act out of gratitude to me, because you don't owe my love anything. My love is like water: it flows endlessly from its source. So don't act as if my love could dry up at any minute, as if you have no love to give back to me.'

I told him that I liked that he'd been living his life to the fullest, travelling from one land to another, from one place to the next. His footprints were impressed onto this body, my maternal body; I could feel his heart beating no matter how far away he was from me.

Siam stayed with me for ten more days; then, one morning, he told me that he had to leave. I told him not to worry about me. He said goodbye, and was on his way.

Not long after he left, the area was struck by a huge flash flood. Water flowed in from every direction: from the hills, from the overflowing rivers, from far-flung places no one had ever been. The earth was inundated with water; crops and houses were destroyed, carried away by the current. The locals were distraught. They have never seen Ganga express such wrath. Luckily, Thai and I had built my home on stilts; the water brimmed over the floor, but didn't quite reach me. Thai came to see me in his boat and tried to persuade me to leave, to go and stay with him. I told him I'm not leaving. He was persistent, but I continued to refuse. In the end, he ran out of patience, telling me not to be so stubborn and just leave the house and go with him. I was quite annoyed with him myself. 'I'm not leaving,' I said. It's only a flood. Why make such a big deal out of it? My words upset him, and he paddled away without saying another word.

What is so scary about a flood? All my life I've been through things worse than this. Thai was worried that I would drown and die in the flood. 'Your mother can't die. Haven't I told you this a million times before?' Thai shook his head in disbelief, convinced that I was talking nonsense. I empathize with him, though. He grew up with hardship: the last thing he wanted was to drift. He needed to settle down, to find security, to do everything he could to deny his previous struggles. His spirit is different from mine. He lives his life according to the rules set by his community; he's a fully-fledged human now, one that strives for success and happiness according to the hierarchies set by human society. I'm not objecting to his choices, but I wish he'd sympathize with me. I'm not human, even though I live in the body of one. My spirit is bound to nature, not humans. Floods, earthquakes, lightning strikes: all these things are familiar to me. Homes, on the other hand, I'm less familiar with: things built on top of a piece of earth, fenced in to mark the boundaries of ownership, all notarized on some piece of paper, so no one else can roam around freely on your piece of land. We've all forgotten that the earth was not made to be owned by anyone. It is only a temporary threshold that all beings must pass through. It is normal for floods to pass through too. The same goes for shrimp, shellfish, crabs, fish: they're all welcome to pass through your land, but snakes? You find them menacing. Humans were the last ones to occupy the earth, but somehow they see themselves as superior to other beings. They issue title deeds to occupy, buy, and sell land, and they do all sorts of things to Mother Earth: her jungles, mountains, and rivers. Never have I seen it happen the other way around. The earth has never claimed ownership over humans, let alone said: 'What right do you have to prostitute my body? These trees grow on me, and you cut them down and reap their fruit before any of the other animals can have them. It used to be that birds, or monkeys, or anyone passing by could simply harvest from me in order to subsist, and I had no problem with that. So when you humans claim to own my fruit, does that mean they alone are allowed to enjoy my fruit? How is that fair?' Mother Earth has never claimed ownership over anyone. That's the core of her love. She has never demanded that her kindness be returned. She is generous to all beings, to the most and least grateful of creatures. She is not interested in the language of debts; the excrement left on her by one creature serves to nurture another. Mother Earth might be split or torn apart but in the future, rivers and canals will fill up those gaping wounds. She is both a continuous cycle and an eternal transformation, for one thing leads to the birth of another, or contributes to the possible emergence of an unknown. Such is she. And who is it that likes to preach about loving the land, about returning her love and denouncing those who are treacherous to her. Isn't it humans? Once life begins for them, humans disrupt the life cycles of all other beings, imposing their own absolute laws onto nature. They plaster the land with their ideas of nation and country, gilding stones and trees to label one sapwood or another as their own property. They claim to love her, to return her kindness. But really, they love the fences that they have erected around her. They love her land that represents their nations. Who is it that loves to laud the land, the land that has never asked for anything in return? Isn't it humans? Ungrateful and vainglorious. I see no other race as treacherous as them. From a human perspective, natural disasters are threatening and wrathful. If that is so, perhaps Mother Earth has had enough of the humans roaming around on the surface of her skin. Perhaps she shakes herself every once in a while, out of irritation.

The flood lasted for about a month before it subsided. As soon as the water dried up, half of the land that Thai had bought me disappeared, eroded by the tide. My house, which had once been some distance away from the river, was suddenly right on the edge of the bank. Seeing this, I remembered that nothing was permanent. Mother Earth was testing me by taking half of the land away. 'I'm not bothered at all,' I said. 'You can take all of it if you want, because this land isn't mine. My stay is temporary, and if it's not possible to live here, I can always move somewhere else.'

But Thai and his wife didn't see it that way. They were infuriated at having lost half of their hard-earned land, and held nature responsible for its cruelty. It must have been bad karma from their previous lives, they thought. In the end, Thai rented a backhoe and filled the flooded area near the house with more earth, which was no easy task. He told me to move out of the house and to go and live with him. It's not safe here, he said. He was going to sell it as soon as the river filled back up again.

So I went to live at his house with his wife and children. It's this house right here. He built a garage attached to it: they do tapping, spray painting, generators, whatever it is that they do. Every day, from dawn to dusk, I am forced to listen to this racket, to say nothing of the unpleasant smell of paint and motor oil that fills the place. I wasn't happy. You kids might say that the smell isn't that bad. Well, it's not so bad today, because the garage is closed. They had something important to attend to, which is why they left you kids here with me, you see? Come to think of it, you're probably used to the smell by now. But I'm never going to get used to it. I can't understand how my son's wife and kids can stand it.

Some days, I would leave the house and wander into the next-door neighbour's orchard for a chat. I told her how pleasant and lush her orchard was, and asked if I could stroll around it; eventually, she was happy to let me spend most of my time there. When Thai heard about it, he said he didn't like what I was doing. He said that what I was doing wasn't right, wandering around someone else's property, and anyway, he didn't like the owner of the orchard, since there had been some conflict between them a while back. He told me to stay home.

I was frustrated, but I'm not going to argue back.

My time is drawing closer and closer, telling me that death is imminent. Its presence has always been palpable within me, but being forced to live somewhere I don't belong has intensified the feeling.

About a month ago, I had a dream about Siam. He was lost in a swirling mist and I heard him cry: 'Mum! Mum! Where are you?' I replied to him—'I'm here, my dear!'—but he couldn't seem to hear or see me, stumbling right past me in the heavy mist. I startled awake and tried to get up, but the lower half of my body was petrified, as if a ghost was sitting on my lap. I cried out to Thai that I couldn't feel my legs, and he took me to see a doctor, who said that my spine had pressed on a nerve, causing my lower half to become paralysed. Look at that, kids! Look at how the human body eventually and inevitably deteriorates with time.

Life still dwells in this body, ancient and complete. Once, it was under the earth and emerged to live inside a gigantic thlok tree. Then, a naga, a tiger, a deer, a stone statue, and finally a human. Now it's time for another change. At first, I thought about leaving this world permanently because my children have grown up now, and are living their own lives. I would become nothing but a burden to them if I continued to stay alive: a burden to you too, right? Your parents asked you to be here with me, to look after me because they have things to attend to, things they don't want you kids getting involved with. Do you want to know what those things are?

Last week I prayed to be put to sleep forever, so I need never wake again. But as I did so, I saw Siam lost in the mist again, crying out for me. That same afternoon, Thai told me that Siam had fallen unconscious while working, and had been taken to a hospital. He has yet to regain consciousness. After hearing that, I told Thai about my dream, which I now see as a premonition. My elder son is lost in another world, and a mother cannot just sit here and do nothing. Right now, your parents are trying to save him, but it seems to me that they're not making any progress.

When I heard my son calling for my help from another realm, I realized it's not right to think about my own desire for escapism. I have to go and help him. I've been through all sorts of things, experiences that I was able to let go of, but not this time. A mother must act when her children are in need. It is high time for me to embark on another journey. I have to bring my son back to this realm.

Do you kids want to help me? If you do, fetch me my medicine. It is time for my medicine. Grab that bundle on the Buddha shelf for me. I can't reach it myself because the shelf is too high. Yes, that's it. Do you remember this bundle? It is the bundle of herbs given to me by the hermit before he left this world. Now, please pour some water into this silver bowl for me. That's lovely. First, I will concentrate and set my heart in the direction of my son. I will find him and bring him back to this world, and then I will take the hermit's herbs to end my life. I will die and be reborn in my true form.

Now, kids, go outside and enjoy yourselves out there. Let me sleep for a while before you come in here again, all right?

Part 2: Dr Siam's Adventures in the World of Conspiracies

Awake

I've never felt so relieved. Oh God! When I realized it was just a dream, I felt fine at first, but then it started to all feel too much. This person wanted this, that person wanted that . . . I'm not a saint who can split himself into parts, who can please everyone equally. Is it so hard to understand this simple thing?

At first, I was sitting by the rocks, the waterfall beating down next to me. The green water was clear; I could easily see the mossy rocks and little fish beneath the surface. Everything was cascading downwards: the cacophonous echo of the waterfall crashing into the grooves of the rock, sending white foam and ripples to the surface. Water vapour was diffusing through the air, dampening my face . . . So cool and refreshing. Crisp sunlight was shining through the steamy air, casting a rainbow. I was sunbathing on the rocks with my legs swinging above the clear water, drying off after diving off the cliff and into the water. Sitting here for a while, my skin turned reddish-brown; goosebumps spread across my arms, chest, and thighs. I was stark naked, shivering. My dick shrunk to the size of my pinky.

When I was dry enough, the skin on my back scorched tight, I slowly got up to balance myself on the slippery rock, preparing for another dive. Last time, I managed three rounds of somersaults, but this time, I wanted to dive straight in like those guys in the foreign films. I knew from before that the bottom was deep enough, so a swan dive would be easy. I called down to my friends swimming below for their attention: 'I'm about to do a swan dive!'

But one of them yelled back that he'd already done it and that I was copying him; another told me to be more creative. The bastards were trying to outdo me. I was insulted. I was the leader of our group, despite being smaller than everyone else. As I tried to think of a better dive, another friend—who else but that bastard Somjai—dared me to dive face-down, spread-eagled across the surface. 'Are you man enough?' He prodded.

Somjai, you fucking bastard. Of course, I was man enough, but what would be the point? Somjai continued to bluff, saying that if I was too chickenshit I should just crawl back down the cliff and he'd do the stunt himself. The other guys were cackling their heads off. My younger brother was swimming with them too. He was looking at me, but I couldn't tell whether he was trying to stop me from jumping, or urging me on.

I'll lose face if I don't go through with it. I know for sure that it's going to hurt, but I won't be insulted. I'm man enough. I steadied myself and prepared to jump. The guys below kept hollering at me. I faltered when I saw someone out of the corner of my eye: another one of the guys, creeping up from behind. I could tell that he was about to push me, so I swerved away before he could even touch me. 'Ha! You idiot!' I called out, triumphant, but my feet slipped off the mossy rock and I fell. 'I knew it, you bastards!' I was cursing at them mid-air, bracing myself for the pain that was about to shoot through my skin: a sting that erupted from my belly that sent spasms down my arms and legs.

It was so deep that I lost track of time. Speed had ceased to exist, but I was still somehow making a slow descent, as if I were falling through sticky, boiling syrup. The air was thick, dense; I was compressed, enwrapped in a sort of vacuum until I could no longer breathe. Suspended, struggling desperately to touch the water's surface, I wanted nothing more but to feel the pain I'd anticipated. I fought violently against the viscous, syrupy air, screaming at the top of my lungs. I mustered all my strength for the last time. I swung my body up again. At last, I woke from the fall . . .

I've never felt so light before. After sitting upright in bed, I feel relief: it was just a dream. I scan the unfamiliar surroundings as the light slowly seeps in, dissolving the darkness. I'm in a room: quite lovely, a cowboy-style bungalow. What's it called again? A log home? The four walls are lined with logs, country-style, with pink curtains drawn over all three of the windows. I'm comforted when I find Dao next to me, sound asleep. I hope I didn't hit her during my nightmare just now. I suddenly remember that we're on holiday together. I've brought her to meet my mother. I've brought her to my hometown.

Wide awake, I get out of bed. I draw the pink curtains back, gazing at the scenery outside. The morning ambience draws me outside, alone. I don't want to disturb Dao; I know she's exhausted and needs her rest. My childhood memories welcome me. They race to manifest themselves, layer by layer, teasing me into recollection, into remembering where it is I'm currently standing, and to whom this land once belonged, and the farmland and orchard it had once been before this bungalow was built. I stroll with pleasure through the familiar rice fields and orchards, passing the big fish pond where I often came to fish as a kid, whiling away hours at a time. I slowly drift across a dirt road on a high embankment, raised above the rice fields and houses which seem to sink down on either side. I feel groovy, walking down the middle of the road like this.

I reach the front gate of a house with two wooden chairs placed right on the bend of the road. A brass bowl with steamed rice is placed on one of the chairs, along with food in plastic bags, candles, and incense sticks; in other words, all the things one needs for almsgiving. The fragrance of freshly cooked rice lingers in the early morning mist. The rice fields are dotted with rice stumps bathed in dew; when the sun trickles through the clouds, they glisten like morning stars. *Oh, Dao. My beloved Dao. Have you heard this story before? There was a petite, gentle girl, with a little fringe and a face smothered in snot. At night, she was scared of the dark, worried that her lover would not return in the morning as he had promised. She cried herself to sleep and the fields were showered with her tears. Her lover, lost in the middle of the jungle, followed the traces of her tears and returned to her, as he had promised.* My lovely Dao, I'll return to you before the morning warmth dries up your tears, so you won't accuse your darling Siam[1] of lying to you.

'Why are you crying for me?' I'd ask you, even though I know you're not the romantic type. You aren't a sweet-talker—others may find your language rough on their ears—but I don't mind it. I think it's beautiful.

I know you'd say: 'Hey, Siam, turn it down a notch, will ya? All this hopeless romantic nonsense.' And I'd laugh at your unapologetic bluntness, because I know that, deep down, you love me no matter what.

'Oh, my dear,' I'd say. 'You're sending me your love with the morning sun.'

Then you'd raise your voice to reply: 'Don't act so stupid, Siam!' But I wouldn't budge. I wouldn't even mind if you were to pinch the skin around my nipple, if it pleased you, because the pain would please me too.

I'm about to continue on my way when I hear someone calling my name from a distance. An old woman is shuffling her way out of her house, shouting something in my direction. She stands by the road, next to where she has placed her alms for the monks. She gestures again, as if beckoning me over, but I'm not sure it's me she's looking for. I turn around to see a monk walking towards me. *Oh*, I think. *The old woman is probably trying to catch the monk's attention, not mine.* I turn back towards her, shooting her an apologetic smile, and continue on my way.

As I'm about to pass the monk, I stop and put my hands together to show him my respect. He looks somewhat surprised before greeting me.

'Where are you off to?'

'Just walking, Father.'

'With no destination?'

'Not really. I'm just in the mood for a morning walk.'

'In that case, come see me at my temple when you're done.'

'Why, Father?'

'They're waiting for you there.'

Who's waiting? I think. *And what are they waiting for?* The monk is acting strange, his voice an anxious whisper, his eyes darting back and forth. Being told that someone is waiting for me has made me instantly nervous. Only moments ago, everything was fine. How brief that was! Thanks to him, I'm now full of anxiety. And I thought monks were supposed to help us unburden our worries! Who on earth could be waiting for me at the temple? I grumbled in English. *NO. SENSE!* What more do they want from me?

Out of courtesy, I tell the monk that I'll stop by and dash off. Thinking back, I've always been a frequent visitor of temples. Whenever I had the time, I travelled all over the country to pay my respects to the Buddha, to make merit and attend all sorts of religious events: *Tod Kathin, Pa-Pha,* the gilding of sacred stones and medals. I'm pretty sure I've accumulated enough merit for this life and the next. The only thing I haven't done is build a giant Buddha statue. Perhaps the monk I've just run into was angling for one for his temple.

I keep walking. Suddenly, a huge, exuberant crowd appears, heading straight for me. A few familiar faces approach me enthusiastically, shaking my hand and congratulating me. But what for? They claim they're my supporters, that they voted for me and helped to spread the word about my talent, my respectability, my charisma. They're confident that I'll be able to secure all sorts of infrastructure for the community—roads, waterways, sewage systems, garbage disposal systems—as well as provide playgrounds for their kids, promote local products, and preserve the community's traditional way of life and cultural heritage. They tell me I emanate charisma, that it's glowing through my unblemished complexion: a sure sign that I am destined for success. They tell me about my powerful position, and how people will be willing to do anything for me: they go on about how I'll be invited to preside over important events, how I'll drink bottles of wine that cost tens or hundreds of thousands of baht, how I'll travel to off-site seminars where I'll receive special allowances, gifts, hush money. Businessmen will have to come to me and offer me bribes in order to proceed with their projects. They'll hand me envelopes filled with gift vouchers, or private passes to casinos in Poi-Pet for me and my secretary, or first-class plane tickets for Dao and me. We'll fly to Hong Kong and go shopping and stay in luxury hotels. The list continues . . . But wait! This doesn't feel right. These sorts of things are unjust and corrupt. They won't lead our country anywhere!

'But . . . But, you see, I can't accept any of this. Brothers and sisters, I understand that you're excited for me . . . I can feel it. But this is all too much. Can someone please explain to me what exactly is going on? I'm overwhelmed by your warmth and enthusiasm, but please: tell me what this is all about.'

Someone steps out from the crowd. I recognize him: he's the deputy chief administrator of the subdistrict administrative organization, or the SAO for short.

'Congratulations, Dr Siam. You've been elected as chief executive of the SAO with a soaring number of votes. Continue with your good work for the people, and soon you'll be elected chief executive of the province. Just you wait! Then more people will know of you, and soon they'll want you as their MP. See? Who said it's too late for people in their 50s to get ahead with their lives? It's only the beginning for us politicians.' He lowers his voice, whispering conspiratorially.

'Start by serving your party. Start by soliciting votes for MPs and before you know it, you'll have people working for you, Doctor.'

I don't disagree with him. My charitable efforts have often gone unacknowledged. This could be a real opportunity to devote myself to bettering our society, and to finally be acknowledged for it. At my age, I think I deserve it.

'Wait! One more thing,' the deputy chief administrator interjects. 'Nothing is official until you report to the ministry. For now, Doctor, you're only the acting chief executive of the SAO. To be officially recognized as chief executive, protocol requires approval from the higher-ups.'

'Is that so? What do I have to do?'

'You report to the ministry,' he said.

I hesitate, suddenly aware of a weighty uncertainty hanging over me. I'm unsure of whether this position will create more obligations for me. But before I have time to finish the thought, the deputy chief administrator eggs me on. 'You'd better go now.'

Everything is happening so fast. The overwhelming support and expectations from the public, the pressure from the deputy chief administrator, and my promotion in the near future to chief executive: an admirable position in the eyes of everyone from close acquaintances to the general public. A small seed of doubt grows inside my head, sprouting into this rather foolish question:

'How much time will it take? At the ministry, I mean?'

'Oh, not long at all,' the deputy chief administrator replies dismissively, as if it were obvious.

I nod. All righty then. Seeing my response, the crowd cheers me on. I make my way to the ministry, secretly hoping that the process will be over quickly; over before the sun dries up those rice stumps and the dew disappears.

---

[1] What happened was rather sudden but, in truth, very straightforward. Someone I knew collapsed without warning. He lay unconscious and half-paralyzed in the ICU for almost two months before dying.

His was yet another life that I could summarize in a single paragraph, much like the countless other lives that barely got a full paragraph to themselves. So why would I bother with some guy who led a pathetic life: a life lived in deep descent, a life that would one day meet its end, falling flat onto the ground, never to rise again?

'You want to write a best-selling book? Write about my life.' That was what he told me three years ago.

I smirked. Here we go again. Another self-absorbed type, convinced that his life was first-class writing material. His proposal had come as soon as he learned I was a writer.

'Don't be a *cock*tease, *Doctor*,' I told him. He cackled and raised his liquor glass, clinking with mine. 'Why don't you write it yourself?' I encouraged him.

I meant what I said. I don't write about other people's lives just because they tell them to me, no matter how interesting they might be. These kinds of storytelling are skeletal, hollowed of flesh, blood, capillaries, lymphs, and hidden malignant cells. I believe it necessary to *feel* and *see*—to empathize with—someone from a story than what is intentionally revealed.

I couldn't really say these things to him, because he would pretend that he understood them all, as with everything. When I told him that I was a writer, he registered it as a ghostwriter. Perhaps he didn't mean it as an insult (but I was insulted anyway) and simply wanted to boast his superiority over ordinary people by bragging about his newfound knowledge of ghostwriters who write about celebrities, actors, and singers, and publish pocket books. He believed that ordinary people would never be able to make that association; they'd probably think that these celebrities wrote their autobiographies themselves. He gave me a pompous wink to signal that he had understood what I was talking about, and offered his life as material for what he claimed would become the best-selling book.

I gather from the implications of his offer that he probably thought that I was his charity case. He probably didn't even mean it as an insult (but I took it as one anyway).

Hence why I told him that he was acting like a cock.

In fact, I wasn't even being rude. I did encourage him to write his own biography: he had already started referring to himself in the third person anyway, as Dr Siam. Whether or not he was a real doctor, I myself am still doubtful.

Mr Siam Duangsuk was fifty-seven years old. Occupation: doctor. He had a freckled, reddish-brown complexion and was 159 centimetres tall. He'd entered our family with an ambiguous role: he was my mother's friend, her life partner, her new lover. One day, he was hurrying to his clinic, where his patients were waiting for their health check-ups. It was 2.05 p.m. He hadn't even had his breakfast. During his session with his last patient, he was hoping for a break, to finally have his first meal of the day. There were many other things he still needed to attend to: unfinished business that lingered from yesterday, last week, last month, and last year. There were countless things in his life that were continually worrying him, waiting to be sorted through one by one, chapter by chapter. Sitting down with your lunch, chewing and sighing away life's knotted burdens: isn't there something wonderful about reflecting on the concerns and obligations that await you after lunch? The knowledge that you'll be able to be deal with them tomorrow, or perhaps after a quick nap, is reassuring. You thank life for the concerns and obligations it has burdened you with, and thank it even more for equipping you with the capacity to deal with them. Concerns give you certainty. Dr Siam, however, didn't get the chance to have his first meal of the day, or to chew and sigh his way through life's concerns. Simple and sudden, cut-throat and direct, like the command written on the back of a credit card—the company reserves the right to cancel without prior notice—he snapped out of consciousness and collapsed. His head hit the tiled floor, and from that moment on, he ceased to move.

So here we are, Dr Siam. I'm writing about you now. Would a paragraph suffice to cover those two months you spent in purgatory? His dynamism changed suddenly into stasis, and so I changed too, moved to abandon my prior convictions.

All right, then. These are my views. They belong to me: his ghostwriter.

Found

How does maturity relate to age? I'd say that the two run in parallel but refuse to acknowledge each other. I say this because I have felt my own spirit mature, all while I have chosen to forget my age. Those with experience would agree that we want to be remembered for our intelligence and talents, not for our damn age!

Life is strange (Ah! Just talking about life exhilarates me!) because changes occur at all stages of living. It may sound formulaic, but the truth is, everyone undergoes their own changes.

Humans are born with a lack. We cry out for this and that. We need to eat, to accumulate, to be educated, and then we reach a certain age where we hunger for things that might fulfill us intellectually and spiritually. As our physical body becomes satiated, our starving spirit grows ravenous. It takes everything: the good and the bad, misery and happiness, the dark and the light. The spirit's ability to gorge itself is fascinating, forceful, and wild. After a while, we begin to feel full and our appetite dwindles. Our body and spirit slow down as we metabolize and analyze, before moving onto the stage of giving, of contribution. This is where we take all the things ingested during our younger years—the first half of our lives—and extract the best out of those nutrients, like they do with concentrated chicken stock or the best liquor. At this stage, we strive to do things for others. Most people with a family will do whatever they can for their wives, their kids, their parents: yet, there are people who want to help those outside their kin. Despite not knowing where their contribution may end up, they are certain of its accessibility, of humanity's interconnectedness without the need for personal acquaintance.

At this very stage of my life, I feel this powerful urge within me.

Doing things for oneself and one's family is good, but doing things for other people is greater.

What do I want to do for others, for humanity, for my fellow compatriots, you ask? I want to expose the crooked system: the attitude, mentality and way of life misshapen by the false belief that people are always inferior to something, always in debt to something, and always obliged to be grateful for something. Quality of life is rooted in this kind of oppression. The system rewards obedience with security and comfort; people grow content, and so they become complacent, passive. If they start to question things, the system claims that they've already benefitted from its welfare and generous patronage, which means they have no right to demand anything else. If they insist on continuing their questioning, the system transfers the burden of dealing with dissidents to other entities: mobs mobilized by the system itself, engineered to brand unbelievers as ungrateful. They will not be exiled but they will rot in shame within the system.

How does this affect quality of life, you ask? It fosters intellectual inertia and dissuades the revolutionary spirit. New and creative ideas do not grow; instead, age-old tradition, norms, and inherited behaviours exist in perpetuity. This is most powerful and best exemplified within bureaucracy, where time flows like an inert electrical current.

There appear to be no shortcuts or bypasses, because these are seen as loopholes for corruption. However, in truth, there is one regular path through the solemn temple of bureaucracy, and then there is the bypass that business men use to secretly take control of the system. Most people are not aware of the latter path: it is like a termite tunnel within a structure that appears transparent and straightforward.

Those who do have a clue (and there are more of them these days) see it as an opportunity: a privilege that few have access to. The system creates privilege, knowingly or otherwise, and rewards those who seek it. Those who make it inside feel a sense of superiority, while bystanders (and there are many these days) can only complain and become green with jealousy. This jealousy has spread through the hearts and minds of those in this country. Successful individuals in our society (what bad luck for them, that their successes are typically only recognized outside the country to which they belong) are resented by their fellow citizens, who seek to wound with their sharp tongues: 'How arrogant they are!' They are accused of burrowing their way through the termite tunnel to success (no chance they'd be on the straight and narrow!) and such accusations are based on nothing other than the values produced and upheld within our own temple of bureaucracy. Their international success brands them as ungrateful citizens: 'Go abroad then. Why did you even come back here?'

You see, people in this country are bitter and jealous: not by nature, but as a byproduct of a system that instilled those sentiments in them.

Those who want access to the termite tunnels, those who desire for privilege—why not just be a samaritan and tell others the truth—that the bypass can be used by anyone? Why reserve this path for their own little clique, rather than providing access to all?

It's their way of sacralizing rules and regulations, of solidifying them into monoliths (for the underprivileged who are deprived of access to the termite tunnels). And yet, these people keep burrowing into these rules and regulations, hollowing them out. They're indulgent with their own written texts, interpreting and enforcing them in ways that serve their vested interests, while commoners are forced to revere the sanctity of the legal language.

In my student years, I learned that the people are the ones who use the law. So, then, the law must be drafted, adjusted, and amended by the people. Laws that come from the powers that be are illegitimate and should not be enforced, and the powers that be who illegitimately enforce such laws should abide by their own such laws. But most people don't know this. Instead of taking control of the law—administering it in favour of justice—they are subjugated by it. The people must assert their right and freedom to use the law and to claim it as their own: to not be intimidated by it.

It's disheartening to me, but allow me to give some examples from two different phases in my life.

I had a part-time job as a student. In those days, I was living in a temple in Klong Thom. Every day after class, I'd walk through the small alleys, which I found charming in a peculiar sort of way. All sorts of damaged goods were sent here: a miscellany of things that needed to be fixed and pulled apart. The damaged parts would be fixed: anything beyond repair would be thrown away, and the rest would be kept as spare mechanical parts. A badly damaged car may be seen as unsalvageable, but its components—windscreen wipers, bumper bar, steering wheel, screws, some parts of the engine—might still be new and functional. There's overall damage, of course, but once these small components are salvaged from the wreckage, they might be given a new life of their own. You could say that the people of Klong Thom are surgeons, recuperators. They're the working-class shamanic midwives of the underground who possess miraculous life-giving knowledge.

I'm fascinated by this sort of know-how. After hanging out in Klong Thom for a while, I was able to become an apprentice. This coven of midwives taught me so much about recovering and selling parts from damaged vehicles and devices. As time passed, I acquired more skills that allowed me to innovate, to create by re-assembling this with that. I made a remote control that worked on every make of television. Later on, I was able to decode and create a cable box. This was my evolution: this is how I gained the ingenious abilities that are now renowned across all realms.

This kind of knowledge revives the working class, and it truly benefits us all. It protects us from big corporations seeking to exploit workers and monopolize the industry. Soon enough, our community felt the consequences of our actions. They accused us of conducting unlawful and unscrupulous business operations, labelling Klong Thom a den of thieves and lawbreakers and copyright snatchers. They tried to turn other businessmen against us, painting us as selfish, unethical and exploitative cheapskates. (But who is really exploiting whom? It's you who exploit us, charging exorbitant amounts in copyright fees and using that money to pay your own taxes to legalize your businesses. These taxes go to the government, to be spent on public goods for a country that claims to be running on 'clean' money, so you believe your contributions have built this country into what it is today. You feel entitled. As for us—the working class—you see us as a part of the problem, as people who are dragging this country backwards: all because the government gets nothing from us. That's the lie that the government wants you to believe.) The fact is, everyone has to pay taxes.

It's strange. When you eat at a restaurant, you don't complain about having to pay both the VAT and service charge. But what if a roadside hawker wants 17 per cent extra on top of your food? I bet you'd make a big fuss out of it, saying you're being taken advantage of. But we're too small to demand something as civilized as that. (You'd fuss over the 17 per cent we should've been entitled to in the first place, just as you do about our fake satellites and cable boxes.)

Black, fake, illegal, unscrupulous . . . You're talking about a class of people seen by those who thinks they belong to a superior class: the sort of people who fuss over paying more taxes than the underprivileged, but shut up real quick when they get to pay less.

Roadside hawkers! Charge VAT and add that extra 17 per cent! Our waiters are foreigners (though you refer to them as immigrants), our chefs cook the cuisines inspired by their roots (they didn't just take a few cooking courses abroad: you're experiencing an authentic feast with their mother's touch) and the roadside view of folk culture is as authentic as it gets (not staged). Our world has been made bogus.

They've tarnished our world. They've branded it a substandard world, a real-life cockfight. They persecute us with their laws and hammer their ethics into our conscience to justify their authority. And let's not forget the superstitions: our counterfeit and illegal products belong to ghosts! Those spare parts are robbed from the dead who might still be possessive of them, even in the afterlife. They say we stole them, that these restless spirits haunt our objects and anyone who inherits them. These stories make you shiver to the core, but you affluents still drift in and out of luxurious hotels furnished with antiques. That 100-year-old teak was probably stolen from some village—so was that likeness of a Buddha's head from the Tawaravadee era—that ancient sword from Ayutthaya (which has tasted the blood of so many of its owner's enemies)—that age-old centerpiece—that cushion from the early Rattanakosin era. And there you are, sleeping peacefully in your air-conditioned suite, unperturbed by the fury of the spirits whose possessions have been stolen from them.

Two identical handbags—one of them costing hundreds of thousands of baht—are made with cheap labour in the same factory in China. One goes through the front gates for export while the other is smuggled out of the back door, possessed by vengeful spirits. Their new owners will be haunted by the ghouls of law, by their shameful lack of conscience and morality: but no one gives a damn about the cheap labour in China. The handbag company might have specifically relocated their manufacturing base to seek cheap labour in China, after their own government raised minimum wage. Still, the prices of those handbags continue to soar, billowing with international exchange rates. So we have the ghosts of taxes and the ghouls of international law, but we don't see hide nor hair of the ghosts of cheap labour!

This is what really disheartens me. This, and—to top it all off—the condescension. They slander us in the name of creativity. They say that Klong Thom is 'typically Thai' because our counterfeits lack 'originality'. They say that Thai people are skilled in forgery, that we operate best underground and not so well in authorized activities. What a groundless accusation.

As far as I'm concerned, Klong Thom is the most original of them all, an unapologetic representation of Thainess. It's like when we speak English. We used to admire those who could speak with proper British or American accents, but this is no longer the case these days. Where is the originality if we speak a foreign language without a touch of our native tongue? Why is it that Thai people are ashamed of their accent, but let those TV hosts get away with putting on pretentious accents? It's gotten to the point where they can neither speak English or Thai clearly, making it impossible to tell what nationality they belong to or even what language they speak.

Take Indians, for example. They've made the Indian accent widely acceptable. Their English echoes the timbres of their roots and culture. Thai English is flat: every phrase and syllable is equally enunciated, as we often hear from taxi drivers, peddlers, stall owners, and bar girls. Thai accents should be widely spoken and recognized. It is the accent of the oppressed majority.[2] Meanwhile, our oppressors desperately try to imitate Westerners. Little do they know that our flat-tongued accent is admired by those they look up to. Those Westerners know what they're drawn to, and in turn, they know what kind of people are drawn to them.

Anyone still ashamed of their flat-tongued accent, but comfortable with imitating Westerners like a bunch of parrots? And, who, may I ask, is more respectable in the end?

Parrots like you only accuse us of forgery only because you've been deluded into believing that your own imitations are seamless. You're too far gone to realize that our forgery has no originality: we remake not to imitate, but to communicate amongst ourselves. For this, you slander us in the name of creativity. You make us out to be tactless copycats. Tactless, lawless, and godless: unlike yourselves.

Try turning the whole thing upside-down! Invert your aesthetics! You'd be surprised to see how things look from our perspective!

---

[2] Years ago, around half past six in the evening, my mother returned home with a stranger.

He was a stout man in a long-sleeved shirt in light green, neatly tucked into black slacks, which were secured by a leather belt. He carried two mobile phone cases around his waist. His trouser pockets bulged with all sorts of things, while his shirt pocket was stuffed with a pair of glasses, folded pieces of paper, sweets, loose change, and half-tucked banknotes. He had different bags slung across his body, which was somehow representative of his restless personality. He was also carrying plastic bags full of food in both hands. Admittedly, the first time I met him, I thought he was a salesman.

My mother introduced Dr Siam to me as her 'colleague'. I'm not sure whether my siblings were suspicious, but the term 'colleague' for me instantly meant something more. I was sure that my older brother, if he knew of this relationship, would have instantly been able to tell that he was my mother's new lover. But my older brother didn't live with us. He was living in Bangkok, and my younger brother, Maitree, was in prison. Both of them were unaware of anything that was happening within our family.

My mother walked into the kitchen and transferred the food into bowls, purposefully leaving me and Dr Siam to get acquainted.

'Have a seat, Doctor,' I said to him, passing him a glass of Regency brandy.

I don't like liquor, but I like wine. Stout too, sometimes, depending on the occasion. I was in the mood for stout that day, so I drank some while I waited to for the wine to breathe. I was celebrating the bank's approval of my housing loan.

Dr Siam started chatting as soon as he sat down. 'Oh, it's great that you drink stout. A can of stout a day is good for your health, especially for circulation and heart function.' What he said sounded sensible enough, at first, but then he began to digress.

'All German beers are excellent. Germans drink beer every day to stimulate their heart. When I was living there, I noticed everyone was drinking it.' Then he looked at me for affirmation. 'The Germans love beer and the French love wine!'

Nervously, he picked up the beer bottle, taking his glasses from his shirt pocket (a hundred-baht note fell out, but he pretended not to notice) and putting them on, squinting at the label. Then he exclaimed:

'Guinness is an excellent German beer.'

Strike one! He put the can down and grabbed the wine bottle I'd opened.

'Wow! This is a first-rate Cabinet from France!'

Strike two! Was he really talking about a piece of furniture? It's *Cabernet:* Cabernet Sauvignon. And the wine? It was Australian. He shifted his attention back to the stout.

'You know the benefits of stout? The key is in the colour, which comes from chicken soup. That's why it's black.'

Strike three! This was torture. Was this guy really a doctor?

I'm not the petty type. I understand that he was just trying to make an impression. But his last comment about the chicken soup was more than I could hope for. I stared straight at him, signaling to him that I was the last person on earth to suffer his stupid joke. *You can be an idiot elsewhere, but not here. I'll make sure of that,* I conveyed silently.

He recoiled a little and let out a nervous laugh, before continuing to chatter as if nothing that had transpired in the last few moments had been at all embarrassing for him. What was it about him that got on my nerves?

I just didn't like his face for some reason. It's not that I looked down on him, or was disgusted by him or anything of the sort, but something about his personality was vexing: chaotic and irritating, like a fly. But he was also my mother's new lover. I had to be respectful and refrain from making him lose face.

From then on, Dr Siam frequented our house almost every week, and continued to do so for years after that. He cooked for us, ate dinner with us, and drank with us, especially with Maitree. Having done his time, Maitree was warned by our mother about his drinking, but this is where Dr Siam tried to win Maitree over. He told her: 'If this young man wants to drink, let him do it at home, where we can keep an eye on him. Please, my dear Dao.'

For hours on end, he would brag to Maitree about his experience with outdoor activities. They both shared a taste for manly hobbies like camping: sleeping in a tent, fishing. They only knew each other for six months before they became camping buddies, taking trips to the beach together and drinking by the seaside, hanging around lounges and karaoke bars.

That was how Dr Siam befriended Maitree: by reading his mind, by divining what he wanted. He played it casual, treating him the way a friend or big brother would: a self-designated father figure. The similarities between the two were uncanny. They liked challenging each other to drink whole bottles of liquor. They liked playing rough, laughing at obscene jokes, and getting drunk until dawn almost every week.

In the early days of his visits, Dr Siam would show us so many of his 'talents' that we lost count of how many he had. He recounted his life experiences as if there were hundreds or thousands of people were living in them. There was nothing he didn't know, not a single experience unlived: it was as if he could stand in several different places at once. From creating a remote control that worked on all types of appliances to predicting the next prime minister, he could do anything, knew everything: the percentage of the world's unforested land, celebrity scandals, the plot of the final episode of the soap opera that was currently airing. He even showed off his palm reading skills. He started by reading my mother's, telling her that she was headed towards success and prosperity because of the guardian sitting in the middle of her palm.

'Where is the guardian sitting in the middle of her palm? I don't see it,' I asked him.

But he quickly ignored my question, saying that he meant it as a metaphor, before placing my mother's hand on the floor and shifting himself to sit on top of it.

'Oh, you cheeky bastard!' My mother blushed and I felt awkward.

I couldn't deny that his wacky company had lightened our once desolate home. My mother was much happier, strangely so. She believed everything Dr Siam told her. When stem cell treatments became trendy, she was his first guinea pig. He took a tube of her blood and left it for a few days to sediment. He claimed that the tube would be sent to Germany, where it would be transformed into medicine, which would later be injected back into her body. 'The body heals best with its own cells,' he said.

There was no proof, but my mother testified that her joint pains were gone and that she felt brisker, better. I don't know if was all a placebo.

One evening, I stopped by to visit my mother and found her having a drink with Dr Siam as usual, so I sat down to join them. I was feeling unwell; my entire back was aching. I'd been working overtime at the factory and it had finally taken a toll on me. As I was drinking with them, I felt a sharp pain shoot up my spine, and I couldn't help but cry out in pain. Dr Siam asked me to lie face down and he massaged me, trying to reduce the tension in my back muscles. He was firm and forceful. The pain was pleasurable. He asked me to sit cross-legged with my hands up. All of a sudden, he pulled at both my hands with some force, and I heard the length of my spine crack. I felt incredibly light, and the pain was gone.

'Oh,' I moaned, thanking him. 'You are what they call in English a *chiropractor*!'

'I'm more than that, young man,' he said, slipping back into his native dialect. 'The massage I gave you was from Wat Po. Those chiropractors have to fly all the way from their home countries to take lessons there.'

(The above view belongs to Chidchai.)

Routing

Another thing that disheartened me during the second phase of my life (which I almost forgot to tell you about) was when I returned home from abroad. I'd shifted my attention towards modern medicine. Let me tell you: every step I take in life, I take seriously. If I have my heart set on learning something, I will pursue it to the marrow without giving a single damn about what others think, even if they say that I'm a good-for-nothing flake.

The world is full of exciting stories and things to learn, so why should we confine ourselves to a single discipline, or equip ourselves with a single set of skills? That's a waste of a life, but it sure does benefit the state, which doesn't want people to move around or change jobs as often as they'd like. They want us to know our place, so they can firmly establish theirs.

It's burdensome, trying to explain these sorts of things. People say I'm spinning conspiracy theories out of thin air. I once tried to explain it to Thai, my brother,[3] who made a face as soon as I began. Somjai[4] too looked like he was being force-fed bitter medicine. Those two don't really believe in what I do; to be more exact, they don't believe in me. The irony is, though, that deep down, they expect their share from my risky business. The minute those two smell success, they'll be straight on the prowl.

Our world has changed drastically. Our days don't last long as those of our mothers did. New things keep springing up here and there across the planet, competing for attention, however brief they may be. Long gone are the days when a movie could be in cinemas for over a year, or an album could sell over a million copies. Everyone has their chance to draw public attention, but only for a few minutes. Indeed, time these days is counted in minutes: not in months, years, or decades.

As humans, our life span has shortened. I will admit, however, that I played a role in causing this inertia and deterioration: through my invention of the all-in-one remote control. I created convenience, underestimating how irresponsible people could be: underestimating their ability to tell themselves that enough was enough, to tell when something was too much. Comfort stagnates the body. Parts that should move freely are made to do repetitive motions, operated like machines. The result is poor health. I've experienced this too. Instead of metabolizing, a body that sits still for too long will accumulate disease and illness. It starts with aches and pains—muscle pain, aching bones, creaking joints—leading to indigestion, sleeplessness, high cholesterol; then come the problems with the lungs, the liver, the kidneys and so on. Our physical condition deteriorates because we hardly move: it's why people these days fall ill and die faster than their ancestors did. Instead of moving with the world, we sit still and leave the rest to our five senses. This, I'd say, is the defining crisis of our times.

I went to Wat Po for a traditional Thai massage, and all my tension disappeared. I was very impressed with this particular discipline of rehabilitation, the healing and recuperation of the body in this way. It might seem basic, but it's in fact sophisticated; profound, really. It deals in both the physical and spiritual, harmonizing the two for good health. Good health leads to mental relaxation and positive thinking, and all of this leads to a good quality of life. That's the dynamic of it all.

After getting a few massages there, I decided to sign up for a course. I completed it within a year and became an expert in the field. It was the beginning of my physical introspection, of scrutinizing what lay within this body of mine. My subcutaneous explorations made me see how muscles are intertwined, how the bones, joints, tendons, and organs are all interconnected. The inside of the human body is miraculous: a microcosm of the universe.

Before switching to medicine, I studied law. That was the education I received within university gates. *In another hand*—as they say in English—I was a remote control engineer and a traditional Thai masseuse, and now, I'm currently studying Thai botany. All these things are stepping stones towards bigger achievements. I know that modern medicine circles have been actively researching stem cell treatment, which involves extracting cells from our body in order to cure it. Our body consists of both good and bad cells—the sinner and the saint—in perpetual battle. Isn't that fascinating? It is as if a whole universe exists within our bodies! I decided to go abroad to study, and it wasn't long before I imported all this knowledge back with me to Thailand, ready to impart them to my compatriots.

I asked Somjai: 'Hey man, are you interested in a joint venture? Stem cells are a miracle of modern medicine!'

Somjai has been a friend for years, and so he agreed, despite seeming unconvinced. I could sense his unease about it. That was also the day I ran into Dao . . . *Oh, my beloved Dao, the first time we met . . . Save our words and let them remain our secret . . .* I saw her in the market and I asked her how she was doing, as it had been over twenty years since the last time we met. She said she was doing fine, spending most of her time looking after her kids (even though all of them had grown tall enough for a dog to lick their arses). She said her husband had died, which I was surprised to hear. I asked her how it happened, but she simply said that death was death, and that there was no point in talking about it. She invited me to drop by her place, and I promised her I would.

And that was how we became close again. *Oh, Dao. A sweet girl who had been living without love. But love is all that I have for you.*

I told her: Dao, you've been through so much. I have something to tell you, and you don't have to believe it right away. All I ask is for you to listen, and to decide for yourself whether or not I speak the truth.

Dao, look at me: look at my complexion. Tell me: do I look older? I don't, do I? I don't look any older than I did a decade ago, when we last met, do I? Look at my scalp. My hair is still thick and black (unlike those other balding fellows). My complexion is clear and lovely (these freckles come with age). How is this possible? My body has the ability to heal itself. With what? Cells! My cells are their own cure. This is the new frontier of modern medicine, far more advanced than the treatments given in hospitals. So, you see, I heal myself using my own cells that have been sent from Germany. This is the future of medicine, which will enable humans to live for more than a hundred years!

Just one shot and you feel instantly energized. My friend and I just opened up a clinic together. Most of our patients who have received the treatment have shown signs of improvement in their condition. It can cure all sorts of diseases, and patients often come back for regular treatment. Those with gout say their joints are no longer stiff or knotted together. That which was once failing regains its functions. A patient's relative also told me that the treatment cured their paralysis. It's effective even with chronic issues like migraines or anemia. Even people who aren't ill can benefit from the treatment, as it can be used for cosmetic purposes. One shot works wonders: saggy, dry skin miraculously tightens, becoming soft and plump; pale, yellow complexions turn rosy and radiant. Unlike the pills or creams they advertise on TV, which work on a superficial level, stem cells recuperate the body from within. Your mental and physical health radiates from the inside out!

You may wonder: if it's really this fantastic, why is stem cell treatment still relatively rare? Why isn't it administered in hospitals? Why must we be rather discreet about our clinic? Well, my patients were also skeptical to begin with. Let me explain that this kind of treatment is a Western innovation: Swiss, to be exact. Maybe you've heard that the Swiss live very long lives and hardly ever fall ill. Doctors in Germany are also interested in this treatment, and they've taken it even further. The treatment is extremely popular in the West at the moment; in fact, it's officially recognized by several countries.

Talk to the top-ranking doctors in Thailand. They all know about the treatment, and yet, it still isn't widely implemented here. This is because it hasn't been approved by the Medical Council of Thailand. Do you know why this is? Just wait and see! Stem cell treatment won't become standard practice for years, despite the countless benefits outweighing the risks, despite the recognition from international medical councils. Why, the Medical Council of Thailand won't be able to agree on how to split the pie! Doctors, hospitals, pharmaceutical companies, the Ministry of Health: all of them will fight over this multi-million business. They'll prioritize their shares over the health of the people. Now do you see? All the top doctors in the inner circle are aware of this; I, myself, am one of them. But I'm not a stakeholder in any of this. The only stakes I care about are in relation to the health of my patients. Humans have to care for each other, but most doctors these days are no longer faithful to the spirit of their profession! That's why I risk importing this treatment myself, practicing it in my own clinic and travelling far and wide to other provinces to offer it to the general public. It's a risky business, but a necessary one. It is every human's right to have access to basic healthcare. All good doctors know this. Did you know that some clinics and hospitals were closed down because they secretly offered this treatment? Those doctors have had their licenses revoked for operating illegal medical practices. They were denounced as quacks. There's nothing wrong with any of it, except the fact that the Medical Council of Thailand can't agree on how to split the money. When the authorities don't approve treatments, they are deemed unlawful and unethical, as this one is now.

Let me give you another example. The same thing happens to streetwalkers and women in massage parlours. What's the difference, you ask? Both offer sexual services, but streetwalkers are more likely to be arrested since the others are protected. The same also applies to casinos: they're legal in some countries, illegal in others. The legal ones are simply those that governments can extort money from. Perhaps these examples are too grim. Okay, let's put it this way. A factory produces two brands of fish sauce: both brands go through the same manufacturing process, but the first is registered and approved by the FDA, but the second isn't, and is consequently labelled as unsuitable for consumption. The FDA warns the public that the second brand's products might be contaminated, whereas the first brand is deemed clean. Now, let me ask you this: what dictates legality? Definitely not the quality of the fish sauce or the manufacturing process. Do you see what I mean?

That's how I explained things to Dao, who listened attentively and believed every word I said. She wasn't like the others: she was the only one who believed in me, in my existence. That was how we came to be life partners.

---

[3] How could anyone trust that good-for-nothing type? He may have gotten ahead of me in life, but only because the abbot gave him the chance to study in Bangkok. Unfortunately, he was ruined by the glamour of it all. I've always wondered whether he actually completed any of the courses he

took. To this day, I've never seen a single diploma or certificate of his. He liked big, wishy-washy ideas. He also loved big words, terms used to critique our social and political systems. We already have democracy, so perhaps his constant criticism hinted towards a different kind of governance!

Don't forget: he was once accused of sharing Communist sentiments and was forced to flee into the forest. After being pardoned by the government, he wasn't the slightest bit remorseful. What did he really want in life? Why didn't he get a decent job and a decent wife to settle down with and stop living in a fantasy? Stop causing so much trouble? He was a nuisance to society: a stinging fly.

He hardly stood on his own two feet; he switched jobs often. He had no security in his life whatsoever, and he had the gall to blame it on the government, to criticize the judicial system and the army that protects our nation against outside enemies. He never knew his place. I learned of many of his scandals from his friend Somjai, who often called me to tell me about them.

Once, he came to my house out of the blue. Actually, he had come for some sort of clandestine meeting with the woman next door. He was acting suspiciously, forbidding me from telling our mother that he had been hanging around. My brother was a complete failure, and I have no idea why our mother still believes in him. He told me once that he wanted to go into politics, to help the people and correct the system. All I could do was laugh at him. Oh dear! Not that long ago, he had been attacking the system and its politicians, and now he wanted to be a part of it all. Like I said: the good-for-nothing type. Anyway, it's good that he showed his true colours. He's the real failure: no one else.

(The above view belongs to Thai, Siam's brother.)

⁴   Siam was the ambitious type. He overestimated himself often. Everyone knew what sort of a guy he was, spinning all sorts of tall tales. He was a liar, always crafting mountains out of molehills. He turned tens into hundreds, hundreds into thousands, and he turned his stories round and round and upside down. Those who didn't know him well might well have fallen for his eloquence: to the untrained ear, he sounded reliable. I don't really know what ideas he put into Dao's head. He disappeared from my radar for two years before turning up at my door with another one of his grand projects. He told me in elaborate detail about his discovery of the so-called fountain of youth. It was disturbing at first, but after a while, I began to really listen to him.

'The vast universe begins within us,' he told me. 'To understand the universe, we have to look at its blueprint: our body. The complexity of our genes is its microcosm. There was no such thing as modern medicine in the primitive days; herbs and plants had been the only cure. Modern medicine came much later. As we know, the antibiotics of today can only slow down disease and prevent them from spreading, but they can never cure them completely. As doctors, you and I know this. Modern medicine is also political: it's entangled with power and money. Curing people, then, becomes a secondary concern. The body can heal itself, so the key to a long life lies within us.'

Siam tried to convince me of all sorts of stuff, starting with human creation and botany before dragging things back to the Buddha's era (blasphemy!) His story shifted back and forth between antiquity and the last 50 years of our contemporary age. He talked about pious forest monks who had lived in the jungle all their lives and never experienced any kind of illness. Those monks, he said, were able to determine when they would die and perform miracles on their bodies so it wouldn't decompose, like Egyptian mummies.

'The Lord Buddha discovered a secret, something which all of his disciples followed,' Siam went on. 'The secret was even recorded in the Tripitaka scripture—"arōgyā paramā lābhā"—and monks were expected to abide by it.' He looked at me and pursed his lips, as if trying to keep the secret from bursting out. 'Drink a glass of your own piss every day and diseases can never touch you.'

Disgusted and confused as I was, he continued:

'New monks were advised to abide by the following four obligations: one, collect alms. Two, wear a monk's robe. Three, live under a tree. And four, drink medicinal liquor.'

That medicinal liquor was meant to be their own urine.

Siam claimed that he had done thorough research and found that Western doctors who were interested in alternative medicine also advocated piss-drinking. Many sources can confirm its effectiveness when it comes to combating illnesses, he said. It strengthens the immune system and fixes whatever deficiencies you may have. Piss-drinking cures colds, stomach ulcers, asthma, diabetes, cancer, and HIV.

Siam also claimed that he'd witnessed marvellous improvements in chronically ill patients who had found modern medicine totally useless. Terminal cancer patients, whose doctors had given up on them, tried drinking their own piss for five years. Now, ten years later, they are still alive and well.

'Charity! What else could it be but charity, borne out of goodness and virtue!' he cried out emphatically. 'Don't look so incredulous. When I tell you to drink piss, I mean to drink the middle of the flow, not the beginning or the end. That's toxic. But your reaction is completely understandable. People aren't convinced the first time they hear it. It isn't easy to do the first time, but you get used to it. The important thing is that piss-drinking allows your immune system to heal itself. Your own cells heal themselves.'

'Are you drinking your own piss?' I asked.

'I am,' he replied.

I thought I could smell the piss wafting on his breath.

He disappeared for months after that, and I eventually got wind that he was in Bangkok, working as a taxi driver. Some said he'd converted his taxi into a mobile clinic covered with stickers, hawking free health consultations. When passengers got in his taxi, he'd bombard them with all sorts of questions about their health before bringing up the wonders of piss-drinking. No one knows just what he gained from all of this, but some claimed he simply did it out of charity.

One day, Siam returned to Kaeng Khoi and asked me to meet him in a pub. He was looking rather depressed.

'I stopped drinking my own piss,' he said.

I understood why.

'I have fucking diabetes.'

I nodded in sympathy and asked, 'What about the clinic you wanted to open? I can help.'

And so Siam opened his clinic again. He borrowed my license to practice and stuck it on a wall behind the counter. I worked there about two days a week.

That same year, organic food, as well as alternative and traditional medicine, became popular. I have to give him credit for always forecasting new trends: it was as if he had a sixth sense that told him just what the next craze would be. The problem with him was that when he started getting serious about something, he just couldn't do it as well as others could.

Like all those times before, his sixth sense detected a new trend again. He asked me to look after his clinic and to spend more time working there. He said that he was going abroad, and then he disappeared for years. When he returned to Kaeng Khoi, he'd changed a lot. He dressed and talked differently, he socialized within new circles. He had started drinking wine and imported whiskey and all that. He stopped sharing his big plans with me, and simply told me that he'd found love. He was planning to set up a business with her and spend the rest of their lives together. He said he'd discovered a new medical treatment, but that he'd rather not tell me about it, not until things settled down a bit more. One day, he brought Dao to the clinic and introduced her to me.

I thought she looked familiar, but I also felt strongly repelled by her. There was something about her: she acted as if we were from different classes. Siam strayed further from his old friends and relatives as he became closer to Dao. He spent most of his time with his new social circle and was hardly home, leaving me to take care of the clinic. Dao eventually tried to manage the clinic, but she was very overbearing; I couldn't take it, so I had a word with Siam.

About this new medical treatment: I heard from my patient that Siam and Dao are investing in a joint enterprise. Ha. Well, all I can say is good luck to them both!

(The above view belongs to Somjai.)

Worming

Change is natural to this earth, and those who resist change resist nature. We all know this deep down. Whether we confront and welcome it or resist it, change will knock on our door no matter what. An old man was once a child: isn't this a form of change? Our world evolves with time; such is change.

And such is change in human life, which we experience at physical, intellectual and ideological levels. I don't see change as unusual; rather, it is those who weather the storm who have lived their lives to the fullest. It is they who have taken immense risk and acquired valuable experiences in return. People who resist change dwell in comfort and safety; they try to create permanence, falsely equating change with uncertainty and the inability to take things seriously: hence their lack of commitment. I, myself, have been accused of it all.

They have attacked me for swaying from left to right, from communist to capitalist. They mock me for the changes I have been through in life, and nothing would please them more than to watch me decline into disaster. They are ready to denounce me; to mock, ridicule, shame, and even dehumanize me for betraying the principles I once upheld. But let me ask them this. What about you? What are you? You're neither this nor that. All of you are nothing at all, just faceless believers in nought but the nail files you use to buff your faces. All of you look the same. You want to feel safe and content with the ways things are, to ensure that nothing changes.

I don't get upset by these people, but I am skeptical of their ideologies. Trust me: I haven't lost faith in humanity yet.

People ridiculed me when I told them that I wanted to go into politics. My acquaintances all play-acted surprise. 'How could you go into something you spent most of your younger years criticizing? The younger you was persecuted by it, but the older you wants to embrace it. What changed? I've seen you riding an ox cart. How come you're driving a Mercedes now? Don't even think about getting an eco-car. You lived in the country, surrounded by rice paddies. How could you end up in the city?'

Listen. Allow me to explain it with a chessboard analogy. It is politics that drives the changes in our country, whether or not we are aware of it. Millions of lives are directed, controlled, supervised, and branded through rules and regulations. Policies trickle down from the mere 0.5 per cent of the population: this small group of people exerts immense influence in our lives, yet they are barely affected by the rest of us. The players claim their seats in parliament because we voted for them, but the irony is that when we demand change, they argue that the majority does not welcome that change. We were once the majority, but we're deemed the minority. The majority becomes an abstract concept: it's the people who haven't cast their votes, who are on the opposite parties. What does the majority vote look like? Why, they all carry nail files to buff the shit out of their countenances until they are utterly faceless, and they won't stop at their own.

Listen to me. We can't deny that humans are social animals. It's true that I once opposed the system, but we must admit that we live in it and we can't escape from it. Rules and regulations follow you, even into the forest. It's essential that you understand how it works. Once you do, you can neither turn your back on it nor simply boast about how much you know. All talk, no action.

I must admit that this epiphany only occurred to me in hindsight I've been following politics since I was a university student living in Klong Thom until now, as a clinic owner. These experiences have urged me to get into politics, to initiate the change that I want to see. As I mentioned, there are termite tunnels within the temple of bureaucracy. I want to expose them and make them accessible to everyone. My first step is to abolish all privilege, but equality—as we all know—is hard to achieve. Most importantly, people should be able to access all that they are entitled to. These are my intentions for this phase of my life.

Hear my declaration!

I will worm my way inside the system. My strategy will be similar to the approach I take when treating patients.[5] Like stem cells injected into the body—into the universe that lives inside all of us—I will infiltrate the system to cure it. As the Buddha once observed, you don't have to know the whole jungle to know the universe. It is enough to know just a handful of its leaves: its microcosm.

---

[5] The first day the patient was admitted to the hospital, I gave him a thorough health check-up. After that, I informed the relative that I had found a small tumour in the blood vessels that supplied blood to the brain. The tumour was blocking circulation, causing the blood vessels to swell. This was putting a lot of pressure on the patient's brainstem. He needed urgent treatment. If left untreated, the condition could lead to other dangerous side effects, and I could see that the right side of his body was already paralysed.

There was only a 50 per cent chance of recovery from that point onwards. Still, I tried my best. We had to consider whether he was even physically able to receive treatment. But the most important thing was that the treatment needed to be done immediately, and the patient's relative had to be informed about the process.

Three days after receiving the treatment, the patient's condition was stable. I explained to the relative that it was necessary to inject the patient with a high dose of medication to dissolve the tumour that was compressing the brainstem. That was all we could do at the time. The patient's pupils remained dilated, but we had to wait a few more days for the treatment to work before deciding on next steps. Unfortunately, we discovered that the patient had hepatomegaly, renal dysfunction, and diabetes. These conditions would be tremendously affected by the treatment: the higher the dose the patient received, the more damage it would do to the functioning of his internal organs. In short, the patient's overall health was in need of complete overhaul, and each issue had to be attended to individually. But dissolving the tumour by compressing the patient's brainstem was the most urgent task. The tumour had caused compression of the sensory nerves, leading to impaired functioning and hemiparesis. Only after we dealt with that could we deal with his organs. I hoped that the injections would dissolve the tumour before the patient's organs began to fail.

I noticed that the relative looked upset, but it was to be expected. Her expressions seemed to shout: What! I brought him to the hospital because he collapsed and was unconscious. I thought you would wake him, but instead you fuss about the things that don't interest me: his liver, his kidneys, his diabetes. Why don't you make him conscious first before fixing all this?

I understood her, of course, because most patients who come to hospital have complications. They come in with one condition that has reached a critical point, but that point is just the beginning for me. As a doctor, I examine a patient's body to find a web of issues, all of which contribute to said critical condition. So, sometimes I have to say:

'How could the patient allow his internal organs to become so damaged? The damage was done before he came into my hands. You should prepare for the worst.' Then I usually follow with a consolation: 'Though things don't look hopeful, we promise to provide the patient with the best treatment possible.'

I also tell them that regular visits—conversations, moral support, loving physical contact—are essential, even if the patient is unconscious and unresponsive. Patients can feel, they just can't physically respond.

Still, there are sometimes physical responses, such as nodding, a squeezing of the hands, or even tears in the eyes. These are merely automatic reactions or a release of bodily fluids, causing what seems like sentience. Relatives shouldn't read too deeply into these responses.

In this particular case, I had an inkling that the relative was already starting to look into alternative treatments for the patient. It's often the case that many people who are being treated in hospital are secretly seeking help from traditional medicine—monks, spirits, meditation, merit-making, vegetarianism—depending on what they themselves deem most helpful. Usually, I let them do what they want for their own peace of mind. It is admittedly frustrating when relatives then blame me for failing to treat the patient without considering other complications that they themselves may be complicit in causing. And then, if the patient does recover, they give full credit to the alternative treatments, as if my contribution was meaningless.

The following week, I was bound to inform the relative that what I'd feared from the start had happened. The high-dose medication meant to dissolve the tumour had damaged his other organs. It started with his kidneys, which were having to work the hardest, before spreading to his other organs. This was exacerbated by the patient's other conditions. His internal organs were failing, so I decided to stop the treatment. His body wasn't able to handle it. Before attempting to dissolve the tumour again, I'd have to focus on his organs first.

'You mean he just has to lie here and wait until his body is ready for treatment?' his relative shot back at me.

I explained to her that there was nothing I could do if his body wasn't ready for treatment. I was ready, but the patient wasn't. 'Do you understand?' I tried to console her by telling her that the patient was being transferred from the ICU to a private room, which was a sign that his condition was improving. In the private room, he'd be under the intensive care of a nurse.

The relative seemed reluctant. I had to ask a nearby nurse to explain the whole thing, to paint a bigger picture that might help the relative understand the difference. The nurse's explanation was succinct. She also clarified the treatment costs incurred over the first week, asking whether the relative could pay this sum first. The relative took the invoice from the nurse's hand, and the nurse started to explain the hospital's weekly payment policy, which existed to minimize the financial burden on patients' families in the end. Better to pay in small installments like this, she said.

The relative flipped through the pages of the invoice, which—of course—detailed the cost of medical tools and devices required for the patient's treatment. It listed the individual cost of drugs, ICU fees, doctor consultation fees: all sorts of services. All this might overwhelm patients' families, but it is necessary to justify what is printed at the bottom of the last page of the invoice (never once do the relatives fail to utter this figure with an expression of utter shock). 'Oh, no! 420,000 baht!' I then heard the relative mumble, 'All my hard-earned life savings, gone in just one week.'

Again, the nurse knew what to say in such a situation: they always do. She swiftly explained that the relative could receive up to 40% off medical treatment fees if she applied for the hospital's membership card, which covers discounts for many types of expenses, such as accommodation. 'Have you read the pamphlet about hospital accommodation? There's information about the different types of accommodation and how much they cost. We have a superior room, and a deluxe room, and breakfast is included with certain packages. Please don't hesitate to consult the pamphlet before making any decisions. I highly recommend applying for the hospital membership card: it really is worth it. There are different types: primary, gold, and platinum. Fees start at only 30,000 baht. You receive the discount immediately upon applying for the card.'

The relative looked pissed off, but left without this option, she'd have to pay for the expenses incurred in full. She had to apply for the membership card, since it would give her up to 40 per cent off (10 per cent off for primary cardholders, 25 per cent for gold cardholders, and 40 per cent for platinum cardholders). It was an awkward situation, I'll admit, but things had to run their course.

I then excused myself, leaving the relative with the nurse. Take your time, I said to the relative before leaving

Two days later, the relative moved the patient out of the hospital. It seemed she wanted to admit him into a public hospital. This was nothing unusual. It's to be expected when you work in a private hospital.

(The above view belongs to the doctor who treated Dr Siam.)

Entering

I'm standing in front of a colossal building that looks like the Greek Parthenon, raised high above ground level, with steps guiding one eye's up towards it. I'm not sure whether this is the ministry that I'm supposed to report myself to. All government buildings look the same, as if built from the same blueprint Parthenon-style—or was it Thai spirit house-style?—structures originate from. Their facades boast splendour, shrouding the ten-or-more-storey building erected beneath it. The interiors make you feel like you're walking round a shopping centre; at least, in my understanding of them.

People are walking back and forth across the front yard. I quickly stop to ask a man walking past me whether this is the ministry I was looking for. 'Yes,' he replies. With my question answered, I hurry inside the building.

A small shopping complex, just as I had imagined. KFC, Pizza Hut, Sukishi Buffet, 7-Eleven, Watsons, a food court, stores selling clothes, perfume, watches, DVDs, CDs: you name it. There's also a movie rental place, photocopying services, Internet cafes, one-stop-service centres . . . I couldn't possibly name them all. I notice a sign: 'Bureaucratic Office, 2nd floor, Atrium'. And so, I head up the escalator.

As I'm about to reach the second floor, an automated voice calls out: 'Queue number 216'. A tired mass is waiting; people are scattered across the atrium, some standing, some sitting. Where to begin? I head to a machine and scan through the different types of services, each written next to a corresponding button. 1, 2, 3, 4 . . . None of them have anything to do with why I'm here. Well, no shit. I'm just here to report myself to the ministry as the chief executive of the SAO. I'm a special case, one that wouldn't be listed alongside other available services on this machine. I'm no commoner. I'm the acting VIP. In fact, someone should have been here to welcome me. How dare they leave someone important waiting around like this? They have an image to maintain!

I decide to head towards Counter 9. A young female government officer is sitting there, doing nothing at all, behind a sign that reads: 'Please contact the next counter.' I have no intention of jumping the queue: all I want to do is ask where I ought to begin. But the minute she sees me approaching, she lets out a huge sigh, gesturing for me to go to a different counter. I haven't had the chance to utter a single word, and already she's trying to get rid of me.

'Oh, no. I just wanted to ask—'

'Sir, you have to get a ticket from the machine,' she snaps.

'I know, but I'm just wondering—'

'You can't just approach me to ask a question, sir. You need a ticket from the machine,' she repeats.

'I didn't mean to jump the queue—'

'Exactly, sir. That's why you need a ticket.'

'Listen. I don't know where to start, so—'

'You can start by going to the machine for a ticket.'

I'm at a loss. This lady is difficult. I have no other choice but to reveal my identity.

'All right, listen. I'm no ordinary guy. I'm here to report to the ministry because I've just been appointed as the chief executive of my SAO.' I didn't want to brag, but she needs to know who she's talking to.

The lady-officer of Counter 9 pauses a little, before snapping: 'No one can claim importance over others in a governmental institution. Societal rules and regulations sanctioned by the public must be obeyed by every citizen, all of whom are entitled to their individual rights and freedoms. Aren't you ashamed, acting like this?' She raises her voice, as if to publicly harass me: 'And you haven't even been appointed yet.'

I wish the ground would crack and swallow me right there and then, but at the same time I'm enraged: at myself and at her. I fell straight into her trap. Maybe it's her prickly personality. She's testing me by pretending to ignore me and purposefully refusing to acknowledge my position, just to damage my ego. She knew I'd be bothered by her insolence, and so I fell straight into her trap by acting all big and important when, in fact, I'm really just the 'acting' chief executive. I've made a fool of myself, but my anger drives me back into the depth of my mind in an attempt to figure things out. Is this sense of superiority new, or has it been integral to the genetic makeup of human beings for all this time?

I'm burning with questions. I can't stop thinking about it, not until I finally come up with a hypothesis: if this desire for superiority is instinctive to all beings on earth, then it must be guided by conscience, by a willingness to do good that prevents us from going astray. In short, it must be directed towards a specific purpose.

In my case—I know, I know![6]—I have flaunted my so-called superiority. But my intention was to find a shortcut into my new position, one that will allow me to turn wrongs into rights. That's my weakness. I was so focused on the outcome that I forgot momentarily about the means of getting there. And the lady-officer of Counter 9 knew the right buttons to press, and she publicly harassed me for it. She didn't have to do that. Talk about teaching a crocodile how to swim!

Dumbstruck, I stand frozen until the lady-officer of Counter 9 yells at me once more: 'Sir, come here!' For fuck's sake. She didn't even have to do that. I'm standing right here.

I walk timidly towards her and sit down, trying not to disturb the chair too much (again: is this a recent development, or is it genetic?) This time, the lady-officer of Counter 9 puts her face rather close to mine and says, in half-whisper: 'I apologize for earlier, sir. It's part of my job to refer to the rules and regulations. Do forgive me, Mr Chief Executive. We have to do things this way so the people who are waiting won't know that you do, in fact, have privilege over others. I'm aware of this now, and I'll do my best to help you jump the queue.' She gives me a suggestive smile before continuing: 'Can you please wait for me in front of the West Wing lifts? They're to your right. I'll meet you there soon.' Seamlessly, she switches back to yelling at me: 'Please go to the machine!'

Man-ee-fique, as the French say! What a superb performance!

Relieved, I nod affirmatively. See what this proves? It proves I was right! There definitely are termite tunnels within the Parthenon: something that only I know about. Everyone else gets information from public announcements alone, not the stuff said in whispers, the stuff I had to be publicly reprimanded and humiliated for, all for the sake of saving the ministry's face. I can just imagine the lady-officer and I cackling together later, behind everyone else's back.

I get up to leave the atrium, playing the role of shameful citizen.

After a while, the lady-officer of Counter 9 meets me in front of the West Wing lifts, carrying a great deal of folders. Instead of getting into one of the lifts, she leads me to an adjacent room.

She drops the folders on a large desk and asks me to take a seat opposite her. She opens one of the folders, quickly scanning through its contents—details about me, I assume—before handing me an envelope labeled: 'Documents and Itinerary for the Orientation of the Executive Chief of the SAO, Nationwide'.

The cover of the first bundle of documents reads: 'Manual for Basic Personality Enhancement'. It outlines the correct use of terminology when addressing people in government; words like 'integration', 'civil society', 'community network', 'voluntary spirit'. According to the manual, these words should be memorized and used frequently. They are encouraged for defusing tension in situations where one is unsure of what to say: in interviews, for instance.

I know, I know! I don't buy into these things either. They don't always work.

Going through nearly ten pages of these documents, it occurs to me that the word 'sufficiency' is written on every page. I let this observation get the better of me: 'Has "sufficiency" officially replaced "adequacy"?'

My question startles her. Her face twitches visibly in response, as if trying to hold herself back from lashing out. But upon realizing that my question was one of naivety rather than provocation, she explains.

'Oh, that's because the ministry's computer system has been engineered to locate the word "adequacy" and automatically replace it with "sufficiency".' Her face is beaming with pride.

I flip through the documents to a page about clothing etiquette. There's a uniform made of royal silk that everyone is encouraged to wear in order to promote Thai culture; ideally, the colour of our silk uniforms should match the colour for each day of the week. There are instructions for appropriate ways of place one's hands in public or in the presence of seniors, with illustrations of various hand positions in the front and back of the body, depending on the occasion.

The lady-officer of Counter 9 notices me trying to memorize the hand placements. She interjects:

'Please don't worry about those. There will be a hand placement instructor present on orientation day. Once you're officially appointed as chief executive, you won't have any problem knowing where to place your hands.'

I nod in agreement.

'Now, let's talk about the important stuff,' she says.

She starts to explain the proceedings. I'll need to fill out a form and submit it to Counter 3, who will hand me a receipt that I'll need to take to the secretarial office located on the East Wing, where it will be officially stamped. I'll then have to proceed to the lower-ground floor to photocopy all my forms and documents and verify them with my signature before returning to this room to see the lady-officer once more.

Since things seem to take longer than they should here, I rush out of the room, anxious to follow her instructions. The rules and regulations of the ministry are beyond my control, and there's nothing to be done about the time I have wasted earlier. I'm also starting to miss Dao.

When everything is done, I return to the first room. I sit and wait for quite some time before the lady-officer of Counter 9 finally enters, pushing the door open. 'What a hectic day!' She complains loudly, perhaps hoping for my sympathy.

'All right, Mr Siam. This is your membership card,' she says, hands me what looks like a business card. 'Please take this card to the registration division so they can make a record of all your details.' She sighs with relief before saying, 'My job is done now. I wish you luck, sir.'

Her job is done indeed; my own ordeal, however, has only just begun!

---

[6] Maybe people hadn't noticed the signs of deterioration in Dr Siam over the last few years; after all, the changes had been subtle and gradual. His eyes brimmed with anxiety and his movements were restless. His limbs were heavy with sadness and his breath carried the stench of decay. He was lost in his thoughts: he'd start when he heard someone call his name, as if recently returned from wandering off somewhere, somewhere far away. But his fright seemed more like a struggle to break free, as if his spirit was trying to escape from the captivity of his body.

He hadn't looked happy this past year.

I think he had too many things on his mind: decisions and deliberations on matters that concerned him as well as others. Dr Siam knew his own situation better than anyone else did, and how it might affect people close to him: my mother especially.

He was very devoted to her, but he also carried the weight of the dreams he had painted for her. I know my mother isn't always easy to live with: she's 'been through a lot', as they say, especially after she lived with my father. His death ferried her through change. She became someone who demanded a lot of attention, especially from someone willing to give their undivided attention: she refuses anything given half-heartedly. She sways from one extreme to another, with no in-between; with my father, things had been completely different.

It was odd—to me, anyway—the way she welcomed someone as sketchy as Dr Siam into her life. She gave him her trust, and he was consistent towards her in everything he did. His devotion towards her never faltered, even towards the end, when it became obvious that he was struggling, taking it upon himself to do whatever was needed to make ends meet. To me, this was proof of just how devoted he was to her. He would overspend just to satisfy her, borrowing from others to turn the hundred he had today into a thousand tomorrow. But of course, debt catches up with you eventually, and that's what happened to his body too, because of the way he treated it. His collapse had been an inevitability.

How should I order the events? Let's try it this way, I suppose.

Dr Siam didn't just treat patients. He was also my mother's personal doctor. Once upon a time, he'd turned up on her doorstep and sold her a dream: he would protect her, care for her, offer her security. And so my mother bolstered herself with that sense of security: it was a firm surface on which to lean, a soft pillow on which to sleep. Dr Siam pathologized her, telling her that she was unwell, that she was traumatized from her previous experiences, that she needed special care. That's how he's always treated her, and so, in turn, she came to embody both his lover and his patient. She would complain about certain symptoms: a headache one day, a pain in her shoulder the next, then a pain in her leg, then in her joints, and so on and so forth. He would impress her with a diagnosis and treat her with pills. When the symptoms returned, he'd give her more pills until she got better. She was often exhausted from work and it took a toll on her neck, her shoulders, her back. He gave her massages to relieve the tension and they made her feel as light as feather, but only for a while. Then the pain would return and he'd give her another massage to make them go away. The most vivid image I have of the two of them is from when the three of us and Maitree would drink together at home, my mother leaning against Uncle-Doctor Siam as if she were his conjoined twin. He held his glass in one hand and massaged my mother's shoulder with the other.

'Honestly, Uncle-Doctor. Aren't you tired of taking care of my mother?' I asked him once when my mother was out of the room.

He paused before answering, acting all light-hearted. 'It's my pleasure.'

What about now? Will you rise from the dead just to give her a massage, to take on her day-to-day responsibilities just for the *pleasure* of doing it for her, for my mother? No one's massaging her now. 'Ow . . . Where's Dr Siam?' she says, crying out for you in pain only to remember that you were unconscious in bed. 'Where have you gone off to? Why aren't you back yet?' she says. I know she means it figuratively: they say that you shouldn't describe someone unconscious as 'dead'. Instead, you should say they've gone to a better place, or gone off to a trip somewhere. I know this, but I think her use of the figurative hints at something deeper.

Another thing that directly contributed to Dr Siam's downfall was his work: the stem cell treatment, to be exact. At first, it all seemed glamorous and exciting, him and his patients queueing up and spreading the news through word of mouth. But, like all trends, stem cell treatment came and went. A year after the sudden boom, his patients began to disappear. He opened several clinics in different provinces, giving him more work and less time to look after their patients. As patient numbers dwindled, costs rose: rent, medical import fees, money for petrol, bribes. The more patients came, the more unwanted attention they also got. Stem cell treatment wasn't a recognized medical procedure, so government officials swarmed around Dr Siam, hassling him for bribes in exchange for keeping their mouths shut. When their bribes weren't satisfactory, they threatened to close down his clinics. A business like that can only last two, three years at most.

Dr Siam was well aware of this, but he wanted to keep it a secret from my mother. He told her it was natural for a business to have its ups and downs, not wanting to disappoint her (and her alone). However, his concerns and worries often spilled out when we drank together, late at night. It wasn't technically a confession, but all his anxiety about work and money would gush out without him really realizing. So I took all the bits and pieces he told me and formed them into a kind of picture of the mess he was living with.

Uncle Siam was a heavy drinker. He could finish a whole bottle of liquor by himself at the end of a long week, not to mention the half-bottle he drank each day. After work or travelling from another province, he would return home restless, hands shaking, finally relaxing after half a glass of neat liquor.

With each sip, he took pleasure in talking about stories from his past.

One night, he said that he felt sorry for the former prime minister. Having learned more about Thai politics in depth, he thought that there were so much wrong with the country: not just the people in it, but the entire system. No one listened to him. 'He's just a commoner, someone whose image has been exaggerated by the opposite side,' he said, before pausing for a while. 'Don't forget, he was legitimately elected by our democratic system,' he continued, flinging liquor into his mouth and pouring more into his glass. 'They changed the entire system just to bully him.'

Then one day, out of the blue, he told us that he wanted to get involved in politics: 'I want to help our fellow brothers and sisters here, since I know them so well.' He planned to offer himself as a candidate in the upcoming election for the local council.

'Does Mum know about this?' I asked.

'Of course,' he replied briefly. 'But I won't abandon the clinic.'

His condition had previously deteriorated to the point where he'd been admitted to hospital. He was diagnosed with diabetes. They discovered that his cholesterol and triglyceride levels were dangerously high, that his heart was malfunctioning from coronary artery disease, that he showed symptoms of chronic alcoholism (that one, I already knew). As a result, he was put on a strict health regimen: healthy diet, no alcohol, and so on. After being hospitalized for a week, he returned home to recuperate but started suffering from depression. When his physical health showed signs of improvement, he started travelling to his clinics in other provinces once more. My mother would drive him, and when he got home, he would lock himself quietly in his room. Unaccustomed to staying still, he became antsy and restless: flicking through all the different channels on TV, reading all the magazines in the house, rummaging through the things in his room. One day, he found an old melodica. For a while after that, his jarring attempts to play the instrument could be heard coming from inside his room: he even went out to buy an instruction book for it. The sound that emanated from his room was out of tune, but full of deep sadness.

After a month of strict dieting, Dr Siam suddenly remembered that he had once been a doctor: one who treated his patients with stem cells. He took the liberty of giving himself a series of injections. The day of his check-up, his doctor was surprised to see his body showing visible signs of improvement. Dr Siam, of course, gave his thanks to the stem cells.

His melodica started making regular appearances at the dinner table, where he'd play us this or that song. He also started to drink again, but only under the supervision of my mother, who couldn't help but feel sorry for his miserable state of withdrawal. She allowed him a single glass of red wine, which was when he began to convince himself of the health benefits of drinking one glass of red wine (and by one glass, I mean a full glass) every night. Having converted to red wine, he developed a sort of superiority complex, discrediting the alcohol he was no longer allowed to have: whatever Maitree was drinking, for instance (even though he used to drink it too). 'It tastes acrid, strange, different from how it used to be,' he'd say. Or he'd simply claim, in his strong dialect, that it was fake.

'It tasted much rounder in the past. It's no good now.'

Having firmly convinced himself and everyone else that the liquor was fake, he finally discovered the real cause of his hospitalization.

Two months later, a glass of wine became a whole bottle again. Then two bottles. 'Why aren't I getting drunk on this?!' he said, confused. Then he asked to try a sip of Maitree's drink. 'Oh, it actually tastes good now!' And that was how he swung back to drinking the same amount as before, even though he remained strict with his diet and everything else. My mother wasn't much help either. On the rare days when he was sober, he would be restless, depressed, and it would be impossible for him to tend to his patients at the clinic. The whole day would be wasted, and my mother, as agitated as she was with the situation, would finally give in and let him have his drink.

Several months before his collapse (never to wake again), Uncle Siam took my mother out after work to visit famous restaurants in all the different provinces. He analysed dishes by taste and ingredients, surveyed restaurant locations, bought recipe books as well as meat, vegetables, and fish, attempting to recreate each dish back home. This was another one of his talents: cooking. Everything he cooked was both delicious and interesting. He had a personal recipe for gravy, to be served with steak, and a special dipping sauce. He was extremely serious about cooking, committed to the point where he had planned to open a restaurant and had starting scouting locations for it. During this time, it pleased him to hone his skills by cooking for others.

'It's called *fusion food*,' he said with an exaggerated English accent. 'It's very trendy at the moment.'

'More like *confusion food*,' I teased him. 'What about wanting to get involved in politics?'

'I'm working on it, but I need things to settle down first,' he replied. 'Actually, you shouldn't call it "getting involved in politics". Call it a service to the people.'

'What about the clinic?' I asked.

'I've made sure that everything will be managed.' He sounded as if he were saying a farewell. 'I'm doing the best I can with it. There should be a full-time nurse and your mother will take charge of management, so I can slowly distance myself. As for the politics stuff, you just have to attend meetings. And the restaurant: once it makes a name for itself, I won't really have to do everything myself. I've got it all planned. Don't worry about you or your mother. Everyone will live comfortably if everything goes according to plan. As for me, I want to get ordained, become a monk: a forest monk, actually, so I can live in the forest . . . '

'But monks aren't allowed to drink,' Maitree teased him.

He paused. 'You cheeky boy! Why ruin it for me?' Then he clinked his glass with both of ours.

According to what I've told you, there were signals that forewarned us of what was to come. Uncle Siam was struggling: working hard, and shouldering the expectations and risks by himself. At his age, he was still acting like a bird, swooping from this branch to the next, going wherever there was food. He had absolutely no security. His eyes glowed with dreams, the sky, saltwater, aerial views of vast fields. Whether those views were captured in real life, we'll never know. They were from a perspective we could never see from.

This time, Uncle Siam collapsed, never to wake again. 'Where has he gone off to? Why isn't he back yet?' my mother would say. Maybe she was right.

Why would he come back? That's the real problem. Why would he return to the trap he set for himself?

(The above view belongs to Chidchai.)

Exiting

I leave the building once more, because the registration office—as the lady-officer of Counter 9 explained—is in another building, behind the main building. The sun is growing stronger as I make my way to the registration office, my anxiety growing with it. The noon heat arrives.

There's a queue that stretches as far as the eye can see. I am taken over by discouragement to the point of numbness. Only when I realize that the queue is moving do I feel slightly relieved. After a while, my turn finally arrives. I hand my membership card to the officer for inspection. He opens a folder in front of me and takes out a few forms. Oh no, not again. What forms must I fill in now? He passes them back to me, along with my membership card.

'Please fill out these forms, then proceed to the underground floor in the main building. You'll need to hand the completed forms to a staff member at T Bank. Next, please.'

The officer left no room for questions. The people behind me are pressing forward. No wonder the line is moving so fast. All I can do is follow the person ahead of me. A throng of people shuffling into an empty room, each of them trying to find somewhere to sit down and fill out their forms. The bloody forms! The same ones we've filled in before, time and time again.

Exasperated, I head back to the main building and down to the lower-ground floor. 'It'll only take a minute,' the deputy chief administrator of the SAO had said. So much time wasted already. Arriving at T Bank, I realize that more time is to be wasted: everyone in front of me is filling out their forms on the spot instead of completing them beforehand. Disgraceful. It's a reminder that, in this society, no matter how far ahead you are of others, you still have to wait for people to sort their shit out before we can all move forward together. That's where equality starts, presumably. I breathe deeply to try and calm myself down. Inhale, exhale. I'm here to change the system, which means that I have to go along with the system first. This is my test.

I glance at the staff member on duty and notice that she, too, disapproves of these disorganized 'acting' SAO chief executives filling out their forms on the spot. This is my opportunity to volunteer to help. I turn to the people queueing behind me. 'If anyone hasn't filled out their forms yet, please do so now so things will flow smoothly, conveniently, and quickly.'

When my turn finally arrives, I throw myself into the chair, exhausted by the whole ordeal. The staff member sitting opposite me seems to empathize. She gives me a dry smile. 'Look around. Everyone's frustrated.' I pause at her words before realizing that I'm a VIP among VIPs. We're all just commoners who have been granted special status.

The bank staff hands me another form. Life insurance.

'Is this really necessary?' I cry.

'Yes, of course. They come in a bundle. Just a few more now,' she says, trying to cheer me up.

I fill out the form, gritting my teeth. That's what that was, then. It's not that people weren't completing their forms in advance. It's that everyone has to deal with this additional life insurance form. I fill it out quickly as I can without even bothering to read its contents, not even the terms and conditions or the mutual agreements in the back. I sense a conspiracy: you're instructed to do the same thing, over and over, until every form feels the same. You get sick of doing it, and you reach a point where you just want to get it over and done with. You make it to the last page where the text is as dense as a forest. You realize you are no longer taking anything in. Your eyes search desperately for that empty space that awaits your signature. There! You're finished. This is a ruse, planned from the very start to obtain your signature. They tire you out with distractions, making you go through tedious loops until you're dragging yourself across the floor like the living dead. At the final stage, you're too exhausted to have any concerns or questions. All you want to do is sign the damn thing. And that's exactly what I did, despite the suspicions I had been harbouring all along. Too late to do anything now. *Siam, you idiot*, I tell myself as I hand the officer back my signed form.

She gives me a cold stare. 'I have to inform you that what you did earlier was inappropriate.'

'What was inappropriate?'

'Telling others to complete their forms in advance.'

'But didn't it help you get your work done faster? I noticed you looked tired, and I just wanted to help.'

'Thank you, but it was inappropriate,' she insists as she gazes down at my form. 'That's my job, not yours, sir. What you did could potentially cause problems within our organization. You aren't in a position to do it. In fact, it sets a bad example for others in your position.'

My arguments have been wrung dry.

She relaxes a little. 'All done,' she says, handing me a T Bank platinum credit card. 'The starting credit limit on this card is 200,000 baht, but you have to activate it first.'

'I still have to activate this bloody card?!' I yell, almost threateningly.

'Please, sir. Be civil,' she hushes. 'You need to activate the card at the telecommunication company or the property company. They're only about ten blocks away. The card has to be activated, otherwise things won't be complete.'

I rush out of my seat and leave the bank. *This. Is. No. Sense*, as they say in English. No more of this bureaucracy, of this worming in and out of termite tunnels, of shortcuts in this bloody labyrinth of shortcuts. This is beyond me. I underestimated it all. But it's too late now.

I arrive and take notice of the employee standing in between the two company storefronts. She's wearing a tight and skimpy outfit. A transplanted car show girl.

'Are you here to activate your card?' Her endearing expression shines through her big-eye contact lenses.

'Yes, doll,' I reply.

'Please take a look at this before making your decision,' she says, directing my gaze to the advertising stand. 'You can choose between these two options, depending on what suits your lifestyle best. Allow us to offer you a very special promotion for someone special like yourself.'

Listen to her. She's eloquent.

'We can offer you high-tech communication devices with fantastic apps and add-ons from the telecommunication company at a special promotional price with 15% off for T Bank cardholders. Alternatively, you can opt for an apartment or a house from Property Company Limited at a special promotional price with 25% off for T Bank cardholders. With this purchase, you are also entitled to special rewards: a complete built-in kitchen, a romantic dinner in Bali, or savings of up to 500,000 baht.'

'But, doll, I've already got a smartphone and a place of my own in a condo,' I tell her, even though what I have might not be as fancy as what she's offering.

'But, sir, to activate your card, you need to choose an option. Choosing is part of the procedure, as are the fringe benefits and privileges given to a chief executive of the SAO such as yourself.'

'Is this really necessary?' I ask. At this point, the girl's charm has faded for me. Even if I pick one of the options she has offered me, I can foresee the next link in the never-ending chain of contract signing and form filling.

'There's not much to be done after this, sir. Once your card is activated, you'll just need to fill in a few more forms and then you can go upstairs to meet with the minister.'

Not in this lifetime. Things will certainly not end here. This has taken me the whole day, and I wasn't even ready for it. I was forced to come here because the people had hopes and expectations for me. I mean, I don't blame them. Whatever else needs to be done, it'll have to be done tomorrow. It's very late now. I'm done for the day.

'Do you know what time it is, doll? Can I come back to *ac-vi-tate* the card next time?'

'Sir, that's not possible,' she cries. 'Rules and regulations are to be obeyed. If you refuse, things will come to a standstill and I'll be in big trouble. I'll be blamed for failing to make you comply with the procedures. Can't you see? I'll lose my job, sir!' She balls up her fists, placing them on the outer corners of her eyes and play-crying in a *kawaii* sort of way. I'm momentarily charmed. God, she's adorable. 'Your delay will damage the organization,' she pleads. 'Please, sir. Please.'

As soon as the word 'organization' falls out of her mouth, it ruins it for me. I snap myself out of it. The ministry has run out of tricks to play on me. *The End*, as they say in English.

I leave because I miss Dao.[7] The ministry will have to wait another day, because today is our day, Dao. The floor is falling out from beneath us. The dew is evaporating. The day is slipping out of our hands. I pace out of the temple that is the ministry, not wasting another minute more.

I step out of the building. Moments later, I freeze on the steps, as a siren blares. I hear an announcement.

'Those bastards!' I curse and flee.

How is this possible? That damn ministry wants me arrested!

[7] 'Keep an eye on her,' I told him. 'You can't trust her with everything. People get involved with each other because they want something. There's nothing sincere about it. Who else can you trust but me? I've been your friend since we were little, and I'm telling you to watch out for that woman. There's something fishy about her. She's from a different class. We're rural folk, whereas she's a city girl. We're honest and we mean what we say, whereas she always has a hidden agenda. Conflicts of interest, double standards. You know.'

I've been telling Siam this since the day I first met Dao. She's not like us. She looks down on me—on Thai—and she's using Siam.

It's become more obvious since he's been bedridden. Sure, she took him to a fancy hospital but her true colours started showing after just one week.

I received a call from her one day, telling me that Siam's hospital bills are adding up. In one week, she'd already paid 400,000 baht. 'What do I do?' she said to me bluntly. 'You're his best friend. What about his relatives? Is there anyone from your side who could help with the costs?'

'Have you spoken to Thai?' I asked her.

She sighed instead of answering me. 'What about you?' she asked me back.

'Of course, I'll help,' I answered.

'How?' She snapped back. 'I can't shoulder everything. You have to help me.'

Who told you to take him to that fancy hospital in the first place? You didn't even ask any of us about it. What kind of business are you two running together? You were making money, building up your savings: that's why no one ever asked you about it. But now you're coming to us when you have to foot the bill? I know what I heard from other people. Siam himself bragged about it. Surely 500,000 baht isn't much in comparison to everything you've got in your secret savings account!

That's what I wanted to say to her.

'So what are you going to do?'

She was persistent. She sighed out of frustration.

'Siam always had your back in the past. Why can't you do the same for him now he's in trouble?'

'What has he ever done to help me? Who told you that?' I retorted.

'Why, he's helped you all your life. That's what he told me.'

'That's not true, Dao. You must've misunderstood.' I ended the call. There was no need to explain further.

As expected, Dao decided to move Siam to a public hospital after one week. Her excuse—yes, 'excuse'—was that she was no longer able to bear the costs. She knows full well that that amount of money is nothing to them. She even said herself that Siam will remain in this condition for a while, and there wasn't much the doctor could do to help. The chances of him waking up grow dimmer each day, and so Dao thought it would be best to move him to a public hospital. It seemed unnecessary, she said, to pay tens of thousands of baht per night in accommodation and medical fees.

And so ended the performance of generosity that her kind of people put on. Laughable, isn't it?

Where else did Dao put her hopes after this? While Siam was unconscious, she waited for the abbot[8] to summon his spirit back to his body. That's right. This lady here turned to superstition. You'll have to excuse me, but it all got rather ridiculous for me.

Thai informed me the other day that when he went to see Siam, the doctor informed him that the chances of his brother regaining consciousness were slim. He'd been unconscious for two weeks. Your organs slowly deteriorate if you don't use them properly (I've known this for a while now!) and Siam might live on as a vegetable or a sleeping prince, as a burden to his relatives. The doctor wasn't sure whether this was preferable to death. Do you know what Thai told me about what Dao said when they found this out?

'Have you thought about who's going to take care of Dr Siam?' she said.

Like she already knew it wasn't going to be her taking care of him. What happened to your love and devotion, huh? Siam, this is the woman you swore your love to. Haunt my dreams tonight and explain it to me, I beg you.

The audacity of her question. We all have our own burdens to carry. Thai's mother just moved in to live with him. Imagine if he took in Siam! Running around cleaning up after both his mother and his brother. Wouldn't that be too much on Thai and his family? Having to nanny everyone around him?

Dao has the most comfortable life out of all of us. Her family's well off and she lives at home with her sons: a home that is right next to the auto repair shop Thai's family runs, incidentally. How inconvenient could it be for her to take care of Siam? Her sons are adults: can't they help her take care of him? Goddamn it. Pull your weight! Let's be frank here. Doesn't Dao have all that money saved because of Siam's hard work? From what Siam told me, Dao has never worked for anything. She was a widow with kids, an average housewife. It wasn't until Siam came along that she was able to finally stand on her feet. He gave her every last baht he earned, leaving himself with nothing but a little pocket money. *She* always got the big bundle, whereas Thai's family and his own mother were only left with occasional scraps.

So what am I supposed to think? If you've already been taking your share of the income he earned through sweat, blood, and tears, then take responsibility for his illness!

The more I think about it, the angrier I get. The other day, she even had the guts to call me again. She was persistent. 'Aren't you going to do anything to help Siam?' Goddamn it, I've been helping him all my life. For once in her life, can't she just take something on without complaining?

'If you're not going to help, then please return the 70,000 baht you owe us,' she said.

'For what?' I was confused.

'The money you borrowed from Siam. Don't act like you don't remember.'

Please, not this bullshit again. What kind of stuff did Siam tell her? 'Let me repeat this to you clearly, Dao. I have never owed Siam any money. Quite the contrary. He's the one who owes me the exact amount you just reminded me of. Do you want to know what it was for? My medical license that he "borrowed" to stick on the wall of your clinic! The medical license that your clinic is "legally" operating under. I didn't think too much of it, to be honest. I just went along with it. He told me he'd give me my share, that's what he told me. But to this day, I haven't received a single baht. Now, who can I demand that from? Can I demand it from you, huh? Not to mention the fact that I work at the clinic two or three days out of the week. Sometimes he pays me, sometimes he doesn't. Now, what if I want my wages in full? Would you be able to pay that for me, Dao?'

'What do you say, Dao? Where's the money you owe me?'

At a loss for words, she hung up on me. I forgive her, though. At least she got a taste of her own medicine.

When I spoke to Thai about what to do with Siam, I warned him: 'Thai, keep a close eye on that woman, especially when it comes to the things that belong to us. Don't let her have them. I'm only saying this because I mean well.'

The next day, I rang Thai to remind him of something important. We talked for about fifteen minutes. I told him: 'Listen, Thai. I want to be frank with you. (Of course. Spill it!) I'm a doctor too, and I know exactly what's going with Siam.'

'Mm-hmm.'

'And I know about your brother's condition.'

'Yeah, I know.'

'All I can say is, he doesn't have very long.'

'That's what I thought too . . . but I don't know how long "very long" is. My mother said she wants Siam to stay with us in the house.'

'Your house?'

'Well, yeah. Where else? I don't really want to do it.'

'Well, that's actually what I'm calling about. It's probably actually a good idea.'

'How is it a good idea? He's going to be a goddamn burden.'

'Listen to me.'

'The situation is a total loss for me.'

'I understand, but I was thinking about it the other night. I figure you're actually winning if you take him home.'

'How?'

'You're his brother. You have all the legal rights to his property.'

'What are you saying, Somjai?'

'You legally own everything that belongs to Siam.'

'Don't be stupid. It's that bitch who owns everything he has! I'm sick of fighting over this property shit, especially with Dao. Going through all that land ownership stuff was traumatic enough.'

'That's what I'm talking about. Whatever your brother has built with Dao legally belongs to you.'

'You're right.'

'Think about it. Think about how you're going to get all our stuff back. That's all I'm saying. Bye for now.'

'Thanks a lot, Somjai.'

I cautioned everyone I knew about this. Call me heartless, but someone had to be the sensible one on our side. We can't all be distracted by the tragedy, or else it'd be too late, when others have managed to take everything. I'd rather be the person who speaks frankly about money, despite being called cold-hearted or whatnot. But I'm not the one to be blamed here: it was Dao who started it. How dare she shove all that responsibility on us and just keep on taking?

All right. In short, I think it's time that we discuss Siam's assets, because he's sure not waking up any time soon. We should decide who is entitled to what. For me, I should get the clinic at Kaeng Khoi.

(The above view belongs to Somjai.)

[8] I'm standing here, at the foot of the hospital bed, looking at Siam breathing in and out through the respirator. I resign myself to the facts of life that are playing themselves out before me . . . It looks like Siam is struggling to stay alive. He occasionally chokes on the air being pumped into his lungs, causing spasms in his arms and legs. He is wrestling continuously with death.

Eventually, there will be a winner.

In my opinion, I'm certain it will be Siam.

It isn't his time to die yet. What he's experiencing is an encounter with his bad karma. All humans have their own karmic creditors. We either create them in this life or they follow us from our previous ones. We are unaware of our creditors in the present life because they live outside their consciousness. But whatever we did in our past lives, our creditors remember. They would tether themselves to our pain, our grudges, and pursue us—their karmic debtors—in our present and future lives with one goal in mind: to bring about our decline, ruin, and—in some cases—death.

I look at Siam, his complexion as pale as death, and all I see is an empty body, a lifeless heap. His spirit has wandered off somewhere and gotten lost. The Siam we know is not present within this body.

A shadow, like a black cloud or birthmark, rests on his head among the sallow skin that covers his entire body: a mark of terrible karma. He will have a long and prosperous life if he can get through this crisis. The question is whether he can make it through.

I've known Siam for a long time, ever since he was little. My family knows him and his family well. They are diligent Buddhists; Siam, in particular, is especially devout. An inquisitive mind, he would always visit me and spend hours learning about all sorts of things. I was generous with my teaching, because he was keen to learn: headstrong, ambitious. I could tell that he would go far, further than anyone else I've ever known. He was always grateful and appreciative. He went on to become successful, but he's never forgotten me. He always came back to visit and did many things to maintain the temple I live in.

You may ask: how did I come to be here? How do I know what I know? How did I end up at the foot of his bed? As I said, I am close to Siam. There's nothing happening to him that I don't know about.

Last week, during my morning alms, Siam walked past me, looking absent-minded and miserable. I knew something bad had happened to him, so I retraced his steps and ended up at the hospital. Did you know I've been stood here since I arrived, extending my kindness to him? His spirit has received just a touch of it: not all of it. That is because his karmic creditor has been standing between us, preventing all of his senses from receiving my kindness. The more I extend it, the darker the shadow across his brow becomes.

The shadow must be vanquished.

That's the answer that I can give you.

You ask me how he is. I will not hold back my honesty. I will tell you the truth: that his condition is bad. Very bad. However, I can assure you that he won't die, because it is not his time. He'll make it to his seventies.

I agree that what you're doing is good. You should continue to follow the Buddhist precepts, and stay on a vegetarian diet: it heals and cleanses your body, your words, your actions. It would be even better if you could wear white and meditate morning and evening, extending your kindness and good merit to him. The more you do it, the stronger the good karma becomes, especially if others close to him do it too. Eventually, the good karma will be strong enough to defeat the creditor.

There's no need to be afraid. I'm here now. I'm here to help you, and I will meditate to set my mind towards Siam. Can you see? His body is present in this bed, but his spirit is wandering elsewhere. The demons have deceived him into believing that what he is experiencing is bliss: lightness, freedom from life's obligations. If he allows himself to be lured further, the threshold between our worlds will close and his spirit will be unable to return to his body. We must all try and guide him back, to make him see the illusion for what it is. We must help each other.

Siam will certainly wake, and I will not abandon him until he does. It is not his time to die.

Let's call it a day for today. I'll come back later and keep you informed of my efforts.

All right. Bless you.

(The above view belongs to Abbot Glab.)

Manhunt

See what happened? Goddamn it! The sun is high in the sky, and the mist has lifted. Dao will have woken up by now and she'll be worried to find me missing.

I only have myself to blame. I was bombarded by everything all at once. All I'd wanted was to take a morning stroll and get some fresh air. I'd been relaxed, peaceful: without a care in the world. Now look at me. Trouble after trouble, tangled together and piled on top of me. To make matters worse, I'm now a wanted man. How did I end up like this? 'Where the hell have you been?' I can imagine Dao's expression when she interrogates me after all this.

Now that I think of it, I should come up with an excuse, but my brain can't seem to function. Oh, well. Can't have it all. Only geniuses can think and run at the same time.

Where the hell am I? Whatever. It's not important: not as important as escaping from the ministry's people. How frustrating, that disobeying their rules and regulations is made out to be equivalent to murder. Now I'm a wanted man. I bet all those forms I filled in are now null and void. I bet they'll use them against me, one way or another. Pfft. At least I got a good look at the dirty underbelly of politics. I don't want anything to do with it anymore, all this dirty business of living up to expectations. There must be another way to help the people, one that doesn't lead you to your own grave.

Think. Think. Think, Siam, you fool! Where on earth are you right now?

I focus hard and steady myself. I recall my own name and utter it out loud. I'm Dr Siam Duangsuk. I'm on a trip with Dao. We stayed the night in a log cabin resort. I had a dream about a waterfall and it woke me up at dawn. I went for a walk in my hometown in Amphoe Song Khon. That old woman—she was preparing to give alms to the monks—she said beckoning me over: 'Son! I'm here, my dear!' Good God! That was my mother! What's wrong with me? Am I

getting Alzheimer's? Then . . . Then I turned around and there was that
monk—'Come see me at my temple. They're waiting for you.'—That
was Abbot Glab, an old friend of mine from the temple school. He
was made abbot after the previous abbot passed away. Shit. My mind is
playing tricks on me. I couldn't recall anything until now. At least I'm
starting to remember things.

I'm hiding inside a tapioca warehouse, which reeks of dampness
and some sort of acrid stench. Old, rusty machines are piled together in
the centre of the warehouse in half-shadow. Faint beams of light trickle
in through the small holes of the corrugated roof. Nothing larger than
a pack of rats have breathed in here. The sound of clicking geckos
pierces through the thick, pungent air. I gather some tapioca in my
hands and inspect it. Is it tapioca, or dirt, or a mixture of both? Am I
just imagining the stench of corruption in the air?

Half an hour later, I'm finally able to catch my breath. I'm quite sure
that no one is following me now. I get up from the pile of tapioca I have
been sitting on and slowly walk across the cement floor towards a small
door on the other side of the warehouse. There are UV lights outside;
bright and blinding, they scorch my eyes. There are only stumps left
on the parched earth of the tapioca fields. Whose warehouse is this?
Who do these fields belong to? I rummage through my memory for the
owner's name—is this information really necessary?—as I brush dirt
and pieces of tapioca off my arms, neck, and face. My body itches and
reeks of sweat. I shield my eyes and scan the landscape before me, but
no one is there. This is a good sign. Scanning from left to right, I see a
figure emerge suddenly from a dark corner of the warehouse.

'Abbot Glab!'[9] I exclaim, paying my respects.

'Greetings to you, Siam.'

I can't hear him very well, so I ask if he can speak up.

'Are you ready to go, Siam?'

'What? Go where?'

'Everyone's waiting for you at the temple,' he says. 'Come with me.'

'I can't go with you now. I have to go back to see Dao. She's
waiting for me.'

Abbot Glab is saying something, but his voice is muffled. He
points west. I see a group of people in the distance. The people from
the ministry! They're coming! I can't waste any more time.

'I'm going back to see Dao first, but then I'll rush to meet you at the temple.'

As soon as I finish talking, I excuse myself and run across the tapioca fields, heading away from the crowd of people.

Do I know where I'm running? No, I don't. I'm just running: running like there's no tomorrow. Humans have a mysterious energy within us, one we can always rely on in an emergency. An instinctual alertness, a pure and primitive vigilance that has been with us for thousands and thousands of years. It's our missing tail—an anatomical lack we often use to distinguish ourselves from wild animals—but my dear Dao, the truth is, that we still have it. A trace of this instinct remains: a tiny stump of a tail attached to our sacrum. Let us make good use of it!

It feels incredible, being guided by your instincts. Free from the dictates of reason, there's no time to ponder. Every move is one of survival. Ha! Finally, I reach the resort entrance. I quickly shift to walking speed, pretending to have just returned from my scenic stroll, despite being drenched in sweat. Whatever. A resort employee is walking along the stone path towards me. She stops and bows. I blurt an awkward greeting at her.

'The sun is strong today, isn't it?'

She nods in agreement. 'Lovely weather for a visit to the waterfall,' she says. 'If you're interested, please ask for more information about our guided tours at the reception desk.'

'Thank you, thank you very much,' I say, as I whistle my way towards my log cabin.

I open the door and discover, to my surprise, that the bedroom is still dark. The pink curtains are still drawn, blocking any sunlight from leaking into the room. Not a single light is switched on. Darkness tricks your body into thinking it's nighttime; my eyes have to adjust to the drastic lack of light. I feel dizzy. My stomach is churning acid, my blood pressure is dropping. I fumble my way to the mini-bar, where I grab a fizzy drink and down it in its entirety. Seeing a packet of sweets nearby, I tear it open to find a lot of small, round, multi-coloured, chocolate-coated candies. I pour them into my mouth. Feeling much better, I sit down and look at the bed. Dao is still fast asleep, utterly unaware of the fact that I just burst into the room, rummaged desperately through the fridge, and devoured all the sweets. What could she be so exhausted from? I watch her as she lies completely still, popping more sweets into my mouth. Then, it occurs to me that I'm being hunted down. I need to get away, to get out of this place. I also promised the abbot that I'd go see him at the temple. I throw all my clothes into a bag. I need to go right now. *'Quick,'* I exclaim in English. *'Quick!'*

I shake Dao's arm gently. 'Dao, wake up.' Her smooth skin is cool to the touch. She certainly has all the qualities of a beautiful woman: long hair, smooth, porcelain complexion. I study her face and notice that women look younger when they're asleep. I try to wake her again, shaking her leg forcefully this time. 'Dao, we've got to go!' No response. I sit next to her on the bed and slap her lightly across the cheek with my right hand. 'Dao! Dao! Can you hear me?' Her eyes are shut tight, but her eyelids are moving. This is ridiculous! Why is it so hard to wake her up? I might have to slap her harder across the face, but I'd feel so guilty seeing her rosy cheeks all bruised. Who in the right mind would want to do such a thing? Now that I think about it, we've spent years working hard together. It wears you out, trying to make ends meet while travelling across provinces seven days a week. When someone has been exhausted for so long, it's normal for them to need a lot of sleep. Not to mention that Dao is anaemic, so naturally, she needs more sleep than others. In fact, there were times where I needed lots of sleep too. Sometimes, after treating my patients, I'd doze off with a glass of beer in my hand. Dao never disturbed me or tried to wake me up; she always wanted me to get a good night's sleep. Once, I slept for so long that I woke up past noon. I couldn't find Dao at home, so I took a shower and caught a taxi to our clinic. I found her there, looking after the patients, greeting those who had just arrived and telling them to come back later. 'The doctor isn't here yet,' she said. 'He should be coming in this afternoon.' When she saw me, she greeted me sweetly. 'Oh, now you finally show up! Have you eaten?' What a sweetheart she is, truly.

Actually, it shouldn't matter if I let her sleep for a while. She needs plenty of rest so that her blood can thicken back to normal. She always lets me sleep as much as I want to, so it would be cruel of me to do otherwise. We belong to each other. We know how to find each other. It doesn't matter if one of us wakes up before or after the other. We both know when and where to meet again.

Dao once gave me some extra money—several thousand—and told me: 'Go and have some fun. You've worked hard today.' You see, she wants me to have fun the way men do.

'It's really not necessary, my love. Being with you already makes me happy,' I told her.

'Don't sweet-talk me, or else I'll change my mind.' She knew what I was up to. I chuckled nervously. 'You go and have some fun. Let those pretty young girls entertain you with their sweet words. I'm too old for that shit.'

'No, you're not,' I protested.

'But no fooling around, or else . . . ' Her voice hardened. 'Or else I'll cut your dick off and feed it to the ducks.'

Dao understands that men have desires. Me, I don't need anything more than a little bit of fun, some time to decompress after a hard day's work. Hearing honeyed voices and getting massages from soft, nimble hands . . . It keeps me young. That's all men really want. And we always know where we'll be at the end of the night: taking on our arses back home to those we love, care for, and are bound to . . . Those who are waiting for us at home.

'Sleep well, Dao.' I told her. 'I must be going.'

It's really not a big deal if she wakes up and doesn't find me here. I'll leave the car here for her. If I'm not at the clinic, then she'll look for me at the temple. If I'm not in either place, then . . . We'll meet back at home.

---

9 All right, all right. Calm down and listen. I have good news.

Two days ago, during meditation, my spirit travelled to meet Siam. It took me some time to find him. He was in another realm, one parallel to ours. a realm where lost souls are found. If left to dwell in that realm for too long, those lost souls transform fully into spirits, at which point they no longer need physical bodies to travel in. In other words, they are left as a wandering ghost. This is disconcerting, to say the least. If Siam lets go of his body in our world, he will never be able to return to it. The realm he's in is full of temptations and distractions, making it easier for him to believe that he's a real part of it. He must reject it, as well as anything within it that tries to enter his soul. As I followed him, I discovered that he was being manipulated by a gargantuan demon in the form of an albino buffalo. It was muscular, with horns as long as three wa and skin the colour of raging flames, and it was controlling Siam, directing him down the road it has built for him. Yes: this demon is Siam's karmic creditor.

I know this is confusing. My mystical sight allows me to see this, but Siam is completely in the dark. He has no idea he's manipulated by the albino buffalo lord. I'm not able to foresee what may happen in the end. To further entice Siam, the albino buffalo lord may transform into a powerful force or a wishing glass orb, compelling him to mistake painful whips for loving touches. However, the form in which appears it will depend entirely up to Siam's own imagination.

Siam is suspended in between the three realms: hell, heaven, and earth. Led by his karmic creditor, he has travelled there to join a long line of souls that have departed from our world. His creditor has managed to smuggle Siam in among the dead. The journey to the underworld is long; there are many stages to pass through until they are finally judged by the Lord of Death. One of the final stages takes the form of a feast. As I followed Siam at a distance, I prayed that he would not reach the feast, nor eat anything served there, for then the dead will see him as one of their own. I pray to you, Siam . . . May you have the strength to see through these temptations! My efforts were not in vain: Siam seemed to struggle against the albino buffalo lord, and managed to flee from him. I don't know where he went, for at the point my soul had begun to return to my body. But we know now, at least, that Siam is finally aware of his predicament. Disappearing elsewhere is better than queuing for the feast.

I returned to my body—can you believe I meditated continuously for two days and two nights?—and shivered as I came back to consciousness, despite having been surrounded by the fires of hell. It took me half a day to recover, for my body to function normally once more. I had intended to return to Siam at nightfall, but my body felt unable to take the journey. I had to alter my mode of communication.

I placed a five-inch Buddha statue in the centre of a large brass bowl, steady as Mount Kailash, and placed the bowl on the altar. I poured holy water into the bowl, submerging the Buddha up to the waist. I lit some incense, cast my spell, and set my intentions on communicating directly with Siam. Finally, I lit a candle to guide his lost spirit. Ohm . . . My questions are the glowing flame of the candle, and its drippings are Siam's answers. 'Tell me, where is thy soul?'

Something miraculous happened! The candle wax cascaded into the bowl, the colours alternating between innocent white and ugly black. White, black, white, black, white, black; they swirled into each other in a most beguiling manner. Incredibly, once the wax touched the surface of the water, it began to flow in a circular motion, spinning anti-clockwise on the water's surface, the white wax drippings chased by the black. White was leading, black was tailing; white fleeing, black pursuing. I interpreted the white drippings as Siam and the black as the albino buffalo lord, swiftly chasing one other in the bowl of holy water: running in circles like the cycle of life itself. Siam was running for his life, tethered to the albino buffalo lord's pained spirit, under the eyes of the Buddha image hovering above them. Instantly, I knew Siam was in the midst of flight, with neither a destination in mind nor a shelter to rest in.

I asked my question out loud: 'Now, do you know that you've been deceived? Do you want to come back?'

One of the white drippings suddenly flowed faster.

'How would you like me to bring you back?' I continued.

The white drippings suddenly slowed, moved closer to the Buddha's resting hand. The black drippings continued to drift around the rim of the bowl, unable to draw closer towards the Buddha.

What did I make of this vision?

Listen to me carefully, my children; especially you, Dao.

There is only one way to defeat Siam's karmic creditor, the albino buffalo lord, and bring Siam back to life. A refuge must be built: a place for him to hide, a place on which to depend, a place to serve as a gateway into the human world. His karma is immense, tortuously so; better deeds must be built with haste. Imagine a seven-layered crystal wall of protection. You must hurry, or else it will be too late.

I've shown you the path towards the light. All of which is to say . . . Make a donation to this temple's main Buddha statue.

(The above view belongs to Abbot Glab.)

Branding

I'm determined to meet the abbot at the temple in order to disentangle this confused mess. What did he mean, 'Everyone's waiting for you?' My head feels like the sun, or a faux hair transplanted on a bald head: eclipsed; misplaced, like a dark shadow.

I arrive at the village temple where Abbot Glab lives. There are about five or six locals standing around the bend, blocking the temple's gate. Some of them are watching their cattle, their buffaloes grazing nearby, while others are surrounded by chickens, pecking on the ground for food, and others still are accompanied by monkeys and pigs. What a strange sight. Aren't there other places people can keep their animals, instead of allowing them to roam around and get in people's way? I cautiously shuffle my way around them, feeling mildly reassured by the fact that they don't seem to be waiting to capture me. I notice two old men standing guard on either side of the temple gate. The man on the left is waving at me, calling me over: 'Come quick! The abbot is waiting for you.' All righty then. I walk through the temple gate. Suddenly, pandemonium: the group of people start trying to force their way into the temple with their animals, begging the two old guards to let them through. The guards prevent them from entering and urge me to walk straight ahead without looking back. There's nothing I can do but follow their advice and leave them behind me.

I head towards Abbot Glab's house by the pond, which is large enough to run an entire lap around. The floating duckweed gives the pond its dark green surface and there are undoubtedly various kinds of fish underneath, all fat and free in a sanctuary where killing is forbidden. In the middle of the pond, the abbot is meditating under a small gazebo. As if my arrival had been foreseen, he opens his eyes and gets up just as I am about to approach him, raising his hand to stop me from walking further. This is odd.

'Not so fast, Siam,' he warns me from the gazebo. 'You cannot get to this gazebo by crossing the wooden bridge.'

'Excuse me? I can't hear you.'

'You can't cross the bridge to this gazebo.'

'Oh, why not?'

'You are too heavy. The bridge will collapse.'

I'm baffled. What's all this? He was the one who told me to come here, but now he's making a big fuss about it. I didn't even want to come in the first place. And where are those people he said were waiting for me? There's no one else here but the abbot.

'If there's something you want to ask me, please tell me now. I have an urgent matter to attend to, so I'm afraid I can't spare that much time.' I become visibly frustrated.

'Slow down, Siam. Your most urgent matter is here. There's nothing more urgent than this.'

Is this some kind of morality riddle?

'But you said there were people waiting for me.'

'Yes, there are.'

'I don't see anyone.'

'The fact that you can't see them doesn't mean they're not here.'

There he goes again, casually spinning riddles like the reclining Buddha.

'There are many things you can't see at the moment. They will only appear if you jump into the water.'

He must be joking.

'What kind of urgent matter would require me to get into the water?'

'Jump in, I beg you. Swim towards me and the others who are waiting for you under this gazebo. The truth will be revealed to you then.'

'*No. Sense.* There's no way I'm doing that.'

'Are you aware that you didn't come here alone?'

Not only does he want me to jump into the pond, but he's also scaring me with all these strange remarks. I look around but there's not a soul in sight.

'You're here with a karmic creditor from your past life,' he says. 'When you were about to enter the gate, you saw those villagers in front of the temple. They are wandering ghosts, all of whom have their own creditors with them; the guards stopped them from entering earlier. You, on the other hand, were able to enter because I asked the guards to let you in. It's not your time to die yet.'

'What are you talking about?' I start to feel nervous. Suddenly, I can sense a black shadow behind me, towering over me.

'You are being hunted down.'[10]

That's exactly what's happening to me! 'You're right, Father!' I exclaimed.

'Now you've understood that part, you just have to break your cycle of debt by jumping into the water and swimming to me.'

I hesitate. 'Why can't I just cross the bridge ... '

'Because your creditor can follow you across the bridge, but they cannot swim in this sacred pond.'

I'm still reluctant.

'Don't waste any more time: it's running out. The albino buffalo lord behind you is about to charge you with his horns.'

A sudden jolt runs through the four joints of my tailbone, shooting a warning signal to my brain at lightning speed. I jump into the water.

My whole body shudders at the piercing cold. It's not just the temperature of the water. Everything feels strange—the pungent stench of mud, the stale, damp smell of water plants and duckweed, the slime of this underwater world—and it's making the hairs on my body stand on end. All sorts of things wash into my face. Bubbles rise to the surface, bursting against me. The water thickens into a disgusting black tar.

'What do I do now?' I yell.

'Swim! Swim towards me, quickly!' the abbot yells back.

I've mustered up the strength to swim, but my body doesn't seem to be able to move. It's as if I'm swimming on the spot for the sole purpose of tiring all my limbs out.

I look back at the edge of the pond. There's still nothing in sight. The abbot's voice continues to urge me to swim to the gazebo. I hear him warn me that the albino buffalo lord has jumped into the water. At that moment, I hear a big splash. Suddenly, I can see a colossal beast with a human body and the head of a buffalo. Its skin is fair and pinkish, and its body, twice my size, is charging towards me. I let out a shriek when, at last, I see him with my own eyes. The sacred pond has revealed the true form of my creditor. The abbot was right all along: except for the fact that my karmic creditor can, indeed, enter the water!

I gather all my energy once more, swinging my arms ferociously to propel myself. I turn to the right and dive below the muddy water, trying to push myself forward while hugging the edge of the pond and holding my breath as long as possible.

I emerge on the other side of the pond, the albino buffalo lord right behind me. I thought swimming around in circles would shake him off, but I completely forgot about getting to the gazebo. The abbot is cheering me on, but I can barely hear him. My ears are ringing with fright. By the time he's audible once more, I'm already on the other side of the pond. I throw myself on the edge, and cling onto it as I catch my breath. With our stamina, humans are not made to live underwater; it drains us physically and spiritually. We are created to dwell on earth: to live our lives, to make a living, to survive on land. I can't take this anymore!

'Last push! Swim towards the gazebo! Last push! Just a little more!' the abbot cheers.

At this point, I've made my decision. Enough is enough, even if there's just a little more left. My hope has run out, and the albino buffalo lord knows it too. I see through his repulsive plan. He has stopped charging at me; instead, he swims around the gazebo, waiting for me to go straight to him. But what's more frustrating is the abbot, who continues to demand from me when he himself is doing absolutely nothing to help. That bloody albino buffalo lord is right beneath him, but he's just standing there, doing nothing at all. He could easily knock that buffalo lord out with his staff or something, and that would be that.

Now that I think about it, everything that has happened in the last several minutes happened because of him. I did everything he told me to do, in spite of my own reluctance. He told me to come to the temple, told me to jump into the pond, told me to swim towards the gazebo. Then came the albino buffalo lord . . . How it all happened baffles me. But all I know is that it's all because of the abbot. He doesn't directly say what he wants from me; he keeps speaking in riddles, withholding information. I don't even know the real reason behind all this exhaustion. Escaping those people from the ministry was tiring, but manageable. But swimming to this bloody gazebo? How could it help me in any way?

I look at the edge of the pond, then turn back towards the vast landscape stretching ahead of me. The latter promises more chances of survival, unlike the abbot, who only gave me one option: to swim to the gazebo. Right. I've made my decision. This is it. *The End. Finale.* Summoning whatever energy I have left, I heave myself out of the sticky, tarry pond, flip myself over, and sprint towards the open landscape ahead of me, leaving the stunned abbot and that bloody albino buffalo lord behind.

---

[10] Brothers, sisters, friends of community radio: this is your host, Chalermlarp, with an important announcement to make. This is an urgent message for all local communities, dispatched directly from the ministry. Brothers and sisters, please keep a lookout for this wanted individual and report him to the ministry as soon as possible.

Official reports identify this individual as Mr Siam Duangsuk, aged fifty-seven. He is a former doctor of traditional medicine; 159 centimetres tall, with a yellowish complexion. His place of birth is in Kaeng Khoi District, Saraburi: in other words, he is a local. Reports say he is suspected of fraud involvement as well as illegal activity undermining the state's authority. Furthermore, recent events have brought to light slanderous sentiments and undemocratic leanings towards a different system of government. For this reason, he is charged as a traitor of the nation, a separatist advocate who wants to overhaul the current regime. His recent attempt to raise questions about certain phrases coined by the state is but one example of his criminal offenses, where his line of questioning stemmed clearly from ill intent and a desire to cause public distress.

I, DJ Chalermlarp, will not be repeating Mr Siam's questions, in order to avoid the propagation of illegal behaviour, inadvertent as it may be. However, I believe our listeners will not find it difficult to infer the sort of questions we are gesturing towards, particularly in reference to certain provocative phrases that could distress and traumatize the nation, thus warranting his charge of treason.

I'm going to be honest with you. I admit that I have met this individual—this Mr Siam—before, although we were and are not close. This man has always been suspicious: records show that he was a member of the Communist Party of Thailand as a university student, and that he used to work in a shady underground business. He also acquainted himself with extreme capitalists: people who were known for their pro-Western sentiments and their contempt of our traditional culture and values. Most recently, he managed to worm his way into a political party suspected of advocating for a new system of government. Brothers and sisters, this individual infiltrated the aforementioned political party: a party seeking to destroy the virtuous traditions and culture of our free nation, the freedoms we inherited through the blood, sweat, and tears of our ancestors. Brothers and sisters, this is a political party unable to utter the words 'gratitude' and 'loyalty' to the ancestors of our land; a political party that is, in fact, a breeding ground for those people we call 'ungrateful', such as Mr Siam. A political party that does the opposite of what it claims, that is dishonest about their objectives: a party that seeks to sell the soul of our country to degenerate capitalists. They worship the rich: those who exploit others, who don't know right from wrong. This party is about to change our country, to put all that our ancestors fought for in the hands of capitalism. Foreigners will have the right to trade and invest in the riches of our land. The next thing we know, we won't have a country left to save!

The government is making every effort to suppress and exterminate those with such hidden agendas who lurk in polite society. It is a long but crucial process, one that is necessary for the happiness of the people. This arrest of this wanted individual—this Mr Siam—is another example of the government's relentlessness. Their thorough investigation will bring about solid evidence that Mr Siam Duangsuk is a parasite who leeches off the aforementioned political party to bring about our country's downfall.

For this reason, the ministry makes the following official announcement: if anyone has seen or heard from this wanted individual, please report him to the authorities or detain him, so that he may be brought to justice.

All right, brothers and sisters, friends of community radio, listeners all: I, DJ Chalermlarp, must end this announcement here. For further information, please visit the ministry's website. People can also access information and updates regarding this individual on our radio station's own website and Facebook page, as a way of doing their part.

Ah. It truly is disheartening, hearing about this individual's behaviour. Let's put on some music, brothers and sisters. Something that will encourage us to love and devote ourselves to the nation. I, DJ Chalermlarp, have personally chosen this song for you all to enjoy before we take a short break: this is 'Scum of the Earth'.

(The above message is from a public announcement made on community radio.)

Lynching

I'm running for dear life, like a bat out of hell, just to get away from that place. If the pond made my creditor visible, then I must assume that he'll be invisible on dry land. See no evil, hear no evil, speak no evil, right?

My escape may seem aimless, but I'm following my instincts, steered by the four joints of my tailbone towards somewhere predetermined.

Eventually, I find myself in front of the log cabin. This time I must wake Dao, no matter what. I storm into the room and see the housekeeper pulling the sheets off the bed. 'Dao! Dao! Where are you?'

The housekeeper is startled and responds with nervousness: 'Who? Who are you looking for, sir?' I explain to her that I'm looking for the lady who was sleeping here. 'Ah! She checked out and left the resort about half an hour ago, sir.'

I'm confused. It's as if I'm being severed from those close to me, cut off from all the relationships I once had. All I've encountered today are strangers and familiar faces whose minds seem completely opaque to me.

I leave the resort and continue my aimless run.

Dusk takes over, and tinting the road a dark blue. There's not a car in sight. With no knowledge of where I am or where I am headed towards, I follow the road, enclaved by hills stretching along both sides of it. Suddenly, I hear the hum of engines and human voices coming from somewhere ahead of me. I quickly jump to the side of the road, hiding behind rows of tall, dry grass. A pick-up truck full with passengers in the back drives past me, followed by a loaded six-wheeler. Everyone is wearing headbands and waving some sort of flag. There's a huge cloth banner hanging from the side of the truck, but it's difficult to make out what it says through the grass. A third vehicle appears—an extended cab pick-up—followed by another, also loaded with passengers.

Just as the last truck is about to drive past me, a voice from the back yells: 'There! He's there!' Then another voice: 'Where?' And another: 'Who are you talking about?' Suddenly, everyone is banging on the side of the truck, telling the driver to stop. They're shouting about the traitor, the suspect. With no more time to waste, I jump out of the dry grass and sprint towards the forest at the foot of the hills, hoping to buy myself some time while those people are still in their trucks. They're wasting time trying to yell at each other about what's happening, but next thing I know, they're getting off their trucks and coming after me. They're about 300 metres behind me when I run, fast as I can, into the grove.

The abbot appears out of nowhere, scaring the shit out of me. He's blocking my way, so I bow and raise both my hands over my head in a *wai*, begging: 'With all due respect, Father, I'm never diving into that pond again.'

However, the abbot continues to corner me, insisting that I return to the pond with him. 'It's the only way,' he says. 'I had to look for you again because Dao told me to.'

I start with disbelief. 'Your story is skewed, Father. How can I believe you when I didn't see anyone waiting for me at the temple?'

He tells me he's in no position to lie, that Dao came to see him just a while ago, worried because she couldn't find me. Oh, my poor Dao. I feel pathetic. I'm miserable and absurdly exhausted. What now? I scratch my head in utter confusion. I'm in crisis. I'm being hunted down.

Suddenly, the abbot puts his arm around my shoulder. 'Come with me.' I'm about to give into to my fate when a whizzing sound rings close to my ear. I feel a heavy blow across the back of my neck. I collapse to the ground, surrounded by two or three men, blocking my sight of the abbot.

I'm struck repeatedly from all directions; I try to get up, but to no avail. I hear the abbot trying to stop the attackers. It's only when I stop reacting to the blows that they finally end.

The abbot is standing in front of me, shielding me from the crowd. Dumbstruck and desperate, I cast blame on the abbot:

'You said you'd protect me!'

He claims he didn't realize the magnitude of the manhunt, of the number of people looking for me. He turns to my attackers, asking them why they have resorted to such violence.

Their response is bitter, full of accusations against me. They say I'm ungrateful, that I don't know my place; that I'm a traitor who has conspired to infiltrate the system in order to destroy it, that I undermine righteousness and challenge the law. After hearing a public announcement naming me as a wanted man, they had volunteered to hunt me down and take me to trial.

'But what you're doing is unjust,' the abbot reprimands them. 'It's far from judicial process: you've just made up your own laws.

Aren't you ashamed of beating him up like this? Don't you feel any guilt? Can you see he's bruised and bleeding?'

'Assaulting a wicked man is not a sin,' one of them shouts. 'Even if we kill him.'

'How do you know that he's wicked? What could possibly justify this?'

'There was a public announcement issued by the government that condemned him as a bad man. He needs to be arrested and brought to justice.'

Once I manage to haul myself up, I interject bitterly: 'But the law you refer to does not give you the right to assault me. You act as if it's personal, as if the justice system has given you the right to take the law into your own hands and attack me!'

'See? He's acting like a smart arse again,' sneers one of the attackers. 'He needs to be beaten up until his smart-arse brain spills out of his skull.'

I notice that the mob has caught up to us. I can feel the oncoming surge of their rage. One of their hot-headed leaders seems to have full power over the mob. He approaches the abbot, as if to negotiate.

'How can I stop this crowd from sharing these same sentiments, Father? Rage unites us. Try and see things from our perspective. We've been victimized, deceived, confounded, led astray: all because this man has disobeyed the law.'

'But that doesn't call for a lynching,' the abbot says. 'How deplorable to witness, in our society, the way you people swarm around a suspect, being told to reenact a crime he allegedly committed. Meanwhile, the police just stand by, watching you bend the laws with your own hands. And if vengeance strikes—if those hands of yours can't help but beat the accused to death—it seems that both the police and the law have the ability to screw their eyes shut. The police would probably say the same thing as you just did: that it's impossible to stop mass sentiment. And those who do not take part are likely to ignore it too. If a crime were committed against their parents, their siblings, their close relatives: they'd probably do the same as you. You've taken the law into your own hands to satisfy your barbaric desires, when none of this is at all personal. I wonder what must be in your hearts and minds, that you crave violence so much without any conscience or shame.'

'Boooring!' the mob leader bursts out. 'I think you should go back and deliver that sermon at your temple. This is a matter of the secular world: something you probably don't know much about. Things can be very complicated out here. Don't get me wrong, Father. I know you mean well. But if you keep shoving your criticism at us like this, we cannot guarantee you any help if you get yourself in trouble. So, my advice to you, Father, is to return to your temple while you still have the chance, unless you want to be charged with treason. Don't get involved with this traitor, believe me. Go back to your temple.'

So this is how things are turning out. As soon as I hear the leader's cry of 'Boooring', I take the chance to flee. The rest of the crowd is confused for a moment, unsure of whether they ought to stay and listen to their leader or to run after me. The mob is growing indecisive. I run from them, but I find myself approaching yet another dead-end.

A steep embankment lies before me, rising about six or seven wa above the river. Without giving it a second thought, I jump into the river and swim to the other side. I hide behind a tree, keeping watch. I can see that the mob has reached the embankment. None of them dare to jump in. Suddenly, a voice booms from a megaphone:

'Turn yourself in, Mr Siam. You won't be able to escape. Those who want you are on this side of the river.'

I poke my head out to discover that the voice belongs to the deputy chief of the SAO.

'I know you can hear me, Mr Siam. Come out and talk to us. The people are begging you. At the very least, you owe it to the people to explain why you made such a decision.'

What bloody decision?! You people wanted me to become the executive chief of the SAO, but when I refused to *ac-vi-tate* my card, you criminalized me, and now you're hunting me down as if I am to blame for every grudge you've nursed in this life and those before it.

'That power was bestowed upon you, but you treated it like it was a joke. Isn't it cruel of you, to break our hearts this way?' a middle-aged woman protests.

'Explain yourself! These are long-established rules and regulations. Who are you to disobey them?' a man in glasses chimes in. 'Isn't that right, brothers and sisters?'

The mob roars in agreement.

'Hold on, hold on, brothers and sisters. Don't threaten him just yet. He still has the right to explain himself. He's only a suspect, after all,' the deputy chief says, trying to calm the mob down.

'You shameless, bitch-faced coward! Admit your wrongdoing!' a woman's shrill voice pierces through the air, crossing the river and plunging right into my heart. What did I do to deserve such slander?

'What have I ever done to you? I don't know a single one of you in this mob. I'm certain that none of you know me personally. So, what reason do you have for hunting me down and assaulting me with such vengeance?'

A loud commotion breaks out from the other side of the river. A voice responds. 'Yes, we don't know you, so you better tell us who you are, and why you did what you did to us.'

'What have I ever done to you?' I cry desperately.

'We're not the ones being interrogated here. You know full well what you did. Deputy Chief, can you please do this moron a favour and enlighten him?'

'You broke the rules. That's what you did, you stupid fuck!'

'Please, everyone, try to calm down,' the deputy chief intervenes. 'Mr Siam, it's understandable for our people to feel outraged in the face of injustice committed against them. They have always obeyed the rules and regulations, and they strive to maintain them unconditionally. When you prance in and refuse to obey the rules, your actions are an offence against the people. You have no right to say you've never offended any of them personally, because what you did encroached upon their principles. That is all I can say for now. In response to your other question, it is untrue that none of us know you. Mr Somjai is also here with us. All right, Mr Somjai. Talk some sense into your friend.'

I watch in bewilderment as Somjai emerges from the crowd.

'Siam, as your friend, I beg you to turn yourself in, or else things won't end here. You're putting your family in danger. The government will seize control of everything you own. How do you expect your mother and brothers to face the world without being consumed by shame? Do you want them to be ostracized? Trust me. Come out and plead guilty and everything will end here. Society often forgives those who show remorse, my friend.'

My mouth and stomach suddenly turn acidic. Never have I felt so alone. In a crisis like this, where are those who are close to me: my mother, my brothers, Dao? The abbot cannot help me either.[11] Worse, my most trusted friend refuses to stand by me. Come to think of it, I always had an inkling of what kind of person Somjai really is, but I tried to ignore it. Now he wants me to swim to the crowd on the other side. When it comes to negotiating with me, he always refuses to back down. It's just like when we were younger, at the waterfall, when he tricked me into diving with that ridiculous pose. Deep down, he just wants me to get hurt and give up.

What is all this about? Pettiness, escalated into some sort of blasphemy: all this hate from total strangers. What have I gotten myself into? Hell. This is what hell feels like: not being consumed by flames, but being subjected to everything that has recurred again and again throughout this day. Utter loneliness, unfamiliarity: a complete loss of control.

'Turn yourself in, Mr Siam,' the deputy says, his voice echoing out of the megaphone.

I don't respond. I've made my decision.

The silence stirs up frustration. The mob is poised, waiting on my uncertainty. Dusk falls over the landscape. 'It's easy being a smart-arse in the dark, isn't it?' someone says. Oh well. They can say whatever they want about me. I can't fix their attitudes. I feel their patience growing thin. Then someone shouts, 'Okay, suit yourself. Stay on that side and don't you dare cross over. You're no longer welcome on this side!'

Those words are a line drawn in the sand. Shrouded in darkness, I stagger down the path ahead of me and disappear into the forest.

---

[11] My heart is in my throat. Before I was able to succeed, Siam was defeated, and now he has passed away. It was a close call, I swear it; only a little more, and his spirit would have been able to return to

his body. Victory had been within arm's reach. Two possibilities must be taken into consideration: either Siam gave up, or he was overpowered by his karmic creditor's vengeance.

I will say this: he was strong. It was obvious that he was struggling to resist his creditor. This is what I witnessed when I travelled to see him in the other realm. I did my best to offer my help. It doesn't matter what happens to your physical body: everything is determined by the strength of your spirit. Even if your body is paralysed, in deterioration, if doctors have told you that the chances of survival are zero: if your spirit is strong enough to struggle to stay alive, it will find a way back to its body. The spirit remains; its contract is not over yet. But what can it do when the body has expired, and there is nowhere to return to?

There are many things wrong in this situation. Yes, Dao; like you, I feel conflicted about the fact that we are the only two trying to help bring Siam back. It isn't right. I don't understand why the others are against it. It's not difficult to let Siam's body lie in the hospital for a while; I even said I need less than a week to tell if we're going to be successful. I even gave them my word. What right does the doctor have to tell the patient's relatives that keeping him here wasn't necessary, that his conditions would worsen? What right do they have to say that we're wasting money here, that it's better to bring him back home? What kind of a doctor would say this? What's worse is that all his relatives agreed with the doctor. They hurried to bring his body out of hospital. I begged them to keep him here, but they didn't listen. Look what happened. He died within a day of being brought home.

What will become of his spirit?

Despite the fact that it no longer has a body to return to, his spirit has not expired. A wandering, uprooted spirit. What a pity. Some of his relatives pleaded with me—'He's in a better place now, right, Father?'—and what could I possibly say other than, 'Yes, yes he is.'

But, in truth, Siam hasn't left us. He lingers here, as alive as ever, circling around and trying to find his way back. His body, on the other hand, is gone. This is the truth, a truth I will only impart to some, and I'm telling it to you, Dao.

Some people's duties have come to an end, while others' have not: they are still obliged to do certain tasks. For example, the doctor's duty is to treat the body, but his duty ends when the body fails him. Your relatives brought the body to the cremation ritual; once that was done, the body was no longer duty-bound to earthly matters. This is not the case, however, for a monk like myself, who is still obligated to Siam. I understand this is not the case for you either, Dao, since there are certain things that are yet unfinished for you both. We all want to finish what we've started, don't we?

Yes, yes. I understand how you feel. You feel betrayed, used; upset that things have turned upside down. We will never know what kind of a person Siam truly was, whether he was as wicked as others had made him to be. However, such matters should not be decided based on the opinions of others. Take me, for example. From my perspective, I can attest to the fact that Siam was a good person. That's how you feel about him too, don't you, Dao? He was good to you when you were living together, wasn't he? My advice is to hold onto that truth.

We must do our best to send him where he's supposed to go. This is not something that can be done half-heartedly, otherwise his spirit will be left to wander, aimless and alone, and it will be us who will have sinned.

Please allow me to be direct with you. I ask that you lend another helping hand to guide Siam's spirit to his final refuge. I will do my duty in directing him, but it is yours to provide him with this final resting place, which can only be brought about through your personal resources, Dao. As we have seen, it would be difficult to ask this from his relatives. Have pity on his spirit, Dao.

The reason I called you is to know whether I can still count on your donations for building the main Buddha image for our temple, as we discussed earlier. If you are, then I can rest assured, as I have already made a start on some of the construction. It would be unfortunate to cancel the project only because Siam's physical body is gone. Like I said, his body is gone, but his spirit is still wandering this world. Our duties towards him are not over. If you can give me your word that you will continue your donations, I will meditate tonight and try to communicate with Siam again, to assure him that you are building him a Buddha statue as his refuge, so he won't end up as a wandering ghost. His spirit will rest there until it is time for him to reborn in a better place.

Let this be our plan, Dao. All right. I feel so much more relieved. Well . . . Don't hesitate to ring me if there's anything you're still concerned about. All right . . . Bless you, my child.

(The above view belongs to Abbot Glab.)

Waiting for Mr PM

The elements are on my side. Tonight, the full moon hovers like a perfect sphere, illuminating the forest. To be honest, this side of the river is less forest and more residential area. I'm walking on a paved road, wide enough for two cars to pass one another with ease. The intermittent hum of the insects is interspersed with the cracking of tree branches. Am I afraid? Not in the slightest. Nothing could be scarier than what I just went through. Now, I'm at peace; no longer exhausted, I feel strangely safe. This place makes me feel as though it is possible to leave the past behind me,[12] including that karmic creditor from my past life, whose presence I can no longer feel.

Guided by the crisp moonlight, I walk towards a sharp bend and notice lamplight flickering about ten metres ahead of me. I stop, squinting. I can make out two men in a makeshift shelter, one lying down and the other sitting with his legs swinging about. Both of them are looking back at me. What to do now? Are they after me too? They can't be trusted. I stand there, frozen in the middle of the road, as the two of them study me. Suddenly, the one lying down gets up and nudges his friend, and the two of them whisper about whether I'm 'the one' they've been waiting for. The second guy looks unsure. Finally, he decides to ask:

'Are you Mr PM?'

In this sort of situation, even if I were the real Mr PM, I'd say I wasn't. However, my answer seems to disappoint them. Their shoulders droop. I'm slightly reassured—they seem harmless—but I remain still, cautious.

'Who are you?' he asks.

'I'm lost,' I reply, taking one step closer.

'Are you also waiting for Mr PM?'

'No,' I answer.

'Then why are you here? Everyone here is waiting for Mr PM.'

The other guy beckons me amiably into the shelter. My intuition tells me they're not with the others, so I decide to join them.

'So, you're both waiting for Mr PM?' I ask.

'Yes,' says the older one. 'We thought you were Mr PM.'

'Who's Mr PM and why are you waiting for him?' I ask.

'Mr PM opens the gate for us.'

'What gate?'

'The gate to the palace,' the younger one replies, pointing to the other side of the road, where a large estate—easily over ten *rai*—sits on top of a towering hill. I see a dark iron gate, burnished with gold; a moonlit concrete path runs from the gate to the palace, which is lit up from every angle. The light refracts, casting shadows that contour the sophisticated corners and crevices of the building. Who is the resident of this grand estate, I wonder?

'So, you really are lost, huh?' the older man observes. 'That's odd. It's almost impossible to get lost here. People only come here to wait for the chance to enter the estate.'

'But you have to wait for Mr PM to enter, because he's the only one who can open the gate,' the younger one adds. 'We've been waiting for him for almost a week. We were thrilled when we saw you, because we thought you were Mr PM.'

I chuckle bashfully, feeling somewhat guilty for disappointing them. *I might not be Mr PM*, I think to myself, amused. *But I was almost appointed Mr Chief Executive with a 'soaring' number of votes.*

'But why do you want to enter the estate?' I ask with genuine curiosity.

'Ours are considered special cases. We're caught in problems that we ourselves didn't cause; we've been misunderstood and falsely accused to the point of public hate. Entering the palace is our last chance to lodge an appeal and be pardoned,' the old man explains.

'It's essential that we enter the estate. It's our last chance to appeal for pardon,' the younger man repeats. 'It's our only chance to return to the other side.'

'We have to plead guilty, despite having done nothing wrong, just so we can have our normal lives back,' the old man says bitterly.

'Hence, we wait for Mr PM,' the younger one concludes.

When I think about it, my case is no different. I was pressured into doing something that, deep down, I know I've always wanted to do. But I fell straight into the trap: I eschewed careful deliberation, and I got too excited. And before I knew it, I was nose-diving.

'Doesn't anyone live there?' I ask. 'Someone who can come out and listen to your appeal, so you don't have to wait for Mr PM?'

'We've been waiting for almost a week and we haven't seen anyone in there,' the older man responds.

'I guess the resident can't just come out to listen to our appeals, especially considering their status. It's probably more appropriate to let someone else present our appeals for their consideration,' the younger man speculates.

'Unless there's no one in there. Perhaps both the petitioner and the pardoner are on the outside. Perhaps they only enter together once in a blue moon.'

'We're completely in the dark here. All we can do is make guesses as we wait,' says the older man.

'As we wait for Mr PM,' sighs the younger man.

'Why don't you wait here with us, in case Mr PM shows up tomorrow?' the older man says to me.

I nod, despite having no desire to wait for Mr PM, or to enter the palace. Regardless, I'm touched by the small acts of friendship that have passed between us three. A friendship blossoming under the flickering lamplight in this makeshift shelter. And so, I intend to spend the night with them, to get to know one another better. We can talk about the hardships we each have experienced on our own hopeful paths, which have now diverged into one.

'Have you eaten?' the older man asks.

'Not yet,' I answer.

'Let's eat together,' he says.

We sit in a circle and the younger man places a bamboo container in the centre. He lifts the lid. It's filled with sticky rice. The fragrance of freshly cooked rice intermingles with the slightly earthy smell of bamboo, transporting my mind somewhere far away for just a moment. The older man unties a rubber band from the top of a plastic bag containing sun-dried salted meat, handing each of us a small piece. The sticky rice, bamboo, and salted meat together give off an aromatic yet slightly rancid smell: a perfect representation of our trio.

Before I know it, tears are streaming down my cheeks. I apologize to the two men, blaming it on my exhaustion. The things I've just been through are too much to process. The younger man tells me to rest after I finish eating, and I thank them both for their kindness and generosity.

As I'm about to doze off, I hear the whispered voices of the two men humming in the background. I imagine they probably greeted each other like this too, and exchanged stories with one another for the first time at the start of the week. Sleeping next to one other in this makeshift shelter, they probably talked about their lives, their families, their people, their hopes and dreams: they probably talked until they ran out of things to tell one other. All that's left to talk about now are possibilities: imaginings, rumours, even the impossible. Perhaps waiting indefinitely for the impossible—and talking about it—is what makes it otherwise.

So, they want to get into the estate: to be part of the system that cared for them before rejecting them. What they're waiting for, then, is to be welcomed back into the system. They endured all the tests administered by the system, and now they anticipate the verdict. Their only choices are to accept or comply. I, on the other hand, have no desire to enter the estate, neither to lodge an appeal nor to apologize, not since I have borne witness the horrific truth: that once you're the system, you can never get out. If you try, you open a whole new chapter of the story, one that goes something like what happened to me at the ministry.

Life is full of knots. The slightest step in any direction simply entangles you in more knots. These two men have made their choice: they have chosen to wait for Mr PM and enter the estate. Having undergone my own adventures, it's not hard to predict that they'll try to escape again once they're let back inside. I've seen it all, and it still scares the shit out of me. But you never know. They might be able to lodge their appeals, and if they struggle hard enough, they might be pardoned. Things might work out for them. Terrible things might turn good. Their wrongs might be righted. Their bodies might disappear into the shadows behind the gate.

All they have to do is wait for Mr PM to let them in.

As for me, I pray for tomorrow to arrive. Life may be messy and troublesome, but one must keep moving forward. It's inevitable. If more trouble awaits me, then let it be something I have chosen for myself, rather than something beyond my control: rather than some sort of form I simply must complete.

All righty then. I'm drifting off. I will rest to recover, and I will continue with my journey when I wake.

---

[12] The death of Dr Siam brought many things to light, including the changes that occurred in my mother.

When Dr Siam was first hospitalized, my mother was genuinely troubled. Everything she did was to help him recover safely. However, her sincere and selfless devotion eventually turned sour when she realized she was doing it all alone. Pettiness bloomed inside her mind like a fungus, becoming more and apparent. Every little thing someone else did would feed into this bitterness. There was no doubt that she not only believed that she was the only one attempting to prolong Dr Siam's life, but that she was also the only one paying the medical expenses, which had drained virtually all of her savings. No one was willing to understand her and support her: especially not her children.

Chidchai and I visited Dr Siam at the beginning, but we stopped after that. I was living and working in Bangkok. Once it got to the weekend, I was worn out: to be honest, I'd rather rest at home than do anything else. Chidchai told me on the phone that it was okay, that he would visit him for the both of us. So, I thought, that's great, give him my regards. That's what we agreed on: that Chidchai would visit him on behalf of both of us. However, our mother didn't see it that way. Whenever we talked on the phone, she would sound upset, and she would make sure that I knew it. There were two things that agitated me about her manner, aside from dropping passive-aggressive questions, all of which were completely self-centred, such as: 'What about you? Have you ever thought about doing something for Uncle Siam?'

The first thing she did was become a vegetarian. She wore only white and prayed morning and night. 'You should extend your merit to Uncle Siam by praying and going on a vegetarian diet,' she would say. I had no response to this. The second thing she did was fundraising for the construction of a Buddha statue as a refuge for Uncle's Siam wandering spirit. To be honest, I was against it from the first moment she brought it up. To me, it was just a way of capitalizing on people's hopes. There was no logic to it. I asked her, 'How much more is this Buddha statue costing you?' About a hundred thousand, she said. 'Isn't that a bit much?' I exclaimed. 'The hospital fees were already half a million, and now you're spending a hundred thousand more on building this Buddha statue. Will you have savings left once you've spent it all on these things?'

I was worried about my mother. She was so vulnerable that she welcomed every semblance of hope that knocked on her door, from stem cell treatment (is there any actual evidence of its efficacy?) to large hospital bills (despite his condition having shown no sign of improvement!) to eating vegetarian and praying morning and night (although she never misses the chance to cast blame on her unlucky stars) to fundraising for a Buddha statue (can someone please confirm whether Dr Siam's spirit will actually move in and reside there?) Wasn't it getting a bit ridiculous? It's completely irrational. Admittedly, I did not wish to be a part of this superstitious affair. I don't believe in it. But all I could do was go along with her, so she wouldn't think that I was heartless for not visiting him, not praying for him, not helping with the Buddha statue. I just didn't want her to feel as if her children were abandoning her too.

She was consumed by loneliness. Anything the other side said deeply affected her mental health. It got worse and worse, especially when they exposed the darker side of Dr Siam's life. The other side testified to these ugly truths, and it was impossible for my mother to defend him. She fought hard in the beginning, trying to convince herself and others that Dr Siam wasn't that kind of person. But they succeeded in planting a seed of doubt within her, which eventually grew into two different images of Dr Siam: one she knew, and one painted by the others.

Lying there unconscious, it was impossible for the man to defend himself. This dark image of him, conjured by the other side, grew over his paralysed body. He was literally stifled by his own image. My mother must have thought that we weren't supportive. The only person she could trust to tell her what was right, to separate the accusations and defamations from the truth, was lying still in that bed. If only he could rise and speak. He was the only person who would stand by her side. When you think about it, she really didn't have any one left to turn to.

Without anyone or anything to hold onto, this loneliness and lack of support brought about another change within her. She turned to Abbot Glab and put her faith in him, while she focused all her hopes on Dr Siam. If only he knew how she looked at him—her gaze concentrated with intensity, the very distillation of love—every time she visited. That love (the only thing she had to hold onto, the only thing they had left for each other) was her only insurance in this matter of life and death. She staked all her love on this final gamble against fate.

Please wake up. It's the only way to win. Wake up.

But Dr Siam died, and so she lost everything she had bet to fate.

And so she finally believed that the picture the other side had painted of Dr Siam was true: that he was a fraud, a compulsive liar, a wicked person, a dishonest man, a burden to society. She believed that not waking up was a way for him to escape the mess he had created. This belief was important to my mother: it was something she could hold onto, a reason to stop loving him. Focusing on his wickedness—his deception, her betrayal by the one person she loved—was the only way to remain indifferent about him, to eliminate him from the picture. It's as if you're being swept away by a current, and you're left with two floats to hold onto. You have to choose one, even though neither of them promises stability but you only realize this after you choose one. Other people may think you made an unreasonable choice, but that doesn't matter, because it was reasonable for you. You don't let go, and so you allow yourself to be carried away by the current on the float you chose. Things are always reasonable when you have something to hold onto.

My mother had lost her love. She had become utterly disoriented as a result, and was willing to latch onto whatever form of hate she could have for him. It was the only way for her to sever her loving ties with Dr Siam.

The other day, I received a phone call from her.

'Did you hear?' she asked.

'Hear what?' I asked her back.

'Uncle Siam is dead,' she said, her voice dry.

I was silent for a while, trying to process the loss.

'It wasn't long since I saw him last,' I wailed.

'It's for the better,' she sighed. 'Staying wouldn't have done him any good. He's in a better place now. It's those left behind who suffer now.'

'When's the funeral?' I asked. 'Let me know what day we're hosting.'

'He's already been cremated,' she said.

'When?' I was surprised. Why didn't anyone tell me about it? Did my mother really hate me so much that she didn't tell me?

'Yesterday evening,' she said.

'Why didn't you tell me, Mum?' I cried.

'I didn't tell anyone. No one from our side went to the ceremony.' She went quiet. 'I didn't even go.'

'Really?' That's all I could say. When had we become so cold and indifferent? 'Why?'

'Don't get me started,' she sighed again. 'There's so much going on. It's probably good that you're away from all of this, like you were before.'

I was hurt by what she said. Tears came to my eyes.

'This mess is finally over. Now we can each move on with our lives,' she concluded.

A moment later, she began telling me all the stories that had transformed Dr Siam's existence into a complicated mess. I was glad that she did that, instead of hanging up straight after saying those hurtful words. I would have left feeling absolutely ridden with guilt, but instead we took a few moments to think about Dr Siam's departure, to indulge in the shared shame and self-hatred we had for not attending his funeral. But then my mother told me that she hadn't wanted any of us to attend the funeral because of something she had discussed with Abbot Glab. He had told her that Dr Siam's death had not been peaceful, that he had been accompanied by vengeful spirits and karmic creditors that wished to harm him, that his death had been caused by so-called black magic. If any of us were to attend the funeral—the day upon which this black magic is most potent—we might absorb its effects. So, the abbot had concluded, not attending the funeral was—in a way—a form of self-protection.

Upon hearing her reasoning, I couldn't help but feel awful. Was it true? I mean, yes: was it true what Abbot Glab had told her? I had no idea how the conversation between them had gone. But was it true that my mother could wholeheartedly accept this sort of reasoning? All I could tell myself was that my mother had simply lost the biggest gamble of her life.

What's scary is the possibility that these stories might all be fiction: penned not by the abbot, but by someone with a gaping hole in her heart.

She didn't just lose the love and trust she had for others. She lost all the love she had for herself, too. If you run out of love for yourself, how can you expect to share it with anyone else?

After hanging up, a cold shiver ran through my body. Sitting at my desk, I felt paralysed. I couldn't do anything. I thought about the words 'attachment' and 'compassion'. Was it possible for these things to dissipate entirely from a person's heart? I felt like I was one of those heartless people. We can't forget that we didn't attend the funeral. The simplest act of courtesy a fellow human being can take towards another, and we didn't even do that. I felt so ashamed!

I recalled the day Dr Siam Duangsuk first came into our house, and the day he left. What traces did he leave behind? How do we remember him? He came into our life and sold us his dreams: as he had done, perhaps, all his life? I'm not sure. What I was sure of, though, was how easily our family could erase him from our memory.

(The above view belongs to Prateep.)

Episode 3: Dao's Destiny

Destiny shivers

The winter of 1974 came with the most brutal chill: the kind of cold that pierces your flesh, down to your bones. The wind whistled through the house, howling through the rafters and the cracks in the wooden walls. It woke me before dawn broke: before the rooster could crane its neck to crow, before the cuckoo's call could echo through the forest. I rose before anyone else in the house. After washing my face and brushing my teeth, I tiptoed downstairs to load the baskets onto the cart. I braved the cold, pushing the cart through the freezing air to get to the village pond. I filled the baskets with water—my hands aching with cold as if they'd been attacked by a swarm of ants—before pushing them back to the house. I transferred the water into our large earthen jar before stirring in alum. After about half a day, sediment would settle at the bottom, leaving clear water above. I went up to the house and into the kitchen to light a fire, ready to steam some rice. The air was thick with smoke. The rooster crowed right at dawn. While Ma came out of the bedroom, Pa stayed inside, going through his morning prayers before starting his day.

Dawn is vivid in my memory: my daily duties, the household chores, making sure that everything was ready for Pa and Ma, to lessen the burdens they were forced to shoulder. Pa reminded me often that he had always supported my siblings, who rarely show up now that they're all grown. My brothers wanted wives and my sisters wanted husbands. Pa and Ma sold their farmland so that my brothers could afford their dowries, so that winter wouldn't be so tough on them. My sisters ran away from home, chasing after boys. They eventually returned with children for Pa and Ma to raise, which meant selling more farmland to pay for their grandchildren's education.

'I cannot take it anymore,' Pa complained in Lao.

'Neither can I,' Ma agreed.

By the time I was born, Pa and Ma had had enough. They couldn't afford to spoil me like they had my siblings. I've been doing housework as long as I can remember. I've been helping Ma in the kitchen since I was five. I've never left home: not even to go to school.

Pa once said, 'What do you learn in school anyway? They're not teaching you to grow rice, that's for sure.'

I agreed with him. When I watch my nieces and nephews poring over their homework, all I see is a waste of time that might have been spent making a living.

My continued existence is living proof that school isn't necessary for survival. Not being able to read or write is a little tough, but I can speak just fine. So, I don't see what the problem is.

In the winter of 1974, I was sixteen. I was experiencing strange, feverish chills beneath my skin. They'd started when I got my period a few years earlier: a clammy shiver that stirred inside me. When winter came around, all I could think about was warmth: the warmth of touch, of skin-on-skin contact. I remember cuddling with Ma. That was the only kind of warmth that kept the cold at bay. Once, when I went to the village pond to fetch water, I saw a boy doing the same thing. He was looking at me. His body—dark, taut with muscle—was completely different from Ma's. I wondered how warm it would feel if we held each other tight. My body turned feverish at the thought.

Pa once asked me, 'Do you know what love is?'

I told him I didn't.

Love, he explained, is what he and Ma had: living together, building a house together, having children together. A child is the product of their parents' love, and so children ought to devote their love to their parents, not a partner. Pa told me he knew that I was becoming a woman and that eventually I would fall in love. Under no circumstances, he told me, should I give that love away to someone else, as my siblings had done. That love, he told me, should be reserved for him and Ma; the highest form of love, a reverent love. He also told me not to worry about the chills I was getting, that they would pass with time.

Every day, Pa left the house and headed for the rice fields. He would be gone for the whole day, returning at dusk. Ma, on the other hand, spent each day sewing and weaving. When I finished my chores, I went down to sit with her, and we listened to radio dramas together.

I once asked Ma why she weaved. I had never seen her wear any of the fabric she made. She replied that she weaved for *him*. Who? I asked. My employer, she said. He goes around villages collecting fabric to sell at the market. What's a market? I asked. A market, she said, is a place for selling things. If you have something to sell, you take it to the market. Where is the market? I asked. In the city, she replied.

The more I asked, the more confusing it all seemed. I couldn't picture it. Each word she uttered was a mystery to me. One evening, I asked my nephew if he knew what a city was. He said that he did, that he was from the city. He'd moved to the country to live with his grandparents. What's it like, the city? I asked him. There are tall, beautiful buildings, he told me, and people dressed up in nice clothes, all crammed together, and all sorts of things for sale. You can buy anything you want, as long as you've got the money. In the market, you mean? I asked. Yes, he replied, there are so many markets in the city. I still couldn't picture it, so my nephew went to get a textbook out of his schoolbag. He flipped through the pages and passed it to me. It was a line drawing of rectangles: lots and lots of rectangles, dotted with windows, all crammed together. At the bottom of the page was a road, swarming with cars. I stared at the drawing, mulling over the differences between the city and our home.

'Is it cold in the city?' I asked.

'Nah. It's bloody hot,' my nephew replied.

The city was warm, just as I thought. That's why all my siblings moved there and never came back.

Radio dramas taught me that there are only a few types of people in this world: self-proclaimed heroes, heroines, villainesses, villains, and those who existed only to come between the heroes and their heroines. I sometimes wondered why villainesses mostly came from the city. How could somewhere so warm make her so envious, so restless? How could it fill her head with such vile thoughts? Heroines, on the other hand, were often portrayed as innocent country girls who (like me) lived simple lives. But that didn't really ring true to me. After all, heroes were also from the city, and they didn't harbour the same dirty thoughts and obscene ideas that the villainesses did. So, it isn't the city that makes people good or bad, it's their own desires: passion, greed, anger, lust (that's what the heroes tell the heroines, anyway). Pa even said so himself. It's one of the Buddha's teachings, he said.

Ma once warned me against listening to those radio dramas. She was afraid that I'd end up a slut like those girls. Again, her words made me wonder: which girls? The jealous girls? If I ended up like anyone, it would be the heroes and heroines, I told her, because they're good people. 'What a load of crap,' she said in Lao. 'Nothing to do with you, child.' She added, 'You can't fight or kill each other over any inheritance or will. I haven't got anything like that for you.'

These dramas, Ma said, are from a different place: a place we'll never be able to go. Why bother listening to them? The more we listen, the more questions we'll have, and the more envious we'll be of those who have what we don't: we'll want the pearl necklaces and diamond rings that the heroes gift the heroines; we'll want to wear nice clothes and drive a Mercedes like the villainesses. Ma said that Nao, our next-door neighbour's daughter, had become addicted to radio dramas. One day, her curiosity finally got the best of her, and she stole away to the city. She came home almost unrecognizable, dressed in garish colours with a ghoulish face full of makeup. Uncle Koon—her father—and the villagers couldn't help but wonder if Nao had gone to the city to sleep with men for money. Ma didn't want me to end up like her.

All day, every day, I went about my chores, lightening my parents' load, as any good daughter would do to show gratitude to her parents. Pa told me I was the apple of their eye. Unlike the other families in the village that sent their daughters off to struggle in the outside world, he took good care of me, wrapped me in cotton wool, all so I could live a comfortable life under their roof. Even so, strange things made it into our home. Peculiarities trickled in steadily through the walls: tidbits about our neighbours, unfamiliar images that felt so different from the home I knew so well. Sometimes I had secret thoughts: feelings and doubts I couldn't help but carry. I thought about Pa telling me my chills would go away on their own, but they hadn't. Whenever it seemed like they were gone for good, they always wound their way back. I thought about the scandals, the cautionary tales Ma told me about the village boys and girls, about becoming something like them. Even though there was no chance of me becoming anything at all—I was here, in this house, with no chance of going anywhere—these things wound their way into the house, continually generating doubts within me.

Things were the way they were, and they wouldn't even let me listen to the radio? I contradicted Pa and Ma in my head, feeling deep guilt at my audacity. They were just secret thoughts, at least.

One day, Ma's employer came to the village on one of his fabric-collecting trips. Our house was the last he visited. As Ma filled a sack with fabric for him, he kept looking back at me. His eyes were fierce. I felt myself grow soft under the intensity of his gaze. He was quiet and spoke rarely, but when he did, his voice was clear and sweet. He was about fifteen years older than me, with skin like brown sugar and a head of thick, black curls. He was tall and muscular, and there was something quite sad about those fierce eyes. His mouth moved, as if to speak to me, but he said nothing. Finally, he said to Ma, 'Your daughter's growing so fast, Auntie.'

Ma froze slightly before asking, 'How's your wife?'

He was silent—a hiccup in the conversation—and lowered his eyes to the concrete floor.

I don't know what I was thinking, but I poked his upper arm. He started a little, and turned to look at me.

'Take me to the market?' I said.

He looked at me silently, a smile playing on his lips. Ma turned and told me to get back upstairs.

I think it was in that moment—in the winter of 1974, the day Ma's employer came to collect the fabrics at our house and I impulsively asked him to take me to the market—that my life began to change.

It came like a slow, silent wave, surging through the few months that followed. Even when he wasn't there in person, his name wound its way into my house, uttered and exchanged in conversations between my parents. His name was Srisak. Ma once told Pa what a good and hardworking man Mr Srisak was, and they pitied him for what his wife was going through. His wife suffered from some strange illness that made her completely helpless. As a result, Mr Srisak had to make a living for them both. When he was done with work, he still had to go home to clean up his wife's piss and shit. Poor him.

A month later, Ma told me that Mr Srisak's wife had passed away after many years of torment. Fortunately, they had no children. A man of unwavering determination and good nature like Mr Srisak would have no trouble finding a new wife. Any woman would want to have him.

The following month, Mr Srisak came back to our house on his usual rounds. He looked at me once more, eyes gleaming with intent, poised as if to speak but remaining silent. Finally, he opened his mouth, words flowering from his lips. Quietly, he asked whether I still wanted to go see the market. Ma turned to him and said, 'Oh, take her so she can finally see what it's like.'

That day, I got to sit in his truck as he drove us into the centre of Udon. He took me around the market; I was breathless with excitement, but the villagers seemed even more excited than I was. They watched me as we pulled away in that expensive car. It was the first time I had ever been that far from the house. Mr Srisak drove me back home. He bought me a bracelet.

This must be what it feels like to be a heroine, I thought.

A month later, Pa spoke with me. I was turning seventeen that year, he said. I was reaching full maturity, I was becoming a woman; Pa and Ma's daughter had grown into her prime, he said, and it was all thanks to their impeccable care. Now, it was time for them to pass on the love I had given them both. It was time for me to demonstrate my gratitude towards my parents by going to live with Mr Srisak.

'But who'll take care of you, Pa and Ma?' I asked.

'Oh, don't worry about us,' he said in Lao. 'Now you take care of Mr Srisak so he can take care of us too.'

Pa told me to be obedient to him, just as I had been to my parents. From this point on, those things I had never known would make themselves known to me.

'Do whatever he says and you'll learn how to do things in no time,' Ma said.

I was quiet with nerves. I had been with Pa and Ma my whole life, and, now, I was going off to live with someone else. I told Pa and Ma my worries. How was I any different from my other siblings, who had left them before? Tears streamed down my cheeks.

Pa consoled me. I wasn't like my siblings, he said. My siblings had run away from home, they had cost Pa and Ma money and land, they had brought only trouble and shame. But in my case, Pa and Ma were sending me away by choice. They had my dowry in return. My marriage relieved them of their burdens. I was an exemplary daughter.

Hearing this, I felt relieved. I wiped my tears away with the back of my hand.

'You'll never be cold again,' Pa said.

From that point on, my journey from the highlands of Isan to the lowlands of central Thailand began.

Life lessons

There were many things I was yet to see or know. My eyes drifted to the scenery on either side of the road as Mr Srisak's pick-up truck slowly drove us into the lowlands. The sight was spectacular, but there was something unsettling about it, because the journey seemed endless. It looked like Mr Srisak was taking me further and further away from my parents' embrace, towards the very edge of the earth. Misery bloomed in me, like something kneading and squeezing my heart until my chest grew tight. Several times throughout the journey, I had to turn my face away from Mr Srisak, leaning my head against the window and pretending to stare vacantly as I swallowed my tears and sobs.

Mr Srisak was a man of few words. He always had been that way: from before we got married, to when we lived together, to when he died. His silent, solemn demeanour was constant. When he did speak, his way of speaking and the tone of his voice conveyed an air of authority, commanding me to listen and obey. Honestly, his words could be better described as instructions, or orders. Everything he uttered was meant as a lesson: something to be followed, and ultimately accepted as true. He was older and wiser than me, so he could tell right from wrong. Pa and Ma had also told me again and again that everything would be fine as long as I obeyed and loved him. Obeying one's superior was crucial to a harmonious marriage.

'Dao,' he called, as I tried to hide my sobs. 'Dao,' he repeated.

'Mm,' I responded.

'Look at me,' he commanded.

I turned my face towards him. Tears streamed down my cheeks.

'When I call you, you must look at me and pay attention to what I'm saying. Do you understand?' He looked at me for a moment before turning back to the road. I nodded, but he missed it. 'Well? Do you understand?'

'Mm,' I replied.

'Yes,' he said. 'No more "mms" when you're with me. From now on, you must respond with a "yes" when I speak to you. Do you understand?'

'Yes.'

'Very good,' he added. 'Where we're going, "mms" aren't acceptable. People won't understand you. You must answer "yes", or "yes?" if you don't understand something.'

I was confused.

'You say "yes" when you understand, or "yes?" when you don't.'

'Mm,' I replied.

Mr Srisak turned to me with a dissatisfied glare. He let out an agitated exhale before pulling the truck over onto the left side of the road. He leaned towards me, winding the car window down on my side with one hand.

'Spit it out,' he commanded.

'Spit what out?'

'Spit out that "mm" of yours right now.'

He was so serious that it frightened me. When he said 'now', I spat out the window.

'Leave your "mms" here for good. When we reach my house, there will be no more "mms". Do you understand?'

'Yes,' I replied promptly.

From that day on, the word 'yes' became second nature to me. It was not because I had spat my 'mm' out the window, but because every time I heard him say, 'Do you understand?' I would automatically say 'yes'. Where 'Do you understand?' was, 'yes' would follow.

He commanded me to pull the window up as he steered the truck back onto the road.

'One more thing. I will only call your name once. Don't let me repeat myself over and over again. As soon as I call your name, you should immediately say . . . ' He paused.

'Mm—yes.' *That was close*, I thought.

'Very good,' he said approvingly. 'Now kiss me on the cheek.'

I was still baffled, but I did as he said.

'This is your gift for behaving as you should. When you behave well, you get to kiss my cheek,' he explained.

Making him smile made me so happy. He looked like a hero when he smiled, and when I made him smile, it made me feel like a heroine.

I was in awe of him. He had the power to make me forget my own sorrows. No long ago, I had been worried about my parents—worrying that I might never see them again—and those worries truly felt real to me. But Mr Srisak pulled me out from the depths of my despair and made me focus on other things. This miraculous power of his had dried my tears and quieted my sobs without me even realizing it. It was as if he had opened a window into my heart, letting light into a place that had been dark for so long. He introduced me to the pleasure of admiration. He let me kiss him on the cheek as a reward, stirring a tingling sensation I'd never felt before.

'You mustn't cry from now on. No one is dead and nothing is lost. Do you understand?'

'Yes.'

'You're about to start a new life, Dao. You're going to start a family with me. You've stepped out of your parents' embrace and into mine. There's nothing to worry about. Everything is the same. Everything you did for your parents, you will continue to do. The only difference is that you are devoted to me now. Do you understand?'

'Yes.'

'Your parents already told you this, didn't they? From now on, you must give me the love, care, attention, sincerity, and obedience you once gave them,' he said, before pausing for a moment. 'It's that simple. The only thing that has changed is the person you are offering your love and admiration to. All the things you gave to your parents when you were young: now, you pass them onto your husband. Do you understand?'

'Yes.'

'The building of a life between husband and wife: that's what marriage is. You have grown from a child into an adult. Soon, you will become someone's mother and I will become someone's father; the same way your parents came together to become a mother and father, to give birth to you and to raise you to one day become a mother yourself, to give birth to another generation. Do you understand?'

'Yes.' I did not understand at all.

'It's okay if you don't understand everything right now, because you didn't go to school. But you don't have to worry. I'll teach you, and you will learn, and you will remember.'

I said nothing, my eyes fixed on the road ahead.

'Dao,' he called.

I turned to look at him.

'Very good,' he commended.

It wasn't that I didn't understand what he was saying. It was just that his manner of speaking made things seem more complicated than they were. His words were inaccessible, even though he wanted me to understand them. Like the proud and determined hero he was, he would rather hold his hands behind his back and stare straight into the horizon than stoop to the same level as his heroine. It was she who would have to stand on her tiptoes and wrap her arms around his neck, pleading with him to lean over just a little—bending him down like a tree branch bearing fruit ripe for picking—so that their lips might osculate just so. Mr Srisak behaved the way heroes behaved towards heroines in the radio dramas I'd listened to.

In actual fact, there was no need for Mr Srisak to bother teaching me with all those complicated words. If only he had uttered these words: 'Dao, we are fated to be together, just as a hero and heroine should be. Everything will happen as it does in the radio dramas. All you have to do is perform the way the heroines do, and I'll do as the heroes do.' Just like that, I would have been able to picture it all. I would have understood everything, and I would have known just how to carry myself.

And this was yet another of Mr Srisak's amazing talents. Thanks to him and his convoluted words, I'd been able to recall the heroes and heroines from the radio dramas. He guided me towards finding the appropriate role for myself. Once again, I was overwhelmed with admiration for him. My ingenious hero!

The first lesson I received from him on that journey from Isan was our first and last long conversation. He never wasted words again. From that day on, he communicated with pointed fingers and fierce stares. His gaze always dissolved something in me.

And so, our journey finally came to an end. I moved to a new place called Kaeng Khoi District in Saraburi Province. He told me we were now in central Thailand. I looked over at him and nodded in response. He drove the truck onto a dirt road and stopped before long in front of a corrugated iron gate. Mr Srisak searched his trouser pockets, handed me a set of keys, and told me to open the gate for him. I got out of the truck and unlocked the gate. As he drove the car past the gates, I took the chance to study the house. It was a large, two-storey wooden house. It seemed dark and gloomy, but perhaps that was because it was already evening by the time we arrived. That would explain the unsettling air. He got out of the truck and told me to close and lock the gate. That was when I came to my senses: I'd been too busy gazing at the house to realize that the house was staring back at me with the same menacing glare that he had. Or was it the spirit of his late wife gazing down at me? A shiver ran down my spine at the thought.

Walking from the gate to the house, I was struck with loneliness. He must have noticed, because he called me over. 'This is my house, and now it's yours too,' he said. 'There's nothing to be afraid of. You'll soon get used to it.' He knew everything felt strange and new, that he was my only constant, my only comfort. He pointed at a light switch on one of the posts near the front steps and turned it on. The eaves of the house lit up and the gloom vanished. He led me up the steps and into the house, pointing out where all the light switches were. That was his way of telling me that it was now my duty to turn them on.

The inside of the house was brightly lit. The dark was driven away, and as he acquainted me with the house, so were my worries.

He leaned against a sofa in the middle of the room and sighed. Standing by the wall, I unlatched one of the windows to let the breeze in. He let out another sigh, this time of approval. I opened the rest of the windows and saw a spirit house set on the edge of the land. I told Mr Srisak I wanted to pay my respects as a new resident. 'Whatever makes you happy,' he said. I made sure to pour him a glass of cold water before I went.

'I expect a cold glass of water every time I come home. Do you understand?' Another lesson.

'Yes,' I replied.

Probation

Mr Srisak would leave all day for work, sometimes for several days at a time. When he arrived home, it wasn't just a matter of having his glass of cold water ready. I had a host of other precise duties I had to complete: all part of what you might call his welcoming ritual.

I never asked him about his day. (I didn't dare.) Only when he was in the mood to share did I learn anything about him, especially regarding his work. To my knowledge, his job involved regular visits to my village to buy fabric, but what he did with it afterwards was beyond me. He might have been a fabric merchant, driving his truck to collect goods to sell at a shop, or maybe he owned a warehouse somewhere. (Probably in Kaeng Khoi, since that was where we lived.) Every time he arrived, there would be a loud honk at the front gate: my cue to open it for him. He would get out of the car, exhausted. His mood was always hard to predict; every time, I would mentally prepare myself to accept him with good grace, whatever temperament he was in.

Once, he arrived back home and threw himself onto his favourite sofa. When I brought him his glass of cold water, he looked at me, agitated, before knocking the glass out of my hands. Fortunately, the glass didn't break. He told me he wanted a beer tonight, and to fetch it for him. So that was what I did. I poured out a beer and passed it to him, and he calmed down.

'I had a bad day today,' he explained. He took another sip. 'That's why I'm in a bad mood.'

I nodded in response.

'The outside world is miserable. You can't trust anyone. You'll never know when you'll get stabbed in the back.' He was quiet for a while, before he turned to me. 'What are you looking at? Go and make me dinner. I'm hungry.'

I walked into the kitchen to prepare his dinner. I set it down on the table in front of the sofa.

'Come to think of it, I wish I was like you. You get to stay home all day and not deal with anyone.' He spooned some rice into his mouth, chewing with relish. 'But I'm the man. The head of the family. It's a responsibility I can't evade.' Feeling the magnitude of his importance, I felt a rush of gratitude. 'Your responsibility is to take care of the house while I go to work,' he said, before slurping some soup.

Then he took three hundred baht from his wallet.

'Spend it wisely,' he told me. 'It's my hard-earned money.'

'Yes,' I replied.

At the end of each week, he would give me my three-hundred-baht allowance for managing the household. Most of it was spent on groceries for his meals. I didn't need to go far to get fresh ingredients: I bought them off the back of a pick-up truck that drove past his house every morning.

My daily life was spent in and around the house. I kept to myself most of the time, and I didn't have any close friends (I still don't). I wasn't bothered by it, especially because I already felt my neighbours' eyes on me; observing me, as if I were a foreign object. They stared at me in silence every time we came out of our homes to buy groceries from the pick-up truck. Sometimes, when they walked past our front gate, they stopped to peer inside. They acted so suspiciously towards me that I couldn't help but feel too nervous to befriend any of them. They made me feel as if I were an outsider, and as a result, I never trusted them. To be honest, I'd lived alone ever since I was a child, so there was no reason for self-pity in this situation. Their distrustful behaviour also affirmed what Mr Srisak had told me before: that people can't be trusted. The frustration he brought back into the house every night made the prospect of going outside and meeting people more dangerous than appealing. And so, Mr Srisak became the only person upon whom I could truly rely.

Over time, the dilemma of whether to serve him cold water or beer became less of a dilemma. After observing his degree of agitation, which varied from day to day, I eventually developed a sixth sense for it. It's something you just learn when you live with someone. In fact, after three years of living together, I learned to make my own suggestion instead of waiting for his order: 'You look like you've worked hard today. You deserve a glass of beer.' I remember the first time I did it. He looked surprised at first, but then nodded in agreement. That night, he gifted me with the best present: he allowed me to kiss him all over his body. Nine months after that night, I gave birth to his second child.

But before we get to that story, allow me tell you about the ritual I had to perform for him before bed.

In the first few days of moving into the house, Mr Srisak constantly reminded me about the duties I had to perform. I know it sounds like he was incessant with his instruction, but actually, he only ever said things once. It was just that my duties as his wife surpassed those I had fulfilled as my parents' daughter.

So, what are the duties of a good wife? That was his big question. Housework was indeed essential, but the most important thing was to devote all her attention to her husband when he returned home. She must tidy the house and prepare a glass of cold water to welcome him with, and she must prepare clean towels and clean clothes once he has showered. While he's in the shower, a good wife must prepare her husband's dinner, or reheat what she made earlier: that which has since grown cold. Dinner must be served hot at all times. This was the welcoming ritual.

Once her husband's dinner is finished, a good wife must clear all the dirty dishes from the table and wash them in the kitchen. While he sinks into his sofa to watch television, her duties continue. Once she's done with the dishes, she must turn down the bed, put up the mosquito net, and open all the windows to let the breeze in. Once her husband decides it is time for bed, he comes into the bedroom and sits on the edge of the bed. The first day of the ritual, he called me over to sit at his feet.

'My hands and feet have endured a hard day's work,' he began. 'Hands and feet are a husband's survival tools. They're what he uses to fend for his wife and children. Without them, his wife and children would suffer. Do you understand?'

'Yes,' I replied.

'In India, there is a custom; something a wife does for her husband.' As he explained, he kept switching between the words 'man' and 'husband', between 'woman' and 'wife'. Only he could use the words 'man' and 'woman'—I was only allowed to use 'husband' and 'wife'— but I'll explain that another time. He continued.

'To demonstrate her reverence towards her husband—for it is he who supports his family without complaint—a wife bathes her husband's hands and feet before he goes to bed. It's an admirable tradition that has been passed down from many generations to the present day. I think it's an excellent way to give thanks to one other as husband and wife. You express your gratitude to me and, in return, I feel thankful.'

He paused for a moment and looked at me. I knew immediately that he wanted me to respond, so I complied. 'Yes, I understand.'

'We live in a Buddhist country. Thai people are Buddhists. We believe in karma, in good and evil, in ghosts and divine entities: all of which we learned from the teachings of the Lord Buddha. But you know, Buddhism originated not in Thailand, but in . . . ' He paused.

'Yes?'

'In India,' he said. 'Thousands of years ago, monks from India travelled to this land to impart the teachings of Lord Buddha, which spread throughout what we now know as Thailand, Myanmar, Laos, and Cambodia. Because His teachings provided virtuous moral guidance to people, the Lord Buddha continues to be worshipped until the present day. If Buddhism was destined to be practiced by Thai people, then this traditional Indian custom must be destined for Thai women to perform for their husbands.'

He commanded me to fetch a bowl of water and a clean towel. I was told to begin by rinsing both his hands, followed by his feet, before patting everything dry with a towel. As I crouched down, my eyes focused on the bathing of his feet, I could sense that he was looking at me with great approval.

After drying his hands and feet, as I went to take the bowl back to the kitchen, he called my name. I turned my gaze to meet his.

'I feel so very thankful,' he said, smiling. 'Now, you're not just any ordinary wife. You're an honourable one.'

Hearing him bestow those words upon me was the greatest honour. This must be how it feels to be someone's honourable wife, I thought. It was a title to which all women aspire. That's what the heroines from the radio dramas would say, and I couldn't have agreed with them more.

'Remember this. You are an honourable wife now, just like the rest of them,' I told myself again and again. I hoped the radio drama heroine in me might hear it too.

Such is the life of a heroine. They all have to go through the same ordeal—and I really believed this, back then—the ordeal of overcoming the obstacle of incomprehension. Heroines are so often misunderstood and miscast by the heroes, thanks to the villainesses who mislead them, whispering nonsense into their ears. In my case, even if the villainess had yet to enter the scene, she was out there in the world, hiding amongst the people who peered into our house. My hero wasn't stupid—although I secretly thought he wasn't particularly perceptive, either—he knew that there were people waiting to 'stab him in the back': an expression that I understood he did not mean literally. Rather, he meant that there were people out there who were dishonest, manipulative; constantly winding him up. And that was why he always projected his anger onto me.

But being bestowed with the grand title of 'honourable wife' by your husband doesn't mean you get to keep it. Sometimes, he took it back—he'd stop calling me it—and sometimes, he gave it back when I pleased him. The title came and went throughout our marriage, and a woman like me couldn't help but feel anxious about when this status might be taken away or given back to me.

When I was first bestowed with the 'honourable wife' title, I was pleased with myself. I was able to settle into my proper role within the household, and quite quickly too, if I may say so myself. It was perhaps this complacency that lowered my guard, made me less careful with my words. I started inserting myself into my responses to his commands; my confidence made me go from a single 'yes' to 'yes, I understand'. The title of the honourable wife brought with it more and more self-importance on my part.

One evening, four or five months after moving into his home, I served him his dinner in front of the sofa as usual. He looked at the food laid out in front of him, bored. It was true that I made certain dishes more often than others, but I tried to vary what I made for him each day. I was sure that my food was always tasty. His disinterest confused me. Then, he said:

'I'm starting to get bored of Isan food.' His eyebrows knitted together. 'I can't have it every single meal. You need to learn how to cook central Thai dishes.'

I listened quietly, knowing that he had more to say.

'I'm from central Thailand, and now you are too. You should have learned how to cook our kind of food by now, instead of feeding me Lao food all the time.'

'Ma and Pa liked it,' I told him. I hadn't meant to challenge him; what I meant to explain was that I made the same food for my husband now as I had for my parents. In my mind, they were of equal eminence.

But he kept staring at me, his eyes cold and hard, as if he were about to pounce and tear me to pieces right on the spot.

'Are you arguing with me?' he raised his voice.

Startled, I shook my head.

'That's right. Don't even dare to think about it.' When he saw that I had meant no harm, his voice softened. 'I want you to be able to cook central Thai food because you're no longer Lao. You're my wife and you live here in central Thailand.' Then his rage surged again, and he was shouting once more. 'Do you understand?'

The complacency that came with the 'honourable wife' title was one thing. The way he kept hammering the words 'Isan' and 'Lao' at me also threw me off guard. As soon as he roared 'Do you understand?', my instinctive response was to panic. I had already wronged him once, and in that state of embarrassment and confusion, I dug a deeper hole for myself. Why it had to be at that precise moment, I really do not know, but in that moment, I slipped and added the Lao word 'khoi'— meaning 'I'—to my response:

'Yes, khoi understand.'

Immediately, the clap of thunder was followed by a lightning strike.

He hit me in the face so hard that I collapsed onto the floor, landing on my backside.

'That's it! I've had enough!' he bellowed. 'Never say "khoi" in this household. It is "I", and only "I". Do you understand?'

'Yes,' I said in tears. 'Yes, I understand.'

'"Mother". "Father". "Husband". "Wife". Educate yourself. There's a television here, so learn to watch it. No more Lao from now on. You must speak the language of the civilized, of the noble. Do you understand?'

'Yes, I understand.'

'This is your punishment,' he said, inhaling deeply. His tone started to soften, transitioning from tirade to lecture. 'When you do something wrong, you will be punished. Punishment is the consequence of wrongdoing. It's cause and effect. The fact that you failed to behave appropriately—that you challenged the authority of the homeowner and broke the rules and regulations of this house, even though this house provides you with a roof over your head—is unacceptable. It is wrong, and you must be punished for it, and that is what I have done. Remember this. This kind of incident would never have happened if you hadn't argued with me.'

'Yes. It's my fault.'

'Very good. You've admitted that you were wrong.' he smiled, satisfied.

After that, he would call me over to sit by him every time he had his dinner. He would teach me how to speak properly, how to call things by their proper names. The rage he displayed that day evaporated completely. He explained why he was entitled to a wider vocabulary than I was. Take what he called me, for instance. He could call me by my name, Dao, as well as a whole range of other things, depending on the situation. (The following year, he called me a bitch, but my behaviour had warranted it.) But I had no right to use those sorts of words. I was only to use 'I' when referring to myself, and 'dear husband' when referring to him. We didn't 'eat' dinner, we 'dined'; we watched the 'television', not the 'TV'. I had to remember to use appropriate language in all my conversations with him. That was one of the conditions of building a life as husband and wife.

The first golden boy-child

Not long after my punishment, he did something strange. He told me one afternoon that I didn't have to make dinner that evening, because he was taking me out. He told me to put on my best dress—or whatever

I considered 'best' from my wardrobe, although he did grumble that I ought to have a best dress for occasions like this—before unlocking a little box he kept hidden inside a large cabinet. From it, he took out a gold necklace for me to wear. He looked quite dapper himself, dressed in a short-sleeved, pale yellow shirt over navy trousers, a gold watch with a black leather strap around his right wrist. His hair was pomade-slick, parted to show off his broad forehead. With his deeply tanned complexion, he looked strikingly handsome.

He drove me into the centre of Saraburi in his pick-up truck. I got to experience the flashing city lights—the hustle and bustle, the buying and selling of it all—for the second time. It might have all seemed spectacular, but in truth, the city made me feel tense, small. Everyone looked beautiful, but I could feel their eyes on me; looking down on me, looking straight past me. I didn't quite know how to act anyway, but the level of scrutiny made my behaviour seem all the more inappropriate. Fortunately, I had Mr Srisak by my side. He helped me compose myself, telling me exactly what to do and what rules to follow in the most orderly manner. In fact, my beloved hero had the natural demeanour of those city folk, as if he were their equal.

Mr Srisak took me into a crowded Chinese restaurant. It was one of the province's most famous places, he told me. He ordered Peking duck, stewed pork leg, and baked shrimp with glass noodles, among other dishes. He taught me how to use chopsticks, but I managed so poorly that he had to ask the waitress to replace mine with a fork and spoon. He showed me how to eat each dish, what to eat before and after, portioning the food onto my plate before proceeding to eat his own in the most natural way possible. He loudly slurped up the glass noodles, resting his chopsticks unselfconsciously on the table so he could peel the shrimp with his hands. I would have looked ridiculous doing the same and he knew it, so he peeled them for me, placing them on my plate.

When he noticed that I'd only taken a few bites of everything, he asked, without bothering to listen to my response, why I wasn't eating more of the food. He kept saying how rare it was to be able to eat this kind of food, that this kind of food was only for special occasions. The way he carried on made me realize that the fact he had brought me here, to this kind of restaurant, meant that this was a special occasion. So with each word he said, I shoved more food into my mouth. To be honest, the food didn't sit right with me at all. Everything was greasy. Each bite made me feel sick. What about this meal made it so special, I wondered? There were no vegetables. It was spicy, sour, sweet, fatty, and hot, all at the same time: completely different from the food I made for us at home, where everything was well-rounded, with vegetables to cleanse the palate. What made this greasy food so much better?

Surely, there had to be a purpose to our visit. As we ate, he started asking me questions about the ingredients in each dish: how I thought they were prepared, whether I could tell one method of cooking from another. I could figure out some of the dishes, like the baked shrimp with glass noodles: noodles, shrimp, pork belly pieces, whole black peppercorns, garlic, ginger, and dark soy sauce. But I had no idea how to make a dish like the Peking duck. He assured me that I didn't need to worry about preparing such a difficult dish. He only brought me here to introduce me to more diverse types of food, so I could occasionally make them for him at home. I was confident that I could make him baked shrimp with glass noodles, but the pick-up truck that sold fresh ingredients never had shrimp. That meant I'd have to go to the fresh market for certain ingredients.

Mr Srisak looked very pleased with me. He told me I was sharp, that I was a fast learner, which was unusual for someone who had never gone to school. Some people learn better from experience, he said.

'Life is like school,' he said. 'You're the student, and I'm the teacher.'

'Yes,' I responded.

'You deserve a reward,' he said.

He ordered Chinese beans in syrup for dessert, to cleanse the palate.

When we arrived home that night, he hurried me into the house and told me not to bother with our usual ritual of bathing his hands and feet, insisting that we get ready for bed. This was always a sign that he was aroused. Usually, I would be the one to start, pecking him on his cheek, and he'd do the same to mine before kissing me all over. Then he would mount me until he was satisfied. But this time, when I pecked him on the cheek, he moaned gently and lay still. I continued kissing his cheek, his neck, his lips. He told me to undress him and kiss him all over his chest, down to his belly. His entire body was quivering, like someone about to pass out from lack of air. He instructed me to caress his lingam with my fingers and lips, and I did so. In the dim light of the bedroom, I could just make out his facial expression. He looked as if he'd eaten something spicy and so delicious that he couldn't stop eating it. He only wanted more and more.

He told me to climb on top of him and slowly take him inside me. I'd never done it this way before, so I fumbled my way through it, but he was too enraptured to say anything, and I was too. I felt a deep, warm sensation. It felt good to be in charge of him, even for a moment. I was in complete control as I mounted him, watching as he moaned desperately. He grew soft in front of my eyes and quickly fell asleep. Perhaps he was only pretending to sleep out of embarrassment. The next morning, he said nothing about the intense pleasure he'd felt. He resumed his role as the hero with no taste for spicy food, convincing himself that sex was nothing but a duty he had to perform with his wife solely for reproductive purposes. He didn't develop a taste for the piquant fire of lust. (I, for what it was worth, ought to take better control of my desire, and know my place.) He forbade me from making such jokes in the light of day. (He tried hard to repress it, but he liked it, and I knew it.) As time passed, he eventually got what he claimed was all he wanted. I became pregnant and gave birth to his first child.

He was the first golden boy-child. He was his father in miniature. They shared everything from appearance to complexion to personality. My son behaved just as his father did, constantly asking for things and demanding things from me. Having to raise my son while also looking after his father was no laughing matter.

Perhaps it was because I was new to motherhood, but the child was impossible. (So different from the two younger brothers that followed.) He was spoiled and bad-tempered; he cried all day and all night, and he bit me when he suckled. He was also sickly, catching illness after illness. It was as if he wanted all the attention in the world for himself.

He was truly his father's son. By this, I mean that he was a second Mr Srisak; Mr Srisak trapped in the body of a child. Having two Srisaks in the house . . . Well, you can imagine what it was like. He stole my attention away from his father almost immediately after he was born. Father and son, fighting for ownership over their lone serf. (Oh, dear. There, I finally said it. It was years until I realized I was nothing but a serf to them both.)

In my mind, father and son were a matched set, and they sent my head spinning. Many years later, his father would die, and my son would take up the mantle without pause, inheriting his ways and carrying on in his place. That's what I mean when I say they were a perfect pair.

And yet, father and son were also perfectly matched rivals. Two people who want the same thing from one person will always end up stepping on each other's toes. Mr Srisak had expressed dissatisfaction towards his son ever since he was a baby. Our child, it turned out, would be my only stumbling block when it came to keeping hearth and home and husband. It was a pill Mr Srisak had no choice but to swallow; this was, after all, his own flesh and blood. He had to yield. That said, it didn't take long for him to return to his grumbling and pontificating and finger-pointing. A baby, he said, wasn't an excuse for not doing my chores. Every honourable wife, he believed, ought to be capable of doing both at the same time. Other wives weren't like this. (Oh, my darling husband! All the honourable wives in those soap operas had wet nurses and nannies to help them. At this point, I'd grown brave enough to talk back to him in my head.) Later, he would take it out on the baby. 'What in the hell does this damn baby want? Just wait until you're older, and I'll teach you a lesson!'

In short, the boy was destined to be another Mr Srisak. Mr Srisak must have known this, for he raised his son within his own exact parameters. If his son disobeyed him, he punished him. The parameters and punishments he set out for his son were no different than he ones he had set out for me.

His father wasn't the only one with the authority to punish his child. I had the same rights. He was my flesh and blood too. I was harsh on him, I will admit, but he was my first child. I didn't yet know how to be a mother. I blame my behaviour on my ignorance. He bit my nipples every time he fed. I was sore beyond belief. When it became too much for me, I rubbed some menthol balm on them. He fussed, wanting to suckle. I told him he couldn't—no, you can't, it hurts—but he refused to settle. His little fists batted back and forth, grabbing my breasts. Suit yourself. He tasted the balm on my nipples and recoiled, grimacing. 'Remember this. Never bite your mother's nipples again.'

My punishments took many forms. When we were alone together, he would clamour for my attention as I tried to finish the housework before his father arrived home. His father's needs were my first priority—that goes without saying—so whenever the baby fussed, I would point my finger him and scream at the top of my lungs. He'd hiccup, startled, before falling silent. As time wore on, this approach stopped working, and I was forced to resort to physical measures. Physical punishment was necessary, just as it was when his father punished me. Punishments teach you not to make the same mistakes again. If Mr Srisak's methods of punishment worked on me, they should work on the baby. With this in mind, I varied between pinching him and slapping him on the mouth.

Everything I did was for his father's sake, for his peace of mind when he returned home. When there wasn't a child weeping, the house was his haven. Everything I did, I did for my husband, to make sure everything was in its proper place for him.

After all, wasn't it my husband who threatened to punish our son when he became too much to bear? I was merely delivering the punishments before his father could. It was better for me to handle our son rather than to leave him to his father's harder hand.

And this son really was a menace. He would stare at me, plotting his revenge. I was sure the taste of menthol balm—not to mention all the ways I had pinched and hit him—lived vividly in his memory. Instead of teaching him a lesson, or making him feel remorse, my punishments fed his silent desire for vengeance, which he might wreak at any time. His behaviour changed. He no longer cried when we were alone together; instead, he waited for when his father got home. Do you see now how spoiled this baby was? And so, one day, his father couldn't stand the crying any longer. He crossed to the cradle, picked the baby up, and shook him. That's when he noticed the bruises scattered across his arms and legs. He asked me what they were. I told him they were mosquito bites, but he was unconvinced. Mosquito bites are red, he said. I told him the baby often thrashed about during his tantrums. Sometimes, he hit the bars of his cradle; sometimes, when I wasn't looking, he fell right off. 'That's not true.'

His father was absolutely certain. In truth, he'd known the minute I gave my first answer, and now he began to cross-examine me more thoroughly. 'Have you turned into a liar?' I panicked, denying everything, but he continued to bombard me with questions. What had I done? What hadn't I done? Exactly how had I done it? Eventually, I was forced to confess.

'Did you hurt my son?' he barked.

'I didn't,' I protested.

'Then where are these bruises from?' he raised his voice.

'Punishment.'

'You cunt!' he roared.

With the baby in his arms, he rushed at me and slapped me hard across the face.

'You have no right to punish my son. Your job is to look after him, not to punish him. Get that into your thick skull!'

'Yes. Yes, I understand,' I mumbled, scarcely audible.

In my mind, I fought back. This baby was my son too, I said silently. Aloud, there was nothing I could do but endure his orders. Worse still—I can remember it still, and I shudder every time I do— the baby, wrapped in his father's arms, chuckled with satisfaction the moment I was cowed into obedience. 'Yes. Yes, I understand.'

And so, finally, that baby had his revenge on his mother.

The second golden boy-child

Remember what hurts, and don't let it happen again. This was my mantra. I had learned so much from my first child. I had received my rightful punishment. I told myself I wouldn't make the same mistakes again with my second.

Even on days when I was overwhelmed with taking care of the house and the baby, I would have a little time to myself when my son napped. During this time—free from my duties to my house, my son, and my husband—I would learn more from watching television.

After having my first child, the television became a close friend of mine, and over time, our relationship blossomed. Before my child was born, I'd been apprehensive of the television: partly because I was barely acquainted with it, and partly because it belonged to Mr Srisak. The only time I touched it was when I had to clean it. Once Mr Srisak gave me permission to use it, I felt more at ease, but I was still unsure about it. When Mr Srisak watched television, I watched him instead: the way he turned it on and off, the way he changed the channels.

Mr Srisak liked to watch the news, game shows, and comedy shows. Sometimes, he'd listen to *luk krung* songs. On Sundays, he'd be glued to the television while I secretly listened to my radio dramas or *luk thung* music in the kitchen. Sometimes he'd yell across the room for me to turn the volume down when my noise interfered with his television. This was how it was.

One day, a pick-up truck parked in front of our house. A group of workers arrived, armed with a television antenna, and spent half the day installing it. After rewiring everything, connecting this cable here and this cable there, they replaced our old television with a brand new one. One of the workers stood in front of the television, shouting up at another, who was on the roof. When the screen finally flickered to life, a smug expression crossed his face. Mr Srisak looked the most smug of them all. Admittedly, I too was excited when I saw the image that appeared on the screen was in colour. I saw skin the colour of skin, trees and fields the colour of trees and fields. Things were no longer black and white. The first colour television came into our house when my firstborn was about a year old.

Needless to say, I became a woman obsessed. Yes, everything was now in colour, but as I flicked through the channels, I made an important discovery. In addition to the news, and the game shows, and the music, there were soap operas on television too. The stories I had once listened to, had once imagined for myself, were now brilliantly projected into images. So that's what the heroes look like. And that's what the heroines look like. And there are the villainesses, and the villains, and the mansions. Seeing all this sharpened my understanding. Everything was clearer, more real. The heroes and heroines had glowing complexions, like celestial bodies in bad disguises. Mr Srisak had taught me the proper word for 'fruit', which sounded the way they looked on the screen: artfully arranged on plates, set beautifully on tables. I learned a lot about proper words and idioms from the television.

Not only did the television broaden my horizons, bringing a distant world closer to my own, it also brought me closer to my neighbours.

One day, when I was sifting through produce from the pick-up truck parked outside the house, I heard the vendor chatting with some of her other customers about the soap that had been on last night. She always talked to her customers, but I'd never joined in before. Normally, I just gestured silently at the items that I wanted before paying for them and rushing back inside the house. However, the next day, I heard them discussing the previous night's episode. The finale was approaching, they said, and all the show's secrets and dilemmas would soon be revealed and resolved. 'We' (if I may use this pronoun) were all trying to guess at the ending; when one of the other customers saw me nodding along, he said:

'Did you watch it too?'

'Yes, I did,' I replied.

That was the first time I ever spoke to a complete stranger. They were surprised by my answer, I noticed.

'Dear me,' they whispered, giggling amongst themselves. 'She sounds like a true aristocrat!'

In the days that followed, these strangers began to greet me with more enthusiasm, adding an extra word or two each time we met. When a new show began, we would talk about it. When one of the strangers didn't turn up to shop at the usual time, I asked the vendor where they were. The vendor replied with a little grin.

'Strangers? You're all neighbours here!'

I felt the word warm my heart. From that day onwards, I began to call these people my neighbours.

The more we chatted, the friendlier they became, asking me questions about this and that.

'What are you cooking for your husband this evening, madam?'

'Oh, chicken massaman curry, perhaps,' I responded.

When I listened to my neighbours chatting amongst themselves, one thing I noticed was the language they used with one another. They spoke in fighting words, as if they were angry at each other, referring to their husbands as 'that bastard', and 'that son of a bitch', and all sorts of other impolite names. I felt slightly more reassured by the fact that they addressed me more politely as 'madam' or 'lady', and referred to Mr Srisak as 'master'. They even complimented me, saying how fortunate my husband was to have such a caring wife, even when he was hardly home. I flushed at their compliments, looking down to hide the smile on my face.

Not long afterwards, a neighbour called Auntie Yeun started asking me about the property that Mr Srisak owned. She offered to ask her husband for his help getting rid of all the weeds, as it was part of his day job anyway. Standing there with her, I looked through the fence to our home behind, confused. I could hardly see any weeds growing at all, and if any did appear, I could remove them myself easily. Auntie Yeun realized I had misunderstood. She was talking about the land on the other side of the fence, she explained, gesturing towards it. She was right. Over the fence, I could see gigantic trees—mango trees, chamcha trees, tamarind trees—and a ground so overgrown it looked almost impossible to walk through. But the land on the other side of the fence was not Mr Srisak's. I asked her why she would make such an offer to me.

'Oh, madam, you've been stuck inside that house too long! All that land there belongs to your husband. Didn't you know?'

I was shocked to hear this from a neighbour.

There was one time where I left the house with a black eye to meet the grocery truck. When one of the neighbours saw me, she exclaimed: 'My God, madam! What happened to you? Your eye is all bruised!'

'Oh, I fell.'

'What! Did you fall face down on a stump or something? It looks just awful,' another neighbour said, unconvinced.

'You say it just like the heroines do in the soaps,' another one chimed in. 'A bruised eye can only mean one thing!'

They all began to talk about how cruel Mr Srisak was to me.

'Please don't blame my husband,' I said. 'I deserve to be punished.'

Poor you, they said, before adding that they would never let their husbands abuse them that way. They would rather die, they said. They would fight back.

Despite disagreeing with them, I was silent for the rest of the conversation. A good woman must accept that her husband may punish her if she has wronged him, and that he will tell her directly if she does so. It was impossible, not to mention inappropriate, to stand up to someone who cared for me and supported me. I was under his patronage, and if I didn't like the way he treated me, then I ought to give up everything he had given me. I ought to just leave his house and leave his property. The other important thing was that he was good to me and our family most of the time; say, 350 days out of the year. Was it really so difficult to put up with the other 15? Just 15 bad days?

I wasn't sure my neighbours would understand if I told them all this. I kept my thoughts to myself, allowing them to feel sorry for me. I was proud to be with Mr Srisak, to be protected by him: to have a good family, and a food home. He owned a lot of a land and he had a steady job. Clearly, acting the way he did brought him wealth and status. His life was always getting better and better, and because I was with him, mine was too. Looking around the neighbourhood, I didn't see any household doing as well as ours.

I kept my distance from the neighbours after that. I greeted them, but just enough to be polite. My husband was on the same page as me. When I told him about Auntie Yeun's offer to have her husband clear the weeds from his property, he was surprised. He hadn't expected me to socialize with the neighbours, he said, and he'd rather have workers do the job than have nosy neighbours snoop around his property. He warned me about those people. Outsiders can't be trusted, he said. They'd only befriended me because they wanted something from us.

'That Auntie Yeun only made friends with you to earn some money for her husband. Don't you see? Sniffing around other people's business.'

He became annoyed, and started to rant at me. 'Is my owning a lot of land a good reason for anyone to snoop around and tell you things'? It was as if I was also in the wrong for knowing about things beyond the four walls of our house.

To stop me from interacting with our neighbours, he told me to buy groceries from the fresh market in Kaeng Khoi instead. I nodded in compliance.

I started going to the fresh market more frequently after that. There was a local bus that went there and back, so the journey wasn't difficult. It normally took just half an hour. The only inconvenience was having to bring the baby with me. When I first saw the market, I was amazed by its size and all the things that were for sale. Surrounded by unfamiliar ingredients I'd never seen on the grocery truck, I didn't know where to start, but believe me when I say that a woman and a market become the best of friends very quickly. It's impossible for a woman to get lost in a market, even if it's her first time there.

Going to the fresh market allowed me to make a wider variety of dishes. Now, I could buy shrimp, crab, shellfish, all sorts of spices. If I didn't know how to make a particular dish, I could ask the vendors, who were always eager to tell me all the things one could do with their vegetables or a single kilo of blood cockles. Everyone there addressed me as 'madam', presumably due to my refined demeanour and how well I dressed. (As promised, Mr Srisak had bought me nice clothes for when I went out.) I also wore my gold necklace (with his permission) and other accessories: bracelets, a wristwatch, things Mr Srisak often bought for me after a punishment.

One evening, I prepared a lavish meal for us as I waited for him to return home from work. When I heard his car horn, I changed the television channel to his favourite and dashed down to open the front gate. After welcoming him inside, I watched him collapse onto his favourite sofa, exhausted and hungry. He asked what was for dinner. I took the opportunity to offer him a beer.

'You've been working hard all day. Why don't you have a beer, darling?'

He looked very surprised. 'That sounds good.'

I poured it into a glass (which I had kept frozen, to achieve the perfect icy consistency) and he gulped it down greedily. He burped so loudly that it made me smile, endeared. He laughed and said that today had been a good day, that everything had gone well. He grew animated once more after finishing his beer, and seemed pleased with how I treated him. I prepared dinner while he showered. His eyes widened when he saw the meal laid out before him. 'Oh, my darling wife!' That day, he had a much bigger appetite than usual.

After tucking our son into bed, I prepared the bowl for our bedtime ritual. I finished rinsing his feet and had barely patted them dry when he grabbed both my arms and kissed me passionately. It felt good to be wanted. I felt proud of myself for behaving so well that day. Everything had worked out in the end, for both of us. I began kissing him all over, savouring every touch, and we made love in the way that left both of us satisfied.

But it wasn't just the two of us who witnessed our pleasure than night. I wasn't sure if he had watched the whole thing unfold from the moment his father had returned home, but even if he had, he was probably too young to understand what was going on. That night, after we made love, I noticed our two-year-old son watching us from his bed. He was lying quietly, sucking his thumb and staring at us both. For a moment, his gaze made me shudder. My husband had fallen asleep as soon as he'd finished. He had no idea.

That was the night our second child was conceived.

The villainess arrives

As I said, Mr Srisak's second child was unlike his older brother in every way. He was chubby and pale. He didn't cry much, nor did he care for attention. I suppose you could say he inherited my looks, my complexion. It brought me great joy to hold him and raise him, but I soon realized that such present joy would be the cause of my future pain. The precious time I had with my baby boy flew by. He grew so quickly that all I wanted to do was to stop time, so he might stay my baby boy forever. Unfortunately, time stops for no one.

Srisak named him Chidchai. Chidchai learned to walk when he was two. I would clap my hands for his attention, so he would walk towards me. He could barely speak, and would occasionally dribble. He was absolutely adorable.

When my first child started going to the local nursery, he grew distant from me. His teacher dropped him home each afternoon on the school bus. That was when things at home grew more hectic. He was violent when he played with his baby brother, treating him as if he were a toy. He would force his baby brother down on his back, pressing his hands and feet hard against the floor until he couldn't move. Chidchai would cry, and I would divert his older brother's attention with other toys. On occasion, I had to bring the baby into the kitchen with me, keeping an eye on him while I cooked for his father, leaving the older one to play by himself at the front of the house.

Oh well, I reasoned with myself. Both boys would have to go to school soon. If only I could spend more time with my youngest.

I remember taking the bus into town every day when Chidchai started nursery. I would meet them both during their lunch break to feed them the lunch I'd prepared. It was difficult to be apart from them, at first. It took nearly a year for it to get better, and eventually, I was able to stop visiting them.

Once again, the house was taken over by silence.

Mr Srisak was rarely home. His schedule became more erratic in those later years. He used to be away from home a few days a week, but this changed to one week, two weeks at a time. When he did return home, I got the impression he'd only come back to see his two sons. He barely looked at me. I would make him a delicious dinner, but his mind was clearly elsewhere. I yearned for his kind words and compliments, but these no longer came. In fact, he didn't want to touch me at all.

He reminded me of the heroes from the soap operas, when they acted as if they didn't care as much as they did for the heroines. The hero would find flaws in his heroine, saying hurtful things to her and looking down on her background with derision. It was clear that the villainess was behind it all. She would seduce him with a love potion, or cast a spell, luring him to her with sweet words of deceit.

Sure enough, my husband soon brought another woman home.

She was one of his business contacts, he told me. The two of them planned to expand their fabric businesses together, through export. She was tall and gorgeous, with a powdered complexion, perfectly shaped brows, and striking red lips. She was fair-skinned, slender, curvaceous, eloquent: a city girl through and through, who could charm Srisak with her words, and I could tell he couldn't get enough of them. He had brought her home so she could try my food, he claimed. He told her I was the best cook. She seemed to enjoy the meal, giving me lots of compliments. Srisak drove her back to the city after dinner (that was where she lived, I suppose) and he didn't return home until two or three o'clock in the morning. His breath smelled like cigarettes and alcohol. There was an unfamiliar scent of soap.

The next day, Srisak told me he had brought her home so I could get acquainted with her beforehand.

Before what? I wanted to ask, but I didn't, and he didn't say anything more. The woman came to our house more frequently after that.

Oh, my poor soul. What could I do? I empathized deeply with the plight of the soap opera heroines. All I could do was keep these things to myself, but as time passed, anguish imploded into agony. Every night, I cried myself silently to sleep, feeling completely alone. I often held my children for comfort, drying my tears on the backs of my boys' necks as they slept soundly, innocently.

The woman was an unmistakable replica of the villainess. That was why I referred to her as such, in my head. She was always by my husband's side, staring after me as if I were her servant. It was pointless for me to try and get to know her; she had never helped with any of my chores, her hands had never touched dirty dishwater. The two of them always ate together, leaving a mess for me to clean up.

One day, Srisak said to me, 'I will ask Suda to come and live here with us.'

I was stunned. *How? Where?*

'As what?' I gathered my courage and asked him. Tears brimmed in my eyes.

'As my other woman,' he said, straight-faced. 'You are my wife, and she is my mistress.'

I shook my head, no longer able to hold back my tears.

'I feel like I'm the mistress here,' I wept.

There were many things I wanted to say, to vent, to ask. *Where do I stand in this house?* He rushed towards me and put his arms around me. It was something he taken to doing recently, but surprisingly, it made me feel a little better.

'You are not my mistress,' he said gently. 'This house is mine and also yours. You gave birth to my sons, who are very important to me. How could you possibly be just my mistress?'

Mustering my courage, I talked back once again. 'But why do you need another woman?' There was already a hero and a heroine. It would be scandalous for the villainess to come into the picture. 'Don't you think it's immoral?'

He was taken aback. He pushed me away. 'You don't know a thing. Don't start preaching me! There's nothing immoral about it. I've always provided for this family. I'm a man, and I'm entitled to some fun in life. Suda gives me pleasure. She is nothing more. You should be grateful I informed you ahead of time that she would be living here. I didn't need your permission.

Was he really asking for my permission? I could tell he was growing more furious. I looked at him nervously.

'What morals are you talking about anyway?'

'I heard about them on my shows.'

'Oh, your silly little shows?' he sneered. 'Those soap operas are full of hot air. Let me ask you a question. Are you saying that Indian men are immoral because they have a large number of wives? Well, look at that. Nothing to say? We don't even have to take it that far. Just look at those period dramas about the royals. Would you say that the kings in those dramas are immoral because they have many wives and concubines, all eager to please them? Do you believe those kings are immoral? Come on, then! Say something!'

I stayed quiet.

'These are simple comparisons. It is your duty to befriend Suda, so you may live together. It's your duty to do so. Do you understand?'

'Yes, I understand,' I said, swallowing.

From then on, Srisak occupied himself with renovations, hiring carpenters to add another bedroom to the house. He purchased a new bed frame, a mattress, a television, and many other things to furnish his new love nest. He watched with excitement as it slowly came together. He spent a lot of time in the unfinished room, daydreaming about its final completion. The huge bed frame he'd bought was in the centre of the room, piled high with sheets, pillowcases, and blankets, all carefully selected by him in lush, lovely colours.

Once the room was finished, he brought the villainess home. Take advantage of this opportunity, he told me. Get to know her. He had promised her a big surprise when she arrived. I think she was surprised indeed.

She went to the trouble of coming into the kitchen and striking up a conversation with me, asking what was for dinner and complimenting the food. I knew exactly what she wanted. I wanted nothing less than to play nice, but I did so anyway, to keep the peace and to keep Mr Srisak happy. She was so good at playing the nice girl, fluttering around the kitchen until Mr Srisak finally told her not to bother me, otherwise I wouldn't be able to concentrate and dinner wouldn't turn out as well. He took her to see their new room. The two of them disappeared into it for quite some time. Despite my best efforts to eavesdrop, they were so quiet that I couldn't hear a thing. I couldn't help but imagine what was going on inside, which disturbed me all the more.

Afterwards, she behaved strangely at dinner. As we ate—Srisak, our two children, the villainess and I—she didn't say a word, and nor did the person who had built her new room. The tension between them was palpable. Mr Srisak abruptly asked me to ask her if she had enjoyed dinner, to which she nodded and smiled. In short, the hero had to force the heroine into speaking with the villainess. I found it odd that they were no longer revelling in the act of speaking to one another.

After dinner, she went out to the terrace. (We were supposed to be something resembling family, but she didn't even bother to help clear the table.) The hero followed her outside, leaving the dishes to the heroine. I could hear them arguing outside. It seemed that the villainess was dissatisfied with their love nest. She wasn't his concubine like I was, she said. Wait, what? Why drag me into this? Typical. She was complicating things and stirring up drama, as villainess tend to do.

She told Mr Srisak she was free to do whatever she wanted, that she didn't have to worry about what others thought. (Well, of course she didn't!)

'Only your wife could tolerate this kind of treatment!' she exclaimed.

Me? What was wrong with me? What was I doing wrong? I was about to hurl these questions at her, when I heard her speak again.

'Don't you feel sorry for your wife?'

I was taken aback. I began to shake. My first thought was that she understood what I had to go through, and I felt comforted by this. But I dismissed the thought as quickly as it came. I wasn't going to fall for her poisonous words.

I pulled myself together. Mr Srisak is my husband. We have two children together. The right thing for me to do is to take his side. She was attacking him, so I had to defend him. I calmed myself down and carried the dishes into the kitchen, railing at the villainess in my head.

'Look at you. Srisak went so far as to build you a room, to give you a roof over your head. What more could you possibly want? Freedom? Oh, my dear. How could you be so stupid as to want what you don't deserve? You can't even see how much more devoted he is to you than to me.'

There was a sharp sensation in my chest. Envy is acidic, and it was tearing me apart. I felt my heart corrode.

The villainess never came back after that. Whether this was a good thing, I wasn't sure: Srisak was hardly ever home, and when he was, he looked miserable. I couldn't help but feel sorry for him.

Alas, I owe it all to the guardian spirits who live in our spirit house. I had prayed for them to protect me and my family from the villainess, if and when she dared to arrive. I pleaded with them to get rid of her and the troubles she brought with her. After they granted my wishes,

I went down to the spirit house and presented them with a succulent chicken, boiled whole.

The arrogant son

Mr Srisak spent his time away from home chasing after the villainess, or so I imagined. It wasn't exactly the same plot I had seen in the soap operas, where the woman clings to the hero in an attempt to seduce him, but there was something in the way Mr Srisak pined for her, trying everything he could to win her back, that reminded me of it. I could tell he was heartbroken when he returned home empty-handed. He kept telling himself that she had misunderstood him completely.

Srisak's business suffered as a result of their relationship. During dinner, he told me that his joint venture with the villainess was failing, that she was likely to flee with the money he had invested when they were in love. Mr Srisak's happiness had taken a grave turn, as had his financial stability, both of which had a large impact on our family. He became a gloomy, bad-tempered man. Not long afterwards, he decided to downsize his business, lamenting the state of the economy. Even though he told me I would never understand his problems, he continued to vent his worries and frustrations at me, at home.

Soon after, he took my gold necklace from me, selling it along with some other valuable assets. He then decided to sell some of his land, to sustain his business and to pay for household expenses.

Throughout those years, even when he was rarely home, he made it very clear that he was sick of me and of our children. To him, our very existence was a nuisance.

One night, he lost it. After tossing and turning in bed for some time, he suddenly sat up and said he was annoyed by the sound of our children breathing. It suffocated him, he said. They kept stealing his air.

'Can't they see that I'm dying? Every day, I toil away for my family, and they can't even let me breathe in peace? How dare they steal all the air from me? I can't take it anymore!' he howled.

I was frightened. I asked him what I should do. He ordered me to take the children away from him.

Both boys were crying at the sound of their father shouting. I tried to console them, telling them that if they didn't stop crying, their father would become even more upset. 'Hurry up, boys. Bring your blankets and pillows, and come with me. We'll find somewhere else to sleep.' I led them into the room Mr Srisak had built for his mistress. I lay down with my children, thinking I ought to stay with them until they both fell asleep. Even before the boys fell asleep, I could hear Mr Srisak snoring. I cuddled my younger son, gently patting his head; his brother, who had turned his back to me, soon nodded off. Relieved, I soon drifted off to sleep.

The next morning, Srisak was irritated with me because I had not returned to sleep with him in our bed. I told him I was worried he might feel suffocated. He looked angry, and told me to watch my mouth.

From that night on, what had once been their father's love nest became our children's bedroom.

According to Srisak, the boys were old enough to have their own bedroom, but I secretly disagreed. Chidchai had only just started his second year of primary school, but I couldn't cuddle him and fall asleep with him like I used to. Instead, he spent every day and night with his older brother, who had never cared for me, who continued to grow further apart from me with age. Chidchai always followed his older brother's lead. They enjoyed playing together. When sons reach a certain age, they no longer want to be close to their mother. This is common knowledge, however painful it might be.

I wanted another baby.

Babies gave me joy. They made me feel able to care for something. Without them, I felt unanchored; empty, lost. Watching my children grow up had been heartbreaking. Look at when they learn to run: the first thing they do is flee from their mother's embrace.

Just look at my two sons, my own flesh and blood. Each half my life, half my soul. We all look alike. But the older they grew, the less I saw myself in them. Let me tell you about my eldest.

As I said before, my eldest saw me as his enemy. He was Srisak disguised as a child, and this became all the more apparent as he grew older. It seemed as though everything he said or did was to hurt me. (I wonder how aware he was of this.) When he got home, for example, he would sprawl across the floor to do his homework. When I approached him to ask how he was, he would give me a condescending look, just like his father's, as if to say I wouldn't understand what he was studying anyway.

'Leave me alone,' he would say. 'Can't you see I'm busy with my homework? Go check on Chidchai and leave me alone.'

I'm not sure why my presence irritated him so much, but I persisted. I approached him again and again, asking how his day had been, if his teachers had complimented him, if he'd done well in his exams. This last question was one Srisak frequently asked his children. When I asked it, my eldest's response cut sharp as a knife.

'Even if I told you, you wouldn't know anything about it anyway.'

'How could I not know about it?' I argued back. 'I know I'd be delighted if my son did well in his exams.'

He said nothing, laughing at me.

I can't be the only one who thinks he thought me stupid. When I asked about his homework, he would brush me off as if I were a bothersome fly, because he knew I couldn't help him. 'You couldn't help even if you wanted to,' he once said. If he held his education in higher, grander regard than he did his mother, he was right. I couldn't help him.

It was unfortunate, the way he felt. He believed I was an obstacle on his path to knowledge. I remember quite clearly what he said to me once, when he was in fifth grade. He had been watching cartoons when I asked him to help with me with some chores. He had already finished his homework, he said, so he didn't have to do anything else. Doing chores was no longer his responsibility. It was as if education had elevated him beyond such menial tasks. When I heard this, I told him he was being unreasonable. As my son, he still had to do as I asked. He refused to give in. He had done his part, he said, and I should get back to doing mine.

'Let's do it this way,' he said. 'I'll do your chores for you, but you will have to do my homework for me. That seems fair.'

I didn't speak. It was incredibly rude of him to say such things. I heard the demon within him laugh at my silence.

'You can't do it, can you?' he taunted. 'It's because you can't read or write. How embarrassing is that?'

It cut deep.

But your child is always your child, even when they're possessed by something darker. There were times when I couldn't love him (I won't deny it) but the bond between mother and child can never be broken. When your child is in pain, he will cry for you. It's an instinctive cry, one he may not even be aware of. When that call comes, will you—his mother—despise him still?

When your son misbehaves or does something despicable, only you, his mother, has the authority to reprimand and punish him. There is no mother who would allow other people to insult or harm her own children, no matter how depraved they might be.

When he started secondary school, he not only looked down at me, but he made it quite clear that he despised me. He despised the way I spoke, he despised my mannerisms. In fact, he despised everything about me.

What happened on this day is still fresh in my mind. It was Mother's Day in August, and students were encouraged to invite their mothers to a ceremony at school, in the main hall. Students would prostrate themselves in front of their mothers, placing their heads on their mothers' feet to pay their respects, while an anthem about a mother's love played softly in the background. My son did what was expected of him during the ceremony, but I knew it wasn't genuine. (I know you think I must be heartless to think so negatively of him.) But I knew he felt this way, because he had tried several times to avoid inviting me to the ceremony, from intentionally misplacing the school's formal invitation to informing his teacher that I was ill. (Later, when I ran into his teacher, she asked me if I was feeling better.) When Mr Srisak learned of this, he told his son that he owed me an invitation. When we arrived at school, I could tell he was ashamed of me. He was embarrassed, and worried that his classmates and teachers would make fun of my demeanour.

Nevertheless, I was there for the ceremony, sitting in one of the many chairs in the large school hall as he paid his respects, his forehead touching my feet. Despite knowing that it was all an act, tears streamed down my cheeks.

My eldest was very academic, and I was usually the one who suffered at the hands of all the powerful knowledge he possessed. It got worse once he refused to do his chores, pushing the responsibility onto his younger brother, who did them without complaint. It was Chidchai who relieved me of my burdens and brought me much joy. His older brother, on the other hand, was frequently absent. He'd come home from school and change out of his dirty clothes, leaving them for me to wash. When he returned, he would slouch on his father's favourite sofa and demand his dinner. (I would do as he asked. He had asked, after all.) When I left the living room to get his dinner, he would change the channel on the television, despite the fact that I had been watching it. He acted as a stand-in for the man of the house.

At times, I would lose my patience with him, and we would argue. He would make hurtful comments about how I'd been brainwashed by soap operas, how I imitated the way the characters talked.

'Don't you feel ashamed of yourself for talking like that? You're so obsessed with these soaps that they've become your entire world,' he said.

'Well, then prove to me that there is a world that's different from the ones in soap operas.' I said. 'Soaps are about love, greed, passion: all of these things are a part of human existence. I might not be as educated as you, but I've learned a lot from them.'

'That's because you're uneducated,' he said.

'So what?' I retorted. 'So what if I'm uneducated? What's the harm in that? Didn't I raise you all by myself? Didn't I look after our family? I didn't need formal education to do all of this. I didn't need to be literate to survive. Let me tell you something: you wouldn't survive a day in my village. You wouldn't be able to grow rice or fend for yourself with what they teach you at school.'

'Ha ha!' he laughed hysterically. 'What makes you think I'd want to live in your village? I'd rather die than visit that kind of place.'

'Stop it! I don't want to listen to you anymore.' I tried to stop him from expressing any more contempt against my hometown.

'You're so gullible. I don't understand why you imitate the way those soap characters talk. Talking in your own dialect is better than copying the way they talk.'

'Your father wants me to talk like them.'

He laughed. 'See what I mean? You're a pushover. Don't you realize that no one else talks like you do?'

'Why do I have to pay attention to what other people do? I'm better off being myself. Look at you, hanging around other people and bringing trouble back into our house. You should just stay at home. Your father does better than most, and still, you never listen to him when we tell you not to hang around with strangers. You just like being a misfit.'

He laughed at me again. This son of mine was impossible! He had to be possessed by a villainous spirit. 'You're the misfit! In fact, this family is full of weirdos. You and Father are both weird!'

'You said Father's weird! I'll tell on you!' Chidchai cried. Even he must have felt that his brother had gone too far.

It seemed to work. My eldest laughed a little, to hide his fear. 'Go ahead, you crybaby. I don't even care.'

Chidchai did exactly as he said he would, and as a result, his older brother was severely punished.

As he grew older, my eldest son's behaviour deteriorated. He grew into an irritable teenager who detested his mother and rebelled against his father, albeit behind his father's back. He made it absolutely clear that he hated this household. It suffocated him, he said. Staying at home was a dead end. All he wanted was to leave.

After graduating from secondary school, he finally got his wish. He passed the entrance exams and was accepted into the faculty of arts at a university in Bangkok. His father was overjoyed, telling him how proud he was of him, that he would bring honour to his father's name. He offered to pay for his son's university fees and gave him permission to leave the house.

I, on the other hand, was not as excited. I still don't understand why he let our eldest son leave so easily. It was always difficult for us to get his permission to go anywhere. I also didn't understand what the outside world had to offer. Some of us are permitted to experience it, while others are not. Mr Srisak was fully immersed in the outside world, and now my eldest would be as well. And now there were signs that Chidchai was eager to do the same. *What's wrong with this place? Why is it such a dead end?*

To me, home is peace, happiness, and safety. What more could you possibly want?

The world's a stage

There used to be a movie theatre in the Kaeng Khoi market that looked like a rice mill. It was a wooden building with a tin roof and a large fan on the wall for ventilation. I once had the opportunity to go, and it was particularly memorable because I had been accompanied by Chidchai.

One weekend, my younger son invited me to the cinema with him. I can't remember the name of the film, but I do recall that my son genuinely seemed to want me to join him. He must have noticed how much his mother enjoyed this type of entertainment, and so he tried to please me, which was so unlike his older brother. He had just started secondary school back then. That day, we held hands as we walked through the market, looking more like brother and sister than mother and son. Chidchai was not ashamed of having a mother who was illiterate.

The film was thrilling and full of suspense. I was exhausted from the excitement of watching the hero and the heroine for just over an hour. The villainess in the film was just as I'd expected her to be: she was so terrible that the audience huffed and puffed and booed whenever she appeared on screen. I think the actress's name was Wiyada; if I'm not mistaken, she won the Golden Doll award for her role as a truly evil woman in the film *Mia Luang* a few years ago. There was a lot of debate about whether awarding her the Golden Doll sent a negative message to the public, with the implication that a villainess might be rewarded for her sins. People said it would lead to the moral degradation of society. Still, the actress went on to act in many other films as the villainess, the heartless harpy, the temptress, and other degenerate roles. She never showed remorse for it, often responding to criticisms with high-pitched, deafening peals of laughter. Later in her career, she would portray the villainess in soap operas including *Prim: A Woman Driven by Desire*, and the whole country would despise her for it.

Not long after I saw the film with Chidchai, a vendor at the market told me our district was a popular filming location. They filmed action movies in the forests and mountains, she said, and romances near the railway station and in small alleyways around the market. Other vendors told me that whenever there were rumours of a film crew arriving in town, they immediately packed up their stalls to go and catch a glimpse of the cast members. They spoke about how handsome Sorapong Chatree was, how skilled he was at dodging bullets and performing martial arts. They praised Naowarat Yuktanant's exquisite beauty. She has the sort of face you just don't get tired of looking at, they said.

Then came the day when I finally got to see a film set for myself. It was during my usual morning rounds of the market when I met the person who would change my life forever.

I saw the crew setting up in the centre of the market. Most vendors had abandoned their stalls and were gathered around the set, hoping for a glimpse of the hero and heroine up close. The hero and heroine were sitting side by side, getting their makeup done. The crowd flocked around them, whispering conspiratorially about why a man would need makeup. I was walking along the outer edge of the crowd, towards a large pick-up truck that had wires hanging all around it. It was there that I saw Wiyada, the villainess. She was sitting on a chair, chatting away to the people around her.

When I saw her face, I was overcome with rage. I could feel myself shaking. I kept staring at her, although it seemed as though I was the only who was: everyone else was preoccupied with watching the hero and the heroine. Good for them, I suppose, but for some reason, my eyes were fixed on Wiyada. The more I looked at her, the angrier I became. Look at her, enjoying herself despite receiving little to no attention, showing no remorse for all the terrible and immoral things she had done. Her shrill voice rang in my ears. I recalled all the obscene things she had said in *Prim: A Woman Driven By Desire*. In fact, I remembered all her films: in every one, she stole other women's husbands, spitting slanderous remarks like an adder spitting venom. She was a true villainess in every sense of the word.

Rooted to the spot, I continued staring at her until it was time for her scene with the hero. I watched them meet in the market. The minute she saw him, she pounced on him, wrapping herself around him, putting her face close to his. I was sickened by the sight.

I couldn't help but think that her breath must have been filled with the stench of the huge bowl of noodles she had been eating earlier. I wondered why the hero didn't shove her away, disgusted by how close she was to him. Instead, he was courteous. It helped me realize that even the hero could be swayed by desire. When desire surges, even the most repulsive smell can be enticing. Such was the case when Srisak followed Suda, wishing for her to return to him, despite the fact that she was no longer interested. I noticed that the wickedness in the villainess was confined not only to her soap opera scenes, but that all the hideous things within her emanated outwards, contaminating even the food she devoured.

When the scene was over, Wiyada returned to her chair, her good mood returning too. It suddenly occurred to me that I ought to seize this opportunity to approach her. With my heart pounding and hands shaking, I said:

'Excuse me. May I ask you something?'

She started a little before turning to look at me. Then she said, in that pretentious voice of hers: 'Yes, darling?'

'I wanted to ask you . . . ' I struggled to get the words out.

'You wanted to ask me . . . ?' she repeated the question and added, 'What to eat to become this beautiful?' She let out a piercing laugh.

'No,' I said, my voice stiffening. 'I want to know when you'll stop being a villainess and turn things around.'

She was stunned. She must have realized at this point that I wasn't being friendly.

'How do you know I'm not a good person? How unfair of you to make such an assumption.' Her true colours were starting to show, I could tell.

'I know you very well. You love to play the villainess: a seductress, a bad person.'

She laughed out loud. 'Oh, my dear. That's acting. I'm an actress. Don't you understand?'

'Of course, I know that it's just acting.' My voice had begun to shake. 'But you love this kind of role, which means that you are like those characters you play. Don't you know it's immoral to seduce other people's husbands and destroy other people's homes? You will burn in hell.'

'What? Is this a curse? Are you trying to curse me?' she said, raising her voice. She called out to the crew members. 'This woman is insane. Can someone get rid of her before I lose it?'

At that point, the crowd shifted their attention towards me, watching me teach the villainess a lesson.

'Going to lose it, are you? I'm not afraid of you,' I said, raising my voice to match hers. 'Why don't you show everyone who you really are? You want to slap me? Go ahead. You want to slander me, go ahead. I'm not afraid of you just because you're a villain. I'm just an ordinary woman. I'm a good wife and a mother. I live a virtuous life and have never once imagined stealing other people's husbands and sons the way you do.'

'This woman is insane. Get her away from me,' she whined.

Some of the crew members approached me, tried to block her from me. The crowd was trying to make sense of the situation. When they heard what I said about being a good wife a mother, about having never thought of seducing other people's spouses and sons, I think they began to form a better understanding of where I was coming from. As the crew members were trying to push me away, I yelled:

'Take a good look at this shameless woman! She's attacking an ordinary woman like me!' I turned towards the crowd. 'Look at what she's trying to do to me. None of us like villainess like you. We despise you!'

Suddenly, a voice from the audience pleaded with the crew to release me, to stop pushing me. People around me said I was merely seeking justice, that I had to confront the villainess about why she had seduced my own husband. They began to side with me.

Things happened so quickly that I didn't have time to explain the misunderstanding, to explain of my true intent, which was to tell the actress to stop playing these immoral roles. The chaos that ensued, along with the audience that had taken my side, left me with no choice. I had to take drastic measures. I was able to break free from the crew. I charged at the envious woman, but before I could reach her, someone blocked me and held me down, lifting me up, dragging me away. The audience roared.

He managed to drag me a few feet away before I cried in pain and anger for him to let me go.

'I'm sorry,' he said, letting go. 'Are you hurt?'

'Yes, I'm hurt!' I snapped. 'Who are you? Why did you do that to me?'

He apologized once more and informed me that he was a doctor. When I looked up at him, I noticed that he was well-dressed, much like a doctor as he claimed to be. He wasn't particularly tall—just a little taller than me—but he had a tanned complexion, a round face, and a friendly expression. He turned to face the crowd.

'There's been a misunderstanding. I'm sorry about what happened,' he said. 'I'm a doctor. My clinic isn't far from this market.'

Some people in the crowd recognized him, and things calmed down. He turned back to face me. He touched the back of my neck and the top of my head with the back of his hand. He checked my pulse. I could tell he was truly concerned.

'Oh, you are on fire,' he said, before turning to the crowd to continue. 'This lady is not well.' He turned to me, his voice gentle. 'Please follow me. You are very ill.'

'I'm ill?' I asked, surprised.

'Please don't ask me anything now. Just follow me, all right?'

He turned to face the crowd and the film crew, apologizing again for the confusion, asking them to pardon me because I was ill. I grew calmer, and instantly felt embarrassed by what I had done. I couldn't understand what had taken hold of me. When I heard him telling people I was sick, I was sure that the illness was what had triggered that other part of me. He took my hand in his and led me away. I followed willingly.

My dear saviour

The doctor took me to his clinic. I clenched my hands around his so firmly that they started aching, pain shooting up my arms and into my heart. The combination of misery and shame, as well as the sensation of my pounding heart, made me feel faint. I found it hard to breathe. The doctor turned to face me once more and exclaimed, 'Oh, you look so pale. You must be very ill.' I felt as though his words were being absorbed straight into my veins. The fever mounted.

When we arrived at his clinic, I saw a portly man behind the counter in front of the examination room, reading a magazine. The doctor introduced him as Dr Somjai, his friend and business partner, before informing him that he was going to examine me. Dr Somjai nodded as we walked past him and into the examination room.

The doctor was very animated. He seemed hurried; flustered, almost. He shook a thermometer and asked me to open my mouth, placing it under my tongue. I was quite embarrassed by a stranger putting some sort of shaft in my mouth. The doctor reassured me that everything was fine, that it was just a thermometer, that he was just taking my temperature. Regardless, I had plenty of reason to be embarrassed: I'd never visited a doctor or been to a hospital before, and I was unaccustomed to the intimacy of medical inspection. I was generally healthy, and had never suffered any serious illness. In the event of a rare fever or headache, I took care of it by buying medicine at the chemist's, getting plenty of rest, and taking the medicinal herbs that grew by our house. That was all I needed to make me feel better.

So when the doctor slipped the thermometer beneath my tongue, a sympathetic look on his face, it felt odd. He stood in front of me for an entire minute, staring at me. I didn't know where to look. Finally, he looked at his watch and said politely that he would take out the thermometer now. He inspected it closely before informing me that I had a high temperature. Then, much to my embarrassment, he pulled my sleeve up to expose my naked arm. He wanted to check my blood pressure, he said, and I allowed him do so, despite feeling that he was getting far too close, almost to the point of harassment. No one had ever done anything like this to me before, apart from Mr Srisak. His touch made my head spin.

The doctor left the room briefly, returning with a sheet of paper. He asked me for my first name, family name, age, and address: all the information required to fill out a patient profile.

'You have a fever, Mrs Dao.'

'Yes.'

'I'll prescribe you something for it.'

I hadn't prepared for such an unexpected event. I only had enough money for my groceries.

'I don't normally take any medicine when I have a fever,' I said. 'Lemongrass tea and rest usually does it for me.'

The doctor laughed, but not in a mocking way. It was more of a friendly chuckle.

'Yes, you're right. Warm water and rest can help you recover, but it'll be faster if you also take some medicine.'

He continued to insist, so I had to be honest. 'But I don't have enough money to pay for them.'

He laughed again before speaking. I could hear the slight lilt in his accent. 'Don't you worry, Mrs Dao. I'm happy to take care of it for you. Please do come and see me again tomorrow. I'd like to do a more thorough check-up.'

'Another check-up?' I said anxiously. 'Do you think there's something seriously wrong with my health?'

'Please don't worry. I'd like to check your blood pressure and blood sugar levels, just in case.'

'Is there something wrong with my blood pressure and sugar levels, sir?' I asked, nervous.

'Oh, please don't call me 'sir'. You may call me Dr Siam. May I call you Dao?'

I nodded.

'Dao, please call me Dr Siam, or even just Siam. There's no need for formalities here. All they do is create a distance between us. It's so pretentious, don't you think?'

I hesitated, before nodding in response.

'But I'm used to talking this way.'

'You're used to it?' he asked. 'Where did you learn it from? Did you get it from those soap operas?'

First my eldest son, and now Dr Siam. Here was yet another person commenting on the way I talk. Why is speaking in a polite manner such a problem for me when it came to communicating with other people?

'It's not just soaps,' I replied. 'My husband has talked to me this way ever since we got first married and started living together.'

'Does this mean you didn't talk like this before?' he asked.

I nodded. 'I'm from Isan, and I used to speak Isan. My husband stopped me from speaking it. He found it embarrassing, so I had to learn how to speak standard Thai.'

'But you're not speaking standard Thai. You talk the way characters in soap operas talk. No one talks like this in real life,' he said.

'My husband told me to learn the proper way of speaking from television,' I said.

I had no idea what had taken hold of me. Dr Siam seemed to have some sort of power that made me feel as though I could confide in him about anything. His compassionate voice and warm laughter coaxed things out of me that I should have kept to myself.

'Is your husband very strict, very controlling?'

I nodded, before telling him about all of Mr Srisak's punishments. He continued asking me questions one by one, paying close attention to my responses. I watched sadness cloud his eyes, and occasionally, he would click his tongue in disapproval of Mr Srisak's actions. Dr Siam's kind attention triggered a surge of emotions within me. I felt the knots within me unravel, and I felt relieved.

'And you believe that villainess on TV are like that in real life?' he asked.

'No, it's not like that. I know the difference between real life and soap operas.'

'So, what happened back there at the market?'

'I simply wanted to ask her when she would stop playing the villainess. It's an immoral role, one that destroys society. She has her pick of other roles, so why keep playing the seductress, the villain?'

'That's because it's her job, Dao.' Dr Siam said. 'We all have different jobs, different ways to make a living and support our families. My job is a doctor and my responsibility is to treat my patients but that's doesn't mean that I won't become a patient one day. I can get sick like other people, suffer from all kinds of diseases like other people. I'm a doctor by profession, but I'm also a human being, prone to sickness and death. Do you understand what I mean?'

I'll admit that I didn't. His explanation felt foreign. It was as if he had taken all that I thought I knew, and rendered it incomprehensible. Talking to him was strange—perplexing—but this perplexity was tempered by smiles, empathy, and a sense of goodwill that I could sense in his behaviour. And so, I told him I'd see him again tomorrow, but that I now had to return to the market to finish my shopping.

That night, I was troubled by an onslaught of emotions. I couldn't stop thinking about everything that had occurred during the day, attempting to string them all together into a coherent chain of events. From confronting the villainess, to the arrival of my dear saviour (if I may borrow a future term for use in the present), to a truly healing conversation, to a newfound knowledge about my illness and a cross-examination of an old world I'd thought I understood.

It was a long, strange night, filled with both shame and exhilaration. They say the human heart is difficult to fathom, even when that heart is your own. I did not dare to explore the fathoms of my heart: it was a fearsome, joyous place. Still, my heart persisted in dragging me down into its depths.

Around noon the next day, I went to see Dr Siam at his clinic and found him alone, without Dr Somjai. As a thank you for not charging a penny for my prescription, I'd prepared him lunch, packing it carefully into a tiffin carrier. He looked congenial, exuberant. He wasn't a tall man. He looked a little stout, and he had a brisk walk. His pleasant disposition seemed to make him move even faster, as if he could fly.

'Sir—oh, I beg your pardon—Dr Siam. I'm ready for today's check-up,' I said.

'No need to apologize, Dao. You can relax with me. Just be yourself. You can speak Isan, if you like,' he said, before greeting me with a few words in Isan. 'Pen jang dai? Sabai dee bor?'

I smiled. 'I'll try, but I suppose I'll need a bit of time to adjust. I'm not used to it.'

'No problem. Just take your time,' he assured me.

His kind words overwhelmed me. He gave me all that I was entitled to, and he was good-natured, despite the fact that he was a doctor and could easily order his patients around if he wished.

'Maybe you should have your lunch before getting to work?' I suggested. 'I only just cooked it. I packed it up and hurried straight here. It's still warm.'

'That sounds great,' he said. I was pleased that he went with my suggestion.

He closed his clinic for lunch and rearranged his work desk so he could eat, pushing all of his medical tools to the side. He remarked how delicious everything looked and asked if I wanted to join him, but I told him that I'd already eaten, that I was happy to sit and watch him eat. He seemed to enjoy the food, expressing his satisfaction in the most natural, charming way. When he finished (having eaten absolutely everything), he carried the tiffin carrier to the back of his office, pretending not to hear me when I told him to leave it. I heard him wash the carrier and gargle some water before walking back into the room.

He took out a handkerchief and wiped his mouth and hands, preparing himself for my check-up.

'I had very little sleep last night,' I told him.

'Why is that? How will you get better if you don't rest? Did you take the medicine I gave you?'

'I did, but I couldn't sleep. There were so many things to think about.'

'What kind of things?'

'Well, what you told me about high blood pressure and diabetes was really very worrying. Listen, Dr Siam. I stayed up all night thinking it all through. I'm not even sure how one gets high blood pressure, so I tried to focus instead on what you mentioned about blood sugar levels in diabetes. It occurred to me that the chances of me having this disease are very high, I've hardly tasted anything sweet in my life. From childhood until now—as a married woman with two children—I realized that I've hardly had the taste of sweetness. There were occasional moments, but they were few and far between. So, this lack of sweetness in my life, I believe, puts me at greater risk for diabetes.'

'Oh, Dao. I feel so sorry for you,' he said with genuine concern. 'I'm lost for words . . . Disturbed, really. I will put my medical opinion regarding diabetes aside for the moment, for I am deeply touched by the sentiment you just expressed. You are so innocent. Your plight saddens me.'

'Why?' I didn't quite understand what he meant.

'Well, you say things from your heart, and your heart has been through so much.' He paused for a moment before continuing. 'All these things that are overwhelming you, pressuring you . . . It's the sort of pressure that builds up in your heart over time and eventually implodes. Let me warn you that this sort of stress can contribute to high blood pressure. Psychologically speaking, my diagnosis of physical health—your high blood pressure and high blood sugar levels—can be explained by the amount of mental stress and pressure you are under: pressure is not being relieved. It's like an air embolus in the bloodstream, blocking the natural movement and flow of things. This stress will first damage your emotional health before spreading to your physical health, causing dizziness and difficulty breathing. You might find your entire body aching, more vulnerable to disease . . . '

'Please don't say anything else,' I pleaded. 'I'm scared.'

He came very close to me.

'Don't be afraid. I'm here with you.'

He pulled me gently towards him, so I could rest my head on his chest. I did not resist, for I was shaken by the severity of what he had just described: an illness that seemed to be able to spread endlessly.

'Don't get yourself worked up about the symptoms. They all stem from one cause. I described the symptoms to you already, but what I really want is for you to trace them all back to their cause. Do you know what that cause is?'

He worded his question as though he were talking to a child. I was curious.

'What is it?'

'You've been put under so much pressure that you no longer know what joy is. Once you find joy, all your health problems will disappear.'

'How can I find joy?' I asked.

'It is within you. Listen to what your heart desires and follow it.'

'I'm afraid it is selfish to do so. My life is not mine alone.'

'When you are happy, you treat the people around you with happiness, with a heart full of joy. When you are suffering, you treat them with a heart full of sorrow. Don't you think so?'

I was beginning to grasp his logic. The way he reorganized my understanding of life, as well as his patience and his empathy . . . He was incredible. I was happy and willing to accept his diagnosis, and to follow it wherever it led me.

The last golden boy-child

The joy I had felt after my encounter with my saviour was fleeting. Things had happened so suddenly; to a joy-deprived soul such as myself, everything good seemed to vanish quickly afterwards.

At the clinic in the market, Dr Siam was nowhere to be found. He had disappeared without a word, without a trace, leaving Dr Somjai by himself. I went to the clinic a few times. I found Dr Somjai odd. It was as if he had something against me. Once, I asked him, 'Is Dr Siam not here today?' He gave a blunt 'no' in response, making no attempt to say anything else, hospitable or otherwise. Another time, I asked him, 'Where did Dr Siam go?' to which he responded, 'Who knows what he's up to. Typical.' I was a little annoyed by his dismissive responses, and began to doubt whether their friendship was genuine. I knew very little about how close they were. All I knew was what Dr Siam had told me, which was that they were close friends from childhood. So, what exactly did Dr Somjai mean when he said that this disappearance was 'typical' of Dr Siam?

I did not step foot in that clinic again.

I returned to the open arms of solitude and emptiness that lived in the house. I had been reduced to nothing more than Mr Srisak's servant and concubine. As time passed, I became the recipient of his violent outbursts. He would disappear from the house and return only rarely, looking darker and stormier each time, like a person marked by their own bad luck. I eventually discovered that he was no longer employed, and that his entire business had gone bankrupt. He was living off his inheritance, selling his possessions to pay off debts. He had a gambling addiction and problems with various women. He would come home, sell some belongings, and drive off to gamble the money away, at which point he would return once more, empty-handed, full of disappointment and dissatisfaction that he would take out on me, often in bed.

My eldest son was also trouble. He was hardly ever home, so making him help me with household chores was out of the question. On the cusp of thirteen, he was nearly a teenager, carried away by his delinquent friends. I worried about him chasing after girls and indulging in drinking and smoking, but as soon as I tried to warn him about anything, he would give me a cold stare, filled with the sort of derision that told me I know nothing anything about this world It was impossible for me to understand his adolescent emotions. He had never done what I asked, even as a child; as he got older, he openly rebelled against me. There was no way to convince him to listen to me, and so I lost the courage to try and change things. In the end, he made me feel the same way his father did.

What is adolescence, really? Adolescence is that which severs the bond between mother and child, and my Chidchai was no exception to the rule. Once a reserved, neat child, meticulous about his appearance, whose first thought would be his mother if anything were to happen, he now devoted much of his attention to girls his own age, and far less to his own mother.

When he was a little child, after I finished dressing him for school, he would ask if he looked handsome, and I would tell him that he was the most handsome boy in the entire world. As he grew older, he continued to dress smartly every time he left the house. Every Mother's Day, he would take me to school, pin a jasmine flower to my blouse, and prostrate in front of me to pay his respects. Two years ago, on Valentine's Day, he ran over to me with heart-shaped stickers and started sticking them on me.

'Don't you want to give them to someone else?' I asked him.

'These are my hearts, and they're all for you,' he replied.

He said these simple words, stuck all his hearts on me, and ran away to do his homework, leaving me in tears. When Valentine's Day came around this year, he spared one heart for me, and kept the rest for his friends at school.

On a lonesome day much like this one, I did not ask for much, but I did ask. There is no such thing as a life without happiness. Dr Siam once said that happiness lives inside us, that we only have to listen to our heart, and to follow it.

So, I followed it, and it led me right inside myself, where my desire was pulsing and warm. My happiness slowly shaped itself into existence, into a new life that lived within me. As the months passed, it became obvious that I was expecting another child.

It was just what I had hoped for. This baby entered my life at a time where I was being absolutely neglected. He came to bring me out of this emptiness, to resuscitate the life of the pitiful woman I had become. Mr Srisak was free to go wherever he desired; north or south, it did not matter to me. My eldest son was free to slander me, to abandon me at any time. As for my dear Chidchai: even though you are becoming a teenager, I know you'll always have me in your heart.

It made no difference, because I would now have someone to cherish, to care for. I waited, full of devotion and anticipation, for the day my baby would open his eyes and look upon his mother's face.

Mr Srisak had been quite excited about the baby, naming him Maitree. Because he was born a full ten years after Chidchai, Mr Srisak jokingly referred to him as the stray child. He had thought it was impossible for us to have another child, but he had been proven wrong, which was why Maitree was eventually nicknamed Lhong, meaning 'stray'.

It frightened me to hear him say it. I'm not used to it still. If what they say about a person's name determining their character is true, then this name should never have been used. If names have the power to seal a person's fate or to magnify their true colours, we should all be more afraid and more careful about what we call others. Fortunately, Mr Srisak is the only one who calls him Lhong. His brothers and I prefer to call him Maitree.

Maitree grew up in the midst of our family's difficulties, witnessing the breadwinner decline by way of gambling and womanizing. From the moment he was born, he looked exactly like me. Mr Srisak spent time looking at the child, trying to find some genetic resemblance between himself and his son. For the first year, he couldn't find a thing. It wasn't until Maitree was able to talk that Mr Srisak felt reassured by the fact that there was something deep within his son that resembled him indeed.

By the time Maitree got to that age, he had learned a few words, like 'Mum', and other word-shaped things that sounded unintelligible at times. Being the youngest child, bullied often by his older brothers, I suspected that Maitree had learned some words from his eldest brother, who liked to swear whenever he was dissatisfied. Maitree took to words like a parrot. When Mr Srisak returned home, I was excited to show him that Maitree had learned to talk. I carried him closer to his father and encouraged him to say 'Mum'. Nothing came out of the baby save a mumble or two.

I persisted. 'Say "Mummy". Can you say "Mummy"?' Then *that* word came out of his mouth: 'cunt'. I was shocked, not to mention frightened by the punishment Mr Srisak would surely in store for me. However, upon hearing the word, Mr Srisak merely looked baffled for a moment, before letting out a hysterical laugh.

'Ha! Look at him, cursing at his mother! Lhong is one hell of a child!'

This was how Mr Srisak came to adore the child, and how he finally saw something of himself in him.

Despite the hardships our family went through, I gave my youngest everything he wanted and all he needed. I made sure he was well-fed, that he slept enough; that he had plenty of warm clothes and toys, all of which were hand-me-downs from both Chidchai and my eldest. Now everything belonged to Maitree. I kept him close at all times, watching him grow from a baby into a toddler, from mumbling to speaking full sentences full of unintelligible words. As he grew from one to two to five, my attachment and care towards him grew too.

Maitree was nothing like his brothers. He was shy and quiet, demonstrating time and time again that he was very comfortable being on his own. Even when he was very young, he would sit very still, as if immersed in his own thoughts. He preferred it that way, it seemed: when the world was quiet, and nothing bothered him. Maitree didn't need the company of anyone except himself. By the time he was one, the child was so silent that Mr Srisak began to suspect that he was mute. The few times he did open his mouth to speak, it was disturbing. Whenever his brothers bullied him, he would swear at them. I would have to stop them from pestering him, from compelling him to swear. Soon enough, it became his way of protecting his personal space from invasion. Cursing and swearing got him his way, and this made him spoiled. He wasn't particularly demanding, but when he had his heart set on something, he would scream obscenities to get it.

Mr Srisak was rarely troubled by the behaviour of his youngest child. Not only was he rarely home, he'd also grown relaxed about the way the household was run. It was as if he'd lost his claws and his fangs along with his attention towards his family. This allowed Maitree's small swearing problem to develop into a personality issue, one that left him spoiled with a tendency to repress violent emotions. I noticed these changes develop over time. He would get into arguments with his brothers and with Mr Srisak, but he never had a problem with me.

Once, Maitree swore at his father. Mr Srisak had also been in a bad mood that day; he raised his voice and scolded his son. But Maitree, unfazed, retaliated with more swearing. Mr Srisak lost his patience, smacking Maitree on the mouth with full force. The boy collapsed to the floor. Tears streaming down my face, I watched my son, desperately wanting to help him while also knowing that this was the punishment he deserved.

But instead of putting an end to Maitree's aggressive behaviour, Mr Srisak's punishment triggered something within him, unleashing far more violence. Later in life, when his father disciplined him, instead of yielding or remaining silent like his older siblings, he would clench both his fists and hit himself with them. Mr Srisak would stand there, stunned and helpless, as his own son harmed himself, before calling me to come and take him away. I would be the one to tell him not to hurt himself in that way, because it hurt me too. But Maitree would continue to cry and cry. It was excruciating to see.

When I started examining the depths of my own heart, I discovered that the vengeful storm raging in Maitree was not entirely his father's doing. His emotional violence—a thirst for vengeance that had transformed into a kind of retribution, of punishment—was mine. Buried away for over a decade, a seed had germinated in the hidden fathoms of my infested heart and it had sprung forth in Maitree. He had grown from the deepest, darkest part of me. Something that had once lay hidden, concealed, had manifested itself in front of me.

Oh, my vengeance.

Maitree was bound to resist Mr Srisak. In this regard, he had nothing in common with Mr Srisak at all. He was not born with the desire to ridicule, to discriminate or dictate; on the contrary, he despised all of these things. He had always indicated that he preferred to be left alone, that he was content with himself. If someone disrespected that, he would retaliate.

Oh, Maitree. You and Mr Srisak are nothing alike. The more you grew, from five to six to seven, your physique and appearance grew even further apart from his. You are not as tall as him, nor as tall as your brothers. You are not as beautiful. Your hair is neither thick nor wavy. It is fine and dry.

You are just like me, and here is nothing to worry about, but if there were to be, please let me bear that burden alone.

You are the true sinner

When the year he had been waiting an entire lifetime for finally arrived, my eldest son got exactly want he wanted. It was the year he could spread his wings and fly away from the safe haven that was his loving family.

This son of mine had a heart of stone, a heart dead and detached from his parents, his brothers, and the birthplace that raised him to adulthood. He was indifferent, uncaring and—if I may say so—downright ungrateful.

Perhaps it was because he had always seen himself as the centre of the universe. As he grew into a demanding teenager—one who spat ruthless insults, one whose words slashed like a scythe when he didn't get what he wanted—he grew all the more indifferent towards his own family. He considered himself superior to his mother and father, and he used his knowledge to bolster his own pride and ambition, elevating himself so high that he looked down upon his own flesh and blood, his own birthplace, which had nourished him and provided a roof over his head. This (I realized later) he learned from Mr Srisak, who spoken often of things that were distant and abstract: things that he thought were important, superior, necessary to humanity; things that he felt could split the world open in the most logical sense; things that were indistinguishable and incomprehensible to someone like me. (He could make me feel immense guilt about my ignorance of a world he claimed he understood perfectly.) Whenever the pair of them disagreed, my eldest son would accuse his father of being a tyrant. It was when I saw them arguing that I realized my eldest was just like his father. If Mr Srisak was the tyrant, then what else could this son become but his usurper?

He said he needed to leave in order to find somewhere better for himself. He was accepted into one of the country's top universities. He would have to study hard there, he said, to earn a bachelor's degree, a master's degree, and then a doctorate, in order to become a professor. As he talked about his ambitions, his eyes were fixed on the future he saw himself standing in.

It was his father who pulled him back to the reality of the present. In a dignified, superior tone, Mr Srisak said:

'I wholeheartedly support your dreams and ambitions, as well as your determination and your discipline towards your goal of pursuing further education. Higher education is important. A degree gives you a better chance at life than others, and a PhD earns you prestige and respect. This I absolutely understand, and I also know that it will bring pride, honour, and dignity to everyone in our family, not just you. You represent our family. But we're struggling financially here. It might be possible for us pay your tuition fees, but going to Bangkok involves other costs, like accommodation and daily expenses. I presume those combined will cost more than your tuition. What is your solution to this problem?'

My eldest son was silent for a brief moment before responding petulantly. 'But isn't that your problem?'

Mr Srisak grew annoyed with his son. He reiterated that this was a question for his son to answer, not one for him to ask.

'But you leave the house every day,' his son retorted.

I was terrified by my eldest son's audaciousness, his unabashed questioning of his father's daily absences from the house. Both my eldest son and I knew about Mr Srisak's secret visits to his private world of pleasure. Confronting his father with this was strategic, a way of signalling to him that his secret world was a secret no longer, that he was willing to expose it to the rest of the family. He thought his father would finally accept defeat, but he was mistaken.

'That's my business. Stay the fuck away from it, or else you'll get nothing from me.' Mr Srisak threatened him.

My eldest son was visibly taken aback. His big head shrunk to the size of his toe.

The fact that he had not thought for one moment exactly how he might afford his higher education—and isn't education supposed to allow one to think for oneself?—meant that he came crawling to me, claiming that it was a parent's responsibility to fully raise and support their children, to get them the best education possible. For him, it was a question of duty, not want; it was about being a good citizen. His voice was piercing, laced with derision. I didn't want to hear it. His attitude did not make me want to help him, regardless of whether helping him was a duty or a desire.

And so, I told my eldest:

'My son. My dear, I have three children. I have to look after all three of you, not to mention your father. I have to take care of the household chores. Look at it from my perspective, won't you? What would I have left for managing all my duties at home, from groceries to you and your brothers' pocket money, if you asked me to give you a share of the money?'

'Then why don't you give me Chidchai and Maitree's share? They live here, they don't have to pay for food or rent. They don't have to struggle like I do,' he said.

'How could you say that? Their education is as important as yours. And I need the money to pay for their food.'

'You always have an excuse when it comes to me,' he said. 'You never have any problems with Chidchai or Maitree. Let's face it. You love them more than me.'

He began to cry, but it was clearly just for show. His sobs were loud, but not a single tear had fallen. My son was strategic; he had built the moment up and gone along with it, so I might fall for it too. Despite my emotional nature, I was not easily swayed, for I was certain that I loved all my children equally. It was he who did not love me, who was constantly pushing me away and saying hurtful things to me. But I did not tell him this.

'You can't say that. How heartless and unfair of you to accuse me so. I love you. Of course I love you,' I said, my own tears brimming.

He was a little stunned by this. He stopped crying and looked at me, as if to see whether I was being sincere. From what he saw, he must have come to the conclusion that I couldn't be relied upon. He sneered at me.

'Just go back to living in your soap operas, why don't you?'

He walked away.

In moments such as this, I knew deep down that this eldest son of mine would be fine. He was clever and resilient enough to fulfill his own ambitions. He was unafraid of his destiny, even if it meant paving his own path towards it. I held this conviction most sincerely in the part of my heart that I held for my eldest son.

And so, he left home to study in the embrace of the capital.

Between him living at home and him living there, I came to prefer the latter. We struggled to send him money every month, but I made my peace with it. Struggling once a month was better than living with the ordeal of having him at home.

Mr Srisak told me that the cost of the children's education was no longer a laughing matter. It was difficult enough paying for our eldest son's tuition, and now, a year later, Chidchai wanted to study in the city too. Mr Srisak put the idea on hold, proposing Chidchai attend a local college instead. I agreed, because it meant I'd be able to see my boy every day, just as I had years ago when he returned home from school. Chidchai was upset at first, but he got over it quite quickly.

Besides, Maitree was to finish primary school in a few years' time, at which point we'd have to pay for secondary school. I must say that our children's school fees rose every year, and it did make me wonder whether getting a good education really brought honour and wealth to one's parents, or if it simply dragged them closer to poverty.

Mr Srisak eventually found a way to blame me for the financial pressure that had gripped our family. I was too comfortable, he claimed, now that all of our children were past needing constant care.

'What do you do all day, really?' he asked.

What a question. Mr Srisak looked at himself: hardly ever home, leaving the house every day to try to make a living all on his own, utterly unaided. And then he looked at me sitting around at home, nothing but a burden. He told me to go out and earn some money for our family, to stop waiting around and asking him for money. He believed that out of all of us, I was the only one living a life of comfort.

I was speechless. There was nothing I could do but attempt to follow his orders. I tried to think of ways to earn an income for the family, but it was hopeless. All this time, I had been doing what I did best, what I had been taught to do—to cook, to do chores—and dare I say, I was impeccable at it. But when it came to making money, I was at a complete loss. Had Mr Srisak forgotten that I was illiterate? Having to leave the house for the outside world was terrifying, but I did it. I found a job that had been recommended to me by someone who said it was easy and paid well.

My new job was selling underground lottery tickets. All I had to do was go to people's homes, and customers would flock around me; sometimes, they even came to my house. You might be wondering how someone so illiterate could have handled a job that requires so many calculations. Let me explain. Being illiterate means that I am unable to read or write, but it doesn't mean that I don't understand numbers. Despite the fact that I had never gone to school, life had taught me how to understand numbers and mathematics, especially when it came to the lottery. Most people here didn't go to school, but they know how the lottery works, especially when it comes to calculating the reward money. You don't need school for this sort of thing: just practice and experience. That's how I became an underground lottery ticket vendor.

I can't deny that the job was risky. After only six rounds, I got caught by the police, put into jail, threatened with all sorts of things. Mr Srisak, who had been in another province at the time, found out about the whole thing and had to drive back to bail me out. When we got home, he made sure to punish me comprehensively. My whole body was covered in bruises. When my sons got home, Chidchai wept, knowing what had happened. There was no need to explain it to him. Maitree, on the other hand, was much younger; only about nine or ten years old. He cried at the sight of me, storming up to the front door and punching it furiously. The noise was deafening. 'Which bastard did this to my mother? I'm going to fucking kill him!'

But it was your father who did this to me, my dear son. Fate forbids patricide. It has happened in other families by way of karma, but it will never happen in this one. Karma works in unexpected ways, and those who have wronged are never exempt from consequence.

I'm saying all of this because the time has finally come. Mr Srisak's existence had continued to deteriorate throughout the many years of life he had been given; at its darkest point, death had finally beckoned him.

Mr Srisak's death came around the end of the year. Rumour had it that he died a terrible death, driving his truck along a lonely highway around Ayutthaya and crashing into a big tree on the side of the road. His truck almost split in half. Mr Srisak died instantly. It was also said that there had been a young woman sitting next to him who survived, but was severely injured. I don't really want to describe the incident in any more detail, for fear of how awful the picture I painted might be.

His death was brutal and unnatural. According to the old sayings, only bad, sinful, vile people die this way. His karma finally caught up with him. I hope his soul may rest in peace.

Peacefully ever after

Mr Srisak's death freed me from the obligations that had once imprisoned my heart and soul. I stopped using formal pronouns when referring to myself. The simple 'I' of the commoner would do now.

A modest funeral was held at a temple near my house. Our neighbours came to pay their respects out of courtesy, but I wouldn't have blamed them if they hadn't. Mr Srisak was hardly friends with anyone in town, not to mention the fact that he had discouraged me and my children from also befriending anyone. He didn't have many relatives. In the end, the funeral was attended by my eldest son, who travelled in from Bangkok, Chidchai, Maitree, some neighbours I knew from the grocery truck, and myself. The neighbours offered their condolences, and help if I ever needed it. They told me not to be a stranger now that I was alone, now that I was a widow, now that I was free of Mr Srisak. Their offers of friendship seemed genuine.

Losing him was devastating because he had always planned everything for our family, decided everything. I was disoriented without him. I was a small boat, lost in a wide expanse of ocean. I didn't know how to go on with my life.

Mr Srisak left nothing for the family. All he had, he squandered. A once-wealthy man, Mr Srisak threw all his money away in aid of his personal greed and lust, leaving his wife and children one house on one piece of land the size of one rai. After the funeral, I was driven almost to the point of insanity, trying to understand how to support my three children, all of whom were still studying. The eldest had one year left, at which point he would be graduating with a bachelor's degree. I hoped that he would help his mother and his brothers out of this crisis, but as soon as the funeral was over, Prateep returned to Bangkok without a word, without any attempts to contact us afterwards. It was I who had to call him, to remind him of his mother and his brothers, to urge him never to forget the family to which he is bound by blood.

That same year, Chidchai decided to drop out of school after receiving a vocational college diploma. He started looking for work. Fortunately, Kaeng Khoi is an industrial town, full of factories manufacturing everything from cement and toilet equipment to processed food and power tools. Chidchai had no trouble finding work. Finally, after Mr Srisak's death, Maitree grew bored with school, skipping lessons until he eventually stopped going entirely.

'Why aren't you going to school?' I asked him.

'It's just a burden for you, Mum. Better for me to find a job,' he said, trying to please me.

So, I let him do what he wanted. It was clear from their actions that both of them sympathized with me, and understood the situation our family was in. After Mr Srisak's death, I also stopped sending money to my eldest, who began to pay for his own university expenses. This loss of funds seemed to not bother him at all, but it showed me that he was at least aware of our situation to some extent.

These were trying times for our family, and we had to work together to overcome them. That aside, I can't deny that I was happy and at peace. We led a simple life with minimal expenses. I had children who loved and cared for me at home, children who worked hard and earned enough to support me. I didn't need anything else. Content in that modest space of ours, my spirits gradually returned to me. I was happy to cook and clean, to wash and iron clothes for my children to wear to work. My sons contributed a portion of their monthly salary to the house. We drank together after dinner, mother and sons. There were no formalities; we were entirely at ease, like friends.

I became the head of the household, and I had all the freedom I could want. Before, my life had been dictated by rules. I lived in terror of punishment. I would never do the things Mr Srisak did to me. I knew enough about the narrative of my life to know, if I were to compare it to the epic twists and turns of a soap opera, that his would be the final episode. How did I know it? I knew it because I had been through so much and for so long, trapped in the most brutal and basest of plots. The most complicated storyline in my life—the arrival of a sinner disguised as a saint, the scene that exposed him for the monster he was, and the final dénouement of his death, brought about by his own karma—had come to an end. What my children and I had been through was traumatic, and all that was left—the final scene left to play—was peace and resolution. The only thing that remained was the sweet taste of happiness. What other scenes could there be?

And I was right. Five years after Mr Srisak's death, happiness greeted us. In 2003, the owner of a food stall near my house introduced me to someone. Her stall was right by the Friendship Highway bend, near the mouth of the narrow alley that led to my house. According to her, a man was looking for somewhere to settle down and start his business. He'd stopped by her stall one day while scouting the area. This area along the highway was a wonderful location, he thought, a good choice for someone looking to start a new life. Because he didn't know anyone here, the stall owner offered to help ask around on his behalf. The man was ecstatic, and started visiting her stall frequently after that.

That was how I met this man, through the food stall owner. He told me his name was Thai, and that he was from Kaeng Khoi but lived in a different subdistrict, and that he was looking for a small plot of land to start his garage business. This area was ideal for it, he said, since it was so close to the Friendship Highway and the cement factories. He asked if I would be willing to sell a portion of my land to him, that he'd offer a good price for an area right off the highway.

I told him I'd think about it. I told Chidchai and Maitree about the offer. The man had offered a large sum of money, enough to keep our family going for quite some time. After hearing this, Chidchai came up with a fantastic idea. He suggested we invest our money in building a rowhouse, with rooms to rent out to migrant workers, many of whom had recently flocked to the district in search of work. According to his calculations, a five-room rowhouse with a monthly rent of 1,000 baht per person would give us a regular income of 5,000 baht per month. I thought it was brilliant, and I told him I would see it through.

The next time I met Thai, I took him to see our land, so he could decide which part he wanted to buy. He pointed to the moringa tree, and said he only needed the area that ran along the alley up to the tree. I was fine with that, and I told him I couldn't give him any more of it anyway, as there was a well in the middle of the land that we'd always pumped fresh water from, as long as we could remember. Thai assured me that he only wanted the area he'd indicated, which was about one *ngan*, give or take. I knew nothing about land measurements, so I took the moringa tree as the basis of our agreement. He seemed like a friendly person too, which made it all the more easy to sell him the portion of land.

From then on, we became good neighbours. I greeted him whenever I walked past his garage, and we sometimes engaged in long conversations about our backgrounds. To my wonderful surprise, I learned that he was Dr Siam's twin brother! I had suspected it, as they looked so alike. I told him I knew his brother because I used to be his patient, before he'd disappeared. Hearing this, Thai's expression grew weary, and he said dismissively, 'That's typical of him.' So I said nothing more about it.

I hired builders to work on the five-room rowhouse, which took a few months to build. Soon after, we rented all the rooms out to migrant workers, and our finances became more stable.

One more good thing followed. One morning, as I was grocery shopping in the market, a familiar figure walked towards me. I did try to avoid him, to be honest, but I was too late. He reached me and asked how I was, one decade later. He was as animated and high-spirited as before, as if nothing in life had tainted him. Perhaps what had happened years ago hadn't left a mark in his memory. So, I said:

'I'm fine, thank you. There's nothing much to say about my life. I'm just taking care of my children. My husband passed away.'

'Oh, Dao, please spare me the formalities! We used to be such friends,' he said. 'I'm very sorry about your husband. When did he pass?'

Many years ago, I told him. He nodded along, as if he didn't know what else to say. I tried to cut things short. 'I'd better say goodbye now, Dr Siam.' He looked hurt, but as I turned to walk away, he raised his voice at me, in the middle of the market. 'Wait, Dao! Can I please come and visit you?'

I didn't give him an answer. All I did was turn and glance at him. I walked away.

It was a strange feeling. I felt brave, vindicated; it was a personal triumph, allowing myself to follow my heart's desire: the desire for happiness.

When I returned home, I waited with bated breath for happiness to arrive. Would my saviour follow the path paved by my desire to find me? I knew he'd show up sooner or later, because he was the only thing left missing from this drama. Peace and happiness were on the way.

When Dr Siam arrives, my life will be complete.

Volume 4: The Problems and Solutions
of the Ghostwriter

19 March 2004

So, my father died six years ago today. What an apt coincidence. I was called to sort out an important matter back in my hometown. My mother's voice on the phone was so full of enthusiasm that I couldn't help but wonder: when was the last time I'd heard her sound this cheerful?

Yes, it's been seven years since I left home, determined to fulfill my educational and professional aspirations. That determination is still there, but those goals have grown dim and blurry since. Once, my naive pride whispered in my ears, 'If you don't succeed, don't even think about showing your face back home'. It was something I'd remembered from some book or another. In my teens, I clung to this phrase with fierce tenacity. But as the years went by, the phrase took control of me, confining me within a cage of arrogance. I refused to do something as simple as coming home once a month. I severed myself from the past, cutting off contact with the classmates and teachers I'd once respected.

Do I recognize my past follies? Am I ashamed? No. I don't waver that easily.

That's why hearing my mother's fretful voice on the phone has been more than enough contact over the past seven years. I was happy to keep my distance.

Since my father died, my mother has seemed much livelier. I can hear it in her voice. I'm particularly cold towards her, I'll admit.

She likes to call and tell me about the time she's spending with the neighbours, the big projects she's dreaming up.

'It's a shame not to do anything with our land. There are cement and lathe factories everywhere these days, and lots of Isan people moving here for work,' she told me eagerly.

'And what are you going to do with our land? Sell it? In your dreams,' I said, stopping her in her tracks.

'Let me finish . . . '

'You're selling Dad's land,' I cried.

'Only two ngans. We'll still have one rai left. Someone wanted to buy it, and open a garage for tractors and mining equipment. I'll use the money to build some rooms we can rent out to workers.'

'Right. Got it. So, what now?'

'You have to come back and sign some land deeds for me. We need three signatures: yours, mine, and your brother's. The land department told me we need all three of them.'

It wouldn't actually bother me that much if she sold the land. I only said things like 'in your dreams' and 'you're selling Dad's land' to make her feel guilty.

It's true: I've been taken over by the middle-class, capitalist mindset. Everything is built to generate profit. It's true, what Mum said. Why waste such assets? The past can't regenerate itself. It lives only in photo albums, kept inside glass cabinets.

I loved my dad, but that love doesn't extend to his land. I feel no attachment to the land I was born in. In truth, I don't really have any affinity towards my hometown, but, there's no reason to hate it, either. It's just a matter of personal frustration and aspiration.

Oh, to reminisce about my hometown . . . The dry spells, and the sun flares that flame over overgrown fields, and the dust that hovers in the air from the roadworks and the cement factories. The pounding of machines and the stench of industrial fumes. The girls I used to date wear factory uniforms now, and if any one of them wishes to be promoted to office secretary, aspires to sit in an air-conditioned room, they must save up for plastic surgery, trade in their old face for a more front-facing one. The boys that used to be my friends once raced each other on their motorbikes. One by one, they die young from car accidents, and those who remain work as cement truck drivers as a front for their real jobs, which is drug dealing. They race their trucks along roads that lead to change. The people whose bodies they bury come from the same villages they once did. Whether they mean to or not, they sell drugs to their own people, crash their trucks into their own people until most of them die out and are replaced by people who have migrated here for the same work. Look at all this change.

There is nothing about this ugly, godforsaken place that makes me want to love it. I don't care for it at all.

But my mother has adapted to accommodate the newcomers. My mother, evolving and enduring amidst all this change.

I told her I wasn't ready to visit the house and the land that once belonged to my father. Not wanting to confront the past I'd left tethered to the earth of my hometown, I told my mother and brother to meet me at the district lands office. Once we finish dealing with the deeds, we'll probably have lunch together at a nearby restaurant, and there I'll ask to leave early, all preoccupied and tetchy and depressed, as if I still haven't been able to come to terms with the death of my father.

And so, my mother and brother walk into the land office. She is wearing a brand-new, tailored dress of iridescent green silk that glows like a metallic-jewelled beetle. The smile lines on her forehead and around her eyes have been filled in with powder, her lips sharply lined a deep red. Despite having walked some way in the sun, there isn't a single drop of sweat visible on her. She is beautiful: probably as beautiful as the day she married Dad.

My brother is sixteen. He is standing next to her, well-proportioned and sunburnt from labouring in the sun. His muscular arms are bulging with veins, contoured by protruding joints. His knuckles are prominent. Dressed in his cement factory uniform, he peers at me, giving me a timid but detached smile before avoiding my gaze, looking down at his own hand, the one holding my mother's arm. I walk towards them and pay my respects to my mum.

'You've grown into a man,' I say, greeting my brother, despite how foolish and meaningless it might sound. He smiles and looks down again, squeezing my mother's arm, beckoning her to say something.

'Every penny he earns, he gives back to me,' she says, beaming with pride.

'Don't you want to go back to school? What qualifications have you got? Fourth grade?'

'That's more than enough. I don't have the money to pay for his studies. It's good that he's working to help me out.'

I shrug, making a face of disapproval.

'You'll earn more money if you have more qualifications.'

'Paying for your education was hard enough for me.'

'Why do you think of it that way?'

'And why do you keep pushing Maitree to want to leave me? It's good that he's here to take care of me. I'm getting old, you know.' My mother raises her voice.

'Yeah, okay. I get it. Let's just sort this thing out,' I say, changing the subject. I walk ahead of them into the district land office.

The atmosphere inside is stressful, to say the least. Office employees speaking in loud, intimidating tones, disorderly queues of people snaking about, and the incessant hammering of typewriters.

Our turn arrives. My mother chats amiably with the woman behind the desk, taking the deed out of her bag and handing it over. The woman flips through it swiftly, asking for other documents and pieces of evidence, her eyes still fixed on the deed in front of her. It seems my mother sorted out the more complicated things beforehand, and all that's left to do is to sign the deed. I'm amazed at how my mother has become an expert at this sort of thing. She dealt with everything before my arrival, visiting all the necessary departments and getting all the paperwork together. All we need to do now is sign.

'This is the one?' The woman asks my mother, giving me a suspiciously friendly smile.

'What? Who?' I ask, startled.

'Oh, have you not discussed whose land you're selling?' The woman's smile disappears. Her face is severe. I turn to my mother, who also looks confused.

Someone is playing games here, I thought. We'll soon find out who.

'Can you please explain to us what it is that you mean?' I ask her politely.

'You want to sell two ngans of the land that the three of you own together, is that correct? Originally, you own one rai—that's 1,600 square metres—and 800 square metres of land. That's 2,400 square metres in total. Dividing that between the three owners, you each own 800 square metres individually. So what I'm asking you is, whose share of the land are you going to sell?'

I nod as soon as the woman finishes her explanation. Crystal clear. I turn once more towards my cunning mother. She meets my gaze, her expression casual.

'Just sign it. I've sorted everything out,' she says, gesturing for a pen from the woman.

'So you want me to sell my share.'

'I live here. Your brother lives here. Doesn't it make more sense to sell your share? The rest of the land still belongs to the three of us. It's all under my name. You're hardly ever here. I don't think you need it as much as me and your brother do. We live here.' She hands me a pen, which I take without thinking.

'Of course I need it, Mum,' I try to explain, before falling momentarily speechless. 'It's Dad's land you're selling.'

And there it is: my accusatory tone. Now I know the truth. She's not selling the land. I am. My signature on this deed is a permanent mark of estrangement. Why didn't I cry at my father's funeral? Why didn't I come home more often? Did I, an expert in human emotion, fail to put on the right sort of performance? Nonsensical questions shoot up like mushrooms. My eyes are fixed on the pen in my hand, hovering reluctantly over the document.

For a moment, I recall an afternoon during the summer holidays right after my high school graduation, where my father took me to my internship at the cement factory.

'Get it right in there, you coward! Do it like a man!'

'But Dad, it's a detonator!'

'That's right, and you better get good at dealing with them, because one day you'll be working here. When you take over from me, you'll be the big boss of the factory. Did you do it?'

'I think so.'

'Let me see. Fine. Right! Now let's get off this cliff.'

'Yes, boss,' his workers said obediently.

It was three in the afternoon, and the wind was blowing hot, carrying clouds of dust that pinched and stung our faces. Next to the crag was a makeshift service station for the excavators, as well as an observation point from which you could see all the cliffs and crags surrounding the cement factory. My father's arms were wrapped tight around my shoulders. We gazed in silence at the scene before us, both trying to hide our anxiety and excitement over what was about to happen. The warning siren rang.

'Watch this. It's the most beautiful thing I've ever seen in my life,' my father mused, before falling silent again. It was as if he had stopped breathing. The siren rang once more, warning the workers away from the very cliffs we were looking at. It rang one last time. My father squeezed my shoulders again.

'Especially since you're the one who planted the detonator. Aren't you proud?'

I turned away in shock. My father's broad hands protected my head from the explosion; I felt my skull shrink and vanish beneath his palms.

As the pen drags its ink along the deed, I hear mountains exploding, tremors rippling through again and again. Somewhere, a cliff crumbles into pieces.

17 June 2007

Of his early diary entries, one dated 19 March 2004 later becomes his first short story. The story is narrated by Prateep, the protagonist. In the story, Prateep returns to his hometown, forced to confront not just his own past that haunts him, but the erasure of his name from the family's land title deed, at the request of his mother. He, his mother, and his younger brother inherited the land from his late father. His mother wants to sell Prateep's share of the land (he'd rarely returned home over the years, and so she felt he needed it less than she and his brother did) and use the profits to build houses to rent out to workers. His mother's argument to sell is not unreasonable; in fact, it is undeniable proof of his shameful indifference towards his own birthplace. Prateep is left with no choice but to sign the document, authorizing the sale of his share of the land. The experience crushes Prateep's spirit, amplifying some inner voice that mocks the severing of his most intimate, most reliable of relationships: his family ties. A punishment for his past derision towards his roots: derision that had stemmed from his teenage years, when all he wanted was freedom from the ties that kept him tethered. But with that eventual, hard-won freedom came a cold loneliness, and an inability to find his way. These are the roads we must take in our youth to forge our own path, to find a way to be true to ourselves.

He wrote the short story in early 2004. At the time, he had been elated by his own work: the passionate turns of phrase, the bold, forceful syntax, his daring, complicated approach to narrative. The story overflowed with energy, brimming with the innocence of ambition and the arrogance of youth. Three years go by. Having reread the story many times on many different occasions, he finds this arrogance to be one of its many flaws. Then there's the limited vocabulary, the heavy-handed metaphors, the supercilious righteousness throughout that reads as dullness, plain and simple: foolish, awkward, unsophisticated. And yet, these flaws were borne out of the fledgling, fiery years of youth. As time passes, they become strengths, daring to capture the emotion, attitude, and spirit of innocence: a powerful surge, a thirst for life that he—at present—can no longer embody. It is a breath of fresh air he can no longer take.

The turbulent energy of youth has turned into profound stillness, his ambitious agility replaced with an appreciation for slowness. He no longer sees life as a destination to be reached, a goal to be won; instead, it is something that lives with him—exists alongside him—from moment to moment. Each passing minute, each passing second, instills meaning, is worth contemplation. His life is no longer driven by the desire to race ahead. Instead, each day brings a different kind of adventure, no less exciting than what the future once promised. He has learned to dwell truly in the present.

Reading the short story one more time, he starts to ponder over which aspects are factual and which are fictional. He's proud of this work of fiction, no doubt about it, but he wonders whether he could use it to recall some past experience, somehow. He was the one who wrote it, after all. He should be able to tell the real elements from the false ones, to discern the parts that can be relied on in this moment where life's realities were competing with narrative constructs.

Thomas Mann makes an insightful observation in 'Tonio Kroger', his rather long short story. He says, 'what the literary artist basically fails to grasp is that life goes on, that it is not ashamed to go on living, even after it has been expressed and "eliminated". Lo and behold! Literature may redeem it as much as it pleases, it just carries on in its same old sinful way; for to the intellectual eye all activity is sinful'.

He is now face-to-face with life's sinful ways, confronting the consequences of writing that short story, despite the fact that he had finished writing it years ago. 'Life goes on [. . .] it is not ashamed to go on living. Literature may redeem it as much as it pleases, it just carries on in its same old sinful way.' He has no choice but to face life; the real-life sequel to his short story.

It has been three years since he has visited his hometown. In fact, Kaeng Khoi is only about 100 kilometres from Bangkok, but the thought of taking a trip has never once crossed his mind when his mother calls to ask how things are going with him. He feels quite strongly that the ties that bind him to his birthplace are all but nonexistent, if you ignore his growing sense of obligation towards his mother and younger brothers as time passes. (Unlike in his short story, he has two younger brothers in real life.) Every time his mother calls, his conscience is disturbed by her expectations, her requests, her pettiness. As a thirty-one-year-old eldest son, he is often haunted by the guilt of not being financially secure enough to offer much help to his family when they most need it.

His mother's phone calls tend to make him tense and anxious, reminding him of his family's hopeless situation: a situation he has tried all his life to flee from. While he has been lucky enough to escape its claws, his mother and brothers are still being dragged down into the depths below, and they are beckoning for his help.

Look at what happened to his little brother, the middle child. Chidchai married at twenty-six, and, since then, he's been drowning in a cycle of debts. The government's economic reform plan convinced diligent youths that their dreams of a prosperous life could be achieved through loans, regardless of the fact that they might not be able to pay them back. Following these dreams, Chidchai and his wife become entangled in debt; eventually, their marriage fractures, then crumbles. He is forced to move out to live with his mother, living once more like a child for whom she cooks and cleans. Day in, day out, he works, putting the money he earns towards his loans. One day, the police come to arrest him, claiming that a loan shark has filed charges against him. The police and the law get involved, all due to his blind determination to start a family, to own a car, a flatscreen TV, to keep golden retrievers—a mundane middle-class dream, reaping its surcharges along the way.

His two golden retrievers are thin and bedraggled. When it gets hot in the afternoons, one of them likes to lie at the bottom of the stairs leading to his mother's door, while the other naps on the cool cement floor of his mother's bathroom. When it cools down in the evenings, they chase his mother's chicks, and she scolds them for it. Not only must she cook for her two sons: she must also feed the two dogs. Eventually, the two retrievers mate with Thai dogs around the neighbourhood, giving birth to a large litter of mutts. Chidchai no longer pays any attention to his dogs and their mongrel puppies. To him, they have come to represent his failed marriage and his futile pursuit of wealth: things he no longer wants to be reminded of.

It is his mother who still looks after the dogs, making sure they are fed, making sure they have enough energy to chase her chicks. They are no different to her sons: despite their failures and their losses, they still have a mother who makes sure they won't go hungry. She simply cannot ignore their suffering.

Chidchai's bitterness grew self-destructive. Late one night, drunk and exhausted, he was driving home from Saraburi when he crashed directly into the back of a parked trailer. Luckily, he only suffered minor injuries; his car, however, was badly damaged. His mother sent it to a local garage for fixing. The hood had to be replaced in its entirety. His mother paid for everything.

As for Maitree, the youngest by about ten years—he was the most worrisome of all. Everyone had been surprised when his mother fell pregnant with him, for by then, his father was already quite old. Maitree had been stubborn and bad-tempered since he was a baby, nearly biting his mother's nipple to pieces when she breastfed him. As a baby, he retained only rude and obscene words, which he later used against those who had upset him. At the age of three, he would throw tantrums and swear profusely at his parents. Luckily, Maitree had been born when their father had become much more mellow with old age. Their father would have never allowed such behaviour to go unpunished with Chidchai or him. They were fully, painfully aware of their father's strictness, his severe punishments. He remembers that once, when they were children, his father had glared at Chidchai and him playing across the dinner table. He had fallen dead silent, his face twitching with rage. He had gotten up and kicked them both, throwing them against the wall before hurling both their plates across the room. As a child, he had experienced all sorts of punishments at the hands of his father. Once, he had thrown a brick at him, cutting his forehead open. As he lay on the ground, his face bathed in blood, pooling dark red and feral, the last thing he remembered was his father walking towards him, admiring his own aim before walking away, unperturbed. He heard his mother sobbing as he lost consciousness.

Maitree was lucky, then, that his father found his aggressive behaviour humorous. 'This son of mine has got guts. He won't give in to anyone. I like it!'

At the end of 1998, when his father died in a road accident, Maitree was in fourth grade. He had never done well in school, which worried his mother constantly. After the death of his father, he stopped going to school altogether. His mother was no match for his stubbornness, his hot-headedness, his disobedience. The constant stream of profanities that streamed out of his mouth knocked her down and kept her there. At the time, he had been in his final year of university in the arts faculty, busy being swept away by the freedoms and rebellions of his generation. The memory of his past was nothing but a painful wound, dehiscing bitter, unwanted agony. He would do anything to flee from his family, his birthplace. Deep down, he felt disowned, estranged from his roots. After his father's death, he believed that the last tie connecting him to his family had been severed; his mother and brothers reduced to images, mere representations of the kind of life he was totally separate from.

When his father died, Maitree went off the rails, causing his mother all sorts of problems. He drank heavily, getting into violent brawls; his mother had virtually no control over him. When Maitree was around fifteen, his mother began to suspect that he was taking speed, which was readily available at stalls all along the Friendship Highway, a popular pit stop for truckers. She forbade Maitree from going near the stalls, confining him to his room. He retaliated by destroying things and hurting himself, before threatening to hurt her. Eventually, she lost her patience.

'I'm your mother. If you dare hurt me, I'll kill you with my bare hands! If you're stupid enough to try those fucking drugs again, I'll slit your throat open while you sleep. You just wait and see!'

She later forced Maitree to look for a job. For a few months, he worked as a temp at a factory, but before long, he went back to hanging around the house, doing nothing at all, until his mother was forced to chase him out of bed with a broomstick. He got another job, but spent all of his salary on a down payment for a new motorbike, leaving the rest of the installments for his mother to pay. She was angry at him, and scolded him for it, but in the end, a mother's love got the better of her. She willingly carried all the burdens he laid upon her, but he was a lost cause. He took to drinking heavily after work. His conscience continued to corrode.

Maitree knew his mother would always be there to help him. She would shout at him for all the trouble he caused her, but she would continue to take care of him, to feed him. She would never kick him out. After a while, Maitree became involved with a girl. She moved in, living with him in one of his mother's rental rooms. His mother was the one who cooked for them, who cleaned their love nest. She even gave him some money for liquor when he asked for it. Maitree and his girlfriend often drank into the night together, and his mother let them do whatever they pleased without a word of complaint. The girl never helped his mother with chores. She didn't even bother greeting his mother; most days, she stayed in their room. One night, however, while Maitree was on his night shift, she invited a man to drink with her in their room. His mother, unable to bear what the girl did, told Maitree. Head over heels in love, he defended the girl, getting upset at his mother instead. Several days later, his mother kicked the girl out, but Maitree followed her in tears, begging her to come back. It turned out that the girl had already found herself a new lover. She wanted to leave Maitree for good.

Maitree was heartbroken. It was as if all the light had gone out of his life. He shut himself in his room, drinking and weeping all day and all night. And who else was there to console him but his mother?

She called him to tell him everything. Full of both fury and shame, he silently cursed his brother—good-for-nothing, useless disgrace—but what could he do to help? Maitree's life was no different to the sad plight of little people depicted in sensational news stories. He felt sorry for them, but he also regarded them as foolish. Some nights, he contemplates the inevitable struggles of the common people; dreams about them, even. What are the cause of these problems, and how can they be solved? Who or what is to blame? The government? Society as a whole? Or individuals? Do people only have themselves to blame if their lives are flooded with trouble? Could it be argued that dealing with problems is part of the struggle of life? Or was there something wrong with the structure of society, something that caused it to sink people's lives into such a state of degradation? How could one make sense of the lamentable, pitiful lives of those people?

And now, that sort of life is unfolding itself before him, seen through the eyes of his own mother and brothers. He can feel its breath on the back of his neck as his mother tells him about the many health problems she's currently battling, from diabetes to coronary heart disease. Later, she begs him—the eldest, most educated brother—to call Maitree for moral support, with sound and sensible advice.

'Teach your brother. Tell him to look to you as an example, so he can stand on his own two feet instead of relying so much on me.'

But what advice could he possibly give to Maitree? What kind of example was he? Look at him: a writer with no security in his life.

Would he be able to lend his mother money if she needed it? What would he do if she fell ill and had to be hospitalized? And if he were to be diagnosed with lung cancer from heavy smoking, he would rather die than let his mother spend any of her money on treating him. He has vowed to devote his entire life to his writing career. He is willing to labour purely for creativity's sake, to dedicate his existence to touching, exploring, unveiling, and comprehending what it means to be human, so that he might articulate the beauty, meaningfulness, sanctity, and dignity of humanity through his words and narratives. He has been working hard, and the thought of giving up has never crossed his mind. His undying faith in the power of narrative has led him to willingly renounce life's other alternatives. By holding on to his belief in creativity, he has chosen a path that cannot bring comfort and security to his mother and his family. He walks this lonesome and selfish path he has chosen for himself, and if he were to suddenly drop dead today, his mother still shouldn't spend a penny on him. If there is anyone who ought to pay, it is fate itself. He will meet it with loud and derisive laughter, with the maddening desire to cling to his very last breath. That is how he will thank fate.

'Tell him to go to hell!' he shouts down the phone. For a moment, he sees his own death and his youngest brother's life colliding into one. Through his mother, he is speaking to his brother and to his own fate.

'How could you say something like that?' his mother reprimands him.

That evening, he calls Maitree and tries to cheer him up, the way an elder brother ought to do for a younger one.

21 June 2007

'Life goes on, [. . .] it is not ashamed to go on living, even after it has been expressed and "eliminated".' Maitree is still unable to stand on his own two feet. Often swayed by emotional outbursts, he never seems to learn from past experiences, repeating the same mistakes over and over.

Maitree moved to Chonburi to work at a construction site, partly in the hope that doing so would help him forget his ex-girlfriend. However, after less than a month, he called his mother and asked her to send him money, claiming that he was broke and that he couldn't wait until the end of the month for his wages. His mother later learned from a friend who worked with him that Maitree had started drinking again. He got drunk every day after work, and he owed the liquor stalls near the construction site a lot of money. Not long afterwards, Maitree returned home for his motorbike and brought it back with him to Chonburi, even though his mother was still paying it off in installments. He used the motorbike as collateral for liquor, and continued getting drunk every night. Two months later, he left his job, returning home with debt for his mother to pay off, just as he had done before.

As the eldest son, he had to not only listen to his mother complain about all the problems caused by his brothers, but he was also the only son who ever sent her any small amounts of cash he could spare. Only when his manuscript was published would he (a ghostwriter) send a larger sum.

Every morning, Maitree asked his mother for petrol money for the motorbike he rode to work and for his liquor in the evenings. After a while, restless and hot-blooded, Maitree got himself a new girlfriend, who was one of his mother's tenants. Unable to withstand his loneliness, he asked her to move in with him. (She stopped paying rent, and as a result, his mother lost some of the income that she used to pay for Maitree's petrol and liquor.) Maitree tried his best to cement his relationship with the girl; eventually, he asked his mother to go with him to visit the girl's parents and ask for her hand in marriage. His mother refuses, despite his claim that the girl's parents had urged them to marry as soon as possible.

'How can you possibly think of getting married when you're still asking me for money?' His mother put some sense into him.

Talking to Maitree over the phone, he bluntly dismisses his youngest brother's dreams of marriage. He says to him: 'Pay for the wedding yourself if you want to get married. Unless you can stop depending on Mum, don't even dream about getting married . . . Get yourself some condoms before screwing that girlfriend of yours!'

His younger brother, Chidchai, also had problems with women. After his wife fled to Bangkok, leaving all her debt behind, Chidchai went back to live with his mother, but found himself a new woman not long afterwards. She was from a well-to-do Chinese family, and was a few years younger than him. At first, Chidchai's new relationship didn't bother his mother, because he kept things to himself, not telling her what was going on with his life.

When his mother learned more about his new woman, as he sometimes brought her home with him, she seemed to be fine with it. Chidchai, however, was unable to forget his ex-wife, even though they were officially divorced. He was struggling to come to terms with their breakup, despite his new relationship. Every week, he drove to Bangkok to see his ex-wife, and he still kept their wedding photo in his room. Large and ornately framed, he had brought with him from the house that had once been their love nest. By then, the bank had already repossessed the house due to their massive debt, and the wedding photo was the only possession and memento left of his failed marriage. When his new girlfriend came into his room and saw the wedding photo, she made fun of him. He felt ashamed that he still could not decide which woman he wanted to be with. Since then, he kept the photo hidden whenever the new girlfriend visited him.

He heard about all this from his mother, who found it both sad and hilarious that her second son still seemed to suffer from unrequited love. Her younger sons were hopeless romantics, blindly subjecting themselves to the strokes of youthful desire and love, despite having hardly any love and devotion left for their mother.

Can he himself deny this depiction? Like his younger brothers, he worships love, despite the fact that he has never had a serious relationship. The sons of this family have all been cursed to be consumed by love. They are regarded as foolish and self-destructive, even in the eyes of their own mother and other people.

His mother confided in him over the phone that she had no idea where her sons had gotten this destructive streak from, because their father had never been romantic. In fact, throughout his entire marriage, their father had been the exact opposite. He never once betrayed any gentleness or passion, showing no signs of affection towards his wife at all. She couldn't understand why her two younger sons were so different. As he listened to her, he could feel it: her mind drifting away, trying in vain to leaf through her memories, searching for some romantic notion expressed by her husband, some spark she thought had faded.

He felt quite sad. His mother's three sons rarely showed any sign that confirmed that they had any love and affection towards their mother. All she saw was their love and devotion to other women.

He tried to make his mother feel better by saying: 'We're men like Dad, but it's because of you that we know of love and sacrifice.'

Does love cause problems, or the other way round? Without a question, the three sons' passionate pursuit of love was moulded from the blueprint of their mother.

In light of his mother's circumstances, he's been trying to understand this. What comes first, love or problems? Things are so bizarre, so baffling. After his father passed away, his mother tried to find ways to fend for the entire family. She came up with the idea of building a five-room rowhouse, so she could rent out rooms to migrant workers. She needed money for construction, and the opportunity to get hold of this money came with a man named Thai, a new settler who wanted to buy a piece of land close to the main road: his mother's land. He wanted to buy about fifty square wa of land from her, but the reality was that his mother knew nothing about measurements, as she had never been to school and could not read. Her solution was to explain to Thai that the land she wanted to sell was the plot beyond the moringa tree, which stood some distance away from the front yard of her house. That tree was thus used by his mother to mark the plot's edge. Next to the tree and closer to the house was an old well, which had been an essential source of water for his family since the early days of his parents' marriage. His father had gotten someone to dig up the well, to pump water up from underground for the family's use. The well and its water could well be considered the family's buried treasure. To his mother, only the plot of land further on from the well—beyond where the moringa tree stood, closer to the road—could be sold.

Roadside land normally fetches a good price; with the passage of time, its value tends to increase. His mother earned over 200,000 baht from selling that plot of land to Thai, and both seemed happy enough with the deal. Next to his mother's property, Thai built a medium-sized garage with a side partition, and the partition was seen as a boundary between their land.

He remembers clearly how he had felt the day his mother had asked him to sell his share of the land. It was as if something inside him had shattered, and later, he had transformed that emotional upheaval into valuable material for his short story. On the day itself, however, he had hardly paid attention to the details of the transaction, overwhelmed as he had been by bitterness and self-pity. He felt angry and saddened by his family's decision to deprive him of his right to inherit his land. He couldn't understand why he he'd been written off the deed, when in reality, he was the one most likely to be able to keep the land for his family. If there was anyone who wouldn't be tempted by an offer to buy the land at a high price, who had the strength and determination to keep his father's land within the family forever, that person was him. Wasn't that obvious to the rest of the family? If his name was no longer on the title deed, there was no guarantee others wouldn't sell the remaining land in the future. They would end up penniless. Indeed, his father's land did grow smaller with time, from about fifty rai in the beginning to a ngan and fifty square wa, when his mother wanted to sell another fifty square wa to Thai. While he was engrossed in his bitterness and self-pity, his mother sold those fifty square wa to Thai.

His real-life anger had triggered him to spite his mother in front of everyone in the land office, yelling out that he had no need to sell his share of the land, and if his mother was desperate for money, then she ought to just sell her share of the land. His mother had been shocked by his reaction, but he'd been too furious to care about her feelings. How could she do this to him? She had asked him to travel all the way from Bangkok just to erase his own name from the title deed! After spiting her in public, he'd stormed out, leaving his mother and brother by themselves. Once back in Bangkok, he'd kept his distance from his family, making no contact with them. In the end, his mother had to sell hers and Chidchai's share of the land to Thai.

His coldness and indifference towards his family's plight at that time has led to unforgivable damage, which he realizes today, as he returns again to sort out the pending land transaction that had taken place a few years ago. The problems began when Thai wanted to get a formal title deed. The land he wanted to claim was not just the plot he'd bought from his mother, but also the plot that had actually been fenced off by his garage. It became clear that Thai wanted ownership of more land than his mother had agreed to sell him, and he claimed that half of his mother's land was actually his. He also had written proof of his claim, stipulated on the land sale document from that day: the day he had left his mother and brother in the land office to return to Bangkok in anger and self-pity. His mother couldn't read, so she didn't know what had been written on that document, and his brother had been too timid, letting his mother handle everything. And he had left them to deal with things on their own.

How could this have happened?

When he arrives at the old family home to help his mother sort out the land issue, he discovers that the top floor of the spacious two-storey house—the top level is entirely made of timber, while the ground level is cement—has been virtually abandoned. His mother and brothers have moved down to live in the three downstairs rooms. The only thing that remains in the main bedroom is a framed photo of his father. Apparently, at night, his ghost occupies the top floor, all alone. His mother only goes upstairs every once in a while to cook during the day; the top floor looks desolate, dilapidated.

Chidchai, Maitree, Maitree's girlfriend, and his mother live in their own separate rooms downstairs. As time passes, his mother's conflict with Thai has continued to worsen. As the hostility and tension between the two parties increase, they remain alert for opportunities to discredit the other.

26 June 2007

Where is the wound, and why has it been left untreated?

Is it because his mother was illiterate? Perhaps this makes her outlook and perception, and the subsequent way she handles things, much like those of villagers from a bygone era. Using the moringa tree as a landmark, she had gestured with her hand, verbally indicating to Thai the exact boundary of the land she wanted to sell. She'd wanted to sell it for 230,000 baht, a deal that Thai had seemed pleased with at the time. Soon afterwards, Thai built his garage on the land he bought, and one of the garage's side partitions replaced the moringa tree—which had been cut down—as the demarcation between the two properties.

His mother's village mentality convinced her that the verbal agreement she had with Thai was clear, definite, and binding. She held on to that agreement with confidence, not suspecting that anything bad could ever come out of it.

Thai, whose outlook was different from hers, had his own way of mapping and assessing the price of the land, which was inviting a surveyor. For her part, his mother had showed no objection, as she thought that he would abide by what they had verbally agreed. Knowing that she couldn't read or write, Thai volunteered to help with the bureaucratic aspects of the transaction. His mother let Thai handle it all by himself, and paid no attention to the written details. She didn't know that the surveyor had measured all the land she had—1 ngan and fifty square wa—and set the price at a little over 400,000 baht. His mother signed, confident of Thai's commitment to their verbal agreement. A few years later, that document she had signed was used against her, stipulating that she'd sold half of her land to Thai: something she'd been entirely unaware of.

They went to the land office together to seal the deal. She didn't suspect that Thai had a different plan, and she went along with whatever they asked her. She feared that she'd look foolish if she asked any questions or showed any doubt about what they were doing. His mother didn't dream of arguing with government officials; in her world, the bureaucratic system and its administrators occupied a sacred position of authority and justice. Thai, standing next to his mother, encouraged her to sign the document, and she assumed that he was acting with good intentions, like any nice neighbour would. It was also earlier that day that her eldest son had yelled at her in front of everyone, causing her to lose face. She felt the need to save face and convince others that her words had integrity, so she urged Chidchai to sell his share of the land together with hers. His mother had no idea what those formal words on the land sale documents meant. The confusing, undecipherable language of bureaucracy! Nevertheless, his mother's inability to question what had been written on the documents she'd signed would lead to the same end as her verbal agreement with Thai: the sale of her land from the side of the road up to the moringa tree, for the price of 230,000 baht. When the land official told her that her share of the land alone wouldn't be enough, his mother was somewhat confused. The official explained further: to get 230,000 baht, she would have to sell more land. At that point, she still didn't quite understand what the official meant, but she didn't hesitate in pushing Chidchai to sell his share of the land too, to reach the 230,000 baht price. Her assumption was that you could sell a piece of land for any price you wanted. She didn't know that before the sale was made, Thai had asked someone from the land office to assess the value of the entire land she owned. That official had told Thai that the value of all her land was 430,000 baht. It was clear that his mother and Thai had completely different transactions in mind. In her ignorance, she signed the sale document, partly because she was intimidated by the land official, who made no attempt to hide her annoyance and her desire to get the transaction over and done with so she could move on to the next person waiting in line. So in the end, his mother signed the documents, and urged Chidchai to do the same.

Looking back, it was clear that from that day on, Thai had already begun to change.

While Thai's garage was being built, he told his mother that she could no longer grow vegetables on the land in between their properties. He also asked her to remove her scaffolding from under the monkey pod tree, and soon after, he put up a fence with barbed wire, marking a clear boundary between their two plots. While Thai's cold and distant behaviour grew increasingly obvious, his mother reacted by complaining to Thai about the noise from his garage. It was open all day and night, it was disturbing her, and he ought to do something about it. But Thai simply ignored her complaints. Worse, he began to say horrible things to her, calling her an illiterate idiot and saying all sorts of offensive things to her face. He remembered his mother telling him on the phone all the things Thai had said to her. She also mentioned that Maitree was upset with Thai, and that they had nearly gotten into a fight. She was worried that Maitree might attack Thai one day, because her youngest son could think of only violent ways to deal with any kind of conflict.

Was Thai's greediness the sole thing that led to all this? Or did Thai genuinely believe that his mother had been trying to cheat? Thai often told others who lived in the same neighbourhood that she was selfish, that she worshipped money more than anything. He even said to her that he had known from the very beginning that she was asking an exorbitant price for the land he bought off her. According to him, demanding 230,000 baht for that plot of land was far too much. It was possible that Thai had had ill intent towards his mother ever since then.

For his part, in order to understand the conflict between his mother and Thai, he needed to piece together the things his mother had confided to him on the phone. On the day he arrived back in his hometown, he visited Thai at his garage to see if he could somehow find a way to resolve the conflict between Thai and his mother. But Thai showed no interest in negotiating with him. Nothing could change his determination to claim ownership of half the land that had originally belonged to his mother. He had taken this trip hoping to help his mother settle her issue with Thai, but it became clear to him after seeing Thai that the latter was not going to back down. Still, he wanted to get to the core and the origin of the conflict.

Thai accused his mother of being unfair to him, claiming that he had trusted her all along. He said she had sold him 50 square metres of her land, which was right next to a canal, for 230,000 baht. However, when he later asked someone from the municipality to mark the boundary of the land he bought, he found that it had been eroded by the canal that flowed straight into his mother's backyard. Thai firmly believed that she benefited from the situation, as the canal had eroded his land and deposited more land onto her backyard. Later, he went to see her, to ask her to give him the land that had been carried away.

She reacted by curtly telling him that she would not give him any more of her land than what they had previously agreed. At that moment, her gut feeling told her that Thai's argument was unreasonable. But later, when Thai's claim was proven to be true according to the information provided by the municipality official who had measured it, his mother decided to consult another one of her neighbours about the matter. The advice she got was that, in practice, the expanded land could be used and occupied by owners of adjacent properties. Legally, however, the amount of land she owned, as registered on the title deed, would not increase. If the title deed stipulated that she owned 400 square metres, then that was what she legally owned, and she had the right to insist upon it, if one day, land department officials showed up to claim the expanded land as public property.

With this new knowledge, his mother insisted that she would not give any more of her land to Thai. Thai was furious, accusing her of being heartless and shrewd. He retaliated by paying truck drivers to unload earth into the canal, blocking its flow almost entirely. After that, he occupied and made use of the filled-up area himself.

As time passed, Thai grew rich and influential. He bought land on the other side of the canal before filling up the canal entirely, joining together the plots he owned on both sides of it. His behaviour and attitude was both intriguing and bewildering. He craved respect and acceptance from people in the neighbourhood. He'd gained more space from filling up the canal, so he expanded his garage. He boasted that many bigwigs, most of whom he was pretty close to, came to his garage regularly to have their cars fixed. Among them, he claimed, were heads of the district organizations, government officials, lawyers, policemen, and military men. Then, one day, a new street sign with the words 'Mechanic Thai's Alley' inscribed on it was put up next to the small, previously nameless alley by the front of his mother's house. Thai was very pleased with the sign, but his mother was obviously annoyed. She described Thai's behaviour as provocative. When chatting over the phone, she poured out her anger against Thai:

'That greedy bastard is a troublemaker who takes things that belong to other people at his liberty. All the guardian spirits here know what sort of guy he is. They can tell crooks apart from decent people. We'll see if they let a crook like him prosper.'

Thai put his mother's guardian spirits to shame by buying another plot of land nearby, forcing her house to be surrounded by land that belonged to him. On one side of his mother's property was Thai's garage; on the other was his newly purchased land. However, things didn't stop there. He went on to pay people he knew from the municipality office to further measure and mark the boundary for his land. He claimed that part of his mother's five-room rowhouse was located on his land, and the people from the municipality office supported his claim, drawing a boundary that ran straight through the middle of his mother's building. Thai demanded that his mother pull down the half of her building that was on what he claimed was his land. His mother had been furious when she rang him, hoping to vent out her anger and frustration. He could do nothing but listen to her. Then he got upset and lashed out at her, making her feel worse:

'See! Everything that has happened is all because of you! You took him in yourself! I don't think anyone can help you out of this mess!'

At that time, his mother, in a desperate state, was about to pull down half of her building. Fortunately, when a surveyor showed up to mark the land boundary, he told his mother that Thai's land didn't extend to where her building stood. When they told Thai this, he was furious, refusing to acknowledge the boundary set by the land office. He claimed that he had asked the municipality office to measure the land, and they had informed him that his land included the area on which half of his mother's building stood. The surveyor grew hostile, telling him coldly that people from the municipality office were not authorized to do such a thing; that authority was only with those from the land department. His mother was over the moon about the fact that things had turned out to Thai the troublemaker's disadvantage. She made sure to profusely thank the guardian spirits for delivering her out of the crisis.

The incident embittered Thai even more, and he accused his mother of conspiring with the land official to take advantage of him.

He later plotted against his mother by trying to ingratiate himself with government officials, especially those who worked for the municipality office, who had previously measured the land for him. These people later helped Thai by pointing out that the documents legalizing the land sale between the two of them indicated that Thai was the co-owner of her property. This meant that Thai could occupy more land; in fact, they claimed that Thai was entitled to half of the land, since Chidchai and she had already sold their shares to him. Thai took this opportunity to usurp ownership of half her land. He came to see her with the land sale documents, threatening to use them to his advantage.

His mother, however, refused to listen to him. She repeated what she had told him before: 'You won't get any more land than what I agreed to sell to you. You still don't get it, do you?' His mother said she could not understand why Thai demanded her to give him more land when, two years ago, he'd only wanted enough land to build his garage on, going so far as to use one of its partitions as the agreed boundary between their properties with no issue. To her, it was bizarre that Thai had suddenly come up with a request for more land after two years had already passed by.

It is compulsory that all land owners are present when submitting a request for land measurement. Therefore, Thai alone could not demand that the land be measured and its boundary established. This matter had dragged on for quite a while, and he himself—one of the co-owners—lived in Bangkok and hardly visited his hometown. Thai had been harassing his mother by asking the government officials he knew to visit his mother's property frequently, under the pretense of inspection. Thai's intent was obviously to intimidate his mother, who still insisted that she would not bend to his demands:

'Over my dead body! This is my land. That is my well. It's a goddamn lie to claim that I sold him half of my land. Try me! I'll go to court if I must, but I won't give in!'

Thai challenged her: 'No court will listen to your rambling. They'll only pay attention to the land sale documents. They'll grant me the right to claim the well and they'll give all the land to me, all the way up to your front door!'

After that trip to his hometown, he dwelled on all the possible factors that had led to the simmering conflict between his mother and Thai over the past few years. When he met Thai, he told him that he wanted to compromise, offering to move the boundary between their properties a little further into his mother's land, although no further than where the well lay. He let Thai know that he made such an offer because he believed that compromise was a crucial thing between neighbours. Thai hesitated a little before rejecting the offer, arguing that he didn't think it was fair. Why should he accept just a tiny strip of land when it was stipulated in the land sale documents that he owned half of his mother's land?

By then, he could see that any attempt on his part to persuade Thai to accept the offer would be fruitless. Thai kept saying that he had been taken advantage of by his mother and her family. He insisted that the canal had caused his land to erode and that his mother had gained more land from the erosion.

As far as he was concerned, Thai was trying to take advantage of his family, and the only way to deal with this was to let the problem drag on without allowing the land office to get involved.

Still, part of him hated leaving things unresolved like that. Deep down, he would prefer finding a way to sort it all out somehow, and if worst came to worst—that is, if his family lost half of their land—one day in the future, he might be able to save up enough money from his writing career to buy a new piece of land and build a small house for his family.

But how would his mother handle the loss of her land? That land was not a mere piece of earth to her; to her, it was her whole life and being. She had lived on that land since her late teens, after getting married. She had raised a young family with my father on that land, and her three sons had all been born there, their umbilical cords buried somewhere within it. Years ago, the three young boys' baby teeth had been thrown onto the roof of the house, and as time passed, they had fallen off the roof onto that piece of earth, where they were eventually buried. His father's ashes were also there. Twenty years have gone by, and his family's history and memories are tethered still to that piece of land, the land from which their lives have since grown and flourished.

Was he truly able to act with indifference towards the plight of his family and his roots?

6 December 2008

It was the middle of the night when his mobile phone, left in the study, rang three times before going silent. He struggled out of bed and went to his study. The clock told him that it was just over one in the morning. He was annoyed. When the phone rang for the fourth time, he picked up and shouted down the line:

'Don't you know what time it is?'

Silence from the other end.

He was about to hang up when a woman with a rural accent said: 'Son, wait!' He was growing tired of late-night calls from strangers who rang by mistake.

'I think you've got the wrong number.'

'It's Mum,' said the voice on the other end.

'You've got the wrong number. Dial again, okay?' he repeated. He hung up before throwing the phone onto the desk, instead of against the wall, which was actually what he wanted to do to express his irritation, but couldn't, because he still needed the phone. He'd had too many stupid calls from strangers recently. Some called to ask if this or that person was there, and when he told them they had the wrong number, they simply hung up without even bothering to apologize.

Last night, his phone had woken him up and all he could hear was a buzzing noise on the other end of the line. After a while, however, it sounded like someone was weeping. A few nights ago, he'd gotten another call from a stranger. This one had sounded like an old woman. She'd asked to speak to someone he didn't know, and told him that she really needed help, because she had gotten lost. He bluntly told her: 'You've got the wrong number.'

Last week, he'd heard the news about a gang of criminals who randomly called people and tried to trick them into believing that their kids had been kidnapped for ransom. The news made him wary of calls from strangers; he felt he couldn't tell whether they were genuine or not. On the other hand, when viewed from a different perspective, this kind of mistrust could also destroy the hopes of people who found themselves in desperate situations late at night and really did need help. What if the person who had been weeping the other night was in a life-endangering situation and genuinely in need of help, only to be mistaken by him as a criminal ruse? She might have been killed in the end. He brushed that possibility off. He could not believe that something like that would happen. If it did, he would never be able to forgive himself.

He cursed when the mobile phone rang again. But when he looked at the screen and realized that it was his mother, his expression changed. He sighed. Why now, at this hour?

'Prateep!' His mother's voice was panic-stricken.

'What now, Mum?'

Out of everyone he knew, his mother was the worst when it came to choosing a time to call people. She often rang him late at night, asking him for help solving strange problems.

It was no different this time. Desperate, she asked him to solve yet another problem. She said that because she didn't have a chance to go to school and his two brothers were not that well-educated, he, with an undergraduate degree, was best suited to figure out the solution to this problem.

'Listen,' his mother said. 'Your brother Maitree has caused trouble. He attacked Thai with a machete and nearly chopped off his neck. I don't know if Thai is dead or not, but last I saw him, he collapsed and was convulsing. Maitree's gone mad. He's locked himself in his room, threatening to slit his own throat with a knife if anyone goes in. It's been over half an hour. His wife and I have been trying to calm him down. When I asked him what he was doing, he said he was packing his stuff because he wanted to run. I don't know what to do! Please help me, son!'

After listening to his mother, he tried to get more details about
the latest, and by far the most severe, trouble his family had found
themselves in. His hands were shaking and his throat felt dry, knowing
that in this sort of life-or-death situation, anything could happen that
might cause more trouble and make things worse. He decided to tell
his mother that everyone should go to the police station right now,
because Maitree needed to turn himself in rather than wait for them to
come to arrest him. *Don't even think about running away because it'll make
things worse. Leave barbarism to the law.* If Maitree continues to act out
of violence instead of surrendering to the power and protection of
the state, he could perish because of it. *Go to the police now*, he said to
his mother.

If all of them kept hanging around at home, it might provoke
Thai's family hurt them in retaliation. Seek protection from the law, he
urged, before adding that he would wait for their call. Once they were
at the police station and had reported the crime, they should call him
immediately. He'd take the trip home tomorrow to see them.

After that, he sat at the desk in the study and tried to imagine what
might be happening. Sangwan, Thai's wife, and Sumon, their teenage
son, and a few of their workers might have already driven Thai to
the hospital. Their shock and fear for Thai's life would soon turn into
anger. (His mother had told him earlier that Sumon had pointed at
Maitree and yelled at him before rushing to the hospital: 'I'm going to
kill you tonight!') After less than an hour, Sumon might leave his father
with his mother and the workers at the hospital before rushing home
on a motorbike. He might creep into his father's bedroom, take out his
pistol, and race towards Maitree's, where Maitree was locked inside his
room. His mother, his wife, and Chidchai would be gathered in front
of the room. They'd beg Sumon not to create more bloodshed:

'Please calm down! Let us not hurt one another anymore!'

That's probably what his mother said to Sumon.

Sumon, enraged, would roar: 'You tried to kill my father. I'll kill
you. Come out, you son of a bitch!'

Maitree would probably be seized with fear for his own life. Was
offering death to others the same as having death handed to oneself?
Perhaps Maitree would be so panic-stricken that he wouldn't be able to

utter a single word. But Sumon would not hesitate. He'd rush towards the front door of Maitree's room and kick it with full force, destroying the door and sending the hinges flying everywhere. While the others were paralysed by fear, Sumon would spot Maitree, and before anyone could do anything, he'd pull the trigger and fire several shots. The dark room would flash momentarily, and then Maitree's body would lay still on the ground.

Barbarism paid back by barbarism. An eye for an eye, and everything would be resolved. The blame would shift to Sumon and Maitree's death would wash him clean from his crime. Eventually, Thai might die, but Sumon, as one who committed another crime, would still be imprisoned. By then, the two families would have suffered enough from the losses, and would never want anything to do with one other again.

But what if the desire for barbarism was elevated in sophistication due to the power of the mind? Maitree's silence might provoke violent desires in Sumon's heart, turning his raw anger and hatred into cold-blooded rage, and a more ingenious tactic—one that would inflict as much pain on his enemy—might come to mind. Sumon's rage and thirst for revenge would not take hold of him; instead, he'd master it, realizing his advantageous position. He'd have a gun, so there would be no need to kick down the door, to force it open. The gun endows him with superiority. He can make the situation unfold any way he wants. (See the result of silence? See how silence might have a significant role in all this?)

'You killed my father! Now I will kill your mother!'

In a split second, Sumon would stretch out his arm and point the gun towards his mother's head before pulling the trigger. (Even if Sumon took his time with the gun and Maitree decided to rush out of his room, it would still be too late, since Maitree's life was no longer what Sumon wanted. What he wanted now was his mother's life, and the consequences that came with killing her. Maitree would suffer in exactly the same way that Sumon suffered. All would be balanced. A parent would be killed, and all the burden would fall to the sons who remain.) He would point the gun at his mother's forehead and shoot her at close range. His mother's lifeless body would lie still on the ground. Another life lost, simple as that, and it would be no different from the way Maitree had taken Thai's life hours prior. This way, Maitree and Sumon would be forced to accept the consequences of their crimes in a more or less identical manner. Sumon would have to go to jail for killing Maitree's mother. An atmosphere of sadness would dominate the two households, and the shocking atrocities would forever act as dual reminders for them to stay away from one other.

Barbarism resolved by barbarism. A just, decisive, and highly efficient solution. He would sit in the tormenting silence of the night, waiting for a call from his family; then, after almost an hour, his phone would ring. When he picks it up, he'll hear Chidchai's pained voice, telling him: 'Mum's gone!'

He would sigh; finally, the problem was solved.

The reality is different. When his phone rings and he picks it up, he hears Chidchai asking him in confusion: 'We're at the police station now. What should we do next?'

A sudden surge of exasperation. His family seems totally incapable of finding a way out of their own mess. They're like thirsty people, asking others what they should do to quench their own thirst. If only he could haul over an entire canal of his own. He'd happily drown his family in it.

10 December 2008

He didn't rush home the next day; instead, he waited a few days before returning. He waited because the police didn't immediately detain Maitree after his mother and brothers went to report the crime at the station. Chidchai told him over the phone that the police gave Maitree credit for turning himself in. They believed that he had no intention to flee so they let him go home and said they would stop by later to investigate the crime scene, to gather more evidence about the case and report them to the public prosecutor.

He rang Maitree to tell him he'd done the right thing, leaving it to the hands of the justice system. *If you'd run away, things would've gotten worse. You've done what a real man is supposed to do, which is to admit when you've done wrong.* Maitree mumbled in agreement—*yes, yes*—and the elder brother continued, warning him to stay away from Thai's family members. *You can still leave home for work and all that, like you were doing before, but try your best to stay out of their way. Try not to trigger their vengeance by flaunting the fact that you're still a free man.*

He also chastised his brother for his heavy drinking and all the drug taking. All this was the consequence of excess. His mother told him that Maitree had been drinking the day he attacked Thai. Looking back, he remembered how often alcohol had morphed Maitree into a destructive monster, turning a quiet and timid young man into a barbaric thing: mad with rage, always looking for trouble. Even his mother couldn't stand him when he was like that. She'd tried to make him change his behaviour, but he'd reacted badly, aggressively. They had fought and nearly killed each other. As his elder brother, he told Maitree to quit drinking, and Maitree promised to do so.

The next night, he called his mother to ask how things were, and whether Maitree was still going to work like before. He also wanted to know if people from Thai's family were harassing her. She told him that Sumon approached her front yard a few times a day, hollering and demanding to know whether Maitree was home or not, threatening to shoot Maitree with his father's gun. At other times, Sumon yelled out that his mother was going to lose her youngest son soon, that Maitree's wife was going to be a widow, that the whole family would never find peace or happiness for the rest of their lives.

He could tell that his mother was very worried, even though she said she wasn't afraid of Sumon. According to her, he kept threatening them, bragging about how his friends in motorbike gangs were willing to help him. Sometimes, they gathered in front of the garage and roared their engines to intimidate his family. They also said they were waiting for Maitree to return home from work so they could beat him up.

His mother's fear for her youngest son's life was palpable. He tried to calm her down. He told her it was best not to react, because Sumon and his family were obviously still upset and looking for revenge. In fact, it was probably better that they were able to verbally release their anger, rather than taking violent action.

His mother then told him that Maitree himself was ridden with fear and anxiety. He couldn't sleep; yesterday, he had had to drink to calm himself down, to keep his fear at bay. Prateep got upset that Maitree had started drinking again. He had told that idiot to quit drinking! But his mother immediately defended Maitree. He drank by himself in his room, she said, and she felt sorry for him, because he had said that he wanted to die. She'd let him drink just to relieve his stress, just so he could get some sleep, and she'd kept an eye on him.

He was speechless for a moment, before telling her that if Maitree got in trouble again because of his drinking, she should never ask him for help. Outraged by the fact that his mother had allowed Maitree to drink again, he began venting uncontrollably. *I can't believe you let him drink again! Do you think he'll let Sumon yell out threats from the front yard when he's drunk? I bet he'll rush straight to him, and when he's drunk, any damn thing can happen!* Then he reminded his mother that he had forbidden his brother to drink again, so he'd be able to gain some self-awareness. Maitree had to be punished by being forced to live with his own fear and anxiety. He needed to reflect on his own life and realize, for once, how reckless he had been, and how that had affected everyone in his family. Maitree had to be forced to acknowledge that his stupid actions had dragged his mother and brothers through hell. They had no peace because of him. If Maitree was forced to confront his fear and anxiety, there might still be a chance for him to change things. But his mother had let him drink to escape these moments of fear and anxiety. She allowed him to walk free from the painful burden that should have been his to bear.

'I'm keeping an eye on him. He won't cause any more trouble,' his mother interrupted. Once more, he was speechless.

He tried to reevaluate the problem again. Maybe the drinking wasn't Maitree's problem—Maitree was who he was. It was his mother! She spoiled him, allowing him to do anything he wanted, without guiding him in the right direction. It was quite odd, the way his mother always gave in to her youngest son, ever since he was born. As a baby, Maitree used to bite her nipples when she breastfed him, and she did nothing to stop him. When he grew a bit older and started yelling profanities at her and his father, she made no attempt to stop him from doing that, either. After his father passed, she couldn't make Maitree go back to school. All she said was: 'He doesn't want to study anymore.' As simple as that! After quitting school, Maitree mostly hung around at home doing nothing. His mother complained a bit, but she still cooked and washed his clothes for him. She gave him money to buy alcohol and paid for his new motorbike. She complained about his good-for-nothing lifestyle, that was true, but complaining was all she did; in the end, she always helped him out and took care of everything for him. Maitree himself knew very well that, regardless of her complaints, she would never cut him adrift. His mother only tried to fix her youngest son's problems according to each specific circumstance or condition. She approached his problems the way you would an exam question with only two choices.

Question 1: Maitree has just assaulted someone. He is really stressed out. What should he do?
    A. Endure the stress and suffer.
    B. Try to find a way to relieve his stress.

Maitree and his mother never tried to think beyond this framework. For example, they'd never ask why they had to address the above question at all, nor would they ask: why did Maitree assault someone in the first place?'

Question 2: 'Mum, can you give me some money for booze? Otherwise, I will . . . '
    A. 'Put it on my liquor store tab.'
    B. 'Do all sorts of horrible things to get the money.'

Earlier, he'd tried to tell his mother that she had been deceived by Maitree into believing that, for each of life's questions, there were only two choices to choose from. The truth is, he realized, his mother had not been deceived by Maitree. She was actually the one establishing this framework for him.

Question 3: How many people can a bottle of booze help to relieve stress and bring about sleep?
   A. One person.
   B. Two people.

Last night, his mother had been with Maitree while he was drinking. Because she was drinking with him, comforting him, letting him know that she shared his suffering, she was sure that he wouldn't go out and cause more trouble.

Two days later, he takes a trip home. He had asked Chidchai to go to a local market and buy him a gift basket, which he plans to bring with him when visiting Thai at the hospital. He wants to meet Thai to apologize for his brother. Based on the phone conversation he had with Chidchai in recent days, he knows that Thai is still alive. Luckily for Thai, he was not severely injured; Maitree had attacked him with a machete, and it had gone straight through his neck, but it had been blunt. The curved part in the middle of the machete had gone into the curve of Thai's neck, fracturing his jaw instead of cutting into his flesh. He had sighed with relief after Chidchai informed him of this.

As he sits on the back of a hired motorbike, riding past Thai's garage towards his mother's house, he notices that Sangwan, Sumon, and a few of their workers are aggressively staring at him. Once he arrives at his mother's house, he sits down on a bamboo bench downstairs while his mother gets him some water to drink. He glances at the machete resting against a cement wall and asks his mother whether it was the one Maitree had used that night. She nods. The machete occupies the same spot it did before it became a weapon in a crime. That spot is near the entrance to the downstairs area of the house, right in front of his mother's bedroom, near the bamboo bench on which Maitree and his mother often sat together to relax. He suspects that the night Maitree committed the crime, he had been drinking with his mother on this very bench. And after listening to his mother recount to him what happened that night, he knows that his guess is right.

It happened just a few weeks after the festivities of Loy Krathong, and people were still enjoying themselves, drinking and having fun through to early December. According to his mother, a party had been going on at Thai's garage for many nights. His mother, Chidchai, and Maitree's wife had been drinking together on the bamboo bench downstairs, and Maitree, who was already a bit drunk, joined them later. His mother told him that the party at Thai's garage had started in the afternoon and, like many nights before, it had gone on into the night, with music blasting and cherry bombs exploding. Cherry bombs were much louder than regular firecrackers, and Thai's guests lit them with impunity, throwing them casually in all directions.

Drunk and enraged by her refusal to give him half the land, Thai had been throwing cherry bombs into his mother's property in the middle of the night for three or four nights in a row. The loud explosions had driven the family to their limits. They had no clue what Thai hoped to achieve from it, but they had tried their best not to react. However, the night the crime took place, their patience ran out. He guessed that his mother could no longer stand Thai's behaviour, and she couldn't help cursing at Thai while she drank with her two sons. Every time a cherry bomb was thrown from Thai's garage and exploded in her front yard, she probably swore at Thai. 'Why the hell does he do that? Driving people crazy with those stupid bombs! Leave me and my heart in peace! Those bombs are going to give me a heart attack!' Listening to their mother complain, Chidchai and Maitree were probably disturbed by her irritation and anger. As sons, how might they help protect their mother from being provoked by others? What could they do to ensure that she enjoyed peaceful sleep at night? When another cherry bomb was thrown, exploding near the bottom of the staircase at the front of their house, the two sons simply tolerated the ear-splitting explosion before continuing to drink, preparing themselves for the next shock. Their mother, on the other hand, got up and headed towards to Thai's garage.

She yelled out angrily: 'Why do you keep lighting those goddamn cherry bombs? You've been doing it for three or four nights in a row now! When will you stop? I would've been okay with it if you hadn't

thrown them into my front yard. What the hell did you do that for? Do
you want to provoke me or what?'

Thai rushed out to swear at her, yelling back that he could do
whatever he wanted. Both got into a heated argument. All of a sudden,
Thai punched her, but just a split second after that, she heard a swirling
sound behind her. She saw Thai's neck being struck by a knife, sending
him to the ground. She turned to look behind her and saw Maitree
standing there. Shock soon turned into chaos as Sangwan rushed
towards her husband, while Maitree's wife and others tried to hold
everyone back. After that, the family walked home in a daze and sat
together in the downstairs area, trying to figure out what to do. It was
then that his mother decided to pick up the phone and ring him.

He remembers that, on that night, after telling his mother that
Maitree should go to the police, she had handed her phone to Maitree,
so that he could talk to him. He'd asked Maitree in annoyance:

'What the hell did you do that for?'

'He hurt Mum!' Maitree had replied.

He wondered why Maitree had been carrying that knife with him
and what sort of demon had whispered into his ear that had prompted
him to attack Thai. Maitree said he'd just picked up what was available
nearby, and that knife had been close to hand. At the time, his instinct
had told him that something bad was going to happen, when his mother
had gotten up all of a sudden and gone straight towards Thai and a
group of men who were drinking together. Apparently, from Maitree's
point of view, picking up the knife and following his mother had been a
reasonable thing to do in that circumstance. In fact, Maitree, who relied
purely on a son's instinct to protect his mother, had simply told him:

'I knew that something bad was going to happen, so my hand
automatically reached for a weapon.'

Question 4: Pick the losing side.
    A. Them.
    B. Us.

That was probably how Maitree had perceived the situation.
Something bad was going to happen—something that will result in

loss—so he has to decide who will be the one to suffer. Maitree made a decision without consulting anyone else in the family.

Our family are the accused, and their family are the accusers.

After listening to his mother tell him about what happened that night, he walks around the house and finds remnants of cherry bombs scattered in the front yard, by the side of the house next to a chicken coop. (His mother's chicks had probably gone berserk from the explosions that night.) His mother certainly wasn't making things up. Nevertheless, he was in despair. Despite the visible evidence that persisted from those cherry bombs, his family remained the accused.

11 December 2008

It was time for yet another uncomfortable confrontation. He couldn't help imagining all the things that might happen when he met Thai's family, but somehow, he mustered the strength to face them. He grabbed the gift basket and headed towards Thai's garage. Once he got to their place, he was surrounded by Thai's family members, all of whom were extremely hostile. Sumon, loitering nearby, tried to intimidate him by kicking stuff around. He tried to stay calm, greeting them politely before sitting down on a granite bench in the yard in front of the garage. He told Sangwan that he had come to see them to apologize for all the terrible things that had happened. They were right to stare at him with utmost mistrust, and to respond to his apology with coldness, with animosity and provocation. They all viciously attacked his mother and brothers, and he had to tell himself not to react or argue back, reminding himself that Thai's family was the victim here, so it was best to let them vent, to let out their anger.

Later, he mentioned to Sangwan that he wanted to visit Thai at the hospital, but she objected, claiming she didn't like the idea because she didn't want to put her husband at risk of fatal assault. He shook his head, put on an embarrassed smile, and told her that someone like him was incapable of murdering her husband at the hospital. Sangwan responded by saying, 'You're all animals! If your brother could attack my husband like that, you can too!'

At that point, all he wanted to do was get up and leave, but he forced himself to stay put. He calmly told them that his family was genuinely sorry for handling the conflict so badly. ('Of course! All of you should feel sorry by now!') The crime had been committed and, as the eldest brother, he wanted to apologize for what his family had done. ('Well, it would be better if you tried to teach your folks, especially your mother, to learn to control themselves!') Their responses rendered him speechless for a while. ('I could easily shoot the motherfucker right here!' Sumon yelled out for everyone to hear.) He put on another stupid smile and said his family was willing to pay for all of Thai's hospital expenses, but Sangwan immediately rejected his offer, adding that she wanted Maitree to serve the longest possible jail term. Accepting money from his family would help Maitree in court: something she absolutely did not want to happen. 'I'm not stupid, and you can't buy me!' she said.

He responded by saying that the real cause of the conflict was the two families' inability to agree on the land issue. 'Wouldn't it be better if we attended to the root of the problem, and settled this issue once and for all? We live close to each other and we see each other every day, and it's probably best not to let the argument drag on. So, should we try to find a way to clearly divide the land in a way that satisfies both sides?'

'Don't you act like a smartarse!' Sangwan snapped. 'These are two different things, so don't you try to pretend that they're the same! Your brother trying to murder my husband is one issue'—he tried to correct her by saying that it was just physical assault, but she wouldn't listen—'and the argument over the land is another. Don't even think about convincing me to go along with you. I'm not that stupid, and I've got a lawyer to help me. In either case, my family is in a much better position to win than yours, and we'll make sure to teach your family an expensive lesson. Your brother is going to jail, and he'll rot there for at least twenty years, and half of the land is going to be ours. End of story! You and your family have no right to negotiate.'

He had no idea how he just sat there and let them hurl insults at him. Afterwards, he got up quietly and calmly, although he was raging inside.

'Even if that is the case, I still want to apologize, and I hope Mr Thai gets well soon.' He didn't mean it, of course.

There are probably people who enjoy benefitting from their own unfortunate circumstances, hoping to gain something from their misfortune by taking advantage of others. They might try to use their own tragedies to get ahead in life. For example, a young girl of not yet eighteen might decide to sell herself, but when she gets caught, she claims that she was lured into the sex industry, that she was raped. She pushes the blame onto a madam or a pimp as she cries for help from a high-profile social worker. In short, she takes advantage of the circumstances and tried to create scandal out of it. Maybe someone whispered advice into her ear, suggesting she might contribute to society by exposing some human trafficking ring. In this way, she is transformed from a girl who wanted money for an iPad into a victim whose plight saddens others. People like this do exist, he believes, and they are more or less like Lolita, Humbert's nymphet.

He was boiling with fury. Maybe he was inherently cruel just like Sangwan had accused him of being. While his brother betrayed such traits through violent actions, he expressed them furtively through cruel thoughts, which often come to him as he acts extremely polite to others, or laughs at something he does not find humorous at all. His mind goes in the opposite direction of his outward expression. Only with his family does he not put on an act, and that is why he treats his family inconsiderately. He chooses to be nice to others outside his family; just a while back, he had been extremely polite to Sangwan, telling her how sorry he was for what had happened. How long could he tolerate his own hypocritical self?

How had this catastrophe fallen upon his family, and how had they passed it on to him? He walked home. When he got there, he looked at his mother. She was the one who had initially handed the problem to him: 'I don't know what to do! Please help me, son!' He couldn't push the problem back onto her, for he could imagine all the worse things that might happen if he refused to help.

A few days ago, he had contacted a lawyer to seek advice. The lawyer had exclaimed, 'How awful! How very serious! Gravely serious!' perhaps in the hope of demanding more pay for handling a difficult case.

But who is going to pay the lawyer?

'I certainly can't afford it. If they're throwing him in jail, so be it!' his mother said, before complaining about how unfair it was that Maitree would have to go to jail for trying to protect his own mother. After learning the number of years he would have to spend in jail, she was shocked: 'If I had known things would turn out this way, I would've just told Maitree to chop off that bastard's head!' In his mother's eyes, if Maitree had killed Thai, the time he would have served in jail would hardly be different to his current sentence. Therefore, it would have been more worthwhile to kill that hateful man. His mother also believed that they wouldn't have to hire a lawyer if they simply let Maitree go to jail. He had to explain to her that things didn't quite work that way, that they would still need a lawyer regardless. 'I don't have any money.' That was all his mother could say. His younger brother Chidchai couldn't offer any help either, because he was still deep in debt. His mother often gave Maitree cash, but he'd spent so much on drinking that he owed several liquor stores a huge amount of money. All the family expenses seemed to be his sole responsibility. Fuck them all! He shook his head, irritated.

What a shame. If someone had died, it could have been a priceless lesson or parable; a sin that continued to haunt one or more of those affected. However, in reality, there had been no death, and the person who had nearly been killed would eventually recover. He pondered all of this bitterly. Why? Someone should have died. Take a look at fiction, where death is of such significance. In fiction, death can the beginning of a narrative, or the trigger for a plot point, or a resolution. Death can be placed anywhere in a narrative to achieve the desired effect. Death is crucial in fiction: it is a necessity, a form of justice, the moral of a story.

But in real life, death is seen differently; everyone tries to reject it, to cast it aside and out of their relationships. Death cannot exist, cannot be real, cannot be fair. Death is incomparable; we merely hope that justice, awareness, conscience, moral lessons, and positive change might occur without death. No wonder reality is suffering. It tries not to die, refuses to die, and heals itself. Life rejects death—that which is so simple and so just—and struggles to find something else to hold onto, something which might give meaning to its existence.

If Thai had been killed that night, or if his mother had been killed, things would have been over by now. Life would not have been prolonged; it would not have been forced to search for other things to attach itself to: things like the law, justice, trials, social vitriol. There is no denying that death is indifferent towards humanity.

Death is sacred in fiction. It sits on its own throne, before life, which stands and waits for justice and morality to be delivered by death's hands. Once death strikes us with its fatal hammer, we simply accept it without question, without appeals or attempts at retraction. Once death strikes us (and commands us to die), we accept it. As simple as that!

As a storyteller (though a mere ghostwriter), it is unsurprising that he desires death, because real life does not offer it to him. In fiction, the deaths of characters are a common occurrence. Characters die in order to maintain their own honour or dignity, or to reinvigorate the reader.

There are probably certain kinds of people who hope to gain something from their own unfortunate circumstances, but he cannot tell whether Sangwan and her family belong in that category. Apparently, his family isn't like that, and neither is he. Nevertheless, because his mother has handed this problem to him to solve, he—as a writer—has concluded that death is neceesary for resolution.

'Tell me what that bitch said to you,' his mother said. He was annoyed by her blunt, hateful, unrefined way of talking about people she disliked. She had probably acquired this way of speaking from watching soap operas on TV. Why couldn't she rise above lowly emotions and try to be a bit more civilized? He felt a sudden rage against his mother.

'It's all because of you! You!' he yelled at his mother. 'You and your greed and stupidity! You can't even read or write and those TV soaps you watch all the time have made a fool out of you. See what happens when you sign anything people give you? They tricked you into giving up half of our land, and there's no way for you to get it back because you already signed the sale documents! If you go to court, there's no way you'll win because no one will listen to you, even if you shout from the top of your lungs that you only sold this

or that bit of land. You have no written evidence, but that family has
the sale documents with Chidchai's and your signatures on them.
You made a mistake but you won't accept it. Your stubbornness
led you to disaster and you brought the disaster onto our family,
nurturing it with your stupidity, your obstinacy, your blind devotion.
No wonder those other two kids of yours can't think. Their faculties
have been paralysed, and they can't stand on their own two feet.
They depend entirely on you because they know that you'll let them
stay with you, that you'll feed them and do their laundry for them.
And they know that you'll clean up their messes for them. They are
utterly hopeless without you!'

His mother sat there, wounded. Her eyes were sad, and her lip
quivered. Lucky for him that he hadn't been pampered by her,
otherwise he'd be hopeless too, just like his two brothers. He'd left
home when he was not yet twenty, managed to get a degree, and had
been supporting himself financially ever since finishing his studies.

He was so upset that nothing but the earth swallowing him whole
could have stopped him from venting his anger. Wasn't that the thing
he secretly longed for? He was hurling abuses at his own mother.
The only person who could compete with him in this regard was the
infamous, matricidal Kong Khao Noi!

'Drag me down! Do it now!' he told the earth silently. He strode
towards his brother's room and started yelling at him.

'It amazes me that you're still alive! Do you have any brains left?
Where is your conscience? You're just an animal, a brute! All you've
done in your life is cause trouble for your mother and brothers. Why
are you still breathing? Why don't you just drop dead? Death will be
good for you, and it'll make the family happy. Your death will unburden
Mum and free me from all the pain you've caused me.' He shook his
head to show his brother just how disappointed he was in him. Maitree
was sitting in the darkness of his room. He looked pathetic.

'And you didn't go to work today, did you? I bet you said you were
too distressed to work, and I bet you'll say the same thing when you
sit down to drink tonight! You bring disaster onto our family! You son
of a bitch!'

He caught a bus to Bangkok. The burning rage inside him slowly diminished. His daily life in Bangkok is not particularly hectic. He struggles mainly with silence and his own thoughts, and on the days where he feels boredom, he often sits on the passenger seat of a motorbike taxi that takes him through the winding and unfamiliar alleys of the city. Then after a while, he usually gets off the motorbike taxi and takes a stroll before catching another motorbike taxi to get home. Some nights he sits at a bar in a Japanese restaurant whose patrons are Japanese men working for Japanese companies in Thailand. The Japanese come with their colleagues or bosses. At first they eat and drink quietly, but they get more jovial after a while. He likes that kind of restaurant. Listening to foreigners laughing and chatting away in a foreign tongue gives him a warm feeling and fascinates him at the same time. The night after that trip to his hometown, he visits a Japanese restaurant and drinks several cups of sake as he chain-smokes, exhaling so much smoke that it looks like a thin mist has spread all over the restaurant. Then, he walks into a restroom, where he cries soundlessly, so as to not disturb others with his sobs. After that, he asks for the bill and takes a motorbike taxi home. There, he resumes his crying. He feels like his heart and entire being have been struck with pain and sorrow, for he has said horrible things to his mother and youngest brother. He will never forgive himself for that. Once uttered, horrible words don't simply affect those they are directed at; they have not been handed over from him to them. Instead, those horrible words still remain within him, and they squeeze his whole being with such force that he is stretched out of shape and starts to fall apart, just like clothes that have been washed by hand and squeezed so forcefully that all their seams are damaged and broken. He feels no different from a shirt—a once-intact shirt, with a neck and sleeves, pockets and all— that has been reduced to a badly-damaged garment, on the cusp of falling to pieces.

He thinks about the terrible things he said to Maitree and his mother. Horrific images of destruction appear in his mind and engulf his entire being.

15 December 2008

He received a call from his mother three days later. 'You must be pleased now!' she said, sobbing. 'Chidchai is dead!'

Chidchai's death is yet another sort of stupid situation, one that has no connection whatsoever to the disaster currently befalling his family, as caused by Maitree.

Chidchai had his own problems, and his death was the result of an accumulation of things, things he had done to himself. His death was independent, cut off entirely from his family. When his mother said that he must have been pleased knowing that Chidchai was dead, her blame had been totally misplaced. He didn't want Chidchai to die. His death was timely, though, as it epitomized the destruction suffered by his family. His mother had taken Chidchai's death as an opportunity to blame him.

However, already drenched in disaster, he went along with the blame his mother placed. Let her believe that his cruel words were as powerful as a court ruling. Let her. There's more where that came from.

Chidchai's outlook in life had brought about his death: a rising middle-class man, aspiring towards a luxurious lifestyle, towards dreams pre-packaged by society. Though that type of dream was commonplace, it made him feel like he was different from those on the lower rungs of society, different from the older generations before him, from the rural life that surrounded him. Those middle-class dreams painted a totally different picture from provincial unsophistication. They were dreams manufactured by state-owned factories, by TV commercials, by pamphlets issued in aid of national economic and social development. These manufactured dreams were force-fed into the hollow brains of the future, where they generated an image of themselves as the more novel, more elevated generation, stuck living in primitive, rural lands. Slowly, they changed themselves, before embarking to change the land they stood on. Such journeys are costly. Thousands have dropped dead along the way, and Chidchai was one of them. What's more, Chidchai's death was predetermined. Death is an unavoidable consequence of those dreams. (It isn't widely advertised, but it's been there all along.) In other words, one cannot exist without the other.

After the bank seized Chidchai's love nest, his wife changed her first and last names and moved to Bangkok to start a new life. Broke and alone, Chidchai returned to his birthplace, where his mother, with her unwavering love, welcomed him with open arms. She cared for him, gradually stitching the shattered parts of his soul together until it was whole again. She also persuaded him to briefly become a monk, hoping that doing so would help rid him of bad luck. Deep down, she also wanted to cling to his monkhood as a means of gaining enough merit to be reborn in a better world after her time in this one had ended. Chidchai went along with her, even though monkhood did nothing to calm his restless mind.

Immediately after renouncing his monkhood, the first thing he did was to head to Bangkok to find out where his wife was living. Once he found her, he gave her all the donation money he had acquired as a monk. He spent a whole week begging her to come back, to live with him, to start their lives together again. Even though he tried to rekindle the romance they once shared, all his attempts at persuasion were unsuccessful. She wanted him to live with her in Bangkok, but he couldn't, because he didn't know how his mother would manage if he lived so far away from her. Chidchai was convinced that his mother needed him and wanted him to live near her, when in fact, it was actually he who needed her most.

Lovesick and pining for his ex-wife, Chidchai returned home, where he lay bedridden for a few days. All the time, his mother was by his side; eventually, Chidchai was able to pull himself together. He got a job at a power plant, toiling day and night to resurrect himself from the bankruptcy of his old marriage. Determined and ambitious, he managed to earn enough money to pay back all their debtors, even the loan sharks who had sent the police to arrest him. His mother couldn't understand why he paid for his ex-wife's debts. 'Why are you so infatuated with her?' she asked him. 'Did she give you a love potion to drink?' In response, Chidchai simply told his mother that once he had sorted out his mess, he would repay her for all she had done for him. At this, his mother's face lit up, and she cherished his words in her heart.

But Chidchai never kept his promise. He created private living quarters in one of his mother's rental rooms, with a very comfortable bed, a computer, and a flat-screen TV with cable. He drank imported liquor and experimented with wine. (His mother and Maitree drank moonshine; indeed, it was only once in a blue moon that Chidchai would share his expensive alcohol with them.) He also bought a brand new car on installment, and soon, there was a new woman in his life.

She was well-off and had her own business as a clothing retailer and wholesaler. Chidchai often brought her home with him and, although his mother was not exactly pleased with their relationship, she did prefer his new girlfriend, who didn't seem to want to control the way Chidchai handled his money like his ex-wife had. She didn't seem like someone who would cause Chidchai trouble, but because of this, he didn't seem to lust after her as much. He was fond of trouble and, deep down, he always looked for it. Chidchai's relationship with the new woman lasted less than a year, and they broke up over something as trivial as his insistence on keeping old wedding photos of himself and his ex-wife, instead of throwing them away.

Chidchai seemed independent enough, either spending most of his time outside or in his room, sleeping. The only time his mother saw him was when he wanted something to eat after he woke up. In short, Chidchai's life was mostly spent outside the home, and his mother had no idea what he got up to each day. With Maitree, things were completely different: she knew everything that went on in the life of her youngest son, whereas Chidchai led a life of extravagance that he just couldn't afford. He ignored his mother whenever she questioned him about it and, if she persisted, he would say that he could look after himself. He purchased all sorts of luxurious items, like that new car. When his mother occasionally asked him to drive her to the fresh market, he'd ask her to pay for the petrol. Everything Chidchai owned was for the sake of maintaining the image of an affluent lifestyle. He had to work extremely hard to earn enough money to keep up. It was, therefore, not the right time to repay his mother as he had once promised

His mother earned very little from her rental rooms. Two of them were occupied by her sons, neither of whom paid her any rent or bothered to help with household expenses. More electrical appliances meant higher electricity and water bills, all of which she had to pay. She also had to find enough money to afford the meals she cooked for them every day. Where did she get the money from? Partly from the monthly allowance he himself sent to her. It was he that his whole family relied on, and it was through a shameful job that he earned his income: his job as a ghostwriter, as one who hides his true identity in the shadows. It was a job he could not be truly proud of, because he wrote in order to please others and to follow their instructions. It was the kind of writing that paid well, but was considered humiliating within its own community. The kind of writing that makes you feel disgusted with yourself when you look in the mirror.

As far as his job was concerned, though, he knew he couldn't blame his mother and brothers. No one had forced him to do this job. He did it willingly because he didn't have the courage to reveal his true identity. That was why he had to keep this diary in secret. What a pathetic, self-pitying person he was!

Chidchai was addicted to nightlife, and he frequented bars and pubs in Kaeng Khoi, Tan Diew, and sometimes the Saraburi town centre. He barely had any friends, so he often went to these places alone, looking for young girls to sit and drink with. One night, he met a girl who was just his type—someone with issues, someone likely to cause him trouble—and he fell head over heels in love with her.

She was only about sixteen or seventeen, almost ten years younger than Chidchai. She was still a student, and at the age where clubbing and partying were one's main priorities; sure enough, she partied hard, and often. They had met at a bar in Tan Diew, flirting until they eventually became romantically involved. She was considered quite the catch, so having her as a girlfriend was seen as a victory for Chidchai.

Chidchai brought her home often. On the phone, his mother told him:

'When they're home, they spend all their time in his room and only come out when they want me to cook them something to eat. I don't know what to say, because that girl is still in her school uniform. She's so young. Chidchai always drives her to school and picks her up, and I don't hear him complaining about the cost of petrol. When he comes home from work, he takes off his dirty clothes and leaves them for me to wash, but I've seen him washing that girl's panties for her!'

What she told him seemed trivial, but it was as if she felt that the things Chidchai did for his lover were actually things he should have been doing for her. She also observed, 'I'm sure he's paying for her studies. I saw him give her money before she went off to school.'

His family's fate was like a snake chasing its own tail. His mother adored Chidchai, but he was the type to always let his infatuation and passion for a woman get the better of him. He was no different from his father, who had also let his infatuation with his mistresses ruin his life. And when his father died, his mother chased after Chidchai for the love and attention she had never received from her late husband.

After the incident where Maitree attacked Thai, Sumon (Thai's son) made sure that he and his family members never had another moment of peace. He did everything he could to intimidate and harass them. Chidchai was a coward and hated violence, something he saw as belonging to primitive folk, something beneath him. When Sumon started harassing his girlfriend, he moved her to a new place, where he paid the rent for her.

But the girl wasn't merely Chidchai's plaything. Growing bored of the relationship, she started frequenting the pubs and bars of her past. She often spent whole nights there. When Chidchai finished his night shift, he would be upset when he found her at the bars, surrounded by school boys. He made sure she knew he was displeased, and grew possessive of her. But this only made her—who by then was already sick of him—even more annoyed, and she wanted him out of her life. She grew very friendly with one particular group of teenagers. When you stop loving someone, but they still believe that you belong to them, a common but undesirable thing often takes place.

Chidchai was pathetic and pitiful. He was a slave to his own troubles. He thought he was a refined city dweller, worshipping at the feet of the middle-class dream, and he expected to be respected in return. He dismissed rural folks as vulgar and crude, assuming that it was possible for everyone to better themselves the way he had with his identity, his attitude, his heart and soul. He was wrong, of course, because some people can't change. He put his own life in the wrong place at the wrong time—you might say it was his own karma that brought about his death—but his mother saw it as the direct outcome of his brother's cruel words, as a vindication of the curse he had wrought upon them.

Chidchai had been killed on the spot, even though he hadn't wanted to die. Those who are scared of death often die like this. He should have just been injured, given a chance to get treatment, to recuperate and continue with his life. That way, he would have gained some life lessons, something he could haved pondered over until he reached old age. However, life no longer loved Chidchai. People like him are destined for sudden death—*bang!*—the kind of death that comes instantly after a bullet from a home-made gun belonging to one of those students goes straight through his chest and into his heart. It was a good shot. (Death happens easily to those who still enjoy being alive. On the other hand, those who are desperate to die might still survive, even after being riddled by bullets.)

After his friend pulled the trigger, one of the teenagers exclaimed in admiration, 'Fuck! Great aim! One bullet and that guy's dead!'

Later, some members of the gang were rounded up by the police, but Chidchai's killer managed to escape. None of them were ultimately charged or found guilty.

As for the killer, he spent ten years in hiding while boasting to others about how he had once killed a man, as if it were some prestigious act. By the time he becomes a middle-aged man, he won't even remember that he was once a killer. When he is married with children, with aging parents to look after, he will no longer remember the wild and violent years of his youth, and this death, this taking of another life, will twist and fade away and eventually disappear altogether.

5 May 2009

There is a strange feeling one can examine and occasionally ponder over as one grows older; over the years, that feeling also grows more distant. That feeling—or term—is 'bloodline'.

Does one instantaneously develop a feeling of attachment towards one's biological parents or siblings? It is true that we humans inherit genetic traits from our parents that affect both our physical appearance and our ways of thinking and feeling, all which are foundational to the development of each individual, which in turn shapes with the experiences we encounter in life. Does that feeling of attachment develop immediately once we are born? When someone looks after us for a while, we start to feel attached to that person, and when someone is devoted to us—sacrifices everything, even their lives, for us—we feel a profound love towards that person, regardless of whether they're our biological parents or not. If attachment is something that can be developed after birth, then what is the true meaning of bloodline?

You may not know you share a bloodline with someone. You must be told, or else see it with your own eyes, to know it to be true. The bearers of such information, those who imbue importance and meaning to this knowledge, are the people we refer to as our parents. It is our parents who name someone our 'brother' or our 'sister'. It is true that he saw his mother throughout pregnancy, carrying in her womb someone who would become his brother, but how can he tell if that brother is his 'real' brother?

But how does one define 'real'? Are we 'real' brothers because we were born from the same mother, from the same sperm? Are we 'real' brothers because we share the same bloodline? Or are we 'real' brothers because we are members of the same family? He might have been adopted, or his brother could have been conceived from the sperm of a man who is not his father. So, does bloodline even matter if they share a brotherly affection with one other? What about their biological parents? Are they important in this case? To him, the answer to both questions is 'no', because the affection we have for our parents happens afterwards. We love, respect, and care for our parents because they brought us up and made it possible for us to survive, not because of some biological process, the act of fertilization. This is most evident in cases where a child is adopted: the child loves the people who have nurtured him, and he refers to them as his parents. To him, they are his real parents, and this is no less real—indeed, it could even be more real—than the relationship between biological parents and their children.

So, what is the crux of the definition of 'parent'? The same question applies to the definition of 'sibling'.

We humans grow up with limited perceptions, listening to age-old stories, but they coalesce within words like 'mother', 'father', 'family', 'bloodline'—to name just a few—and eventually, they lead us to the definition of those words, which enable us to comprehend our position in life. But comprehension alone is not enough. We need to be aware of the significance, of the grand definitions behind some words: words whose meanings we dare not explore, change, or question, as if by simply questioning them, we might be branded as ungrateful.

We learn of these stories with our limited perceptions, we learn the value of these big words and their meanings, but what we don't learn is how meaning is constructed into terminology. Words like 'parent', 'family', 'sibling', 'bloodline': they were not distilled within us like sweet nectar, but poured into us from the outside. From a jar of syrupy substance (honey, perhaps), our own parents spoon-feed us these words, saying before each spoonful: 'This is honey, my dear. It is so sweet.' We then associate honey with sweetness: honey equals sweetness and nothing else. We then accept this supposition as the truth or the norm, and we contort our personal experiences to fit these meanings that have been imposed on us. This is how we humans scrape and polish our own experiences. If we try hard but still fail to normalize our experiences, we may have to cut out or erase some of them. We have been brought up to embrace traditional definitions, not to construct our own meanings for things.

What was he playing at? Sitting here, trying to cram oceans into canals? His younger brother just met a tragic death, but he feels no sadness. All he feels is that it serves him right. He feels neither love nor attachment towards the lost life of someone he once called his 'brother'. Maybe that was why he was trying to come up with elaborate tricks of logic and reason to justify his lack of grief towards the death of his own brother.

Let's not forget that he's also still trying to fix the chronic stream of problems handed down to him by his mother. He realizes that he is yet to escape; in fact, he is still stumbling around within the confines of the problem, trying to figure out a solution. But he was starting to see a larger terrain of possibilities that might lead to a way out of the problem. His mother handed him the problem, after all, so she ought to accept his method of handling it. Chidchai's death was just a prologue to the real, imminent disaster. Blink and you'll miss it! If his mother really wanted to know, he wouldn't mind telling her right now: the truth is that those who repeatedly beg for death won't be dying anytime soon. Those who want to live, on the other hand, will be the ones to leave this world, abandoning those who desire death, leaving them to continue existing in paralysis, unable to think or do anything except to watch the drowning, devastation, and annihilation of those who wish to live. Those who wish for death must live to bear witness, to learn their lesson.

This is his rough solution to the problem that his mother has given him to solve.

You know what, Mum? He's had his suspicions about Maitree for quite a while now, and today, he is going to find the answer to them. Chidchai's death has revealed to him that sharing the same bloodline with someone does not automatically create a feeling of attachment towards that person. And when it comes to that brainless troublemaker Maitree, well: cutting him off will be easy.

During his second trip home, he learned something regarding Maitree's case. He and his mother had been consulting the lawyers he'd hired to help out with the case when Somjai—Maitree's girlfriend, who had been there the night he'd assaulted Thai—walked past where they were sitting, on the way to her room. He noticed that she had put on weight and was walking rather slowly, so he asked his mother what was wrong with her. His mother beamed and told him that Somjai was pregnant. When he asked who the father was, she said, 'Who else could it be?' He supposed that his mother was already imagining herself with a new grandchild in her arms, and that was why she looked so pleased.

But he was not at all pleased, especially when he remembered how events had unfolded on that disastrous night. He remembered that

Maitree had been harassing his mother to organize his wedding with Somjai, and had also asked her to help pay his dowry. Later, on the phone, his mother had asked his opinion, and he'd told her that he disapproved of her helping Maitree.

Even though Maitree and Somjai weren't married, the two had been living together in one of his mother's rental rooms like husband and wife, and it was now obvious that they had consummated accordingly. He remembered yelling at his brother to use condoms. Now, he felt like he'd been slapped back and forth across the face with those same condoms until he was numb with pain. It was clear that Maitree and his wife hadn't bothered with condoms; in their eyes, they were husband and wife, so there was no need for them. However, it was also possible that their refusal to use condoms was actually an ingenious gamble, and if that gamble paid off, their stagnant fates would creak to life and shift anew. And Maitree had won by successfully creating new life: the foetus sleeping in Somjai's womb. This foetus would become a baby and a grandchild, one that would break his mother, force her to yield. This grandchild would be the sticking point, an obligation that acted as a bridge, formally linking Maitree and Somjai together. In short, the birth of Maitree's baby would force his mother to make the necessary preparations, to help Maitree pay his dowry and to arrange his wedding, to make it all real.

This is how one uses consequence to justify cause. This is how one uses consequence to dismantle reason, to force it to fit present reality.

Such was the ingenious plan his wild imagination had conjured up for them, but in truth, he believed that his brother and Somjai had not planned this. Instead, they had just taken one of the two options available to people who were used to living their lives with only two options to choose from. Still, there are moments in life where coincidence rewards you with something both brilliant and worthwhile.

He asked his mother how far along Somjai was. Around five months, she said, according to what Somjai had told her after she'd gone to see a doctor. He tried to figure out when the baby was conceived, and once he arrived at the date, he felt the sting of the condom slapping him round the face, even more painful than before.

Over the past five months, his family had been bombarded with problems, starting from that early December night when that stupid Maitree had committed that disastrous crime. If that night was the starting point . . . Aha! It all made sense. The final missing jigsaw piece had clicked into place, completing the whole picture. This final jigsaw piece—this ingenious coincidence he had previously been unaware of—had been created amidst all this crisis.

That night, after Maitree had attacked Thai with the machete, his mother and Somjai had dragged Maitree home, forcing him to stay in his room. His mother had tried to calm herself down before calling him. He'd suggested that they take Maitree to a police station, which they did. Seeing that Maitree had no intention to flee, the police had recorded the crime and allowed Maitree to return home with his family. That night at home, everyone was shaken; tense and confused. His mother had ordered Maitree and his wife to stay in their room, while Chidchai and she remained downstairs, keeping an eye on things. Sumon, Thai's son, had been enraged. He'd walked back and forth in front of their house, venting his fury by yelling out threats and all sorts of abuse.

In the hellish atmosphere of that airless, moonlit night, Maitree had been unable to sleep, pacing back and forth in his small room. Somjai was crouching on the floor, her back against the wall as she kept an eye on Maitree, who had begun to weigh the options of fleeing or taking his own life. Actually, the first option was no longer available to him, as he had convinced Maitree to turn himself in, and deep down, he knew that he was too cowardly to commit suicide. His mouth was dry and his throat was phlegmy. He had gulped down plenty of water but he was still thirsty. He'd been desperate for a drink, believing it was the only thing that might help him feel less tense and anxious, but he remembered that he'd been forbidden to drink by his eldest brother, who had told him that drinking would only drag him down further into a disastrous abyss. He also remembered that he'd promised his brother he would quit. But half a bottle of moonshine was still in his room, and he felt it could give him another option. He wouldn't have to choose between death and running away, because the moonshine would allow him to cope with what he had so recently done; namely, turning himself in, which had not been his preferred option at all, and something he'd been forced to do by his family. At this moment, he had been tormented by the thought of jail, of being in chains and being forced to share a cell with other prisoners. It was not at all the option he'd have up with, but he'd have to accept it. In order to come to terms with his future, he needed to drink, because drinking would relax him just enough that he would drift into sleep. He'd picked up the bottle of moonshine, but Somjai tried to stop him. 'Pity me,' Maitree said. 'I'm the only one who has to bear this hell. I have to suffer all alone.' Feeling sorry for Maitree, Somjai had let him drink, moving closer to him to indicate that his suffering was also hers, and that she was worried about her lover's future. She then picked up a glass and poured some moonshine into it so she could drink with him. In this way, the two had bridged their plights together, and together, they blamed fate for playing tricks on them.

'Will you leave me if I go to jail?' asked Maitree.

'I'll never leave you. I'll wait for you,' Somjai said.

'I'm so scared,' Maitree said. 'I'm sure you'll leave me,.'

Somjai wiped the tears from Maitree's face with her hand, moving closer to him to hug him. Then they made love.

In that airless, moonlit night, while Sumon yelled hysterically outside, a new life had begun.

6 May 2009

In the midst of a crisis, a life had been conceived, and despair embraced it like a womb. Nine months later, that life would come out into the world.

In his opinion, under such circumstances—a new life entering into existence just as its entire family was going downhill—how could this baby be a gift to its parents? How would it feel when it was grown up? Would it feel that its birth was a gift, when its parents had brought it into this world but were incapable of raising it? It would be born into a basket already shredded by fate. It seemed to him that no one had paused to ponder whether the birth of that child would bring more hardship, or whether it would offer the dim hope of redemption.

Redemption from what? Right now, Maitree's lawyer was trying to conjure a date of conception for the life in Somjai's womb that might help the process of witness interrogation. The lawyer would magic Somjai into being three months pregnant on the night of the crime, hoping that this, along with other details he planned to fabricate, would reduce the severity of Maitree's sentence. Was it redemption from the couple's illegitimate relationship? Indeed, the birth of the baby would prompt his mother to pay for the dowry and to organize the wedding for Maitree. To him, however, this baby would not offer any redemption and its birth would not benefit anyone. Still, the baby seemed a significant possible solution to the difficult problem his mother had asked him to fix, for the baby's blood was mixed with the blood of a mysterious stranger.

He recalls his father's sudden death, years ago; now, he feels it was most opportune. If his father were still alive, what would he see? Would he see this the way he, the elder brother, now sees it? What would he do? He has no answers to these questions. He has witnessed this thing for his father who couldn't, but there is nothing he can do about it. That is because he is no longer part of this family. He is merely an observer. He is able to piece things together, but is unable to interfere with his family's affairs; now, his mother is the one who steers the family's destiny.

What does he see? He sees something odd, secretive; he sees an attempt to conceal it, even though it may not be obvious. Still, with the passage of time, this thing reveals itself more and more in a way that is hard to ignore.

His father died and did not have the chance to watch Maitree grow up. If he saw Maitree now, he would certainly be able to tell.

When Maitree was a kid, he'd looked like his mother, and his father had complained that he saw no physical resemblance between himself and Maitree. As time went on, his father assumed that Maitree had inherited his fearlessness and sharp tongue from him. He was, in fact, totally mistaken, as those traits had been the first sign of Maitree's desire to challenge and destroy his father, Chidchai, himself—the eldest son—his entire family. Maitree wanted to ravage his father's bloodline, ensuring that only his and his mother's remained. He was washing the old bloodline clean for a new one, and it is unclear to him who was behind all of this. The mastermind had masked himself and his intentions using Maitree's barbaric act. It seemed uncomplicated on first glance, but the truth was not quite so simple.

It is rather obvious to him that, as they grew older, Maitree's personality was quite different from that of Chidchai's and his. He and Chidchai were similar in their keen pursuit of higher education and their desire for a more affluent life. They both deliberated over the problems with careful reasoning instead of resorting to physical violence. Maitree, on the other hand, had no interest in studies and lacked ambition. Short-sighted, he was content to live a lazy life, satisfied by what little rewards came his way. He often relied on physical violence to deal with things.

He himself likes drinking, but it doesn't make him aggressive or violent. He knows when he ought to stop drinking, and he doesn't feel the need to drink every day. When he is drunk, he never wants to raise his voice, beat someone up, or have a heated argument with anyone. (He cannot understand people who, when drunk, want to pick fights and lash out at others. Could it be that they felt crushed or trampled by some mysterious force, compelling them to do the same to others?) He couldn't imagine himself getting drunk, grabbing a knife while demanding money from his mother to buy more booze, throwing tantrums and wrecking things when she refused to do so. Only a thug could do something like that, and his brother was one of them.

Still, out of all her sons, his mother seems to love Maitree the most, is most protective of him. Why?

It had to be because he shared her bloodline. It had to be because he was not his father's son!

Maitree grew up to be very different from his brothers. The physical differences were especially evident: the two brothers (Chidchai and himself) were tall and thin, whereas Maitree was quite stocky. The brothers (Chidchai and himself) had yellow undertones in their complexion, while Maitree had pinkish-brown. Maitree's facial features also bore little resemblance to his brothers' (his and Chidchai's) to the point where one could help but wonder whether he has any trace of their father's genes at all. The shape of his skull, cheekbones, and nose seem to have come from a different mould. Another puzzling thing was his hair, which in his early twenties, started to thin out: a clear sign of future baldness. It was a mystery as to where Maitree had gotten this genetic trait, since their father had thick, curly hair, and their mother's hair was also quite thick. Unlike Maitree, and like their parents, the brothers (Chidchai and himself) had thick hair.

From his physical appearance to his temperament, Maitree bears no resemblance to his brothers and their father. What a pity their father had died when Maitree was a just a kid, that he hadn't been able to witness the difference, but he was here, and he was able to witness them. He could see the difference with his own eyes, but there was nothing he could do.

For years, a stranger's genetic traits have infiltrated his family. He is sure of it. Maitree bears no similarity to him, which will make it easier for him cut him off.

But all of this is his own hypothesis, and he has yet to find other evidence to support it. So far, it is all based on his own suspicions that there was something wrong, something out of place within his family. That which corresponds with his suspicions is Maitree's total dissimilarity to himself, and he cannot accept something alien into his (here imagined) family. He probes further, looking for more evidence, only to encounter contradictions and things which undermine his suspicions. But he does not give up. On the contrary, he becomes bolder in his thinking, in his conviction that Maitree is not his father's son, that he had been fathered by his mother's secret lover, who had vanished after impregnating her.

There are certainly things that make this hypothesis appear unreasonable, not quite right. His mother doesn't seem like the type of woman who would be bold enough to do such a thing. She'd been completely under his father's control while he was still alive, and she couldn't possibly have done anything he hadn't been aware of. Even freedom of thought hadn't been possible. Still, his mother has the tendency to do things differently these days, to behave in opposition to the way she had done whilst living with his father. After his father had passed, the change in her was dramatic. It was as if she had transformed into a different person, and she has since made it clear that his death had freed her from the oppression she'd endured throughout their marriage. She was no longer the prim, polite, and submissive woman she had once been. She has become a sharp-tongued, loud-mouthed, upcountry woman. Sometimes, she reverts back to the dialect of her birthplace. In short, she has rejected everything his father once imposed on her.

Nevertheless, being free of her husband's oppression had not really improved things for her. It was as if she had been freed from one type of domination, only to fall under the control of another. Her life has grown totally disorganized, no different from an abandoned, overgrown plot of land. Its divots and mounds are never filled up or leveled. When birds fly past this plot of land, dropping seeds as they go, those seeds grow freely into big trees, which remain there undisturbed. In the same way, his mother has allowed fate to make a mess of her life by allowing it to determine its own course. If her life appears more complicated now, it is less a demonstration of her free will than it is a consequence of allowing fate to do whatever it wanted, again and again.

There will be plenty of time to ponder over his mother, to piece together the fragments of her life. For now, he shifts his attention to Maitree.

He is certain that Maitree and he have different fathers. Let us consider the full picture of his family once more: there were once three sons, but the middle one met a tragic death, so now, there are only two sons still alive. It seems very unlikely that he, the eldest son, would marry anytime soon, but the youngest son is soon to be a father. The blood that flows within this new life is a mixture of Maitree's blood—imbued with the stranger's blood—and Somjai's blood. The new life that these two have created, their baby girl, is untouched by the blood of the late owner of the land the two reside on. A new family was going to displace the old, to take over land that was not theirs by blood.

To be honest, he severed his family ties long ago, back when he was a teenager. He hardly feels any emotional bond with his family, and their contact was limited to matters concerning loss and familial disaster. (Could that painful, limited sort of contact count as family ties?) And now, he is convinced that Maitree has a stranger's blood in him. They share the same mother. But who was Maitree's father?

9 May 2009

Was it that important to him, knowing who Maitree's real father is? He has spent a great deal of time thinking about this. Was knowing the identity of the man in the shadow essential to finding a solution to the problem? Or was the most significant thing perhaps the realization that Maitree does not have his father's blood in him. That ought to be enough for him to proceed to the next stage, to solve the problem the way he wants to. He has devoted a lot of time to piecing things together in the most logical way possible, contemplating the relevant details and making his hypothesis sound. Initially, he felt that it would be worth spending more time trying to bring the identity of Maitree's real father out into the open, but that feels no longer necessary.

He feels he is becoming obsessed with the matter. Now he isn't sure whether the disaster that happened to his family has depleted his energy, or reinvigorated it. At first glance, it might be a bit of both, but as he gives it more thought, he realizes that it is he who is the real source of disaster. Bad things have happened because of the evil words he uttered; those words were an incantation, an articulation of his rebellion and defiance. He remembered that he had yelled accusations at his mother, blaming her for causing all the awful things that had happened to their family. Not only had he wanted his mother to feel bad, he'd also hoped that his hurtful words would trigger supernatural forces—the law of karma, or any other higher power—to turn, to shift their attention to him and trample him to dust. He wants to hear their terrifying cries as they curse him and sentence him to a horrible death, to cause him more suffering than the suffering he had caused his mother.

He implores those forces to compel Mother Earth to drag him down to his death!

But the earth does not split beneath him and pull him down. Supernatural forces do not manifest themselves that way.

In today's world, supernatural forces do not exercise their power grandly, outrageously. They are cold-blooded, but mercilessly so. Those supernatural forces have heard his defiant words, and they have been watching him. When the moment comes, they will carry out their sentence, they will plunge their stings into his skin. He becomes conscious of the fact that his whole body feels completely numb. He can no longer move.

'Are you happy now?' asked those supernatural forces.

He moaned. Yes, this was how he wanted to solve the problem his mother had handed to him. Is he happy now? Yes, he is in a state of complete bliss. This was the result he wanted.

In uttering his defiance, he has rendered himself infirm. One day, his limbs went limp, and he fell over, where he laid unconscious for a long while. When he regained consciousness, he tried in vain to move. He was overcome by panic. He tried to calm himself down, forcing himself to lie still, hoping that the paralysis would leave him. He grew hopeful when movement returned to the right side of his body, but his left side remained paralysed. By the time dusk crept in, nothing had changed, so he tried to crawl to his desk, grabbed his phone and called an ambulance.

And this is how things unfold from there.

The doctor diagnoses him with a clogged vein in his right brain, which has impeded its ability to control the left side of his body, leaving it paralysed. According to the doctor, there is a chance of recovery, but it could take a year or two, depending on the kind of treatment he receives. He spends the next week in hospital, depleting almost all of his savings.

Throughout the week, he is visited by some of his friends and acquaintances, who each spend fifteen to thirty minutes chatting with him before excusing themselves. It is clear that he cannot stay at the hospital forever. The doctor tells him that he needs to be closely monitored, and that involves expenses: something he cannot afford.

He doesn't have the money to pay for full-time care; because of this, he must endure the pathetic and humiliating act of relieving himself in bed.

His mother calls him. As he picks up the phone, he feels somewhat pleased. She was probably expecting him to help her with something, but he has nothing to give her now that he has become a vegetable, and he tells her as much.

Imagine this: a woman—one who has never ventured out beyond the small provincial town of Kaeng Khoi—now must travel to a big city like Bangkok, along with her youngest son, who, like her, has never been there before. The only thing she knows is the name of the hospital she's supposed to go to. So, mother and son undertake a small adventure, and in the end, they arrive at their destination, despite their upcountry manner and outlook. All the mother knows is her small world on a small plot of land. She takes her eldest son out of a much bigger world and returns him to that small plot of land: the land he should have cherished and valued.

Hatred fills his heart, flooding it more and more each day. This feeling of hatred takes the place of sensation within his limbs, sensation that has since been taken away.

Now, he occupies one of his mother's rental rooms, the one next to Maitree's. He who ran away from home and his family has been forced to return. He does not want Maitree to look after him, to ask what he wants, to offer to do anything for him. He does not want to see Somjai or the baby she is carrying. He hates it when his mother touches him, wipes his skin, cleans up after him. He does not want to listen to her sorrowful words or sobs, nor does he want to see her weep. He hates everything. He realizes that he has become a burden to others. Such a reversal of roles, compared to when he used to complain about shouldering responsibilities for others. But this is his fate. This is what he deserves.

At first, he thought that his plight would bring great suffering upon his mother, who has always seemed unable to rely on herself, continually handing over her life to fate and to others. She had depended on his father, and then on him (her eldest son) to support her crumbling family. Now, he does nothing to help the family, and he waits for it to collapse before his very eyes, but nothing of that sort seems to happen. It is as if things will remain in this state forever, refusing to collapse. After three months, the pain and torment that he thought would affect his mother slowly retracts back into his own heart, and it becomes increasingly clear that it is he who suffers alone.

He has been transformed from a free man with a thirst for life into someone deprived of all he used to have. He starts to think it might be better to be a sleeping prince, unaware of anything that went on around him, unburdened by any and all responsibilities. Right now, his condition is no different to that of a fish stranded on land: still alive, still able to see, hear, and feel, but completely helpless. His condition multiplies his suffering and exacerbates his torment. He wants to die.

But remember the terms previously set? Death spares those who desire it most. He wishes for death, and so his wish will never be answered. All he can do is to lie still in this shabby room in this half-dead, half-alive state. It is what he deserves.

One day, his mother walks into his room, carrying a bowl of water and a towel. She starts to clean him up, rubbing his face, neck, and ears with the damp towel. She moves on to his arms, hands, chest, stomach, legs, and feet, before making him lie on his side. She cleans his back, both sides of his body, and his backside.

Later, she tells him that he has turned into a newborn baby that needs her to give him a bath and put on his clothes. As she cleans his feet for him again, she recounts to him the story of her life when she was a young girl who had to clean her husband's feet before he went to bed. He does not want to hear stories like this and, before now, he had tried to tell her to stop, but his stiff neck and drooping mouth rendered his words unintelligible.

Today, like before, he tries to stop her from telling these stories, but all that comes out is gibberish. The effort makes him drool. Seeing this, his mother says to him, 'Please don't say anything. When you try to talk, you dribble, and then I have to clean you up again. Just listen to me, okay?' She continues telling him her stories, the stories he does not want to her at all.

His rage and hatred push him to wrest control of his voice box once more. He focuses on forming words, forcing them out as clearly as possible while his mother is still wiping saliva from his neck and chin:

'It's all because of you!' he cries. 'All because of you!'

He is about to continue, but his mother won't let him. She covers his mouth with the towel she was using to wipe his saliva. All he wants to say slips back into him. She covers his mouth like this until he starts struggling to breathe, and suddenly he realizes that it would be excellent if she were to cover his mouth just a little longer. But she lifts the towel and lets the air in, leaving him struggling for breath, unable to say anything anymore.

He remembers his mother once said that a mother has the right to kill her own child if it does something truly terrible. When Maitree got drunk and violent, she told him she'd kill him if he tried to hurt her, his own mother who gave birth to him. To her, to hurt one's own mother was an unforgivable crime, and the monsters who do so will go to the deepest abyss of hell. She would kill him to prevent him from committing the most terrible of all crimes. She would rather become a monster herself than let him become one.

He isn't exactly sure when things started going astray, when they diverged from his initial plan, from the story that would end with his mother witnessing the death of each of her sons. Instead of dying, he is disabled. That was fair enough, he supposed, but when he tried to gather all his strength in the hope of uttering something cruel, something that might have a devastating effect on his mother, he failed. It was because his mother would not allow the story proceed the way it should. Instead, she intervened by covering his mouth and nose, depriving him of the ending that he yearns for, the ending he believes would have been utterly heart-breaking, excruciating, cold-blooded, and soul-shattering; the kind of ending that reveals to us that the more we explore the human soul, the closer we get to the depths of hell, to a barbaric time, to an ancient world dominated by animal instinct, a world in which morals and conscience do not exist.

And now, the burden is on him to find a new ending.

8 June 2010

' . . . What the literary artist basically fails to grasp is that life goes on, that it is not ashamed to go on living, even after it has been expressed and "eliminated". Lo and behold! Literature may redeem it as much as it pleases, it just carries on in its same old sinful way; for to the intellectual eye all activity is sinful.'

Thomas Mann was right! The problem with writers is that they try to capture and express life's realities through their work, hoping that once they are captured on paper, those realities won't repeat themselves. This kind of hope stems from the belief that acts of writing and reading will make us realize that all things are sinful. But the truth is, they are only sinful when contemplated from a spiritual perspective, and still we are powerless, unable to prevent reality from running its course. And we humans must continue to witness degradation and loss, unfolding in real life for an unending length of time.

And this is how his family's reality unfolds.

Three months after the crime that took place in early December 2008, Maitree was still able to lead a normal life. He went to work every day, and it seemed he had matured after that horrific night. Then one day, he receives news from the prosecutor: a lawsuit has been filed against him. Accompanied by his mother, his wife, and his eldest brother, Maitree appears at provincial court. Maitree's lawyer insists that he will fight the case, arguing that Maitree had committed a crime of passion, because the plaintiff had assaulted Maitree's mother first. He would try to change the prosecutor's attempted murder charge into the less severe charge of physical assault.

He (the eldest brother) goes to the courtroom with everyone else, to be informed about upcoming court dates. The room is quite small and crowded, with hardly any space to walk or move around. People can only sit or stand. Worse still, the courtroom, which is roughly 30 square metres in size, is also crowded with people involved in other cases. The courtroom looks like an apartment in a slum.

It couldn't have been more different from the grand, awe-inspiring courtrooms he had seen in foreign films.

No one, including Maitree himself, had imagined that Maitree would be handcuffed after hearing his upcoming court dates. He is taken to a jail beneath the courtroom. It is a very hot day, and all the family can do is hang around the front of the jail until noon, when they would be allowed to see Maitree again.

While his mother goes out to buy Maitree new clothes, sandals and some lunch, he (the eldest brother) asks the lawyer what they should do. He advises them to bail Maitree out. As he has been charged with attempted murder, they would need to pay at least 40,000 baht in cash or assets. He hears what the lawyer has to say, and he is at a loss as to where to find such a large sum of money.

But once again, Maitree's mother turns out to be his fairy godmother. After spending three nights in jail, he is released on bail. His mother had asked for help from a neighbour who agreed to use her land title deed to bail Maitree out. His mother is now indebted to this neighbour, who gave Maitree his temporary freedom back.

Eight months later, at the end of 2009, a court hearing takes place: three consecutive days of interrogating witnesses of behalf of both the defendant and the plaintiff. The plaintiff has character witnesses, including the policeman who had been in charge of the criminal case and the doctor who had provided Thai's medical care. The defendant has only his family members as witnesses, making it harder for him to fight the charges.

He (the eldest brother) is present for the court hearing, which lasts from morning till late in the afternoon. He notices that the judge started showing signs of tiredness in the afternoon, when he not only had to listen to the interrogation but to summarize the details of the exchanges between lawyers and witnesses. With the microphone close to his mouth, the judge sums up the goings-on in dense legal jargon; meanwhile, a court official stationed below his bench types up the judge's summary. The whole process did not flow smoothly; in fact, it was rather tedious and, as the late afternoon wears on, he can tell that the judge was getting bored of listening to the same questions being repeated by the lawyers in their attempts to ascertain the truthfulness of the witnesses.

The only thing that is even slightly similar to what he had seen in foreign films is the prosecutor. He raises his voice when questioning the defendant's witnesses. He makes it clear that he looks down on them, blatant in his attempts to mock, intimidate, and disrespect. It is all intentional, so the judge might see the defendant's witnesses as unreliable, not worth the benefit of the doubt. He notices that Maitree's wife is most affected by the prosecutor's questioning. He mocks her and tries to make her lose track of proceedings by asking misleading and confusing questions. His strategies work, as Somjai grows extremely nervous and unable to answer properly. Her voice shakes and her answers come out all wrong. The prosecutor does not seem to have any sympathy for her, despite the fact that she is heavily pregnant.

Witnessing this outrages him. He sees these people who have nothing to do with the terrible event acting as if they're the experts, but the truth is, those people—the judge, the lawyers—had more or less dismissed the event, focusing their energy on showing others how smart and knowledgeable they were. They are players in this legal chess game, and the plaintiff, the defendant, and the witnesses are merely pawns for the players to move around, so they can boastfully demonstrate to the others just how well they know the game.

His mother, however, reacts differently from Somjai when she is cornered by the prosecutor. His loud voice fails to intimidate her, and when he mocks her, she fights back, responding to some of his questions with defiance and aggression. Although doing so had helped his mother to feel a little better, it puts them at a disadvantage. His mother had fallen into a trap set by the prosecutor, by appearing very emotional and unable to control her temper. This made it easier for the prosecutor to claim that she was the one behind all the trouble, the catalyst for the attempted murder that night.

In the courtroom, your destiny is handed over to those who bend and distort it, before passing it back to you once more.

Of course, the defense's job is to convince the judge to agree with him. However, he can see that his brother's lawyer did not do a good job in the courtroom. Yet, the lawyer exuded confidence when talking to Maitree, his mother, and himself, telling them that he could argue against any and all the points raised by the prosecutor. Perhaps he did so in order to convince them that there was hope, even though such hope did not really exist. And sure enough, desperate people often run towards whatever hope they might glimpse, whether or not it is real or imaginary.

However, the two parties could agree on one thing. The prosecutor informs them that the plaintiff will drop the charges against the defendant if the defendant agrees to pay for all medical expenses as demanded by the plaintiff. Since it's a criminal charge, the case won't be over even if the plaintiff decided to drop the charges. It will proceed until the court passes a sentence. Still, if Maitree agrees to pay the medical expenses, there's a higher chance of a lighter sentence.

Maitree was just an unskilled worker. He didn't make much, and only had 3,000 baht to spare each month. Because of the condition set by the prosecutor, Maitree must pay all the medical expenses before the court delivers his sentence, which would be in six months from now. He (the eldest brother) couldn't see how Maitree would be able to pay all that, almost 100,000 baht in total, by the deadline.

And this is his youngest brother, the one who used to ask for money from his mother to buy booze. Now, he is asking for money to buy his freedom. His mother had to ask a neighbour to help bail him out, and he himself had to pay for the lawyer, and now, they will have to help him pay the medical fees by the deadline. He also remembers what the lawyer told him about his 50,000 baht fee: that this fee applied only to the lower court, and if the case went to the court of appeals, he would have to pay more. He cannot understand how he allowed himself to be dragged into this mess.

On the day of Maitree's sentence, he prays for the lightest possible punishment for his brother. He feels that Maitree should serve a substantial prison term to pay for the crime he has committed, but he thinks it should be less than 10 years. He can see that Maitree has become much more mature, especially after Somjai had given birth to a baby girl named Maya. Maitree's sense of responsibility has increased, as he now has to father a child. He brings his baby girl along with him to provincial court, and when he looks at her, his eyes are full of love and concern. Maitree's affection for his little daughter is evident to him.

Thai and his family members are not present at court that day. Maybe they don't want to know what kind of sentence Maitree is going to get. Thai has fully recovered from the injuries; the shattered bones of his lower jaw have been properly fixed and are back in place, no longer damaged and broken from the force of Maitee's machete. Even if Thai is fine now, it is undeniable that Maitree's machete could have killed him, and this fact could greatly affect the sentence Maitree will soon receive.

Maitree is sentenced to ten years for his crime. He is handcuffed again and a policeman leads him out towards the back door of the court: the door that convicts use to pass through to their cells.

The judge found the prosecutor's arguments convincing, unlike the counter-arguments put forth by the defense. Maitree does not get a reduced sentence, despite the fact he has paid all the medical fees. The judge claims that the proof of payment did not get to him in time. According to the judge, the details of Maitree's case were sent to the central court, who read them, passed the sentence, and sent them back to the Saraburi provincial court. The judge's duty is merely to read out the sentence decided by the central court. Worse, after the sentence has been read, the judge tells Maitree that if he wants his sentence reduced, he must apply for it later. This implies that Maitree's case would have to proceed to the court of appeals: just as Maitree's lawyer had wanted, just as this ridiculous legal process had intended.

The judge also informs Maitree that he needs written proof from the plaintiff that they have received all the medical fees from him, and that he needs to submit that proof to the court before he can start the process of appealing for a reduced sentence.

He remembers the day he paid a visit to Sangwan, Thai's wife, to apologize for what his brother did and to let her know that his family was willing to pay all the medical expenses. What she said to him that day comes back to him:

'I don't want your money! I want him to rot in jail. If I accept the money, your brother will get the upper hand in court. I'm not stupid, and you can't buy me!'

Yes, that family wanted Maitree to be punished by the longest possible jail term, and that must be why they hadn't arrived to collect the medical fees on the date agreed by the prosecutor and the defense in front of the judge. They will collect the money after the judge has passed the sentence.

This is how things should go. Such is the outcome when a person physically hurts another without the grounds to do so. That was what the court based its judgement on. The court only pays attention to life as revealed through photos, through words written and spoken, especially the ones spoken by the trustworthy. These things were passed onto the judge, who dominates the stage where real life has no place.

The court found the claim made by the defendant's lawyer unconvincing. According to the lawyer, before the crime took place, Thai had been provoking his mother every day, calling her a stupid, illiterate Isan bumpkin that had signed half her land over to him. When Thai tried to claim his land, his mother had refused. Thai had hired a lawyer to help him to file a lawsuit against her, and later bought a property right next to hers, hoping to disturb her as much as he could by doing all sorts of things: making lots of noise with his machines, releasing polluted water into her property, attacking her dogs. In short, his mother and her family had had to endure all manner of things from Thai. And then Thai had thrown cherry bombs into his mother's yard, one after another, until his mother could no longer contain her frustration and anger. She had gone to his place and yelled at him in rage. He'd retaliated by punching her, but Maitree had rushed towards them and attacked Thai with the machete, sending him to the ground.

The court, however, insisted that Maitree used excessive violence. Thai's actions might have been provocative but they were not life-threatening, so Maitree's sudden outburst was unjustified. The court also claimed that the defendant's family could have pressed charges against Thai for provoking them, but since they hadn't sought legal help, they had no one to blame but themselves.

Is that what they should have done? Could a villager simply go to a police station and tell the police that he had been insulted and verbally abused? Do you think the police would have taken this matter seriously, or would they have simply laughed in his face? It is most likely that the police would not have seen the villager as having enough dignity to be insulted, and they probably would have just told the villager to go back home and sort the matter out themselves.

Even if the police agreed to recognize the complaint, the next step was a time-consuming and costly legal procedure involving lawyers and courts. The villager would be pushed into a world of law and order and judges, where one has no choice but to rely on legal professionals. This world is a chess board, and there is only one group of people with enough expertise to play the game, and to make the game their job.

It's just the way things are, he tells himself.

'Let him go to jail, Mum,' he tells his mother.

'If I'd known that he'd have to stay in jail that long, I would've told him to just kill the bastard,' she says.

13 August 2011

During Maitree's first week in jail, his eldest brother was tormented by awful thoughts. Thinking about Maitree's loss of freedom and his life as a prisoner took a terrible toll on his mind. Nevertheless, he was not the one being physically imprisoned; after a week had passed, thoughts of Maitree troubled him less. A month passed quickly and normally enough, and soon, a year had gone by.

In the beginning, his mother and Somjai visited Maitree three or four times a week, and they tried to make sure that he got everything he needed: things like sandals, blankets, cigarettes, even some money for personal use. Initially, Maitree wept every time he saw them and asked Somjai to bring their baby daughter along, as he wanted to see her. That was the only thing he wanted, he said. After a month had passed by, the frequency of their visits reduced to a few times a month, as Maitree adjusted to life in jail. His mother didn't have to provide for him. All she had to do on her visits was remind him not to get involved with drugs, otherwise he would lose his chance at a reduced sentence.

He never visited his younger brother in jail, but his mother often called him to talk about how Maitree was doing. He promised that he would go to see him in jail, but he never did. He simply asked his mother and Somjai to give Maitree his regards and transferred some money to his mother so that she could give it to Maitree in case he needed it.

Around late August last year, his mother called him and said that Maitree wanted him to withdraw their appeal, because he believed it was no use, and he was willing to stay in jail until he completed his sentence. He didn't want to be released, only to have to go back to jail again. According to Maitree, the appeal that seemed to go nowhere also made him ineligible for the annual pardons that were granted each year with great pomp and circumstance. After that phone call with his mother, he rang the lawyer to ask for advice, and was told that if the court approved the appeal, the reduction of Maitree's sentence would be far greater than the one he might get through an annual pardon. He then told his mother what the lawyer said, so that she could pass it on to Maitree when she next visited. However, when his mother rang him again, she said Maitree had very little confidence that the court would grant with their appeal, and if his appeal was rejected, his sentence wouldn't be reduced at all.

He was quite annoyed by Maitree's attitude. He had put a lot of effort into helping Maitree with the appeal, but his efforts had gone unappreciated, and were even seen as attempts to increase the severity of Maitree's punishment. By the end of 2010, it became even more obvious that the family blamed him for what he had done to help Maitree. His mother told him over the phone that he was the one who had made Maitree ineligible for the pardon he deserved. She wanted him to tell the lawyer to withdraw the appeal immediately. She also added that since he wasn't the one imprisoned, he could not possibly know what it was like to spend each day in jail. Maitree was the one in prison, and if he wanted something concerning his sentence to be done in a particular way, there was no reason to deny him that.

She said, 'Maitree seems to believe that you want him to stay in jail for a long time.'

'How did he come up with such a warped idea?' he raised his voice. 'Is that what he really thinks?'

'It's because you never try to see things from his perspective!' she said. 'You never listen to what he wants.'

How could he listen to someone like Maitree, who can't even tell what is best for himself?

Then, one day in June of 2011, the witnesses were asked to appear in court to answer questions that would help the court determine how to divide the plot of land among the parties involved. The root cause of the terrible disaster that had befallen his family was the conflict over this tiny plot of land, following the arrival and invasion of some guy named Thai. To him, this guy was just his family's karmic creditor, a hanger-on from their past lives. Since the day he had been allowed to live on their land, he had turned their wheel of fate, ensuring that his family suffered terribly time and again.

On that day, Maitree, Thai and he had to appear in court together, as they shared ownership of the land. Witnesses for his family and Thai were also there. His family fought for the land based on their occupancy rights and their active use of the land, while Thai claimed that he had the right to the land based on the official land sale agreement.

The trial lasted three days, with Thai as the plaintiff. (Once again, Thai played the part of the karmic creditor, taking control of his family's fate, and because of Thai, the word 'plaintiff' would continue to haunt him for the rest of his life.) The first part of the hearing, where Thai was called before the court and interrogated, one and a half days. Then it was his family's turn, which took another one and a half days.

At first, the judge tried to encourage the two parties to negotiate with one another and come to a compromise. He said he was aware that the land conflict had created a lot of tension between the families, that it had triggered Maitree's assault of Thai, resulting in the former's jail sentence.

The judge's speech reminded him of the day of Maitree's trial, when he was sentenced to ten years in jail. That day, the judge hadn't taken the land conflict into account, and he felt that his family had been treated unfairly. Because of this, he stubbornly refused to negotiate. He was surprised by his own reaction, since he had already tried to reach a compromise with Thai's family before. Perhaps because Maitree already received the maximum sentence Thai and his family had hoped for, he felt no need to stay on friendly terms with them anymore. So the trial carried on.

On the last day of the trial, Maitree was taken out of jail to appear in front of the court. He was in a faded red prison uniform. He was shackled. After the trial, he was led by a policeman to a prison truck that would take him back to jail. Maitree said nothing to him. In fact, he didn't even glance at him. Regardless, he didn't give much thought to Maitree's coldness.

On the day the court issued a verdict for their case, the small courtroom was fully packed, as many other people were awaiting verdicts on their own cases. Everyone looked the same: they were all nervous, atwitter with both negative and positive speculations about the verdicts soon to be delivered by the court. He was no different from them. He thought about what the worst possible verdict might be for his family. He told his mother that if the court ordered them to split the land in half (one half to his family and the other half to Thai's), they would have to go along with it, as the court's decision was final. According to his lawyer, it was enough for him to be present for the verdict, so they didn't apply for permission to take Maitree out of jail and to the courtroom that day.

As the judge sat on his bench and read out the verdict for their case, he was confused. He couldn't quite keep track of what the judge was saying. The ruling was lengthy and formal, and the decision made by the court was left till the very end. As he listened, he grew more anxious and worried. Things didn't look good for his family, especially when the judge pointed out that the conflict was unlikely to be solved even after the land was divided between the two parties. This was due to the fact that the plaintiff and the defendant lived next to each other, and a new conflict could easily occur in the future. Dividing the land between them, then, would not get rid of the root of the problem, which was that both parties refused to give in to the other.

According to the judge, having taken everything into consideration, the court had decided that the land would be put up for auction, and the money earned would be divided equally between the two parties.

His heart sank when he heard the verdict. Was this really the best solution the court could offer to his family? They had lived on that land for a long time, and now they would have no home. Their fate had been decided by that verdict; or, more accurately, fate had forced them out of their own land on that verdict.

He didn't want the money from the auction. It a small amount of money, not worth anything significant in life. He wanted the land back for his mother and brother, the land that had his family's history etched into it. He didn't want to make new memories on a new plot of land. He glanced at Thai's family, and noticed that they didn't seem particularly emotional. Thai owned the plot of land adjacent to the one in question, so he and his family only needed to walk a step or two, and they would be back on their own property. But where would his mother and brother go? His heart cried out in agony, and he looked at his mother, whose expression clearly betrayed her shock. Her eyes were moving back and forth in panic, but her face seemed paralysed. It was the same face she had made that day, when he had yelled that he wasn't in any hurry to sell his share of the land, and that she should sell hers if she needed the money. What happened that day in the land office became material for his short story, which depicted a fictional situation in which the protagonist is eventually forced to sell his share of the land. In the story, he compares the act of holding a pen and signing away his right to the land to the cracking open of a cliff, following the arrival of cement factories and the subsequent industrial era. The invasion of the factories signified the arrival of new things, things that shattered local legends, history, and memories before transforming them into cement, tiles, gypsum boards, bathroom fittings, coal, energy: all the things needed to build a new house. The earth's spirit is cracked open and shattered in order for new memories to be made.

Those were the messages he wanted to convey in his short story. There were things in that short story that did not take place in real life, but their existence within the story had functioned like a bad omen. It was as if he'd borrowed those things from the future to use in his short story, and that borrowing had come at a price he would have to pay back seven years later. History repeats itself, and fiction can be a retelling of real life. But sometimes, real life is, more or less, a retelling of fiction, like on that day, when he stood in the courtroom, transfixed, after the verdict had been issued. The judge told him that he could sit down, but he remained standing until the judge left the bench and another judge was about to take his place, to read out the verdict for another case. Other plaintiffs and defendants in that crowded courtroom were shifting around, and he realized that he should leave the room, as his case was over. Everything had been done quickly, and there was no room for whining, arguing, or appealing. The judge for his case had disappeared, and he should stop attracting attention, and allow other complainants to take centre stage.

Then a two-page document was pushed in front of him. His lawyer had passed it to him with a pen. It was the written verdict, and he was supposed to sign it, to acknowledge the court's decision regarding the case. He took the pen and signed.

Yesterday he received a letter from Maitree, sent to him from jail. He guessed that it had already been opened and read by prison authorities. He opened the envelope to find a piece of paper on which a short message had been written.

I wrote this in tears.

I don't really know whether I should remember or forget the fact that I once had a brother like you.

It's all because of you! All because of you!

I hope the rest of my time in jail will help me to forget you. I want nothing more than to erase all my memories of you. Wish me luck with it.

Maitree's message was muddled and very emotional. It was possible that Maitree had been drunk as he wrote those words. If that were the case, it just goes to show that you can't change some people's fates, even if you put them in jail.

Folder 5: Maya's Birth and Existence

Images

Time, as we know it, is made up of the past, present and future. Knowing where we stand in time, however, is a different story. Many people dwell in the past, while others fantasize obsessively about the future. Is it any surprise that only a few of us live in the present? I'm talking about emotion. Most of the time, emotion propels the physical body into action; other times, emotion ignores the physical body to which it belongs, drifting instead to where it wants to go—somewhere between the past and the future—leaving its body to wither away in the present.

Humans live least in the present. They lack continuity; they are disjointed, like a dotted line that fades and blurs from sight. That is why the Buddha's life and teachings are so magnificent. Throughout his life, he drew a precise and continuous line, marking the present—an awareness of every passing moment—with mindfulness, recognizing and sustaining every moment and action. He lived a life centred around the body, pulling emotion away from the distractions of the past and future. The Buddha's teachings are a sublime thing, because they realign humanity back to its present. It sounds easy, commonplace; his teachings might seem like something any person can contemplate if they put their mind to it, but knowledge alone will not suffice. Not without practice. Practice is everything: that's why so many knowledgeable people continue to live in the past and dream of the future, leaving their present lacking in precision and continuity.

I, too, began from contemplation. At this very moment, my thoughts are appearing before me, forming a mass—a substance—fleshing out into form. Slowly, I am gathering my thoughts back into the present, establishing my awareness of my own body.

I'm standing by a glass window, looking out absentmindedly at the disorderly scene before me: a vast field, a dried-up pond. In the distance, an overgrown garden; houses, scattered across the landscape. The houses are made of bricks and cement, with roofs made of brightly-coloured tile and sheets of corrugated iron. Some of the doors and windows are glass; others are hewn from a material that resembles wood. Houses are rarely made with real wood these days, mine included. My feet are resting on tiled floor. The table, cabinet, bed, and cupboards are all factory-made and assembled, made not with real wood but with a blend of plywood and other materials, like Formica and laminate: common materials that most families can afford.

I'm standing by the glass window in my bedroom, which is furnished with only a few objects from the past—the distant past, my own—photographs and knickknacks from childhood. Whenever I return here—to my bedroom, to my birthplace of Kaeng Khoi—the damp smell of the past leaps at me like a dog that has been waiting for its owner to arrive. Maybe I'm imagining things; maybe it's nothing more than the smell of mothballs in cupboards and disused corners of disused rooms. Mothballs have their own distinct smell, one that absorbs and intermingles with the scent of objects past. When we smell mothballs, we also smell the past. I doubt the past smells as pungent as mothballs do, though.

I only visit my hometown once or twice a year, during the summer holidays. I'm studying at a university in Nakhon Pathom, majoring in education. In a few months, I'll turn twenty in 2029.

So, the question is: how did I end up here, standing by a glass window in my hometown in apparent contemplation? Why did I choose this place? (There are moments when our actions become a mystery unto ourselves. We might believe in supernatural forces: omens, gut feelings, whatever other things that might be hard to explain. Sometimes, if the mood takes us, we might allude to these things to avoid explaining ourselves. At other times, we might act in accordance with some image buried deep in our memory. In the latter situation, I like to think of myself as Tereza in *The Unbearable Lightness of Being*. Or is it Thomas who stares out the window, contemplating the life that has been and the life that will be?). The glass window is shut, but the sight of outside sunlight warms me up from within. I don't feel very hot, but I tie my hair up anyway, to let the back of my neck cool down. Today was a chaotic return home. My body is acting up, and my period has come. It is also the same day I cut myself off completely from him. My words are still ringing in my mind. 'Let's break up,' I said, before telling him to leave my room and locking the door behind him so that I could be alone.

I packed my clothes and necessary belongings into a bag and then came here. I was shoved here by the past to confront another past, one that pounces at me like an excited dog. I'm standing by the glass window with the past pressing in on all sides, as if I'm the owner of several dogs that want to sniff me and lick me all at once, and all I can do is to stay still and pretend to ignore them. If the past were a pack of dogs, most of them would eventually lose interest and leave, but a few would remain. They'd lie down beside you, a few paces away. At the slightest movement, their eyes would snap open: alert, on edge. It's that kind of past we need to watch out for.

Why does my thinking start with the past, present and future, you may ask? And why all these references to the Buddha? It's because these are topics we've been debating a lot lately; 'we' being my lover and I. He goes to the same university, but belongs to another faculty.

He's good-looking. He's tall, slim. I fell for his caring personality: his sweet words, his sense of humour. He isn't the pensive type, but he does like to demonstrate his strong (if narrow-minded) opinions. To be honest, with all I've said, I've painted him as your average guy, and yes, he really is just like all the other guys. It was easy to fall for his sweet words and his sense of humour in the first few months of the relationship, but things eventually changed when we started sleeping together. He was no longer interested in what I had to say; worse, he made out as if my voice was like daggers to his ears. And he couldn't take it when I sat silently in thought. It made him anxious. It made him feel like an inadequate lover. When things got to this point, that's when I realized: that was it. He thinks only of himself, cares only about himself. Because what could be so upsetting about me simply sitting in silence, in contemplation?

A week before the end of the semester, we were still excited about getting to spend time together. Then, little by little, these seemingly trivial things started to spread, like drops of ink blooming across damp paper (I used these exact words to explain the issue to him, and he found it all intolerably outdated, not to mention the metaphor gave him the creeps), and at the end of the week, he blurted out that he was going to be ordained.

'When?' I asked.

'Next week.'

'That's so soon. Why didn't you tell me earlier?'

'My family wants me to do it.'

'You don't want to be together anymore?'

His face contorted, as if I'd done something wrong in pulling him back, and he began to feed me all sorts of implausible reasons for why he had to get ordained.

He explained that it was something that every man had to do in his life, out of respect for his parents and for long-standing tradition. After completing his education, a man must enter monkhood, and then marriage. These are the stages of life. He said, among other things, that he was trying to teach me about the duties of men. To persuade me, a lot of imperatives—plenty of 'must's and 'should's—were used.

'But do *you* want to become a monk?' I asked what I really wanted to know.

I'd asked the wrong question. He pulled another face again. It's not a question of want, he said, but a question of duty. 'When your parents offer the chance to make this kind of merit, it would be sinful for a son to refuse.'

That's not true, I thought. He's just found the opportunity to be away from me; indeed, the perfect opportunity.

'Who's carrying the pillow during the ceremony?' I asked. I had no interest in being that person. I only asked him because I was frustrated. I wanted to provoke him.

'You can carry it if you want.'

Was that the best answer he could give? I could see the picture he had envisioned for himself, a picture without me in it, and I was hurt, because he made it sound as though he had been forced to say it: 'You can carry it if you want.' Oh, please! The words of a young boy about to take on the great responsibility of monkhood, a young boy about to become a 'real man'.

So this was the way the road was turning. This was the script we'd been given. One sinner, and one saint. He's too weak to play the devil, I thought. Too weak to admit defeat. So I let him play the good guy.

'I don't want to carry it. Do whatever you want. It has nothing to do with me anyway,' I said.

'Oh, so this is how it's going to be.' That was all he said, looking at me with disdain, as if he'd never met this girl before, this she-devil.

But hey! You're only a saint because I let you be.

He took a deep breath to calm himself down. I didn't have anything else to say, so I walked home.

He disappeared for two days. before showing up at my place this afternoon. He knocked timidly at my door. Quietly, I let him in.

'I want to get ordained so that I can marry you.'

This was the excuse he'd come up with after disappearing for two days? Did he really think that I wanted to get married, and to him? Did he really think that his words would make me go weak in the knees? He came closer to me, pulling me into his arms. Let's make up, he said. I love you, he said. Then he started slowly caressing me, taking off my shirt, unbuttoning my trousers. I didn't say anything. I just let him proceed. He'll stop in a minute, I thought. But he didn't. He kept going, even though I was on my period. He kept going until he came inside me. I was hurt. I stung, I ached, and it hurt.

After he finished, he went into the bathroom to get dressed. When he walked out, I told him, 'Let's break up.'

I told him to leave the room. 'Leave. Get out of my life.' And he actually did.

What he did to me was him making the most of his final days of secular life. No doubt about it.

Representations

I've been looking at the footprint at the Temple of the Buddha's Footprint for ten minutes. I decide to leave the pavilion and walk around the temple grounds instead. A mysterious force drew me here, you could say. When I was still living in my hometown, I never even thought to come here, but when I returned as an outsider (that is, someone who no longer lives in their hometown), I immediately felt the urge to return here too. I thought it was a tourist impulse, at first; after all, I'm here as a tourist, not as a local.

I photograph the temple from every angle possible, then edit and upload them to my personal page. I also take this opportunity to make merit by providing money for monk offerings as well as other items available around the temple. After making a full circle, I come to a halt at the pathway leading up to the pavilion, admiring what is considered to be a popular tourist attraction. You can't help but take photos of the scenery, and even though it's been captured countless times before, it doesn't stop you from taking more.

I sit down in the shade to admire the steps. What a mysterious force this is, I think to myself. First, I break up with someone who is going to be ordained as a monk, and now, I'm sitting in front of a temple. Not the temple he'll be ordained in, but a temple in my hometown, and a temple I'm visiting for the first time, at that. There's something uncanny about this enigmatic force. It's like I've led myself into this scene—this scene in which I'd been scripted to appear—only to slowly, gradually, notice something else coming to the surface. This is how I feel as I sit in the shade of the trees, hearing some voice, some ancient voice, resound inside me: 'Ask your parents to bring you here so you can see for yourself.'

At the foot of the steps leading up to the pavilion that houses the Buddha's footprint, there are four five-headed naga sculptures. Their golden bodies gleam in the sunlight. I pay close attention to them. You can see these naga stairs in almost every temple, not just in Thailand, but in almost every ASEAN country that is predominantly Buddhist. According to Buddhist history, a naga once transformed itself into a human in an attempt to be ordained as a monk, but the Buddha was able to see through its disguise, proclaiming that beasts were not able to enter monkhood. Ever since then, it has been customary to ask someone who is about to be ordained whether or not they are human. It is said that the naga confessed that it wanted to become a monk to free itself from the lowly form it had been given at birth, and the Buddha took pity on it. He told it to guard the temple's main hall; that doing so would be the quickest way of escaping its base nature and becoming human. And so goes the story of how the naga steps came to be.

Later stories have said that the naga, forbidden to live as a monk, pleaded the Buddha that its namesake be used to refer to the person who are about to enter monkhood, and that's why men who are about to be ordained are called nagas.

As a woman, I don't have the option of becoming a monk, but I wonder if the person who is about to become one is even aware of these stories. I mean, no offence, but I really don't believe he does. People who have the opportunity and the privilege to do certain things and become certain things usually take it for granted, whereas people like me will spend time digging through the reasons why we must be deprived of such things.

As I sit there, spurred by the competitive impulse that comes naturally to a sinner like me, I look up more information about the Buddha's origins on the internet, because I'd collected some scattered observations about the story that bothered me. Why does the story attribute the naga's desire to transform itself into a monk to dissatisfaction with its lowly birth, its beastly nature, as if humans are the noblest of beings? I watch a temple dog walk past me and I think, does this dog want to become human? What about the herd of ants climbing that tree? Do they want to become human?

The Buddha forbade the naga from becoming a monk because it had been born a beast, and would have to be reincarnated as a human in order to be ordained. Was the Buddha implying that humanity was a virtue, that to be virtuous was to be a sentient being with intention, free will, and the awareness to reach enlightenment? Can I infer from the Buddha's remark that being born as a human implies that we have more attributes and access to knowledge than other beings?

But what about that dog? Does it aspire towards humanity? Those ants, too. I doubt they have that kind of desire; on the contrary, humans are the only species to tell themselves that they are the noblest of all creatures, and they impose this view on other beings, such as that dog.

Nagas are unable to chronicle their ancestors' history in a language or method that is intelligible to humans, so we cannot truly know what they are thinking. All we know about them comes from our perception of them as humans. So this claim that the naga was dissatisfied by its lowly birth, and sought a way of becoming human: this was a human explanation, one presented to elevate the supremacy of our own race.

After reaching this point in my analysis, my face suddenly grows hot. I slow my thoughts. The naga transformed into a monk in order to glorify the prestige and power of Buddhism!

There it was. I found the answer to my trivial little challenges in the Jataka tales about the Buddha's five hundred previous births, which recount the Buddha's stoic spiritual practices and modes of accumulating merit. The Buddha lived as a naga for three lives altogether: the Naga Bhuridatta, the Naga King Champeyya, and the Naga King Daddara. And what do these tales tell us? To know that he was once a naga was enough for me.

From what I've learned, the word 'naga' is etymologically linked to 'nog', an ancient Indo-European word which means 'naked'. This word appears throughout many other languages, like 'nudus' in Latin, 'naked' in English, 'nagna' in Sanskrit, and 'nanga' in Hindi. There had also once been a tribe of people called the nagas living in the easternmost part of India, known as the Naga Hills. The nagas didn't wear any clothes; in other words, they were a nudist tribe, and it is said that they were looked down upon by the Aryans. 'Naga' in Assamese also means 'bare', or 'naked'. Is it possible, based on these observations, that the term 'naga' was used to refer to indigenous people, forest dwellers, uncivilized folk, savages?

But I wonder whether the naga was just a metaphor for indigenous people, for so-called savages. The naga was a gigantic serpent found throughout ancient Asia, particularly in the southeast region. According to the legend of the Phanon Pagoda, this region was 'home to the nagas'. The origin story of the Mekong River, as told in Cambodian mythology, depicts nagas helping to build cities. Naga tales also circulated throughout Thailand and Myanmar.

Then I learned that it wasn't customary in India for men to become nagas before entering monkhood. This practice was only found in Southeast Asia, the ancient 'home of the nagas', where people worshipped ghosts and nagas as the true owners of all lands and entities. Indigenous people had held this belief until the Buddha arrived in the region to impart his teachings, and with him came progress and civilization.

But it wasn't as simple as just replacing old beliefs and ways of thinking with new ones. Miracles had to be performed, dissent had to be suppressed, and evil had to be eradicated. It required force and benevolence both: some things had to be completely destroyed, while others called for compromise. It was necessary in order to allow the old and new to coexist.

The Buddha left footprints in countless places across Thailand; not just in Saraburi, but in other provinces as well. All of these places claim that their footprints are authentic, despite their varying sizes. According to the measurements of these footprints, I figured that the Buddha had to have been tremendous in stature and multitudinous in appearance (but of course, the Buddha had the power to shape-shift, to shrink himself, to travel through the air). These relics were manifestations of the miracles he performed, ones that were strategically used to convince the indigenous and the primitive to convert to Buddhism.

The transition from naga to monk is exclusive to this region, which was once known as Suvarnabhumi. The transformation tells of the might and merit of the Buddha's arrival. Historically speaking, Siam was younger than Laos, younger than Myanmar, Cambodia, and even the Lanna kingdom. But the journey of Buddhism can be traced back even further than the birth of China. One could say that the prosperity of the Khmer kingdom had touched the Siamese city of Lopburi, bringing civilization with it. When the Buddha first arrived in this region, he vanquished the previous proprietors of the land—the ghosts and the nagas—taming them so they could be converted to Buddhism. Following that, he convinced their devotees (indigenous peoples, forest tribes, savages who worshipped the naga) to convert to Buddhism (that is, to become civilized). But the Buddha didn't force the people to renounce their ancient beliefs, and so, the ceremony of transformation from naga to monk remained.

The arrival of the Buddha also marks the arrival of early civilization. It condemned primitivism, establishing humans as distinct from non-humans. It was the arrival of the ruler and the subject, as well as the arrival of immigration, civilization, politics and governance, capitalism, progressivism, global networks, and whatever other names we've given to these concepts throughout history. A handsome man from a different class and country falls in love with a native girl who doesn't really know herself. There must be some external power responsible for humanity's elevated status. I think there has to be some universal formula that can explain every change throughout human civilization, through every life cycle. A formula that works even for the plots you see in soap operas on TV.

Will he know any of this, on the day where he'll be robed in white as a naga, dressed in the Brahmin uniform (not Buddhist!): Brahminism, Animism, and Buddhism all jumbled together? Presumably he'll be sitting in his chair, surrounded by relatives waiting in line to cut his hair. His mother will be standing behind him, one hand holding a pair of scissors for the hair-cutting ceremony, happy tears streaming down her cheeks. Her son will finally be ordained for her sake, and rest assured, she'll be able to hold the hem of his yellow robe as they fly towards paradise when she dies (she'll have this image in her mind, you can be certain of that). What isn't certain, though, is the source of this image; I don't know when it became a part of human consciousness, but it is firmly imprinted on the hearts and minds of almost all Thai Buddhists, casting aside all I had previously described, all I had learned, studied and researched. The image of the parent holding onto the hem of their son's yellow robe as they ascend towards heaven, a realm that is neither where the Buddha resides, nor the realm of enlightenment.

The image of a family flying to heaven, all streaming tears of joy for the token of civilization and their near-emancipation from their non-human condition.

'Are you dissatisfied with your birth?' I ask the colony of ants, before turning to face the pavilion of the Buddha's footprint once more. Look at me, sitting in the temple grounds but hardly paying any attention to all that's around me. Instead, I'm wasting time researching through this civilized gadget that I had brought with me, as well as having an argument with myself. A true sinner: props to me.

Great Grandmother's rebirth

The voice slumbers in the heart of some distant memory. When something triggers it, stirs it somehow, it sends waves up from the depths, up to the surface: 'Ask your parents to take you there to see it for yourself.' The voice echoes from inside me, as I'm at the Temple of the Buddha's Footprint. What I initially thought was a mysterious force drawing me here turns out to my own competitive need to challenge some philosophical concept, which is connected to some deep-seated sense of rebellion against my ex-lover. An unexpected thought uncoils itself from the shadowy depths: my visit to the Temple of the Buddha's Footprint isn't just about my breakup. It also satisfies some mysterious desire from the past. It's as if this visit is filling some once-empty space, like a jigsaw puzzle, where every piece fits together perfectly, making an image whole again. It's triggering the inner workings of some slowly revolving thing that's akin to the wheel of life.

I've answered some desire from the past by stepping feet first into its pit.

The stories my great grandmother once told me are starting to come back, piece by piece. The voice is hers, she who once told me to tell my parents to take me to see the Buddha's footprint and image, so I could see whether these relics she once depicted in her stories existed.

It happened around a decade ago, probably in 2015, the day all the children had gathered at the house that belonged to my great uncle. It was on this exact same plot of land. It used to be an old house, but it's been demolished since, and a new house has been built in its place. I was old enough, about six years old. My parents and relatives had left me with my friends and told us to to keep an eye on Great Grandmother, to see if she needed anything, and to fetch it for her if she did. She could no longer walk by then, only lie down or sit up.

I was quite clueless back then, and only found out later why our parents had left us to go to the temple that day. Grandfather had died that day, and there were things to manage and things to be done. Everyone at the temple must have been busy with cleaning and dressing his body in preparation for the bathing ceremony at his funeral. Nobody had dared to tell Great Grandmother the news of his death at the time. Our parents had presumably agreed to wait for the right time to tell her, for fear of something happening to her when she found out.

My friends and I kept her company. Apart from the fact that she couldn't walk, she seemed to be in great health and good spirits. Her memory was failing her, and she couldn't remember our names or what certain things were called, but that was normal for someone her age. It was actually Great Grandmother who took care of us, making sure we stayed put and keeping our attention with fantastic stories about her life's adventures. As young as I was, I'd listened to her stories as much as my attention span would allow, which wasn't very much. Whenever I got bored of listening, I'd find somewhere farther away from her to sit and play. We could still hear her voice from a distance; besides, her eyesight was almost gone, so she probably hadn't even realized that all the children had stopped listening to her. Still, I would return to sit with her from time to time, listening to her stories and providing some companionship.

I remember that day, with Great Grandmother half lying and half sitting on the mattress, her body leaning against her triangular pillow. Her room was gloomy, tinted by greenish-blue light emanating from the fluorescent bulbs on the ceiling, which was covered in smoke stains and dead insects. On the wall above her head was a small shrine to the Buddha. The air was thick and damp, and it smelled like something old mixed with the stench of oil and motor, enveloping all of us inside that ancient cave-like room.

When Great Grandmother told us how she'd transformed into a naga, and the sort of movement she'd made as she slithered along the ground, I was ecstatic; it still excites me to this day. I've never heard of other elderly folks telling stories like that; in fact, the generation that came after her didn't seem to have these sorts of fantastic tales. Later, I read somewhere that stories about extraordinary transformation were usually told by those born before the 1960s, that stories from those born later tended to be more historical, more realistic. In other words, later forms of stories were more aware of injury and death: storytellers after the 1960s only had one life.

Great Grandmother lived multiple lives, through countless transformations. She used to be a naga, and a deer, from what I recall, before she became the human Great Grandmother: elderly, decrepit.

Did she foresee the way people of the present generation would read her births and lives? Did she anticipate how the story would be received by the younger generation, such as myself, when she told us she used to be a part of the earth before becoming a naga? These stories had to wait a decade while I matured into a young adult with the intellectual ability to interpret them in a new light: not as fanciful, mindless tales, but as stories with meanings and symbols for analysis. I think the part about Great Grandmother's existence as a naga, and how she dedicated her life to meeting the Buddha, is somehow connected to the fact that my ex is about to become a naga himself.

Is it possible that her life (her story, rather) serves other ancient narratives that predate her? Had she woven herself into the fabric of other stories she wasn't even conscious of? What if there was a grand narrative, vast as a galaxy in its own right? Or was it more like a womb, where a sperm swims to find a compatible egg to fertilize a new narrative? In that case, there must exist some author, content in their anonymity, who picks up a pen to connect these dotted lines into coherence. It's like when I look up at the dark starry sky and, with my eyes, draw virtual lines to connect one star to the next until a mysterious shape appears in my mind. That shape is mine, but it could also be inadvertently similar to someone else's. I'll never know, but this ignorance doesn't change the fact that they're the same.

I wonder—despite the gaps in my memory—about the purpose of Great Grandmother's stories. When someone begins to tell a story, there is a destination in mind, but whether or not they get there isn't important. What's more important is what motivates them to go there in the first place. As I reach this conclusion, other things begin to take shape in my mind, rising from an ancient place that had slumbered, or been forgotten.

Slowly, I start to draw the connecting lines. My existence in the present isn't a coincidence, not once we take the time to acknowledge the things that came before us. I exist partly to serve the past: connecting with it, disclosing it, unforgetting it.

Now I realize that I play a much greater role in it than I thought . . .

In 2015, our family suffered devastating losses: Grandfather's death, soon followed by Great Grandmother's. This tragedy that struck us twice was unexpected by all of us.

Let's continue drawing the lines. That afternoon, the relatives had probably busied themselves with cleansing Grandfather's body as it lay lifeless and naked on a table in a temple pavilion, before patting him dry and dressing him. They would have put him in something he liked wearing, something that made him look respectable: his royally-granted uniform, or slacks with a long-sleeved, light green shirt. Would they have put his doctor's gown on for him too? Then they would have applied his makeup, restoring some colour, particularly the darker tones, to his now breathless, lifeless face. 'Look, it looks like he's just sleeping,' a relative might have commented, and that would have marked the end of preparations. Grandfather, properly clean and dressed, appearing respectable—just sleeping—ready to welcome all the visitors who'd arrive in the late afternoon to participate in the bathing ceremony. After the ritual, they would lay his body in a coffin, along with his treasured possessions and other items he might need, before sealing it and setting it on a raised platform.

When that part of the ceremony was done, the relatives had probably discussed how they could break the news to Great Grandmother in the least traumatic way possible. And they'd probably figured something out, pictured how it would go from start to finish, only it was too late.

Great Grandmother's death followed so suddenly and unexpectedly. When the relatives returned to the house, they discovered her lying motionless, not breathing. Tragedy had struck once more. They bombarded me with questions, demanding to know what had happened and how it could have happened under our watch. I was singled out for questioning: my great uncle grabbed my arm, yelled in my face, and struck me repeatedly. All I could do was cry; no words would come out of my lips, so I wept, until my parents came and put a stop to it all.

Dad gently asked me about it, and I told him that Great Grandmother was with Grandfather.

'She's going to help him,' I said.

All of the relatives there heard the exact words I'd uttered, and they whispered among themselves: 'See? It's a miracle that Great Grandmother foresaw this, before anyone else had to tell her.' Then Great Uncle remarked bitterly that his mother loved his brother more than him: so much so that she was willing to die to be with him.

Upon hearing that, I corrected him, speaking to my father instead of directly to Great Uncle: 'Great Grandmother didn't die. She told me that she's going to be born again.'

I was so convinced that I refused to let anyone tell me she had died. I repeatedly argued that she was going to be born again. But that year, I had little time to argue my case. I remember Mum taking me to live with my maternal grandmother two days later. After that, any memories I have of my birthplace are cut short.

At that time, I thought Great Grandmother had lived multiple lives: as the earth, a naga, and a deer before she became the Great Grandmother that I knew. She was immortal, having lived for thousands of years and gone through many transformations, over and over. When she'd asked me to fetch the bundle of herbs from the shrine above her mattress, I had simply done what she had asked . . .

The word 'juti' literally means 'to die', but it also refers to the act of moving from one place to another. The former meaning is reserved for deities, not humans; the death of an angel is a migration from one place to another, it is to be born again, to shape shift, to transmute from one matter into another.

I didn't lead Great Grandmother to her death; rather, I helped her rebirth. More importantly, I had only done what she had wanted.

But, oh . . . In a month, I'll grow a year older, and turn twenty. Time progresses into the future, but right now, I am allowing my thoughts to wander into the past, into a space of lost memories, where I discover that I had some part to play in this past of mine. I don't think this is a very good birthday gift to myself.

But why I am thinking about these things now, at this very moment? That's the question.

Time heals all wounds

I spent around four years in Isan, living at my mum's birthplace until I finished primary school. Mum brought me there, but she returned to live with Dad less than a week later, leaving me in the care of my maternal grandparents, who explained to me that Mum had to go back to help Dad with work, and it was easier for children to change schools than for their parents to change jobs.

My parents visited me frequently during the first half of my first year in Isan, but as time passed and they saw that I was settling in with my grandparents, their visits were limited to long public holidays like New Year's or Songkran. My grandparents' house was spacious; it was in the town centre, in a community known as the Red Shirt Village, which was highly active in organizing activities and protests until the coup in 2014, when everything was suppressed. I, on the other hand, was making new friends at school and starting my own life.

My grandparents told me that they were part of the new democratic spirit, which saw citizens as the rightful owners of the country, rather than the few high-ranking officers and aristocrats who governed as though they knew what the majority needed or didn't need. My grandparents considered themselves as part of the masses who had turned derogatory labels used against them by the ruling class—terms like 'serf'—into words of pride.

They were there at the protests in the city from 2006 to 2010, historically controversial years marked by a chasm between two groups who held two completely different versions of the truth. After that period, the country was blanketed by discourse on good and evil, on good people defeating corruption, on angels defeating demons: the country's politics were steeped in images and ancient accounts of the Buddha's life. The years of 'the absolute rights of good people' were also the years of 'democratic dictatorship': two phrases that emerged from two opposing groups, two impossible definitions that clashed and converged. The whole population was submerged in this impossibility.

Deaths and casualties among Red Shirt protestors erupted after the government—led by the prime minister with the pretty face—ordered the police to 'secure the area'. My grandparents were injured and traumatized; not long after that, my grandmother was diagnosed with a colon tumour that turned into cancer. One of her sons, who held opposing political views, suggested that the cancer was karma, punishing her for not knowing her place.

'You're no better than I am,' she scolded him in her native dialect. When he dies, she threatened, he would become a *pret*—a hungry demon with a mouth as small as the eye of a needle—for all the horrible things he had said about his mother.

After her diagnosis, Grandfather took good care of her; he made sure they never travelled to the city or participated in any other protests, unless they were organized within the community. But Grandfather never left the countryside again. This is the story of the ancestors on my mother's side.

Dad came to visit me shortly after I finished primary school, and told me it was time for me to return to live with my parents in my hometown, Kaeng Khoi, where I'd start secondary school. He told me that I should prepare to return home, that they'd missed me terribly every day, that they'd wished they could bring me back home from the first day they'd sent me away. Still, they couldn't, and all they could do was wait an excruciatingly long time for things to settle down, until Great Uncle and his other relatives forgot about what had happened that day.

He said this was our second long-term separation, and he hoped it would be the last. He promised not to talk about what had happened that day and told me to stop arguing with Great Uncle, to ignore him no matter how aggressive, sarcastic, and nasty he was to me. There was no use arguing, Dad reasoned, because my great uncle was going to die soon anyway. Dad didn't get along with Great Uncle—there was some history between them—so he was extra cautious around him. I kept these observations to myself that day, since I was more than glad to learn that I would be returning to live with my parents. There was something else that piqued my curiosity.

Dad said that this was our second time being apart, and that it was because of me. But what about the first time? Had I also been the cause? Why had we been separated, and why didn't I remember anything?

He said that I'd been too young to understand, that it had happened shortly after I was born, when I wasn't even a year old yet.

'You were living with Mum and my mother then,' he said. 'They both looked after you.'

'So where were you?'

'Somewhere else. Somewhere unpleasant.' He went silent for a while. 'Your mum and your grandma brought you along when they came to see me.'

'But why were you there?'

'I was forced.' He fell silent again. He was riddled with discomfort and shame, but he also realized that he could no longer keep me in the dark. I persisted with my questions, so he made his decision, and told me: 'I was in jail.'

'You were in jail.' I repeated his exact words.

'Yes, I was a prisoner,' he said. 'Charged for attempted murder, despite the fact that it was nothing but a quarrel.'

'The court sentenced me to ten years in prison,' he continued, 'but I only served a little over three years, because my sentence was eventually reduced due to good behaviour. There were also several important dates each year, auspicious days, and I was granted a royal reduction in sentence on one of those. So I was released much sooner.'

'Who put you there, Dad?'

'Your grandfather's brother. Great Uncle Thai.'

I'll never understand how family members could go to such lengths to hurt one another. Great Uncle Thai was the reason why Dad was in jail for almost four years, and this probably explained why their relationship turned sour, despite living together in the same compound. Dad wasn't as possessive towards the land as Great Uncle Thai was. Perhaps it was because Dad felt he'd wronged Great Uncle Thai, because the way Dad acted around him seemed to me to be an inadvertent admission of guilt for what had occurred between them.

It now made sense to me: why I'd always felt intimidated by Great Uncle Thai, more so than anyone else, whenever I visited my hometown. He owned this land for a long time and everything that was built on it had been earned by his own blood, sweat, and tears: the garage, the corner shop, the building he rented out to migrant workers . . . Even the small road in front of our house was named after him, called 'Mechanic Thai's Alley'. He had built little houses around the old house so that his relatives could live together, as harmoniously as possible, in the same compound. This little kingdom, the kingdom he'd built for himself with little more than determination and his own two hands, stemmed from an ancient force that had remained with him since he was a young boy who had promised his mother to build a house for her—a promise he had since fulfilled—and now, in his old age, all his dreams had come true. He possessed the future, the present, and the past, all as a result of his hard work, ambition, and personal history.

The next day, I try to find the right time to speak with Great Uncle Thai, despite knowing that I wasn't his favourite grandchild and that I had been sent to live somewhere far away because of what I had done to Great Grandma. But that was a decade ago, and all I could hope for was that his hatred for me had faded with his old age.

At this time of day, Great Uncle Thai usually spent time in the prayer room, meditating and passing his merit onto others: whatever helped to cleanse his spirit. I wait for him in front of the room and pretend to be passing by when he comes out.

'When did you get back?' he asks.

'Two days ago.'

He seems to want to end our exchange there. I call out to him as he starts walking away.

'Great Uncle!'

He shoots me a glance before continuing to walk away. I follow him until he reaches the kitchen. He sits down and asks me why I'm bothering him.

'I'm going to be frank with you, Great Uncle, because I know you'll find a way to yell at me anyway. The thing is, there's something I want to ask you.'

'Go ahead, ask me then.'

'Do you remember the thing that happened between Dad and you?'

'Which thing? There are many.'

'The one that sent him to jail, just after I was born.'

'That motherfucker.' He inhaled deeply, calming himself down, the good Buddhist that he is. 'He was an arsehole back then. The good-for-nothing type, not like how he is now. I think he only improved when he had you.'

Now, Dad works for him at the garage.

'He was always drunk and high,' he continued. 'Always getting into fights, even with his own parents and relatives.'

'Did he start a fight with you?'

He falls silent, and all I can hear is the sound of his teeth grinding. His jawline grows prominent. His breathing is loud; I notice he's having trouble with it. I don't want to breathe like this when I'm old.

'I forgave him for all the times he'd wronged me. I stopped thinking about past conflicts. Your Dad is family. He's my brother's son.'

So, it turns out that what I'm searching for remains locked up in the past, under the shroud of forgiveness. Great Uncle Thai has now chosen to follow the Buddhist path of letting go. He's chosen non-attachment, and the acceptance that comes with old age. We all carry our pasts and the pain that comes with them, but as we get older, we seal them with forgiveness and pack them away into boxes. Those boxes will never be opened again, at least not any time soon.

I might try asking Dad about it again, although his bitterness makes it hard for him to remember what happened, like someone with a chronic wound. The past can't be dressed with forgiveness; instead, the wound festers, ready to dehisce and create new hurts at any time. So, he holds back on disclosing his past, and all I can do is make delicate contact, to extract only what I need to know. Any more than that, and I'll aggravate the wound and the past will bleed out from it. Dad could die from the loss of blood.

The two parties have forgiven each other. Is there any point in trying to interrogate the others who were part of the situation?

But what about me? Where do I fit into this equation?

Ancestral miracle

This is the story Dad was willing to tell me, and I will narrate it as follows:

Grandmother was from Isan, although from a different province than Mum. She fled poverty to look for a job in Saraburi, where she worked in a textile factory. She was beautiful, naive, and illiterate. She started working at a factory when she was sixteen and, less than a year later, she moved in with some guy.

He was the foreman at the textile factory, so Grandmother imagined that being with him would give her security. They lived together unmarried for several years without her parents' knowledge, but she sent them extra money each month, and so they didn't worry about her.

During those years of living together, Grandmother's life was far from blissful. She was abused by the foreman, who had issues with drinking, drugs, gambling, not to mention all his other women. It wasn't even a year before he revealed his true colours, physically beating her until the other folks in the neighbourhood grew fed up with him. But Grandmother endured it all because she believed that the rest of her life depended on him, that he could fire her whenever he wanted.

They had two boys together. When they were born, Grandmother wanted to take them to see her parents. The foreman, however, was against it, claiming that she was trying to force him to see her parents. Deep down, Grandmother thought this was exactly what she did want. She wanted her children to meet her parents, yes, but she also felt it was finally time for him to ask them for her hand in marriage. It was the customary thing to do, especially as they already had children together.

Despite his objections, she secretly took the children to see her parents anyway. When she returned, she was severely beaten, fired from her job, and thrown out of the house.

She was in hospital for almost a week. That was when she met Grandpa.

Grandpa worked as a full-time doctor at the subdistrict's public hospital, as well as running his own clinic near the Kaeng Khoi market. He was a reputable, respectable, and progressive doctor, who pioneered the use of traditional Thai medicine to treat his patients. Despite having spent years abroad studying modern medical technology, he acknowledged and valued local wisdom.

Grandpa adored Grandmother, more so than his other patients; he sympathized with someone who had been through as much as she had. He was the one who found her work at a Chinese restaurant whose owner he knew, and he also found her a new place to live.

Grandmother was a good cook, as was Grandpa, but he never had the chance to show her his culinary skills. She cooked his meals and brought them to the clinic in tiffin boxes. He genuinely enjoyed her cooking, and it was an excuse for him to see her more frequently.

Later, he would pay her a visit at her apartment, and it was during this time that Dad was born.

In the end, the foreman managed to find her. He came to drag her back home to look after his children. He started a huge row and threatened to strike her again, but Grandpa interfered and beat him up first: 'Son of a bitch! You only have the guts to hit women. Get the hell out of here and don't you dare show your face again.'

Grandma never saw him again.

Grandpa was an exceptional man: knowledgeable, skilful, perceptive. He was intelligent and physically strong. He was a perfect man. Perhaps too perfect for someone of Grandmother's status in the view of others, particularly Great Uncle Thai. But none of this bothered Grandpa.

Great Uncle Thai looked down on Grandmother, saying she was uneducated, calling her an illiterate country bumpkin. He also didn't like how Grandpa Siam brought her to live in Thap Kwang, on the land that belonged to Great Uncle Thai. After they moved here when Dad was only three years old, Grandpa Siam disappeared.

Rumours flew. They said he went abroad to study, that he was a volunteer doctor stationed at the Thai border, that he had been driven insane by the field of medicine, that attempting to combine traditional Thai healing with modern medicine had made a huge mess of everything, and so he'd vanished into a cave in the jungles of Kanchanaburi . . . Or so they said. Years later, Grandpa Siam returned, perfectly sane and even more charismatic than before.

He returned with new knowledge and skills he'd gained during his absence. He upgraded the therapies at his clinic, incorporating new stem cell technology, which people got excited about. News of it spread through word of mouth. He began seeking new franchises for his clinic, with a focus on aesthetics and enhancing beauty from within. He had a massage parlour and a spa, as well as a store selling health and beauty supplies. Grandmother worked alongside him, taking care of the business, and they spent their prime years together.

'What a quack,' Great Uncle Thai commented. 'It's dishonest, making money out of people's hopes and dreams.'

It was superficial, according to Great Uncle Thai. It was a job that offered neither security nor sustainability. In fact, it wasn't even a real job: it was consumerism!

A few years later, Great Uncle Thai would refer to it as 'vile capitalism'.

Grandpa Siam, he thought, was taking advantage of the poor: people he saw as uneducated and short-sighted, people who wished to change their skin colour in the blink of an eye and were therefore willing to believe in the miracle of stem cell treatment. He said that even if the treatment could return movement to their previously paralysed limbs, how could we be certain that the medication would not poison them in the future?

A year later, Great Uncle Thai stopped using the phrase 'vile capitalism', replacing it with 'the destruction brought by populism'.

Great Uncle Thai set up a satellite receiver and tuned his television to a channel that broadcasted attacks on the then-populist government all day and night, slandering, fabricating conspiracies, and rousing its audience with obscenities. Great Uncle Thai always wore a yellow shirt and carried a plastic hand clapper around with him, which he occasionally clapped as he stood in front of his house, directing the sound towards Grandmother. Every once in a while, she would retaliate with her own pair of plastic clapping feet.

Great Uncle Thai's house was filled with direct-to-consumer products advertised on that satellite channel. He only used some of what he purchased; the rest were kept sealed in their packages, bought only as a way of donating to the movement: the People's Alliance for Democracy. Things were not so different at Grandmother's house, which was also furnished with products she bought to support the opposing group, the United Front of Democracy Against Dictatorship.

This fracture in the two brothers' relationship solidified itself into something more concrete. Their conflict wasn't at all ideological; rather, it had been triggered by a mere fraternal disagreement.

Great Uncle Thai travelled to the capital city with his fellow allies to participate in a protest, aiming to overthrow the puppet government that allegedly sought to change the country's system of governance. They thought they would wage their final war, but to their disappointment, the election that took place after the 2007 Constitution resulted, once again, in the victory of the much-hated political party that haunted Great Uncle Thai, and other Yellow Shirts, like a spectre. Great Uncle Thai and his allies set up their headquarters near Makkhawan Bridge, a stone's through from the Government House. Later that evening, they would join forces to overthrow the government once and for all. The People's Alliance's leader announced on stage that their mission would be aided by several 'invisible armies': the Vanguards, the Small Army, and the Pisadan Army.

The following day, they divided and occupied various government buildings, beginning with the Ministry of Finance, then the Ministry of Agriculture, then the Ministry of Telecommunications, then the government's television station. Finally, they captured the Government House.

Grandpa Siam and Grandmother thought it unacceptable how far those people had gone, so they decided to take a ride into the capital with their Red Shirts comrades from all over Isan, including my mother and her parents. This was the event that brought my parents together. They hit it off right away and fell in love.

At Sanam Luang, Grandpa Siam, Grandmother, and their comrades joined other Red Shirts. He urged her to stay with the crowd while he went off with smaller groups of Red Shirt protestors to find out what Great Uncle Thai and his Yellow Shirt supporters were getting up to later that night. A brawl broke out in a small lane near the Ratchadamnoen Boxing Stadium between Great Uncle Thai's and Grandpa Siam's factions. Each of them charged at the other, throwing punches, flag poles, rocks, and other weapons, before gunshots rang out and Grandpa Siam's Red Shirt fellows collapsed to the ground.

Grandpa Siam was gravely injured; his right eye was bleeding, and he had a head injury. He was certain it was Great Uncle Thai's doing.

Both Grandpa Siam and Grandmother returned home, defeated. Dad also asked Mum to come back with him.

The fact that Grandpa Siam had been attacked was infuriating for Dad. His young blood boiled with vengeance and loathing for Great Uncle Thai. He began drinking every day and stopped working completely, lounging in the front yard waiting for Great Uncle Thai to return from the capital.

At the end of that year, after the Yellow Shirts successfully seized the country's two largest airports, the constitutional court disbanded the ruling party. The court barred them from political involvement for five years, forcing the then-prime minister to retire immediately. Soon after, an opposing party's prime minister came into office. He was Thailand's youngest and most handsome prime minister to date, and he spoke perfect English. (All of these traits are well documented in the history of the administration of the country.) Great Uncle Thai returned home shortly after the new prime minister took office.

It was the beginning of December. Dad had been drinking and playing with firecrackers since Loy Krathong, and when he saw that Great Uncle Thai had finally returned home, he throwing firecrackers at his house. He kept on doing it to provoke the old man. (Don't judge me, Dad said to me. I was a hot-headed teenager back then, and I hated Great Uncle Thai so much but I've changed.) When Great Uncle Thai couldn't take it any longer, he stood in front of his house and yelled obscenities at Dad:

'You don't have a future. I'm the one who put a roof over your head, and you're still ungrateful. This land is mine, so don't even think about revolting against me. You and your folks should just get the hell off my land and serve that treasonous bastard, like the slaves you are!'

Grandmother couldn't just sit there and listen to Great Uncle Thai. Both of them starting cursing each other from the front of their own house. Things quickly got heated, and Grandmother started making her way into Great Uncle Thai's front yard. Dad, who was drinking but watching from a distance, could tell that something horrible was going to happen; he was certain that Great Uncle Thai was capable of hurting his mother in the same way that he had hurt Grandpa Siam.

He grabbed the machete that was leaning against the wall beside him and charged. Dad was right. He saw Great Uncle Thai punch his mother several times until she lost her balance. At that exact moment, there was an opening between Dad, Grandmother, and Great Uncle Thai. Dad swung the machete and struck Great Uncle Thai in the neck, intending to kill him. The curved blade hit Great Uncle Thai's jaw;

his neck was caught in the machete's curve, but the knife was blunt. His head remained intact, but the force of it still knocked him to the ground, where he lay unconscious in his own front yard.

Dad was imprisoned for almost four years as a result of that single scene.

Now I understand why.

Great Uncle Thai said that he had forgiven Dad. Still, I'm not sure if Great Uncle Thai is entitled to offer him that forgiveness.

The arrival of the two brothers

In the midst of a crisis, there is always good and bad timing. Dad told me that. Like when Mum realized she was pregnant with me several months after Dad assaulted Great Uncle Thai. I was a precious gift during that difficult time in their lives. Dad said that Grandmother, Grandpa Siam, and both of my parents eagerly awaited the day I would come out to greet the world. I was the only thing that made them feel like life wasn't so unbearable, so terrible. During those dark days, I was something for them to look forward to.

But there was also bad timing. The arrival of the two brothers—the sons that Grandmother had with the foreman—came out of nowhere. Both of them wanted to meet Grandmother. After searching for her for so long, they wanted to meet their mother.

Grandmother learned that her two sons' father had passed, leaving them with nothing but orphanhood as their inheritance. Their father had squandered all of his assets—property, possessions, and money that should have been passed down to their children—on women and gambling. The two were left with almost nothing, not even relatives to turn to: with the exception of their grandmother and mother, whom they had managed to find.

At that point, they were no longer kids; they were older than Dad and had already started university. Dad said that he had no idea what they wanted. On that first day, Grandmother allowed them to stay with the family. Grandpa Siam didn't mind either, because they were considered Grandmother Dao's children. They only wanted to spend time with their mother—to talk to her for a few days—and then they would leave our family alone.

However, their stay grew longer, and they became more and more involved in family life. They helped Grandmother and Grandfather manage the household when the pair of them left for work. Both of them, especially the younger brother, Chidchai, offered to help Dad find a competent lawyer to defend his case in court, to get him out of the mess he was in.

One day, when Dad was drunk, he bluntly asked the two brothers: 'What the hell are you two doing here, anyway? Nowhere else to go?'

Dad sensed that they were sly and insincere. In fact, he was suspicious of their intent to help manage things for him. The next day, the eldest brother, Prateep, told Grandmother that his half-brother's drunk behaviour was concerning. They were persuasive enough to convince her, and she told Dad: 'Maitree, listen to your brothers. They know better than you.' Dad was frustrated with the fact that he now had to live under the same roof as the brothers, so he did everything he could to let them know that they were not welcome.

Everything Dad suspected about the brothers came true. Their arrival portended the total devastation that would befall our family. Although they didn't seem to be the main cause, they were the catalysts that transformed calamity into something that seemed almost natural, inevitable.

For starters, the lawyer they found for Dad doomed him to a full prison term with no reduction. So Grandmother lost one of her sons, but she gained two more, both desperate to claim the household as their own. They eventually infiltrated the family and, little by little, took over certain things while Dad was in jail, unable to protect his kin. His child, wife, and parents were on the other side of the fence, together with the two brothers.

During Dad's early days in prison, Grandmother took me to visit him once a week. She told him that her eldest son had left the house to pursue his studies, and Grandpa Siam was paying for him.

'What about the other one?' Dad asked her.

Grandmother remained silent. He looked at Mum, who was holding me as she looked down, sobbing, and avoiding his gaze. The tension suggested that the other brother was still at home. When Dad realized what was going on, he made a promise to himself that he would drag Chidchai out of the house as soon as he was released. If he could, he would murder him. Being sent back to prison didn't concern him in the least.

In our property, Chidchai had a small room of his own. He dropped out of college and used his meagre qualifications to find a job in town. Chidchai always drove Grandmother and Mum to visit Dad in prison, but he never went in with them. During one visit, after he had spoken to Grandmother, Mum, and me, Dad asked to speak with him alone. Chidchai sat down opposite him, a large glass panel between them. As soon as he picked up the phone, Dad said:

'I know what you're up to.'

'Do you?' That was all Chidchai said, indifferent to Dad's rage.

'You bastards came to replace me, to take my property,' Dad said. 'I know all about it. Next, you'll get rid of my wife and kid. You'll get rid of everyone so you can have it all to yourselves.'

'Typical,' Chidchai responded. 'This is the kind of bullshit only people like you can come up with. I'm your brother. I've done everything for you, you ungrateful bastard. Look around! You're here because of all the fucked-up shit inside your head. What's it to do with you if I choose to stay here, anyway?'

'You're fucking dead,' Dad threatened him quietly, aware that the prison guard might be listening. 'Just you wait when I'm out.'

'That's what I'm saying. Your kind is only good for being locked up.'

From then on, Dad heard nothing about the two brothers. Grandmother stopped mentioning them during her visits, since she knew it would only upset him. But being kept in the dark was just as tortuous as knowing what they were up to. During the long days and nights of his prison years, Dad repeatedly asked himself the question: 'Could I really kill them? If I find those two still lounging about in my house when I'm out?'

But by the time Dad was released, they were no longer there. Grandmother said that Chidchai now lived in a house of his own in the suburbs of Saraburi.

This came as a huge relief to Dad. He never wanted to resort to violence, but if the situation demanded it—like the case of the two brothers who had invaded the family, wreaking havoc on everyone's lives, especially mine and Mum's—then he had no choice but to protect his family. Although Dad no longer had to worry about the two brothers' intrusion following his release, he still had to deal with Great Uncle Thai, the owner of the land.

Dad did everything he could to avoid Great Uncle Thai. He couldn't find work at first, so he spent his days hiding in the house while Mum worked. It was Great Uncle Thai who made the first move. He appeared in front of our house, asking Dad how life had been in prison, and whether he turned himself around. Dad avoided looking at Great Uncle Thai. He refused to answer his questions, but he could sense that the old man meant no harm, and no longer held a grudge against him. To Great Uncle Thai, Dad had paid for his crimes and his karma by doing the time. Great Uncle Thai approached Dad as an elderly relative, one who had come to forgive and make peace. Then, Great Uncle Thai asked if Dad could help him with work at the garage, and so, Dad followed him. Since then, Dad has been working at Great Uncle Thai's garage. Grandpa Siam and Grandmother were also happy with the ways things turned out.

Then came the year 2015. According to Dad, that was the year of our family's greatest disaster, which occurred after the arrival of the two brothers.

It was the year Grandpa Siam fell unconscious in his clinic. Grandmother took him to a private hospital, but when his condition showed no signs of improvement, she later moved him to another hospital. Everyone knew about this, even the two brothers who came back to visit Grandpa Siam: everyone, that is, except Great Grandmother. Dad said Grandmother tried everything to help Grandpa Siam regain consciousness. It happened just as he was about to enter local politics. He was paralysed in the middle of his glory days. He lost it all, along with his consciousness. After many months, he passed away.

As far as I know, Grandpa Siam didn't go alone. That year, Great Grandmother went right after he did, and that was why I was sent away to live with my maternal grandparents in Isan. That was where things took a violent, tumultuous turn.

Great Uncle Thai's vengeance and rage resurfaced, almost to the point of insanity. He hurled curses at my family, especially at Dad and Grandmother, who no longer had Grandpa Siam to look after them.

He should've known, Great Uncle Thai said, cursing us. We'd been waiting for this, he said. We the ungrateful, the treacherous, the vengeful: we'd been waiting for this moment to get back at him, to crush him deeper into the ground, to watch his life crumble. His relatives and close friends had to come and stop him, to try and calm him down. But he had suffered so much loss. His heart brimmed with venom. He claimed that Dad had never stopped thinking about seeking revenge, and that was why I did what I did to his mother. (What a cruel accusation! She was my great grandmother too.) He said that these wretched children and grandchildren—not just Grandpa Siam's but also the other two, from Grandmother's previous relationship—had brought nothing but more disaster into the family. Those people enter his land, he said, and then they leave with 'their stories and utterly shameless lies'. They lived off lies, fabricating truths from falsehood and selling them to people who were ready to believe whatever things they wrote.

'My heart is wounded by these ungrateful children, and it's no one else's fault but their bitch mother!' Great Uncle Thai cursed.

He accused Grandmother of bringing about these losses, for carrying destruction in her womb and giving birth to it, again and again. All that destruction, slowly consuming Great Uncle Thai's land and spirit.

Dad was no longer violent. He knew he had a kid, a wife, and relatives to take care of. He admitted that he was angry at Great Uncle

Thai but, given his situation, which had now drastically changed, he couldn't afford to be impulsive like before. He also knew that Great Uncle Thai's bark was worse than his bite, so he let the old man rage.

I'd already been sent away to live with my maternal grandparents. By the time the funeral proceedings were over, Great Uncle Thai had calmed down.

Great Uncle Thai's outburst, on the other hand, was the final straw for Grandmother. She couldn't take his insults any longer. With Grandpa Siam gone, she believed she deserved nothing but peace in her final years: something this household could not provide. One day, Grandmother decided to bid Dad farewell, telling him that he was now a father with a family for which he was responsible, and that she no longer worried about him. She planned to leave the house for good, to leave my parents to raise their child alone. She went back to live with the son of her first husband: Chidchai. That was why she was not there when I returned.

Contemplating lies till they become truth

After hearing what I'd just heard, my curiosity was piqued, especially when Dad recounted to me the disaster caused by the two brothers, and how much it had wounded our family. I was also intrigued by Great Uncle Thai's relentless cursing of all three of Grandmother's sons for bringing catastrophe into the family. I asked Dad whether he still has that book. He isn't sure and tells me to search for it; perhaps it's in one of the piles of old newspapers and magazines somewhere in the house. Neither of my parents like to read, so these sorts of items are left scattered about everywhere.

This is the place where I was born and brought up. My parents didn't see the use of reading, so I grew up inherently indifferent to it. It's genetics. Strangely enough, though, it became one of the reasons I wanted to pursue my studies in the field of education.

Dad tells me that it might be better to look through Great Uncle Thai's bookshelf, which I agree with.

Finally, I find it in a bundle of books in the corner of a room, along with books about dream interpretation and astrology, as well as ultra-nationalist books about Lap Luang Prang, Thailand and Cambodia's territory dispute. Two decades had gone by, but fortunately, that book I was looking for had been quietly waiting for me in this damp room.

The book is titled *The Shattering of the Curse*, written by Prateep P., first published in the year 2013. It's thin: a novella of just over a hundred pages. That night, I spend two hours reading the entire thing.

The Shattering of the Curse is divided into thirteen chapters, each of which is dated like a diary entry to indicate when it was supposedly written down. All thirteen chapters interweave various incidents into a story about the lives of three brothers and their mother, all of the same bloodline. What's remarkable about the book is the vivid depiction of each character's personality, and it's these contrasts between the brothers that make it more interesting. The plot was convincing, full of tension, which worked to develop the reader's sentiment while raising important philosophical questions.

Central to the story is the land that belongs to the late father, as it represents the three brothers' conscience and their attitudes toward their birthplace, as well as the arrivals of intruders who try to expropriate their land. The land also serves as a geographical and psychological place that unites all the characters in the story together.

Violence is employed throughout the plot, driving it towards a traumatic ending. All in all, a very interesting work: but not exceptional.

In terms of narrative techniques, it's rather postmodern (which, in 2013, was no longer considered innovative). The text attempts to combine the old and the new, as evidenced by the diary form, which specifies the date each entry was supposedly written (by the narrator, or the ghostwriter; these dates, too, are significant to the incidents in the plot). It also asks minor questions about the way real life and fiction are interrelated. The plot attempts to take readers down a route never previously taken: at least not by any author in their right mind, who would never write such misery into their work. It's as if the ghostwriter is attempting to ask: if the lives narrated in the story were predestined by an invisible hand, would the reader accept it as a literary convention and a matter of chance? In other words, could fate's terrible curse befall any family? In this story, the ghostwriter (who wants to remain anonymous but is called 'Prateep' by his mother, although he refers to himself, irritatingly, in the third person) is also intimately connected to the story. 'He', as the eldest brother, also has blood on his hands, from forecasting misfortune upon his family and, by extension, his story. Despite his insistence to the reader that the story is fictional, the effect is quite the opposite: it feels real and unsettling, a product of the storyteller's cruelty.

The ghostwriter takes up his pen, drags it along the piece of paper that is meant to be someone's life, and moves it towards an extraordinary destination. The conflict and chaos within his own heart are passed onto the reader. When a true story is diverted towards the deserted path of fiction, the storyteller takes on two roles: the elder brother and the author of his family's fate. From Chapter 5, '6 December 2008', the narration shifts from storytelling to another mode in which the crisis in the story becomes a problem that must be decoded and solved.

As I said before, this book isn't exceptional as a piece of creative work. No further information, apart from the stuff published on the back of the book, comes up when I try to search for the book's title and author.

In this sense, *The Shattering of the Curse* doesn't seem to have created enough impact to have affected the public.

In fact, the entire book is full of contradictions; it straddles the line between professional and amateurish, just as it does the line between reality and fiction. Personally, I don't believe it indicates a skilled writer; rather, it betrays his hesitancy, uncertainty, and, more than anything, the nascence of his ideas. This is the book's greatest flaw. Think about it. When something is published into the world and it isn't powerful enough to outshine the other works of its era, it becomes a dying light in the larger universe of literature. Its own light, however, shines bright enough to illuminate the real lives of those who are behind the story.

Every character in the story is named after real people who live here, including myself (except the storyteller, who avoids using his name and identity.) All of the incidents in the story are rendered from the same material, but they take a tumultuous turn. Great Uncle Thai becomes a vile expropriator, and Dad becomes a love child. Can a literary work that disguises deceit as truth be regarded as genuine? He—the writer—reconstructs memories into a new history, dismantles an archaeological ruin into a new piece of architecture. Our lives—my own, my parents', grandparents', and ancestors'—are reconfigured.

What a pity. Other readers know nothing about this backstory. For me—for us—we feel a terrible pain that cuts deep into our ancestors, our stories, our memories. I'm not surprised that Great Uncle Thai, like Dad, feels the need for vengeance.

I can't sleep all night, disturbed by the things I read. Even though it happened a long time ago and our family has found peace among ourselves, the sediments of the past have now been stirred up. Age-old rust is slowly corroding into the steel core.

I search through as many websites as I can to find more information on this anonymous writer. I found that the literary scene in 2013 was very barely active, which is ironic, given that was the year Bangkok claimed itself to be the 'Book Capital of the World'. Then, I stumble onto a website that sells old books, and a title catches my attention. I stare at its cover for a long time, as though I might be able to see through it and read its contents. I look at the author's name, and it's not the one I initially had in mind. The author is not Prateep P., although it's possible that it might be another one of his aliases. I'm convinced that it is, for some reason; perhaps it's the title: *Dr Siam's Adventures in the World of Conspiracies*. I click the order button.

Two days later, I have the book in my hand. It's in bad shape, covered in damp spots here and there. The low-quality paper also betrays that the book doesn't just appear old because of time: it was also poorly designed, with an old-fashioned front cover that shows a two-toned woodcut artwork of a running man. Generally, it looks like a cover typically used for books that belong to the 'Literature for Life' genre. The author's name, Tai Pudpard, stands out from everything. Considering it was published in 2016, the design, title, and author point towards the same intention: to satirize the book itself, as well as that of the society it depicts.

And I'm right. After speeding through the book, I find that both the contents and the cover are indeed satirical.

When the anonymous writer discloses himself as the ghostwriter in the first chapter, the reader is confronted with a contradiction (anonymity vs. disclosure). He recounts the story of Siam, a man in his fifties, a fugitive seeking to survive in the afterlife, or rather, an invisible world that runs parallel to the real world. Dr Siam is caught in the middle, 'bound' by the obligations of the real world while desiring the freedom to inhabit his other, ideal world. Despite being an 'invisible' world of his own creation, Dr Siam's world is intruded upon by many things. (How awful!) His identity becomes a blank canvas for others to paint over, to define him; gradually, all of this seeps into Dr Siam's invisible world.

This space that was supposed to be his becomes tainted by other people's 'opinions' of him. Slowly, they tighten their grip on Dr Siam's wandering spirit, crushing it completely. These opinions sought to explain his identity, eventually subsuming him into one of those explanations.

The form also works well to convey this meaning. Through the use of footnotes, an academic convention, the author seizes the main narrative (as told by Dr Siam and written as a manifesto of sorts, which is undercut by his sometimes overdone, childish sense of humour). It might be said that Dr Siam is an unreliable character, and that even the author undermines his credibility by mocking his accent and his failed attempts to show off his mediocre English with the mispronunciation of things, like 'no sense' instead of 'nonsense.'

The use of footnotes is quite effective (despite the way it interrupts the reading experience) because, in every chapter, the footnotes are longer than the main narrative. This reflects the 'grandiosity' of reasoning that violates the main narrative, undermining its credibility and seriousness with tasteless jokes. We, as readers, tend to be indifferent when an unreliable character is prone to injury and death, especially when this character is cornered and killed by a reason or explanation that is bigger than themselves. We quietly acknowledge and ultimately accept their deaths when they are justified by the hand of reason.

For me, this is an utter tragedy. Not only is the character victimized by the other characters around him, but he is also persecuted by the author who created him. If the story does not offer this character any hope, then perhaps the underlying message is that the author himself is also unreliable.

While *Dr Siam's Adventures in the World of Conspiracies* employs creative narrative devices, the ideas within the story are outdated, reaffirming the ideals and anti-establishment attitudes that have since been exhausted. It can even be said that the story perpetuates the same set of individualistic ideals that can be traced back to the works of Kafka and Beckett. Anyone who has read *The Trial, The Castle,* or *Waiting for Godot* will find the imagery, as well as the character's motifs and surrounding conditions, strikingly similar.

I won't mention how my family is related to this novella. It becomes obvious, upon finishing it, that Tai Pudpard is Prateep P.'s second alias. The three years that passed between the publication of the two works corresponds to the events that occurred in this house and on this land. (The author didn't even bother to change the names of the characters, and all who appear in *The Shattering of the Curse* reappear in this novella.) These two stories, once again, undermine and dismantle the truth about my family. In turn, they distort my memory and my identity.

Having read both works, I can confirm that they are written by the same author. It's not important to distinguish which one of them is fact and fiction. I won't stand here trying to prove that he's wrong and I'm right. He fabricated stories about his ancestors in a particular place, a particular land, while I too have my own stories about my ancestors, ones I heard in that same place. Our worlds inhabit the same space, despite being in different dimensions, different hierarchies.

A thought occurs to me—a result of my contemplating solely with reason—which works like a flash of light, coming in to dispel darkness. These things 'matter', even when what is considered unreliable perishes before your very eyes in the name of reason, justice, virtue, the triumph of good over evil. The Buddha's defeat of the demons, religion's eradication of superstition, land taken by new owners, brothers that switch bloodlines . . . I can't just let him die and be forgotten.

Towards the end of *The Shattering of the Curse*, the ghostwriter suffers from paralysis, while Dr Siam is forced to disappear at the end of his story. Yes, they 'matter' to me. There might not be any concrete space for the defeated—the unrefined, the evil, the unreliable—but they continue to resound. I am its witness. We are its witnesses.

Sins and karma are subjective. I don't think that those who are already dead possess the mental faculties to form connections like the living. Animals don't believe that humans are superior. Death doesn't believe that life is superior. Everything I know is perceived through my own thoughts and feelings about myself and the world.

I am Maya

Who am I? I ask myself. The answer is not in my name. Names are used to identify things, to label them superficially. They're not substantial. So, what I mean is, what substance do I carry within me?

Going back to the moment I was born, before I became myself, the substance that eventually would become me took shape inside a warm nest. This biological substance slowly became whole, until it reached full capacity in that place I eventually came out from. Did I know who I was at that point? I don't think I did, and I would continue to not know for centuries. The world was full of the unknown, and I didn't think about questioning anything, I just felt them through the senses I'd been equipped with. This body, this biological substance, was able to feel warmth, just as much as it was able to desire it. I didn't want anything else. For many years, I had no desires of my own. Only my body desired: it desired to grow, to be fulfilled, to be prepared.

Then I started learning about my surroundings. I named everything using words, ones that I'd heard other people use; in turn, I learned to describe things the same way others did, including what to call 'myself'.

Words came pouring in: 'Dad', 'Mum', 'flesh', 'blood', 'life', 'family', 'home', 'land', 'country', 'world', 'universe'. Things are expressed through words—'once upon a time . . .'—and they create existence. The past exists, memories exist, histories exist. Words bring the past to me, from a time when I didn't know what I was. The past brought back the night I was born, placing it right in front of me, through words uttered by my parents. I might have been impressed, moved by them: not because I was aware of them at the time, but because of those words. Words created my memories, my past, me. And I started to use the past, along with all my senses, to explain surrounding phenomena: that which I know I'm participating in. They are my experiences, conveyed through words. The 'now' exists. The present awakens.

During the days when I learned of the present, my biological substance continued to grow, nourishing itself with other things, becoming aware of its desires. In fact, I started to know what I wanted: not just carnal things, but other things that I couldn't always have. So, I started hoping; dreaming of them, imagining what it would be like to have them. The light of tomorrow began to dawn on me. The future turned towards me.

Now I know that the place I'm standing is the present, which is in turn is situated in space and time. I'm walking to Great Uncle Thai's house through space and time. Nothing is taken without loss. Space and time put everything into balance: everything that is here, in the present, from the time when you're a child, to when you grow into a young woman, to old age. While I accept that everything unfolds in the space and time of the present, I also try to resist it. I resist going along with the present. Instead, I dwell in the past, in my memories, and in the future, with my imagination and my hopes. In one single day, I travel to different places in a blink of an eye: outer space, the universe, the galaxy, the Milky Way, and other Milky Ways. Small clusters in the utter darkness of the universe, moving, orbiting, crashing into each other to form a black hole that swallow everything in its horizon. The more it swallows, the smaller it gets, until it's as small as the size of my body in the womb. So incredibly small. The entire universe lives inside a mother's womb, all of it compressed into an atom. Smaller than an atom. A quark. Smaller than a quark. They don't know anything, these seeds, these essences of immeasurable substance. They don't know that they're this small, that they're living inside a maternal womb. Sometimes they're even smaller than that, more or less the size of a handful of padauk leaves in the Buddha's hand. He stretches his arm and scatters those leaves. The breeze carries them towards the Buddha's disciples. The Buddha is sitting there, under a large tree, moving his hand to scatter the padauk leaves into the wind. He is aware that his hand is moving. He follows its motion. His whole body is aware, focused on this spot, on this hand, in this present moment. Undotted line, uninterrupted, unfading. The present flows like a stream, continuous. There is neither past nor future.

Who am I? What substance am I made of? I have a past and a future, but are they really mine? I'm aware. I appear. I'm standing here in my room, in the house where I was born. I'll be twenty in a few months this year, the year 2029.

My past slowly weaves itself, taking form. If I remember and recall, staring straight into the horizon of events, different stories arrange themselves into images, events, and phrases. I become aware before I ask the question: 'Who am I?' I come to my senses, like I'm waking up from sleep, or being born out of emptiness. When I ask about myself, the stories start rushing in.

Do stories predate me, or do I predate them? Do the past and future exist before me, or do they exist because of me? I'm not the kind of person who runs in circles, and this question isn't meant to be contradictory. This is a serious question.

Do we know ourselves from the moment we are born, or from when we ask ourselves: 'Who am I?' If it's the latter, then I was just born a moment ago, at the age of nineteen. And the stories exist, because I asked.

Perhaps stories already existed before I asked, or before I was born. Once I was born and began to ask questions, I formed a bond with them. I become a part of what has come before: the past, memories, stories, misery and happiness, struggle and indifference, victory and defeat. I become a part of that grand narrative, a mere cog that drives forward what has already been written as history. Am I a part of the grand narrative?

Fate, or destiny: the ancient belief that some other force is writing and driving the course of our lives. Those who refer to it often do so when they encounter something unexpected, something beyond their control: things like repeated misfortune, sudden death, or natural disaster. We don't plan or design for these things to happen to us, and yet, sometimes they do. Those who are drowning in poverty and debt may never surface for years and years. All of a sudden, you could be hit by a car or a stray bullet. Thousands could be wiped out in a flash flood or an earthquake. We didn't design these things ourselves. They are destined. But by whom? Lord Brahma? Fate?

I don't think they have anything to do with it. We humans are to blame. We all play a part, creating ripples that connect us to others, whether we're aware of it or not, whether we're aware of them or not. Even natural disasters are man-made. When something occurs in one place, it affects other places. We are all part of one other, affecting and connecting each other.

I feel the rippling effect of my family's legends and histories being passed onto me. I'm not the cause of these conflicts and wounds, but the fact that I am part of them is inevitable. I have been part of them since I was born. They are my heritage, they are what constitutes as me.

I'm just a minor narrative that exists within the immensity of a grander narrative. But actually, it feels much more forceful than that. I feel like I'm just a character within my own minor narrative.

I exist in the moment where I ask myself who I am. Suddenly, all the events arrange themselves before me. I'm standing in a room in my old house, having travelled from Nakhon Pathom after breaking up with my boyfriend who was about to become a monk. The naga made me recall Great Grandmother's ancient stories, as well as the Buddha's footprint. Stories were fed to me, making me into someone, tethering me to the stories that came before. There are stories in the present, that happened to me: like the one where the fight I had with my boyfriend somehow drives me to serve a past that I didn't create, drives me to become a part of the story, to begin investigating and tracing back, to listen to all the stories about things that happened a long time ago. The past crashes into me. Am I responsible for them—the tales of my ancestors, the stories enveloping me—for the ties and obligations that come with them? I'm neither their creator nor their cause, but I was asked to remember them, forced to memorize them, to live my life as a continuation of the past.

What about my present? You didn't think to write about that in your grand narrative.

I'm faceless and my physical appearance is obscured, mainly because I don't rely much on physical form. I move with my thoughts and, in turn, they indicate my identity in this story. My surroundings—like objects, like shadow and light, like weather—are ambiguous. These things lose their shape and disappear if I stop noticing and scrutinizing them.

I wonder if I have any beliefs or faiths. I critically expose things through comparison and connection. But if I believe in something or have faith in it, that thing may be irrational. Will *you* let me keep it, if that's the case?

Will *you* free me from this story and the stories that came before it? I'm just someone who came after them.

Those stories are ancient, so ancient that they're like complete strangers to someone like me. My memories are short-lived and fleeting, and there'll be other stories to remember. My time moves faster, it does not span as long as it did in the past, just like how present space is less vast now. In fact, I bear no attachment to the land, to territory, ownership, home, to the long history that these deep attachments stemmed from. Even the earth is foreign to someone like me, someone who lives in a square room in a condominium. We all share living space now. We've have moved far beyond those conflicts of the past. We have love, attachment, possessiveness, beliefs that are uniquely ours.

And those conflicts of the past, the societies to which they belong: they appear too archaic, too wild, too barbaric. They slumber in their bygone caves. If they're still relevant, if you're curious about them, if the past is curious about me, then the years on which I stand still contain my stories. My stories are no better or worse than yours, but we have hope and faith (terms borrowed from your time). The sediment from the past is here in our present.

I haven't forgotten the past, but I manoeuvre in the present.

You have to set me free so that I can be born again, in my own story.

Juti

Too hazy. Too obscure. The fine mist of darkness lingers. Once open, my eyes slowly adjust to the dimness of the room. The weather is cooler than usual; even with the air conditioning on, I can feel it. The weather outside affects it too. The morning feels cold and damp. I curl up into a ball under the duvet.

Light seeps through the window and the double-layered drapes. The calls of an Asian koel can be heard from afar. I reach for my phone, which is lying next to the pillow, and turn it on. The screen illuminates my face. The time is presently 06.11 a.m., the temperature is 20 degrees Celsius, and the sky is gloomy and cloudy with a high probability of rain. A tropical depression from China has spread across the country's north, north-eastern, and central areas. Meanwhile, the Thai Gulf and its surrounding areas are humid, with strong sea winds and large waves. Thick clouds form due to the clash of two different types of air masses. Significant rainfall is expected in the southern region, as well as showers in the central region.

My finger taps the camera icon on the screen, focusing the camera on my face. The face of a person who has just woken up is an unpleasant sight: sleep-covered eyes, bad breath, cheeks creased from rubbing against pillows and sheets, unkempt hair. But this is my face: yellowish complexion, wide forehead, thick brows (that need trimming), eyes that are neither too big nor too small, a tiny mole under my left eye. From where I'm lying, my nose looks huge and my lips look thick. This is not my angle. I shouldn't take any pictures of myself from this angle. Everyone knows their best angle.

I close the camera app, fighting the temptation to browse my different accounts. I get out of bed. I open the door to the terrace. From the ninth floor of my building, I can see that the sky is cloudy, just as my phone predicted. The weather is cool, but a humid breeze flows through the building, making a low whistling sound as it travels through the window. The Asian koel's calls echo louder than usual. There's no movement from the yard below. It's probably too early for anything to be awake. A silent crowd of parked cars and bicycles take up the majority of the space. The earth appears darker than usual, possibly because of the rain that fell yesterday night.

I have several potted plants in the corner of the terrace. All of them are rosemary plants, and the largest of them all is the 'mother': the one whose branches I chopped off and planted in the other pots. They looked so withered in their first week, as if they were dying, but eventually, they flourished. I was so glad to see them slowly sinking their roots into the soil, to be able to touch them, smell their fragrance on my hands. It seems no watering is needed this morning.

Back in my room, I prepare some herbal tea for digestion. I get easily constipated, so I drink my tea every morning before I do my business in the bathroom and get ready.

I intend to go to the university library this morning, even though what I'm looking for can be found online without having to leave my room. But today it feels necessary. I feel inspired to move, to travel across space and time. I think we need to go after what we want, rather than allow ourselves be bogged down in passivity. It's like the weather forecast: the figures displayed on my phone are only a threshold, a window or a framework through which to view the things we wish to know. They aren't knowledge in and of themselves. They're just a window into it. I open my window, letting my body luxuriate in the cold, damp air. It isn't exactly the same as the figures I read on my phone, but the actual sky feels more or less the same as what the machine computed. Still, we tend to put our beliefs in these machines, these windows. We see them as unmistakable oracles that calibrate, filter,

think and feel everything for us. We transfer to them the information
that we find important, so we don't have to remember them. More
importantly, we let them become our instincts. That's why I feel it's
necessary to use my own judgement, rather than let myself become
heavily dependent on the machines.

People are still at university, even though it's still the holidays.
Activities have continued as they do during the semester. The halls
are teeming with students, some who remained on campus over the
break, and some recently returned from home. Restaurants and cafes,
as well as some other services on campus, remain open. I leave my
halls and walk along the path towards a restaurant, surrounded by
lush trees with dark brown trunks. I catch the scent of damp grass
and stale mud from a nearby pond. A millipede moves along the
edge of the path on its hundred or perhaps thousands of feet. A
snail drags itself across the damp road, leaving a trail of glistening,
iridescent slime. A squirrel jumps from the trees onto the power line,
sprinkling drops of water onto my face and arms as it leaps. The
bell rings and I look over my shoulder, before giving way to a few
cyclists. A middle-aged man in a tracksuit is jogging towards me from
the opposite bend and, as he comes closer, I recognize him as one
of my lecturers. He nods and smiles, and I raise my hands in a wai.
After I pass the bend, I come to a little cafe with several tables and
chairs set up across a narrow yard, where a few of my friends are
already seated. I order a breakfast set that includes a hot Americano
and a croissant sandwich. The employee repeats my order with a
foreign accent—she's Cambodian, I'm guessing—and proceeds to
tell me the price in English. I pay for my food and take a seat at an
empty table, ready to spend the next half hour here as I wait for the
university library to open.

The students at the table next to me are ASEAN citizens like me.
There are two women and one man. They're all speaking in Vietnamese,
their native tongue. I remember finding the language unusual the first
time I heard it, which was last semester, in my ASEAN literature class.
I listened to another student read a Vietnamese poem. The cadence
was mesmerizing. The word 'mother' in Vietnamese is pronounced

'mae', which I find remarkable, because it sounds similar to the same word in other languages. They all start with an 'm': 'mother' in English, 'maman' in French, 'mutter' in German, 'mātaraḥ' in Sanskrit, 'matha' in Pali, 'e-mae' in Lao, 'māma' in Mandarin, 'gun mae' in Khmer, 'ummi' in Arabic, 'omma' in Korean, etc.

Language is preceded by sound, the former's more primitive instinct. If language reflects human's consciousness, creativity, and civilization, then sound is language's more ancient instinct. Utterances have no ethnicity, nationality, or country. They have the ability to reach out to all humans in all emotional states, whether we're laughing, crying, screaming in fear, or moaning in pleasure. We can all make sense of sounds, whether they are heavy or light, high or low. For this reason, when I listen to my classmates read poetry in their native tongues, I may not understand the meaning at first, but their sounds give me an idea of what the poem is trying to convey. This is what distinguishes poetry from novels or short stories: its potential for sound to resonate with meaning, language's instinct and primitive need to express itself. This is not to say that sound is more raw or more fresh than language, but it works against the purification of words, drawing them closer to their origins.

Chewing a croissant sandwich while contemplating the origins of sound is a simple joy on a late morning like this. The velvety feel of the cheese and the smell of the butter in the croissant—its hundreds of layers of pastry sheets, expertly folded, yet paper thin and full of air—is wonderful.

The university library is now open, but I want to stay a little longer at this cafe. I watch my determination drift away, making more room for chance. I know I have things to do, that I've started doing them, and that I'll get them done. I also know that, beneath all the fabulations about Grandpa and my family, particularly in the first chapter of the ghostwriter's footnotes in *Dr Siam's Adventures in the World of Conspiracies*, there is one truth—a truth palpable in the air—in fiction:

'Isn't there something wonderful about reflecting on the concerns and obligations that await you after lunch? The knowledge that you'll be able to be deal with them tomorrow, or perhaps after a quick nap, is reassuring. You thank life for the concerns and obligations it has burdened you with, and thank it even more for equipping you with the capacity to deal with them. Concerns give you certainty.'

Yes, this is exactly how I am feeling right now. I'm sitting in the present, with the past driving me forward into the future, which I hope to reach, to stand on, and make a present of. In a world full of dotted lines and incoherence, I want beginnings and continuity, so I bind myself to them. That is how we pave our course, our time, our place, our stories.

More people enter the cafe, talking loudly amongst themselves. I dust the crumbs off my hands and examine the lines on my palms: they cut deep and shallow, across mounds and folds, like the earth in microcosm. 'Look at them,' an ancient voice resounds. 'Touch them if you want.' It's my great grandmother's voice. 'It's old and wrinkly. I'll be dead soon,' she said. But she's not dead. She's immortal, like she told me, and she will be born again and again. I think to myself, Great Grandmother will be born right here, from the palms of my hands. Keep this image in focus and magnify it until it resembles the ancient earth, when she was only a spirit. 'I'm here, buried underground.' Yes, the 'I' is primitive: proud, ancient.

Raindrops are falling on my palms. I look up at the gloomy sky and I get up, as do other people, to move and find shelter. Then I decide to walk through the rain. A bicycle bell rings from behind. I look over my shoulder. The cyclist pulls up next to me and asks, 'Where are you going?' I mention the library, and he says he's headed there too.

January 2011–February 2013, January 2015

Translators' Statement

The Fabulist is set in the author's hometown of Saraburi in central Thailand, home to descendants of Mon, Khmer, and Lao diasporas. In the words of the 'miraculous old woman' in Book 1, Saraburi is 'a land twice severed and sutured simply to be named at your tongue's convenience'.

Not only is this an apt analogy for the sacrifices a translator must make when she chooses which components of the original language to carry across, it also raises a key question regarding the very enterprise of translation: for whose convenience do we translate? The two of us translate in the hope that our work resonates with a global, English-speaking audience: one that is aware of English's capacity to contaminate the other tongues for which it so often speaks.

As the only country in Southeast Asia that was never officially colonized by European powers, Thailand remains riddled with nationalist narratives, language, literature, and a false sense of pride. Paradoxically, we as a nation also possess a well-developed inferiority complex, planted within us by Eurocentrism and exacerbated by attitudes of Thai royals who studied abroad almost centuries ago. Caught between two extremes, it is not surprising that Thai literature has yet to make an impact in the English-speaking literary world. We are caught between disdain and reverence for the English language, between shame and pride in our own.

Contemporary Thai authors like Uthis Haemamool are harnessing literature as a means of unlearning and learning from the constraints of traditional Thai culture. *The Fabulist* revels in the dissonance of Thai history, grappling with paradoxical national narratives as it playfully subverts the temptation to present sanitized, convenient narratives for the sake of propriety.

Translating this novel from Thai to English over the past three years has underlined its timely significance. As the characters try to reclaim their narratives through different acts of storytelling, a new generation of Thais are reclaiming and redefining their understanding of nationalism and democracy. When this project began in mid-2020, at the height of the COVID-19 pandemic, a new and unprecedented wave of dissent was surging across the streets of Thailand, marking a new era in the country's political history. The new generation isn't just making history through unflinching criticism of the monarchy, the military dictatorship, and other governing bodies. It is also retelling and remaking history: debunking myths and fallacies that have long dominated Thailand's depiction of itself, and imagining potential futures beyond the confines of censorship and compulsory veneration.

In its unravelling of suffocating narrative seams, *The Fabulist* entangles readers in the loose threads of many modes of fiction: myths, legends, and folklore, as well as contemporary phenomena shared by other cultures beyond our borders. Translating this novel has been an attempt—a balancing act, a conjuring act—to bring the complexities of Thai literature and culture to a wider audience, and we hope it resonates.

Palin Ansusinha and Ploy Kingchatchaval

Further Notes

The characters in this novel sometimes speak in local dialects or with non-standard Thai pronunciation, either on purpose or by the slip of the tongue. In some instances, we chose to indicate this phonetically. An example of this is the old woman's use of the interjections *der* and *ner*, and the kinship title *ee-la*, which is Isan and Lao for 'young girl' or 'youngest daughter'. When used together, these terms help to convey the old woman's endearing tone as she recounts old stories for her great grandchildren in Book 1. For readers unacquainted with the language, we italicized such terms at first mention. Our intent is to signpost vernacular as something incongruous, but not secondary, to the standard vocabulary and grammatical rules of both Thai and English.

We also used italics to highlight foreignness: not in relation to the English language, but to a character's native tongue. Dr Siam, Episode 2's unreliable narrator, boasts often of his self-proclaimed worldliness, but cracks in his confidence are revealed to the reader through malapropisms and mispronounciations in English and French, which we chose to italicize.

When dialect is used in dialogue, things get a little more complicated. Dao in Chapter 3, for example, grew up in Isan, a province in the northeast of Thailand, where her parents spoke to her in Isan dialect. Isan (like all Thai dialects) occupies a complex position within the sociopolitics of Thailand. Thai is an inherently hierarchical language with regard to gender, age, class, and caste, and these dynamics are crucial to *The Fabulist*. We were unwilling to simply translate various dialects into

361

'broken English', as if characters were simply mispronouncing words or speaking 'ungrammatically'; instead, we added descriptors after relevant dialogue.

References

I am thankful for the following sources of information and inspiration that have been immensely useful for writing this novel.

1. *Saraburi: Culture, Historical Development, Uniqueness, and Local Wisdom,* published by the Fine Arts Department to commemorate the 6th anniversary of King Rama IX's birthday on 5 December 1999.

2. *The Royal Chronicle of Ayutthaya* by Phanchanthanumas (Jerm) and *The Royal Chronicle of Ayutthaya Luang* by Prasert, Khamhaikan Chao Krung Kao [คำให้การชาวกรุงเก่า, *Testimony of the Inhabitants of the Old Capital*], *Khamhaikan Khun Luang Ha Wat* [คำให้การขุนหลวงหาวัด]. Published by Sripanya.

3. Khwam Roo Rueng Mueng Siam [ความรู้เรื่องเมืองสยาม, *Knowledge About Siam*] by Sor Sajjawatee. Published by Sarn Sawan.

4. *The Royal Chronicle of Thonburi* by Phanchanthanumas (Jerm), Jod Mhai Rai Wan Thap [จดหมายรายวันทัพ, *War Diaries*], *The Miracles of Our Great Kings* [อภินิหารบรรพบุรุษ] *and Other Documents*, published by Sripanya.

5. *The Legend of Phra Phuttachai* recounted in a sermon, available from http://www.watphraphutthachai.com

6. *A Collection of Chronicles Volume 7: Khun Klone's Account of the Buddha's Footprint* [ประชุมพงศาวดารภาคที่ 7 คำให้การขุนโขลน เรื่องพระพุทธบาท].

7. *Where did nagas come from?* [นาคมาจากไหน] by Sujit Wongthes. Published by Post Publishing.

8. *The Defeat of the Naga by the Garuda* [ครุฑยุดนาค] by Sor Plainoi. Published by Pim Kham.

9. Thomas Mann, *The Story Teller* [เมื่อโธมัส มันน์เล่าเรื่อง] Chulalongkorn University Press, from 'Tonio Kroger', translated into Thai by Pussadee Srikiew.

I also like to express my thanks to *Matichon Weekly* for publishing this novel into a series, and everyone who was involved, including Parnbua Boonparn (Khun Yen), Suwapong Chanfungpetch, Anusorn Tippayanon (Pi Ton), Duanghathai Esanasatang, and Associate Professor Dr Duangmon Jitjamnong for the etymological suggestions for some of the words mentioned in this novel.

Glossary

arhat

In Buddhism, an arhat (or arahant) refers to one who has advanced along the path of enlightenment and is liberated from the endless cycle of rebirth.

arōgyā
paramā lābhā

Taken from Dhammapada verse 204, the Sanskrit phrase translates to, 'Health is the ultimate profit' in English.

der, ner

Interjections used at the end of a clause to emphasize that it is an entreaty or command in Isan dialect and Lao.

Dong Phaya Fai,
Dong Phaya Yen

A mountainous region in Phetchabun, Chaiyaphum, Lopburi, Saraburi, and Nakhon Ratchasima Provinces, Thailand. It used to be covered by thick forest and was formerly known as Dong Phaya Fai, or the 'fiery lord', for its wild and dangerous reputation, especially amongst travelers who exposed themselves to malaria and other illnesses passing through it. During the period of deforestation and railway expansion in the mid-nineteenth century, Vice King Pinklao changed the name of the forest to Dong Phaya Yen, or the 'cold lord', to signify that the wild forest had been tamed.

ee-la	An endearing way to call a young girl or the youngest daughter in Isan dialect and Lao.
Kong Khao Noi	A Thai folk legend about a young farmer who hits his mother on the head in a hunger-induced rage after noticing that a lunchbox his mother prepared for him seems to contain only a tiny amount of rice. He later finds out that the lunchbox actually contains so much tightly packed sticky rice that it is impossible for him to finish it all in one meal. To his shock and great sadness, he soon discovers that his mother is no longer alive. The blow on the head has killed her. To show his repentance, he builds a stupa in honour of her.
Loy Krathong	A festival celebrated throughout Thailand, Laos, Shan in Myanmar, Northern Malaysia, Sri Lanka, Xishuangbanna in China, and Cambodia where people float decorated vessels to give thanks to Ganga, the Hindu Goddess of Water.
luk krung	Literally translated to 'child of the city' in English, luk krung is a Thai popular music genre. It typically includes topics regarding people in the capital, with a more polished, urban style compared to its folk counterpart, luk thung.
luk thung	Literally translated to 'child of the field' in English, luk thung is a genre of Thai popular music. It consists of poetic lyrics that often reflect the rural lifestyle, cultural traits and social patterns in Thailand.
ngan	A Thai measurement unit equivalent to 400 square metres.
rai	A Thai measurement unit equivalent to 1,600 square metres.

sok	A Thai measurement unit equivalent to 50 centimetres.
Tod Kathin, Tod Pa-Pha	Tod Kathin is a Buddhist festival that usually falls at the end of the rainy season in October. It is marked by a three-day Festival of Lights commemorating the day when Buddha returned to earth after his three-month stay at the heavenly place known as Tavatimsa.
	Tod Pha Pa, or 'forest robe' in English, can happen at any time of year. In the past, monks only wore clothes made from old rags of dead people, so Buddhists sometimes placed clothes on the tree branches in the forest as an offering.
uwa	An exclamation for something unexpected, denoting a feeling of disappointment.
wa	A Thai measurement unit equivalent to 2 metres.
wai	A gesture of greeting or respect in Thai culture, where one presses their palms together in front of their chest or over their head.